CALL ME
HUNTER

CALL ME HUNTER

A NOVEL

JIM SHOCKEY

EMILY BESTLER BOOKS

ATRIA

New York   London   Toronto   Sydney   New Delhi

EMILY BESTLER BOOKS

ATRIA

An Imprint of Simon & Schuster, Inc.
1230 Avenue of the Americas
New York, NY 10020

First Emily Bestler Books/Atria Books hardcover edition October 2023

EMILY BESTLER BOOKS/ATRIA BOOKS and colophon are trademarks of Simon & Schuster, Inc.

For information about special discounts for bulk purchases, please contact Simon & Schuster Special Sales at 1-866-506-1949 or business@simonandschuster.com.

The Simon & Schuster Speakers Bureau can bring authors to your live event. For more information or to book an event, contact the Simon & Schuster Speakers Bureau at 1-866-248-3049 or visit our website at www.simonspeakers.com.

Interior design by Kyoko Watanabe

Manufactured in the United States of America

1 3 5 7 9 10 8 6 4 2

Library of Congress Cataloging-in-Publication Data has been applied for.

ISBN 978-1-6680-1035-8
ISBN 978-1-6680-1037-2 (ebook)

For Louise,

To my dying day and my last free breath,
Every heartbeat is for you.

Fairy tales are real.

PREFACE

While you read CALL ME HUNTER, you should pick random names and places, or a given situation, and google whatever it is you chose.

Please, I encourage you to do so.

If you happened to choose the name of the *WKRP in Cincinnati* TV star and wife of Burt Reynolds, Loni Anderson, feel free to reach out to her. She cannot deny being in Vancouver, in the restaurant with the other two TV stars and the beautiful woman in CALL ME HUNTER. Nor can she deny that Laszlo George, the Hungarian photographer, was there . . . as well as *Icarus*.

Just as Wolfgang Porsche cannot deny that he flew to New Zealand with the richest man in Romania, Ion Tiriac, on Tiriac's private jet. Ask either of them. Nor can either of them deny meeting with CALL ME HUNTER's antihero, Tsau-z, the *Man of Sores*.

Ask Goldie Hawn if what is written about her in CALL ME HUNTER is true. She will remember the Our World Operative Icarus, but of course, like the others, she will know him by a different name. And yes, she does have a cute giggle.

Look up the past iTunes blues charts. The same person those above cannot deny spending time with undeniably did write, record, and perform a song that went to the top of those same blues charts.

That character in CALL ME HUNTER, the antihero, did indeed travel to Kabul, Afghanistan, and rode in the US Black Hawk helicopters during the *Surge,* and he did indeed wear the high-ranking uniform of an officer in the Canadian Armed Forces for six years . . . a rank that was bestowed upon him.

And yes, the character Icarus, in real life, was a *Vogue* model.

Truthfully, I did not have a story to tell when I first sat down to write this novel, but after *living* for well over a half century, I do have a story to tell.

This is my story.

I mean that figuratively . . . but also literally.

For many of the *facts* and situations in the novel, there is photo documentation to corroborate what is written or at least some form of proof, even if the *proof* must be confirmation from the people mentioned.

Those *facts* that cannot be *proven* are generally facts that can only be confirmed by people who are, God forgive me, deceased. Many of these are facts that would cross the thin line of plausible deniability and would incriminate characters in the novel.

My original thought process in writing CALL ME HUNTER, in creating this *abstract* thriller, was to write in a manner that made the situations identifiable, but barely so, conflicted, to turn it into a work of art with the true perspective altered . . . like cubism.

My goal was to mix up the provable facts of one person's life with facts that may or may not be fiction; to create a slurry, that like quicksand, catches the reader, holds them fast, and if they struggle, if they fight against suspended reality, if they doubt the veracity of what they are reading, they will feel compelled to search for the truth . . . and in so doing, will only sink deeper into the novel's hold.

It is my sincere hope that someone of great influence and re-sources, reading this novel, will get *caught* in the slurry and endeavor to research deeply into what is written on the pages of CALL ME HUNTER, so deeply that in the end, they come to the only possible conclusion . . . that this novel might not be a work of fiction . . .

. . . that it might simply be the story of a life lived beyond where imagination can exist.

Truth?

Maybe.

Maybe not.

CALL ME
HUNTER

Zhivago is dead.

I hunted him down and I killed him.

The police are gone and the street is dark now. Quiet. I stood right here and watched them carry him away. No. Watched isn't the right *word; I enjoyed* them carrying him away. He will never say "exqui-*site" again. He will never hurt you.*

Zhivago is only the first. Before this is done, they will all know me as fear.

You knew me a long time ago by another name. Know me now as Tsau-z.

I am the Man of Sores.

All this you need to know.

Soul Catcher.

This is all you need to know.

1

2020

PINEHURST, NORTH CAROLINA

A car passed. The driver didn't wave. A crow cawed and in the distance the not-there, but always-there, white noise of the city droned on. Nyala noticed none of these things. The high pines filtered the afternoon sun, muted the day, and held back the heat of the North Carolina fall. The mailbox was silver-finished tin, rusting now and canted slightly on the square white post, dug into the ground at least two decades before.

Nyala frowned.

The package wasn't all that unusual for her to receive; it was rolled slightly to fit through the squeaky top-hinged mailbox door. It would be magazines normally, but they didn't usually come in plain brown manila packaging. She'd actually had a thought when she'd pulled the package from the mailbox that somehow she'd been sent some pornographic magazine by mistake, and not just one magazine, several. The package was heavy.

Ha! She'd smiled to herself. That was a joke. Even if she was so inclined, who had time to look at dirty pictures? She felt a pang of regret; when was the last date she'd been on, a month ago? Oh wait, that's right, never. Work, always work; no time for indulgences, she told anyone who asked. No dates. No relationships. It had to be the right one or nobody; she'd felt that way for as far back as she could remember. She'd stopped trying to figure out why she was saving herself. She just was. It was one of her secrets.

The package didn't have a return address, only "Tsau-z" in black pen. *Tsau-z?* A place? Never heard of it. Weird. She turned then, holding the package, curious, slowly ripping the wrapping as she walked back to her house, careful not to slide her thumb along its edge. Crazies out in the world these days; someone she knew, or at least someone a friend of a friend knew, had received an envelope from an anonymous sender, a card with razor blades taped to the edge of it. She shivered. Ugly. What a screwed-up world.

But there was no razor blade. Only what appeared to be three or four hundred typewritten pages, loose in a heavy file folder. She turned the package over in her hands again, looking more carefully at the brown wrapping this time. No return address, just the single word *Tsau-z* in the top left corner and "Occupant" with her address under it, written in precise penmanship on the front of the package. But something was missing.

No stamps; no parcel postmarkings on the packaging material at all. That was strange. Last time she checked, snail mail delivery, as slow as it was, still required some sort of payment and proof of payment on the outside of any letter or package.

Just a little creepy; not razor blade crazy, but still disconcerting.

A bird flitted through the branches of the flowering shrub close by, startling her.

Ugh. She shook her head. Get a grip. She ripped the wrapping enough to pull the file folder out and flipped through the pages once quickly, then returned to the first page to read it.

Jesus, what was this?

Zhivago is dead.

I hunted him down and I killed him.

Zhivago? Killed? And *enjoyed it?*

Suddenly she felt anxiety crawling out from the dark place where she fought constantly to keep it under control and cornered. It was a living thing inside her. The feelings of hopelessness and despair had always been there in waiting, since she was a child. They were her constant companions.

Shit. It was from a crazy. A stalker? Some nut bar who followed her home from the city and put the package in her mailbox? Had to have put it there himself; if it even was a "him." It was always a "him." Great, exactly what was missing in her life.

Nyala twisted her head around to look behind her. Was the creep watching her now? Jesus Christ. Who needed this? She scanned the surrounding forest. Branches overhung the paved laneway she'd walked down from her house to get to the mailbox at the main road. Wonderful. Paranoia. Just what she needed to add to her collection of neuroses. Solitude was good for the soul, but now as she stood, looking for movement, or telltale horizontal lines in the underbrush and still pine forest around her, she rued her choice to move to the country, to get away from the bright lights and action of the city.

"Shit." She said it out loud this time. And then said it again, but this time chastised herself for the bad habit. Come on, girl. It's a stupid manuscript. Somebody knew she was a journalist, that's all; somebody who wanted to be mysterious. Tsau-z. Whoever that was, probably somebody she knew, someone who was too insecure to just come up and ask her to read their work; probably because it sucked.

With a look over her shoulder and a flip of her head in defiance, she turned to walk back down the cracked and weathered asphalt drive that led to her rented home.

Nyala smiled to herself then.

Had to give whoever it was credit. You had me at *they will all know me as fear.* Not bad, whoever the hell you are.

Tsau-z.

Kind of a dumb name though.

———

"Coffee?" Nyala's roommate was her best friend. Unlike Nyala, Luba was short, "five feet plus," she would say, "barefooted and bouffanted," and she would laugh every time at her own dumb joke. Nyala loved her. They'd been friends since they attended journalism school together, Carleton in Ottawa, Canada. Speaking of dumb, Luba chose the cold Canadian university when she could have easily attended any American Ivy League school. Unlike Nyala, Luba's family was rich. Oligarch-money rich.

Unlike Nyala? That was a joke. Nyala didn't even have a family, let alone a rich one.

"What's that? What'd you get?" Luba hadn't bothered to wait for Nyala's answer on the coffee, she never did. "Here. Enough cream to gag a lactose-intolerant vegan."

She rolled her eyes.

"How do you stay so slim? Oh that's right, two hours every day in the gym, discipline, and salad. Barf. I hate you."

She slumped down on the overstuffed chair that was the only thing she'd contributed to their country house furnishings.

"Well? What is it?"

"Not sure." Nyala held the offered mug in one hand and the file folder in the other. "Some kind of a manuscript, I think."

Luba crinkled her nose.

"Whose?" She jumped up from the chair and sidled up to her friend, attempting as she did to see around her much taller friend's arm.

Nyala turned slightly, blocking Luba.

"Don't know."

"Let's see!"

"No."

"Why?" Luba made the Valley Girl deeply hurt face she always did when she didn't get her way. "Fine. What's the big secret?"

Nyala wasn't sure why she said no. They always shared. In fact they knew more about each other than anybody else knew about either of them. Or at least they both knew a lot about Luba. She was Ukrainian; her name was short for "love" in that and other Slavic languages. She emigrated from Ukraine to the United States with her parents when she was five years old. They wanted her to go to an American private school, but mostly they wanted to protect their little Luba from the post-glasnost chaos and anti-Ukrainian sentiment that pervaded Russian thinking.

Luba told Nyala that she chose Canada for her university education, instead of the US, because she liked the sound of the country's name, Canada. She loved saying "Ottawa" too. Ottawa. Canada.

Geez, if Nyala had Luba's opportunities, she definitely would have chosen a school to attend for better reasons than that the name sounded nice. And then to purposely choose journalism as a major? Especially with the idea of working for a newspaper? Nobody in their right mind would do that. Present company included. The newspaper industry was not a growth industry; its relevance was steadily declining as social media platforms and the all-day news channels sucked up eyeballs.

The industry hadn't exactly been helping their own cause though. Nyala firmly believed good journalism died the day Watergate hit the news. From that point on, journalists wanted the fame, recognition, and wealth that went along with "breaking the big story." Damn the truth. Damn the facts. Fake news. That was what motivated virtually all their journalism peers.

The small, privately owned newspaper she and Luba worked for was holding its own against the flow, but mostly because they served a niche market, the older Raleigh citizens who had an aversion to entering the twenty-first century. People who still wanted to hear both sides of the story and make their own decisions on a given issue. "Holding its own" was maybe sugarcoating it. At least the checks hadn't started bouncing yet.

Not that the money mattered to Luba. Journalism was a lark for her, like her life. She couldn't care less about being a good reporter.

Nyala was different. She knew she was a throwback to the days of old-school journalism, an anachronism. Without a truth of her own, she knew how fundamentally important knowing the truth really was.

"Honestly, I'm not sure. I want to see what it's about. Then I'll let you read it."

Luba wasn't the most attentive at the best of times and when she didn't get her way, she was positively bipolar.

"I'm going for a run. Wanna come?" Luba brushed by Nyala, placing her own half-finished coffee on the kitchen counter.

The country house had an open floor plan, with the kitchen, dining room, and living room all in the main room. Other than the location being exactly what she was looking for, the roomy openness was why Nyala signed the rental form. She hated confined spaces, tiny rooms stacked one on top of the other in the city high-rises, like cells in a prison, like tombs. Those were the only places she could afford in the downtown core, where the newspaper offices were located.

She hated all cities. She always had, though she didn't know why. The fresher air of the country and the freedom, the space and wild animals, the green, the trees, those were the things she had a deep appreciation for, a sensitivity that was deadened by the smell of concrete and asphalt.

It was strange, but when she was out hiking in North Carolina's Blue Ridge Mountains, it wasn't like she was in nature, it was like nature was in her. Somehow she felt she was home. It was the weirdest thing; deer didn't run from her. Neither did rabbits hop away as she walked by. Unless she was with her friend. Then everything fled, probably to get away from Luba's complaining pretty much every step of the way.

When she'd informed Luba, who would happily live in the middle of a shopping mall, that she was looking for a rental in the country, she'd expected her friend to kiss her goodbye. But she hadn't. Luba was her best friend, her only real friend.

"No. I'm good. I'm just going to do a little work. Have a good run."

Nyala sat in the same chair that Luba had just vacated. She set her coffee on the low table beside the chair, opened the folder, and started reading.

2

1960s

UNDISCLOSED SMALL TOWN

Do you think our son is slow?"

It wasn't the biggest house on the block, but it was their house on the block. Bought and not quite paid for, actually hardly paid for at all. From where they stood, looking out the front window of their 1,100-square-foot, 1932-era brick bungalow, Pete and Rose could see the fronts of five similar-sized homes facing them from across the street. They could see their driveway and their own front yard, cut grass marred by several fairy rings, despite Rose's best efforts to get rid of the ugly mushrooms.

"Don't say that!" Rose stood in front of Pete. The question from her husband wasn't a joking matter. She wasn't angry about it. Worried? Not exactly, more like trepidatious. Trepidation mixed with resignation. "Never say that again. He's your child."

She knew her spouse of ten years was well aware that he was never to go there, the topic was taboo. Chastised, he reached around Rose and wrapped her in his arms, pulling her in close, looking over her shoulder. She responded by leaning back into his chest and body, holding his arms against her. He held her, but it was she who squeezed his arms tighter to her as they watched their son.

Neither spoke for several minutes.

That Hunter was different was impossible to deny, but she didn't want to admit that something might be mentally wrong with him.

Not that. Please not that. They watched him until Rose took a deep breath, steeled herself, and then broke the contemplative silence. In spite of what she'd just told her husband, in spite of all the years of denial, there was no putting it off.

"His teacher told me he's not reading. She said he can't read. She says maybe something's wrong." If Pete had been able to see his wife's green eyes, he'd have seen them begin to well with tears. "She said we need to take him to a doctor."

Rose shuddered when she felt her husband stiffen. Her chest heaved involuntarily and the first tear slowly rose and broke free from the corner of her eye and slid down her cheek. Another tear fell and then another, and then she began to silently sob.

Pete just continued to look out their large double-paned front window, over his distraught wife's shoulder. She knew it wasn't fair to show Pete how upset she was at the teacher's comments; she knew if he received bad news and it was something he couldn't control, he wouldn't be able to cope with it. He'd close his mind, block it out. He was a road construction foreman during the summer and a heavy-duty mechanic over the long, cold prairie winter, good at both, they said, but this? This was something he couldn't fix with a hammer and a welding torch.

Lord. Just a normal child, that's all they wanted.

Rose knew her husband wanted a son who played ball and wrestled with his dad; a kid who got dirty and wouldn't make his bed; a kid who played with other kids and did normal kid things.

And this is what he got. No, this is what *they* got.

Pete seldom said it out loud, but she knew he thought it all the time, that something was off with their son. They both thought it. Rose, ever the nurturer, ever the positive one in the home, would never say something like that out loud and she didn't want Pete to say it either. Their son was the eight-year-old elephant in the room. Since birth he'd been different.

It wasn't obvious at first. True, he didn't cry, ever, and unlike other infants she'd seen, he didn't smile or giggle, but they didn't think much about it then; they were so in love with their beautiful baby boy. The birth had been easy enough. Rose was in labor for nearly twelve hours, but there was nothing about the ordeal that might have caused him to turn out like he did.

The whole birth-of-a-baby wasn't her husband's thing, "not his department," he told her, but he'd at least been at the hospital in the waiting room when their son was born, something he tended to bring up when Rose, upon occasion, said he was being "insensitive" about something or other. She was happy that he'd made the effort to be there at the hospital, but already knew by that point in their marriage that her husband kept a tight rein on his emotions. He tried to be the rock that waves broke upon.

She wasn't in the waiting room to share the wondrous moment with her husband, but Pete did tell her later how excited he'd been when the doctor came in and told him that his Rose had just given birth to a baby boy. A boy! Holy cow! A boy! For a moment at least, she knew he couldn't have been a rock. For a moment, a fleeting moment, he had to have felt overwhelmed, like she was when the nurse handed the tiny swaddled bundle to her.

Not that Pete wouldn't have been happy with a girl, she was sure he would have been, but she was also sure he was hoping for a boy. Motorcycles. Cars. Engines. She was positive he'd planned in his mind before the birth that if he had a son, they would do the things his own father never did with him, like buy a car together someday and fix it up. Without doubt, he hoped for a boy who would want to play sports. Not the sports she knew he hated, like soccer, but manly sports like baseball and football. Maybe he'd make the all-star team. Of course he'd make the all-star team. Home runs. And touchdowns.

And his wish had been granted. She'd given her husband a boy. But it wasn't the boy her husband expected.

It was the boy they were looking at.

A dog trotted by, tail high, and then slowed when it saw their son. It stopped for a moment and then seemed to nod at Hunter before it continued on its way. It was so strange how animals seemed to say hello to their son. Pete was probably thinking the same thing. He was shaking his head.

They lived on a crescent and their house number was 18. Except for a few hundred square feet difference in size, there were sixty-four nearly identical homes on the curved roadway, but their home was the only brick one. Rose had been so excited when she saw the house. It was her dream home. Besides being brick, not stucco like all the other homes on the quiet street, it was in a nice neighborhood and there was a good public school only two blocks away.

Pete had never been to the school even once in the three years their son had attended, never met the teachers or the principal. She didn't judge him because of his seeming lack of interest; he had a lot on his mind, not the least of those concerns being the constant worry that he might get laid off. He didn't want to be the failure his own father predicted he would be and he would never want to break Rose's heart by having to move the family back into the small trailer they'd lived in up until three years before. That's when they'd laid out their combined life's savings to put a small down payment on the home they now stood in.

Several children, older than their son, walked by, laughing and bumping each other. She couldn't be sure, but it looked like they were laughing at Hunter as they walked past; they were certainly pointing at him. She could feel Pete tense up again. It made him instantly angry, the ridicule. It hurt her husband almost as much as knowing that the neighbors felt sorry for them, the parents of a strange child.

With one last involuntary deep, hard breath she pulled away from Pete and reached into the pocket of her pretty flowered summer dress. She and Pete loved each other, but they were opposites. She was always a lady, always proper, delicate, and feminine; her job was to keep the family together, take care of her husband, and raise their son. Pete was hard, big, and coarse and his job was to provide for them, for their boy.

Rose dried her eyes with the tissue she pulled from the pocket and then, composed again, looked out the window into the warm June afternoon. The lawn was dappled with sunlight where the sun rays managed to find a way through the leaves of a big poplar. When they bought the house, she'd told Pete to build a tree house. "It will bring you together," she'd said to Pete.

But it hadn't. Hunter wasn't interested. He'd barely looked up when Pete, so proud of his creation, pointed out the structure he'd built entirely in one weekend. Rose didn't think she'd ever seen such overwhelming sadness in her husband's eyes as she did that moment. He'd failed again.

It, he, their son, Rose always felt, was the reason they hadn't had another child.

Outside, a robin flew by, landed on the lawn, hopped twice, and saw the boy on the driveway, but it didn't fly away. Birds never flew away from their child. For whatever reason, birds, in fact all animals, tame or wild, seemed drawn to him, like he was some kind of Dr. Doolittle or Pied Piper. He could and often did walk up to the Taylors' big scary German shepherd without an ounce of fear. The dog, what was his name, Bismarck? The dog was a barking brute on a chain, frightening, but it would not only allow Hunter to approach, it would also wag its tail and whine in anticipation of being patted. She'd seen their son seemingly holding court in their yard with half a dozen cedar waxwings or small birds at a time, and not just once, she'd seen it often. Like he was a part of their natural world and not the world everyone else lived in.

The lady across the street, Mrs. Dimertz, came out onto her lawn then and moved a sprinkler to another location. She wasn't a bad neighbor. Older than most on the block, she lived with her husband, but woe be it to any child who dared step on her grass. Dogs were verboten as well; literally verboten. Nobody in the neighborhood talked about it, but they did whisper about it: everyone felt that Mr. and Mrs. Dimertz were Germans who'd somehow escaped the postwar Nazi inquisitions. They were the right age and they did speak German, but Rose didn't like when people spread rumors.

Their son hadn't moved. In fact he hadn't moved for the last two hours. He was still sitting inside the cardboard box, the one he'd dragged out onto the cement driveway after lunch, the one he barely fit in and the one that Rose brought home from the local Federated

Co-op store loaded with groceries the year before. It was his boat. He was still holding the wooden yardstick out over the edge of the box and was still dangling the string he'd tied to the end of it, over the cement.

He was fishing.

Rose knew their son would continue to sit in his cardboard box on the cement, like he'd done for so many hours, for so many days and weeks in the past, until she called him to dinner.

3

Saturday morning. Rose set the plates on the kitchen table. She wished the year had 365 Saturday mornings.

"Breakfast is ready!" She turned to the stove and lifted the frying pan. Pete liked his eggs prepared his perfect way: soft, no shoes, over easy. "It'll get cold! Hurry up!"

The Saturday morning ritual. Rose loved it because these mornings were normal; normal like she imagined they should be. She heard her man and her son making their way toward the kitchen.

"Oh yeah!" Pete went to grab his wife.

"No, don't! The pan is hot!" Rose turned to protect Pete from getting burnt. She couldn't exactly get away from him; one hand was holding the frying pan handle and the other the spatula. "Careful! You'll burn yourself!"

"I don't care. Gimme my beautiful wife!" Pete had Rose at his mercy and didn't hesitate to take full advantage of the moment, wrapping his arms around her and leaning in to kiss the back of her neck.

Rose bent away, laughing now, and Pete pulled her in, grinning. It was a game they played, her coyly resistant and him blithely insistent. It was a balance that so far had resulted in nearly perfect matrimony.

"Okay! Enough! Get your plate. Hash browns are in the pan on the table, get your own. French toast is in the tureen, but don't yank the lid off! It was my grandmother's dish. Be careful!" Rose twisted away from her husband's grasp; her voice was stern, but she was still smiling. "Hunter! Breakfast! Hurry up, or your father will be leaving without you!"

Rose was carefully flipping an egg onto Pete's plate when their son entered the room. Pete hated broken eggs, so she couldn't turn to greet Hunter.

"Get your plate, honey." She was focused on the egg transfer. "And I've made you French toast, just the way you like it!"

Their son was worse than Pete. He liked his eggs exactly the same way as his father but was even more adamant that they be perfect.

"Here you go, just the way you like them!" She carefully, far more carefully than she had for her husband, slid the over easy, soft, no shoes egg onto her son's plate. "Get some hash browns before your father takes them all."

"Don't eat so fast!" Rose wasn't talking to her son now. "It took me an hour to make breakfast, at least enjoy it."

"We gotta go! Time's a-wastin'! Right, Hunter?" Pete took a big gulp of his coffee. Black, not too hot, not too cold; the way he liked it. "Hurry up! All the best stuff will be gone!"

Saturday morning. Garage sale day. The only day their son seemed to come alive. It was also the only day of the week that he and his father found common ground.

The thought that maybe it wasn't normal for an eight-year-old boy to like "garage sailing" entered her mind. But it was normal in a way, because Pete loved it. He even left her apartment early, on the Saturday morning after they'd first spent the night together, before they were married. Rose blushed slightly at the memory. She hadn't been much of a proper lady that night. He'd said he had to go "sailing" and would call her later. Sailing? She remembered thinking it was a touch off-the-wall; they were hundreds of miles from any lakes. But he was honest and there was something about him that made her feel needed, so off-the-wall wasn't a deal breaker. They'd called it "sailing" as an inside joke ever since.

He did call her that afternoon and they were married a year later. Rose smiled to herself; he'd never missed a Saturday morning of sailing since, not that she could remember anyway.

Pete and Hunter both shared a same interest and that was good enough for her. If it made them happy, then she was happy. She leaned against the kitchen counter and watched her son carefully cut his food into small pieces, then mix just the right amount of egg with

CALL ME HUNTER / 17

French toast and then wipe the fork through the syrup, until it was perfect. Only then did he raise the fork to his mouth.

Rose's mother had always told her that one day Rose would have a child just like she had been and that would be payback time. But her son wasn't like her. He wasn't like his father either. He was . . . different. Rose turned then, she hated that, hated that it always came down to that same ugly word when she contemplated her only child, *different*. She hated even thinking it.

"Go," she said, over her shoulder. "Go and good luck!" She turned on the tap to fill the sink. She could hear the chairs scraping back from the table and knew her husband would come over to where she was standing, watching the water.

"Today is the day! I can feel it! Last three weeks have been lousy for sales, but today it's gonna happen!" Pete hugged his wife from behind. "Thank you for breakfast. Thank you for being my wife! Gotta go! See you this afternoon!"

"Don't spend too much," she warned over her shoulder. "And don't forget to keep an eye on Hunter."

She didn't expect an answer; she knew her warnings fell on pre-occupied ears. Pete was too excited to listen to anything except his own thoughts, his hope that somewhere out there at some garage sale he'd find the deal of a lifetime. Rose shook her head and she turned to begin clearing the plates from the table. If it made him happy and if it made her son happy, then what was the harm? She stood for a moment and then set the plates back on the table and walked to the living room window.

Her men were at the sidewalk, getting in Pete's old '52 International Harvester truck. He was so proud of that old green truck. He always parked it on the street the Friday night before their Saturday morning outing, so he didn't have to waste time backing out the driveway. She shook her head.

She watched Hunter reach up and open the passenger door. It was a stretch, but he managed to get his foot up inside the truck and was hopping up and down to get enough momentum to pull himself inside. She sighed. All he had to do was use the running board, it was there to help him, but as usual he was marching to his own beat. *It's my life*. He wouldn't say it out loud, but he did say it in a way, by his every action. He was growing so quickly. He was going to be a big guy when he grew up. And good-looking. Rose crossed her arms and held herself as she watched her son struggle into the truck his father was already in, waiting impatiently to start up the engine.

Pete needed a break. He would be looking for mechanic's tools, carpentry tools, lawn mowers, old diesel-powered pumps, as he always did; anything to make a buck on. He even brought home a small tractor engine one time because it was "dirt cheap," he said. She'd chastised him that day, saying they couldn't afford it and that he needed to be more responsible about the money he spent. She smiled to herself remembering the day he sold it for $300 more than he'd paid for it. "I told you so!" Pete, bless him, wasn't a businessman. He'd spent nearly that in parts to restore the engine, and then added in at least twenty hours' worth of his own time for labor.

Still, she loved that he tried.

They needed money. It wasn't easy making ends meet; Rose knew that. She did the family bookkeeping and paid the bills. He was a hardworking man, but an academic scholarship to Harvard was never in his future. Not his fault, she knew. Unlike her family, Pete's family wasn't inclined toward schooling and education. Nobody in Pete's family ever went past grade 12, so Rose knew well the life she was marrying into when she said yes at the altar.

As she watched him now, she felt a warmness that wasn't from the morning sun just now starting to heat up the neighborhood. He was a good man, but he needed a break, deserved a break. Life hadn't been easy for Pete. She'd only met his father a few times, but those few times were enough. He wasn't nice to Pete and he wasn't nice to Pete's mother. No matter how hard Pete tried, or how well he did, his father, usually intoxicated, ridiculed him. The saddest part was that he did it in front of Rose, purposely embarrassing Pete.

Maybe that's part of the reason she always did her best to see the good in her husband, why she married him, to nurse him back to the man he could have been with a nurturing father instead of the father he was born to. Pete was like a bird with a broken wing that she'd felt compelled to look after, to help.

Despite his hard work though, she knew money wasn't just getting tight, it *was* tight. She didn't tell her husband, but they wouldn't make the mortgage payment next month at the rate things were going. Pete needed to find a good deal, a really good deal, or she would be stealing from their food account to pay the bank. His yard sale habit didn't normally hurt the family finances, but it didn't always help either.

She watched Hunter pull the truck door closed. Hunter. Not a common name and certainly not a name that had anything to do with the action of hunting. Pete, as much as he was salt of the earth, was definitely not a hunter. Not that he had anything against it; he just wasn't inclined to use time chasing around in the outdoors, when he could be indoors, tinkering on this or that treasure he'd picked up on one of his Saturday morning excursions.

No, her son was named Hunter because she herself had insisted he be called that. She'd known the instant the doctor handed her the tiny bundle that was her newborn baby boy. She was crying with joy, but not her baby. He was silent; looking at her; like he was hunting for something in her eyes, something inside her.

Hunter Powell Cotton Johann; the second and third names she had insisted on as well, leaving Pete to contribute only Hunter's last name. It wasn't like her and she'd been a little surprised at her own determination, but she wasn't going to back down and Pete didn't even try to change her mind. Hunter it was. Powell Cotton for their son's middle names was harder for him to swallow, but he'd acquiesced on that as well when Rose explained that Powell-Cotton was her family's actual last name. Not just Cotton like she used for her maiden name.

She had a Great Uncle Percy, Percy Horace Gordon Powell-Cotton, an explorer, hunter, conservationist, museum curator, and family legend whom she'd always admired. Mostly she'd admired him for the respect and fame he'd brought the family back in England. Although he died in 1940, when Rose was Hunter's age, Great Uncle Percy's story, told at family gatherings for years afterward, struck a chord with her younger self.

She sometimes, like now, felt that had she been raised in another time, or another place, or if she'd been born a boy, maybe things would have been different for her. As she always did, Rose felt a ripple of guilt; it was folly. If things were different, she wouldn't have all that she had. She forced the thought out of her mind and waved as her two boys pulled away.

*S*top.

Listen to me now.

Before you learn more, you need to understand something.

About me. About you. About beauty.

True beauty isn't something that can be seen.

True beauty is something that can only be felt.

The feeling of color; that is how I "saw" true beauty.

I didn't know it then. How could I? Eight years old. It all started then. I remember her waving. I remember driving. I remember stopping and I remember stepping into my future that day, into your future.

I remember being happy.

My world, not the world I live in and the world you live in, but the world I see, is different than the world you see. Everything in the world I see is a tone of brown. It's a sepia world, except when there is something of extraordinary beauty. Then color like no color anyone can ever understand. Color. I have tried to explain it so many times. Nobody knows. How can they? They do not see the world I see. They do not feel color.

That day should not have been any different, but it was.

Brown and brown. Brown and brown. Brown and brown.

And then I felt it. Color. Impossible to miss.

Color, radiating, pulsing, so magnificently obvious in the brown and brown that was my universe.

I picked it up.

Maybe it wasn't the only event that set so much in motion. Maybe it wasn't that one object that caused it all. Maybe it was fate and destiny, contriving together to bring me to now.

Maybe it wasn't that one object that caused you.

That caused you, Nyala.

4

2020

PINEHURST, NORTH CAROLINA

Holy shit!

Nyala looked down at the manuscript she'd just dropped on the floor. What the frig was this!

"Jesus Christ! This creep knows my name!" She said it out loud, as if maybe in saying it out loud, somebody would explain to her what the hell was going on. "He knows my f-ing name!"

Nyala looked down in horror at the manuscript.

"Hey, Ny Ny! I'm back!" The front door was barely opened before Luba announced her arrival. "I am unworthy! No discipline. Didn't even make it to the gas station! I'm going to be a blob."

Nyala barely heard her friend. She was still trying to assimilate the information. This clown knew where she lived and knew her name. It wasn't a mistake; it wasn't a coincidence that she received the manuscript.

What the heck was this thing?

She looked down at the pages and frowned. Who was this guy Tsau-z? And why was he writing in first person to her in what was obviously a long narrative? Was it that moron Scott? He'd always struck her as a harmless weirdo, but she could be wrong about that. Could be a mass murderer for all she really knew. Was it him? She shook her head. Scott might be a Starbucks nonfat, nongluten, decaf organic mocha, reusable-soybean-fiber-cup-drinking goof, but he wasn't sinister. Way too insipid.

"Hey! Like I'm here! Hello? Wake-up time. Luba calling La-la-land! Helllllooo! Come in, Ny Ny!" Luba threw her water bottle on the couch, not slowing on her way to the fridge. "I'm famished! Feels like I just used up ten thousand calories! Want a carrot stick?"

"Whoever wrote this, wrote it to me." Nyala didn't look at her friend when she said it. She'd been shocked when she read her name, then horrified, then disgusted, and now she was getting angry. "This asshole knows my name. He's probably the one who dropped it off here, so he knows where I live and he's including me in some kind of deranged fantasy."

Nyala finally turned around, leaving the manuscript where it had fallen. Outside she could hear a blue jay squawking and a gray squirrel chirring. Probably displaying for each other as they competed for the seeds and suet she religiously left out for the birds and fox squirrels, though not so much for the gray squirrels. For a fleeting moment she lost her train of thought. It was funny how when everything was hitting the fan, the sounds of nature always seemed to reach her, no matter where her mind was at that moment.

Luba was munching a carrot stick but leaning forward now, looking at the manuscript on the floor. "What does it say? Is it creepy sexy or just plain old creepy? Any hot pictures?"

"Luba!" Nyala frowned and shook her head. "This is serious; I feel violated. Nobody knows I live here. It's not cool."

They both contemplated the possibilities.

The squirrel and the jay stopped their chattering. The two friends didn't hear the jet engine churning the stratosphere into a long contrail cloud far above.

"Well, we could move back to the city where it's safe!" Luba wasn't joking.

Nyala knew her friend wasn't a country girl and wasn't sold on the quiet and solitude of their chosen home. Not that she would ever leave Nyala alone out here with the bears and tigers and whatever else Luba thought lived in the surrounding woods.

"Stop it! This is real! I'm being stalked by someone! That's just a touch scary to think about."

Again they contemplated.

Luba couldn't resist and leaned down to pick the manuscript up off the floor at her friend's feet, reading the first page as she did.

"What's it about? Who is Toozee? And who is Zhivago? Wasn't that a book or a movie? That's it! It was a movie with Vince Lombardi or someone like that!" Luba was a movie buff, but anything prior to the Marvel Comics Hollywood productions was way, way outside the box for her. She took a seat at one of the two chairs at the table and started to read. "Mr. Creepy, here we come!"

Suddenly, for no good reason, Nyala felt possessive of the pages that Luba was just starting to leaf through and making fun of. It was Nyala's story and she felt a twinge of ownership; even thinking that her friend would read the words before her made her more possessive.

"No. I'm going to read it first. You can read it when I'm done." Nyala didn't exactly snatch the pages from her friend, but it was enough of a grab that Luba sat back in her kitchen chair.

"Whoa! That was rude! Not like I'm planning to steal your secret lover or anything, I was just going to read it." Luba looked hurt, but she wasn't. "So it is sexy! Isn't it! That's why you won't share! Too personal! Old lover? Oh yeah! That's it! That's why you don't go on dates! Gimme!"

Luba's halfhearted attempt to take the manuscript back wasn't meant to succeed, only to make a point, but Nyala turned and walked toward her bedroom-cum-office door, located off to the side of the one main living area. As she walked, she held up the back of her hand to warn Luba not to push it.

"Fine. Want anything from the city? I have hair with Dwayne today, at two o'clock, but I'm free for dinner if you want to catch a bite in town later at the Golden Dragon? Or how about Tosca's? The Portuguese joint! They make the best french fries! We can have whole crab and fries!"

But Nyala was ignoring her friend. She was already leafing through the pages as she walked, finding where she'd left off. What did this guy mean by "that caused you"? That was disconcerting.

Caused me? She frowned as she shut the door behind her and sat at her desk.

She didn't hear Luba say goodbye.

Maybe it wasn't that one object that caused you.

That caused you, Nyala.

5

1960s

UNDISCLOSED SMALL TOWN

It wasn't a big city, more like a big town with big-city hopes and dreams. The streets were lined with well-kept homes, small but sweet, elms and lawns, pretty flower boxes and ladies in floppy hats bent over flower beds; men pushing two-wheel lawn mowers, grass clippings springing out behind the clattering rotary blades. There were dogs every second house, running free and children running even freer, not a care in the world. Hide-and-seek; Cowboys and Indians. Tag and Simon Says "do this" and "do that."

"Check it out, Hunter, have to be treasures in this part of town!" Pete's enthusiasm was obvious in his body language as he leaned forward to read the address on the sign nailed to the weathered telephone pole. And it was just as obvious that he was talking to himself, not to his son, who stood on the floor, holding on to the dashboard, looking out the front windshield, trying to see the sign his father was talking about, even though according to his teacher, he couldn't read.

"That's only three blocks away! I can feel it! What do you think, Hunter? Excited?" Pete wasn't actually asking a question, nor was he expecting an answer. First off, Hunter didn't talk much; second, it was about Pete, not Hunter. Work all week. Now was his playtime, his release.

As per garage sale protocol, this one advertised with signs out on the nearest busy road, the one Pete was driving the truck along. Unlike most garage sales, when they pulled up to the address, it wasn't a newer cookie-cutter type house; it was older and was in a slightly older neighborhood. The lot was bigger too and the trees taller, probably one of the original homes in the area, Pete figured. It had to have been built before the rest of the street was surveyed and subdivided into perfect rectangular lots; must have been rich people. And there weren't any kids playing on the lawn, not that there would have been room, since the tables and boxes and stuff covered most of the front yard.

Pete pulled in behind the last of four cars on the right side of the street across from the garage sale house. There were seven more cars facing the opposite direction, parked on the same side as the house.

"Damn it. We're late." Pete shut the truck off and hit the parking brake. He was about to pull the door handle when he stopped and remembered his son. Reaching into his pocket instead, he took out four quarters, but then put one back. Then he hesitated and put another back in his pocket. "Okay, here's fifty cents. Don't buy anything stupid and don't leave the yard."

Pete didn't wait for his son to exit the truck on the passenger side. He'd already slammed his creaking door behind him and was halfway across the street before Hunter managed to push open the heavy passenger door and turn, to let himself carefully slide backward out of the old truck. His toes touched the sidewalk about the same instant the friction from his belly-on-the-seat slide out of the truck let loose. If his feet hadn't touched the sidewalk when they did, he would have fallen backward from the truck.

Stop. Look and listen. Be careful. Be careful. Don't walk out from between cars. Before Pete's son made it across the street and down the cracked cement driveway and into the aisles of offerings, his father was already deep into negotiations with the homeowner, a small, slender man who looked completely out of place at a garage sale. Actually the owner looked totally out of place in the neighborhood; in the entire town more like. Pete was brandishing a large and by appearances well-used, red-painted pipe wrench.

"Twenty-five cents." Pete was a pro at this and as such was convinced that the louder you negotiated, the more you cowed the owner into selling whatever it was you wanted, for cheaper than the sticker price. Usually the prices at garage sales were written on a piece of masking tape stuck to whatever it was you were interested in, but the prices at this sale were neatly printed in pen, on round, sky-blue "fancy" stickers. Pete was in his glory.

His philosophy, the one that had held him in such good stead over the years of treasure hunting, was first to find something that you knew was worth four times the price out in the real world and then try and talk the owner down to a quarter of that price. On a good day, Pete would push for one-tenth of the sticker price.

"See! It's got rust here and the mechanism is sloppy."

The gentle-looking owner stood only as tall as Pete's shoulder and looked shocked when Pete shook the wrench at him to demonstrate how loose the metal jaws were. Several people, who'd looked up when Pete boomed out his offer, now shook their heads and went back to their treasure hunting. Loud and aggressive wasn't normal garage sale behavior. Most buyers were stealthy, to the point of appearing sneaky to an observer, like they were hiding a secret, which was their inviolable intent if they found something they knew was worth more than the sticker price.

Someone holding a lamp was waiting for their turn to discuss the price with the slight but well-turned-out owner; they were standing just close enough to ensure that Pete could see them in his peripheral vision. Pete turned slightly to ensure his back was toward the waiting customer, making it clear that he didn't care about what they wanted; it was all about him.

"Fifty cents. Last offer. Here." Pete pulled the two quarters from his pocket, thanking himself silently for saving them from his son. "Done deal. Lots more where that came from! Good deal for both of us! Gonna buy a lot more!"

Pete didn't wait for the owner to agree; he literally reached out with the hand holding the quarters and tipped his palm to 90 degrees. The owner didn't have a choice; he reached out and let the two shiny coins drop into his hand. Pete turned to walk away in one motion. It was a gamble that he'd won many times in the past. If the owner didn't hold his hand out to catch the money, it would drop to the ground, which would be embarrassing to Pete, but everyone always held out their hand.

It was kind of like public shaming. Make the owner as uncomfortable as possible, by talking in a voice loud enough that every person in the yard couldn't help noticing. And when everyone turned to see what was going on, basically force the owner into accepting a lowball offer, just to remove them from the limelight. Perfectly executed!

Pete, still chuffed about buying the pipe wrench for at least two dollars less than it was worth, was checking out another box of tools when he noticed his son standing beside him. Standing beside him and holding some dumb thing or other that he'd picked from an obscure corner of the sale. This kid would drive you nuts. It didn't happen often—in fact near as Pete could remember, maybe once a month, probably less actually, one in a hundred garage sales maybe— but when it did, when his son would walk up with some useless piece of crap that he wanted to buy, it somehow always irritated Pete.

"You don't need that. Put it back." He turned to look at the tools but knew his son wouldn't put it back. In fact Hunter would continue to follow him around the entire time, not saying anything, but always there. Pete shook his head and tried to ignore him, walking away, farther down the table, reaching for an old silver-handled flashlight. He clicked the button to see if it worked. It didn't.

"Young man? Do you want that?" It was the owner. He'd been watching Hunter from across the yard and had walked around the tables to stand at the end of the aisle.

Hunter looked up at the man and nodded.

Pete stopped looking at tools and turned to look at what his son was holding.

"How much is it?" He reached down and held out his hand, expecting his son to hand over the goods. It was a white dish with some kind of blue designs on the face. "What is it? An old plate?"

For a fraction of a second, it looked like his son was going to pull it away from his father, but he didn't. He handed it over.

"Ha ha! Are you kidding me! Ten dollars! Are you out of your mind?" Pete handed the plate to the owner. "He doesn't want it."

Dismissive, he turned back to his tools. For Christ's sake, what did his kid think they were made of, money? He was more than irritated now; he was getting angry; a normal kid, that's all he wanted. A plate? God Almighty, this kid was going to make him crazy.

Overhead a flock of starlings flared and flew off. Someone down the street was calling for a child and a dog barked. Four more cars pulled up in front of the house and two cars pulled away.

"You like it?" The owner was still standing there, turning the plate in his hands, looking down at the young boy. "It was my mother's. She traveled around the world on a ship when she was young. I think she brought this from England, but it's probably Chinese. Old, I would say. What do you think? Old?"

The youngster looked up at the man, who was smiling slightly. It was a soft, sincere smile, not intended for anyone alive; it was a smile in honor of a memory. Nor was he expecting an answer to his question. He was instead for that instant preoccupied with the memory of the mother he'd recently lost.

The boy waited, as if aware that it was not his right to break the spell. When the man holding the plate returned to the moment, the boy nodded his agreement; the plate was old.

The plate was very old.

"The kid's not interested." Pete was on the far side of the table now, beside another man who was rummaging through the same box Pete had been searching through. He was feeling possessive, or more like the owner was in his face, overstepping his bounds. "Can't even read yet. Doesn't like to be teased."

The owner ignored Pete.

"How much money do you have?" The man wasn't teasing. He'd made a decision and wasn't about to let the young boy's father bully him a second time.

Hunter reached in his pocket and took out the two quarters his father had given him. He showed them to the man.

Pete was watching now. It was an ugly plate, but if the owner was stupid enough to give a ten-dollar plate away for fifty cents, then he was even more gullible than he looked. A deal was a deal.

"Hmmm. That's a pretty hard bargain you are driving, young man." The slender man frowned and said, "I'll tell you what. If you pay two quarters for this plate, you must promise me that you will be very careful with it and won't break it for as long as you own it."

He was smiling now, holding the plate out to the boy.

"I think she would have liked you. And I think she would have wanted you to have this."

The boy handed the two quarters over to the man and took possession of the plate, holding it to his chest.

More junk, Pete was thinking to himself; just what they needed. More junk headed for his son's bedroom. Maybe Rose could convince Hunter to let her use the plate for setting a plant pot on, or for a lid on a pot, something useful instead of sitting on a shelf in his kid's room with all the other crap he'd wasted the family money on over the last couple of years.

"The kid appreciates it. Let's go, Hunter." Pete had seen all he needed to see. "Spent enough here already."

He waved the pipe wrench at his son, directing him like a street cop at an intersection. No good deals left, too many people, too many other sales to hit before the day was done. Another three cars were looking to park across the street. Pete didn't wait for his son; he was on his way out of the yard, headed toward the truck. He didn't pay any attention to the heavy, unhealthy-looking man walking in the opposite direction, toward the entrance to the garage sale yard.

The man stopped in the middle of the road and turned when Hunter walked past.

"Excuse me?" The guy now walked back toward where Hunter had stopped at the back end of Pete's old truck. "Excuse me."

Pete was already in the truck, about to slam the door.

What now?

"What?" He was holding the door. "Something I can help you with?"

"Is that your boy?" The man was breathing heavily from the exertion of turning and walking back across to the truck. He stopped and pointed at Hunter.

Pete was really getting fed up now. One day of the week, was that really too much to ask? One day when he could do what he wanted, when he wanted, as many times as he wanted.

"Yes, he's my kid. Hunter, get in the truck."

"No, wait. That plate. Can I see it?"

Pete nearly said no, but he caught himself.

"Why?"

"Sorry, but I'm an antique dealer." He pointed at the truck parked two cars behind Pete's International. "Willisford Dowan. Indefinite Art Incorporated. That's the name of my shop. I pay top dollar for antiquities. I specialize in finer pieces but of course am interested in anything that is old and good quality."

Pete looked back over his shoulder at the truck the man was pointing to. It was a panel van more like, with a roof rack. He couldn't read the sign on the side of the truck from his angle but could see it was there. For a second he thought that maybe he could make a quick sale on the pipe wrench. It was definitely old, but he didn't offer it up quite yet. He took the proffered hand and gave it a cursory shake; soft grip; easy target.

"Nice to meet you. Why do you want to see that old plate?"

The man had already started toward the back of the truck and was reaching for the plate. Hunter pulled away, shielding it from the man with his body. The man stopped, a gentle, reassuring look on his face.

"It's okay. I just want to see if it's what I think it is." The man held out his hand.

Hunter didn't move for a moment. Then, he saw the watch. He still didn't move, just stared at the watch face, and then, as though he'd accepted the man as a kindred spirit, held out the plate to the fat hand. The blue ten-dollar sticker was still stuck to the face, covering part of the cobalt flower blossom decoration.

Hear me again, Nyala.
    Before you go on. You must know this.
Brown and brown. Brown and brown. Brown and brown.
I handed it to him and . . . I killed him that day.
I didn't know. I couldn't know. I was eight.
It was our fate . . . yours Nyala . . . mine . . . his.
He was only the first.
In the darkness now, lying all alone. A lifetime of regrets.
I am sorry. These are things I should have told you all along.
Too late now to right those wrongs.
    I can live it again now, close my eyes, and I see how it started and I see the watch on his wrist again. Color, brilliant, impossible not to see. Mesmerizing in its singular beauty. Hands of time perfectly balanced, set to perfection, it was the essence of . . . essence. I could feel it.
    Brilliant. Bright. Color.
    I have felt that essence since, many times. Perfection, so rare. So transient. Ethereal. Created by artists, artists of God maybe, artists who have God living within. I don't know; I am not an artist. God made me to feel His work. Feel His beauty. I don't know. I didn't know.
    I was eight.
    And I was a death warrant.

6

"Porcelain! Qing! I knew it the instant I saw it!" The antique dealer reached into the pocket of his jacket, pulling out a spectacle case, taking care to keep the plate firmly pressed to his chest as he pulled the optics from the case. "Let's see how old."

Once he had the glasses in place on his surprisingly fine nose, the large man turned the plate over to look at the back. His fat hands looked soft, almost feminine. Pete was taller, so he could see over the man's shoulder, but other than the fact that they were both standing in the same street, the two grown men had absolutely nothing in common.

"Ha! Look!" The antique dealer pointed to the markings on the back of the plate. "Yongzheng!!"

The dealer gazed at the plate. The young boy stared at his watch.

"I've never seen one. At least I haven't seen one outside of the big museums out east. He was a great emperor, early 1700s. Qing Dynasty, Great Qing. After the Ming Dynasty. His father passed on the throne to him when he died. Yongzheng loved art. I can't believe it. Young man, do you know what you have here?"

The large man looked over his glasses at the boy.

Pete moved around to stand beside his son at the back of the truck.

"What's it worth to you?" Pete had never been the brightest student in class, at least the classes that he'd attended, and the fat guy might as well have been talking Martian for all he understood about what he was saying about the plate, but he knew all about dealing with people who wanted something he had. "Make us an offer."

The man holding the plate now looked up at Pete, over the glasses on his nose, sizing up the rough-looking character in an instant.

"How much do you want for it?"

They stood their ground, unflinching, locked in each other's line of sight.

It was the boy who broke the standoff, stepping closer to the fat man and tugging at his sleeve. He was pointing at the man's watch. Both the antique dealer, still holding the plate, and Pete looked down at the boy who'd butted into the middle of their negotiations. Pete's feelings were easy to read; it was like he was looking down at the dumbest person on earth. The antique dealer was looking down at the young boy with almost the exact opposite look.

"My watch? You mean this one?" Bemused, he cocked his wrist toward the boy. "You have very good taste, young man."

He laughed and placed the precious plate to his chest, holding it there with his left forearm, then, as he'd done to pull the spectacles from the case, he undid the wristwatch strap with his free right hand. He was about to give the timepiece to the boy, when he hesitated.

"It was given to me by a friend." He still held the plate against his chest with his left arm but was now looking over his glasses at the watch. "A very dear friend. His name was Jean. He raced cars. He died doing what he loved; a long time ago."

The dealer looked down at the watch now, with a different emotion showing on his face. Loss? No, it was tender, more than just loss. It was tragic loss. More. Tragic love lost. So long ago, he'd been young then, he'd been beautiful, beautiful like Jean. But time, as it ravaged his body, eroded the memory. It was still there now, but the big hurt was gone. It was only a memory of loss now, just a memory, still there, but mixed with a lifetime of newer memories. Then the moment was gone, and he felt the plate against his chest.

"It's called a Zerographe. Made by a company in Switzerland called Rolex. You don't know that company, but they've been around for almost fifty years. It's kind of like your dad's Timex, but different." The antique dealer tried not to smile at his own joke. He detested cheap and functional, especially something named after such modern-day proletariat icons as *Time* magazine and Kleenex. "It's not new; it was made before World War II. It was a gift to my friend who raced cars, from the owners of that Rolex company I told you about."

When Jean gave him the watch, he'd of course been giddy and thankful. Back then, it was just another piece of jewelry, a splendid piece, but everything was splendid in those days and everything came easy; jewelry, haute couture, art. Was it really so long ago that Robert Piguet was postulating to all of them at Les Deux Magots over a fine bottle of 1931 Armagnac Sempé, saying that elegance was born of simplicity's virtue? Christian designed Robert's "Café Anglais" dress, but Christian was still pretty much an unknown art dealer at that time and a good friend. It was years later that he became "Dior" and left his friends behind.

Money meant nothing to the rest of them. Why should they care about money? They all had enough for their needs, for their fun. He had the least, but his rich friends were happy to take care of him. His lot had changed though. He'd fallen for the wrong person and his life started to fall apart, unravel. He'd moved and moved again and again.

The beauty of his youth faded and here he was, in the middle of nowhere. Nobody cared, nobody wanted to know his story; obese; scratching to make a living. Wasting the last of his life begging to buy and begging to sell. On bad days, drinking alone at night, in his apartment above the antique shop, he'd bitterly admit to himself that he'd grown up to become an alchemist, trying to turn cheap junk into expensive junk.

Only the watch he now held in his pudgy, liver-spotted hand remained of his former life and self. At first he'd kept it as a token of the love it represented, but over time and need, he'd looked into selling it to pay whatever pressing "final warning" bill he'd received. He never sold it though; he couldn't. Not because he didn't have the will, but because he didn't have the knowledge. He literally couldn't find any information about it and, more importantly, what it was worth. Of course it was valuable, he knew that for a certainty, but how much? He researched it as best he could, but there were no records of it in Switzerland; at least not that he could find. He'd sent them at least three letters over the years, all with the same result: "Sorry, we don't have any records of such a watch being produced by us here at Rolex."

He'd even taken it to two experts in the watch field whom he trusted as much as you could trust anybody in the business and they'd both said the same thing. They'd never heard of it, and they'd never seen any advertising for such a watch from the Rolex watch company in Switzerland, ever. It had to be a pieced-together copy, they had told him, made by a great watchmaker to be sure, but far less valuable than a real Rolex.

Jean wouldn't have given him an imitation Rolex. Would he?

So many more memories, triggered by the watch in his hand, pushed their way out from the recesses of his mind, but this wasn't the time. Tonight, if he wanted to reminisce, he could do so with a bottle of wine, unfortunately not good and not vintage. And even more unfortunately, by himself.

"It meant something to me once, but not now. Here, have a look."

The boy took the watch.

"The strap isn't original."

The boy didn't say anything, but the antique dealer raised his eyebrows when the boy looked up at him as if to say, "I know. That's obvious."

"Of course you would know that. And if you know that, then I don't need to also tell you that it is a very valuable watch!" He laughed and made a decision. "I'll tell you what, young fellow: I'll trade you. Straight across. Your plate for my watch."

Pete couldn't take it anymore.

"Now listen, what's he going to do with a watch? He's only eight." Pete raised his voice. "Twenty-five dollars. That's his final offer. Cash! Won't take a check."

The antique dealer looked at the man. It wasn't disdain exactly, but there wasn't the tiniest bit of respect in his countenance either.

The boy abruptly reached out to give the watch back to the fat antique dealer and held out his other hand, motioning for the man to give the plate back. They made the exchange.

"Goddammit." Pete shook his head. His damn kid meant it and

Pete knew it. For whatever reason, the kid never wanted to sell any-thing he found. Wasted space and wasted money, sitting on the book-case shelves in his bedroom. Pete knew better than to push though. The result would only be bad; when the line in the sand was drawn, slow or not, his son's stubborn streak was all Rose.

"Okay. Don't sell it." Pete was disgusted. He was sure the guy would have paid even more than twenty-five. "But I'm telling you right now. Never again. You think your mother and I are made of money? We can't afford to have you throw money away on any more crap."

Pete wheeled and climbed back in his truck, slamming his door, not out of habit this time. He was pissed.

"Get in, Hunter. We're leaving."

The antique dealer and the boy looked at each other. The man held out the watch to the boy again. The boy didn't hesitate. He handed the antique dealer the plate and took the watch. He turned without a second look at the large man, who now held his plate, and as he walked around the back of the truck, to the passenger side, he was staring at the watch, obviously mesmerized.

When the boy left his sight, the antique dealer walked to Pete's window and tapped on it. When Pete didn't lower the window, he reached into his pocket and pulled out a card.

"I have a proposition." He said it loud enough that Pete could hear, but instead of answering, Pete just stared at him through the window. The dealer reached into his pocket with his free hand once again and pulled out a five-dollar bill. "Sorry, I couldn't help but hear you say your son bought other 'crap.' "

Pete wasn't sure what was going on, but he recognized easy money when he saw it. He was only making two dollars an hour as a me-chanic. He rolled down the window.

"What other kind of things does your son have?" The antique dealer handed Pete the card and the bill. "That's my number."

Pete looked at the money and ignored the card. Then, without even acknowledging the man standing outside his window, he an-swered.

"All kinds of junk. Small stuff. Like that plate. All crap." Pete put the bill in his pocket and threw the card on the dusty dash. It wasn't until then that he looked out at the antique dealer. "Small paintings. Jesus and God stuff. Weird statues. I don't know, African. And some beaded Indian things. And a bunch of old books. Like I said, I don't know; it's all junk."

On the far side of the truck, the dealer could see the young boy bobbing his head up and down, gaining momentum for the big step up into the truck and onto the bench seat. The boy was holding the watch tightly in his small hand, which made getting in that much more difficult.

"Call me. I may be interested in some of your son's things. Did he pick them up at garage sales?"

"Yep. Comes with me every week."

"Call me." The antique dealer tapped the open windowsill and then turned to cross the street to the garage sale house. There were a dozen cars in the street now and double that many people carefully looking through the offerings on the tables.

Pete watched the dealer walk away. Then he looked at his boy, who was still staring at the watch, caressing it, turning it over and over, feeling it. Whatever the heck just happened, Pete wasn't angry anymore. Five dollars was five dollars and there was still plenty of time to hit more sales. It was already a great day! He had the pipe wrench and a $4.50 profit on the two quarters he'd given Hunter. Not bad.

Not bad at all.

The antique dealer slid the plate into the big pocket on the inside of his jacket and turned to watch the green pickup truck pull away. He noted the license number. If he didn't hear from the kid's father, he'd tap Justin his buddy at the cop shop for a favor and find out where they lived. Justin collected Murano art glass and would pretty much do anything to stay in the antique dealer's good books.

Qing Dynasty; Yongzheng!

He held his hand up against where the plate was now safely hidden in his jacket pocket, almost to make sure it was still there, that it was real. He wouldn't need to work for the rest of the year if he didn't want to. He could get a new van and go on a holiday too! He could do anything his heart desired.

He was thrilled and patted the plate through his jacket again. Then he frowned.

Strange kid. Very strange kid.

The thrill was still there, but thinking of the kid dampened the joy somehow. As he turned to walk over to the garage sale, he looked at where the watch had been on his wrist for so many years. For a moment he felt the shadow of doubt, the shadow of every antique dealer's nightmare. Did he make a mistake?

No way.

Not a chance.

Qing porcelain plate; over two hundred years old; perfect condition. Most valuable thing he'd found in all the years he'd been forced to turn his formerly manicured hand to antique dealing. Yongzheng mark too. Best day of his pathetic life in this pathetic town!

But he was still frowning as he began looking at the other offerings at the garage sale, making his way toward where a youngish, at least younger than him, well-dressed man was accepting money from a dowdy lady holding an old copper boiler. He noticed the young man bore a striking resemblance to Yves, another friend from those halcyon days he'd spent in Paris dancing the night away, wearing one of Robert's "Café Anglais" black and white *pieds de poule*! Those were the days. Yves was big-time now. The fat antique dealer heard he'd started his own haute couture house.

The memory would have normally made him feel a sweet melancholy, a longing for the sun to return, even for a moment. He knew in his heart that he would give up a thousand tomorrows for one more yesterday.

But he didn't feel the sweet melancholy brought on by the fond memories, not this time.

He couldn't shake the shadow of doubt.

7

2020

PINEHURST, NORTH CAROLINA

Did you send me something? To my house?" Nyala was still in her room, sitting at her desk; mobile phone, faceup, beside her computer keyboard, speaker on.

Scott worked with Nyala and Luba at the newspaper. He wasn't much of a writer, but he was an exceptional researcher and so Nyala often leaned on him to find the facts on topics she was reporting on. He was also a millennial, with a touch of hipster thrown in. Basically he was a gender-confused loser with a man bun, beard, and plaid shirt. Ugh. The guy was everything Nyala found revolting in the New Age males from the city. On the other hand, Nyala was everything Scott found irresistible in the New Age women of the city.

"No, not a card and *no*, I don't want a card." Nyala rolled her eyes. "I just want to know if you sent me something, like something you wrote."

Nyala picked up the phone and walked to the window overlooking the lake that formed the back property line of her wooded lot. From her bedroom window, she could often see ducks, geese, and sometimes a blue heron waiting patiently for a fish or frog or salamander to swim to within stabbing distance. Scott was kind of like a salamander. Glabrous. A salamander with a beard. Yuck. Luba found him cute. Nyala found him repugnant, albeit useful.

"No, I said I don't want a card and *no*, I don't want you to send me flowers. And no, you didn't do anything wrong." What was with these guys nowadays? Nyala knew she'd have to change the subject or else Scott would probably get so upset he'd pee on the floor. "Never mind about that. Are you going to be at work tomorrow? I may need you to look into something for me. Don't tell anyone. Top-secret story I'm working on. Good, okay, thanks."

Asking Scott a favor would incentivize him to hang around her even more than he already did. Ugh. So as an afterthought she added, "Oh, and Scott, Luba says to say hi. Uh-huh, yep, she likes you."

She pushed the red button on the phone face and felt a small pang of guilt. That wasn't nice. Scott was so lost, looking for hope, that even the tiniest intimation of affection would turn him into a slobbering puppy dog, but at least he'd be Luba's slobbering puppy dog, not hers. The guilt passed. Luba was attracted to Scott for some reason that Nyala couldn't for the life of her understand. Gross.

She took a last long survey of the lake waters. No wind today; blue sky. She could see two wood ducks swimming by and some grass carp slurping flotsam at the surface near shore. She knew she could walk out and the normally skittish wood ducks would not fly away. Nor would the squirrels scatter or carp boil the surface to escape like they did when Luba walked out.

Even though Luba was the fashionista in the family, Nyala was pretty sure the antique dealer with the watch was probably referring to Christian Dior and Yves Saint Laurent. Pretty cool if it was true. She let herself imagine hanging out in early midcentury Paris with race car drivers and fashion designers.

"If you are lucky enough to have lived in Paris as a young man . . ." She let Hemingway's quote fade, unfinished in her mind. The "young man" part irritated her, but still, he was an amazing guy, good writer, not as great as everyone held him out to be, but his life! How would Luba put it? Hashtag goals? Adventure and travel to crazy places. Discovery and exploration.

Even the hunting he wrote about intrigued her; safaris in the green hills of Africa. Now that would be supercool. Totally politically incorrect as it was among her college friends and coworkers in the city, Nyala had always been fascinated with the idea of hunting, providing for herself, and self-reliance. Somehow it seemed to her that true hunters did the former and exhibited the latter. Hunters appeared to have a spiritual connection with the wild things, a connection that was missing in all her city friends, in spite of their avowed love for wild animals.

Pivoting back to her desk, she sat and pulled the laptop toward her, typing "Qing Dynasty" into the Google bar. Habit. Google Search. Click. Once a journalist, always a journalist. When the screen popped up, she scrolled down to the Wikipedia information. Click. Normally she wouldn't read through anything, she'd scan, but this time she read.

An hour later she was still reading, refocusing her search every few minutes. "**Yongzheng.**" Interesting. "**The Age of Harmony and Integrity.**" Nice. Wouldn't it be great if some of Yongzheng's karma rubbed off on today's leaders? So at least some of what was in the manuscript was real. She sat back and clicked through the information on the screen. Yongzheng did rule during the Qing Dynasty from 1722 to 1735. He wasn't just the Chinese emperor; he was also a patron of the arts, and she confirmed that there were porcelain plates made during his reign. No big stretch there; easy as pie to find the online references. Her natural curiosity took her deep into the Google underworld. Value of a Yongzheng plate. Click.

Nyala whistled under her breath.

Too bad the kid didn't find a Yongzheng bowl. $564,000 USD at a Sotheby's auction a few years back. Plates were less valuable; it depended on the quality. From the little information provided in the manuscript, Nyala figured the plate was probably worth $3,500–$10,000 in today's market. More if it was something as special as the antique dealer thought. Today it was worth that, but there was no way of knowing what such a plate would have gone for back when the boy found it, probably the same relatively speaking, if you factored in the buying power of a midcentury dollar. Enough to buy a van probably, a year's wages maybe.

Nyala took her hand off the mouse and reached for her pen. From what she'd read, she'd assumed the manuscript was talking about the 1950s, but it could be 1960s. The truck was 1952, she thought she'd read. Had to be after that; the truck was old when the kid found the plate. She wrote a note to herself. Check when motorized lawn mowers came on the market.

No need to check on what "Simon Says" was. She knew it was a kid's game, a game she'd never played as a child. Who would she play with? She didn't have a family. No sisters or brothers and she didn't make friends easily, still didn't. Orphan problems. She suffered from them all. Foster kids are us.

She opened the manuscript until she found what she was looking for and then reached for the keyboard. Rolex Zerographe. Google Search. Click.

The first hit said it all.

"Rarer Than The Holy Grail. The Rolex Zerographe, Reference . . ."

Nyala, fascinated now, clicked on the link and scanned.

Rare was right. Only seven made for sure, maybe twelve; only four known to exist today. So obscure, almost no literature available, even in the venerated company headquarters archives. No period advertising.

Nyala sat back and considered what she was reading. If what happened in the manuscript was real and if it happened more than half a century ago, like she figured, there would have been no internet. No instant everyone-is-an-Einstein gratification. It didn't exist back then. So it was possible that an antique dealer, especially in the small town where it appeared the narrative was set, might not have been able to find out what she had with a few typed words and the click of a mouse.

She scrolled down, clicked a new link, and stopped.

"Reported to have been given to the famous race car drivers of the day. Bugatti for one."

She typed Bugatti. Click. **"Ettore Bugatti, founder of the famed car company. Died 1947. Suicide."**

"Son Jean."

She took a breath and blew out a silent whistle. Jean.

Nyala entered Jean Bugatti and clicked.

"Died at age 30, Aug 29, 1939 test driving the car that had just won the 24 Hours of Le Mans." Nyala looked closely at the photo on the screen. He existed. He was a race car driver and there was a connection to a rare Rolex watch.

As an afterthought, she typed in Rolex Zerographe value.

Then she did whistle, and not under her breath this time.

8

1960s

UNDISCLOSED SMALL TOWN

The five-dollar bill was sitting on the table. It couldn't have been more obvious than if Pete had flopped a whale on their kitchen tabletop; beside it was the business card. Willisford Dowan. Indefinite Art Incorporated.

"What should we do?" Rose looked up at her husband. "That's a lot of money."

Pete was holding his beer bottle, already half-empty. She knew he wasn't a fan of the new stubby bottles, way preferring the bigger quart bottles that beer used to come in. Rose was thankful her husband would never meet the people in charge of the "asinine baby beer bottle" decision, or for that matter, anyone who made decisions he thought made no common sense.

"Could have been more, should be thirty dollars on the table right now, but your kid wouldn't sell the plate to him." Pete pushed back his chair, stood up, and drained his beer. He walked to the fridge, setting the empty on the kitchen counter before opening the door and taking out another beer. "What the hell are we going to do about that kid?"

It wasn't a question, and she knew he didn't expect an answer. Pete rummaged in the drawer for an opener.

"I think we call this guy and get him to buy all Hunter's junk." Pete returned and sat at the table across from his wife. "Probably nothing he would want, but at least we should see."

Pete popped the lid off and bent over to pick up the bottle cap from the floor, before sitting at the table again.

"Shhhh. Don't talk so loud. Hunter will hear you. He's in his room."

"Looking at that stupid watch. You should have seen him. The guy gave me five dollars and was going to pay twenty-five for the plate!" Pete was shaking his head. "It's not even a Timex!"

Again, Rose kept her opinions to herself. She knew he needed to vent. He'd fumed all through the evening meal, railed about everything really; she knew the real reason for his mood wasn't their son's trade or the five-dollar bill on the table, although it would have been burning a hole in Pete's pocket all morning. Not finding something to spend it on would have irritated him.

Other than that strange encounter with the antique dealer who wanted Hunter's plate, Rose knew it hadn't been a great day. That always made him cranky. She watched as Pete took another long swig from the third bottle he'd opened since dinner.

Before her boys left that morning, Rose had mentioned to Pete that she had had to skimp on the food budget lately. It was her gentle, roundabout way of letting Pete know that he probably shouldn't be spending money on things they didn't need. At the time, optimistic as he always was at the beginning of any garage sale day, he listened to her, but didn't want to hear what she was saying, preferring to believe he'd find the deal of the century that would fix the money situation.

But he hadn't and now he was feeling guilty.

She knew her husband well. Pete felt guilty because he knew he shouldn't have even gone looking if money was that tight. Her words were finally hitting home and now he was feeling sorry for himself, feeling that he was a failure when it came to his one real responsibility, providing for his family.

Rose knew the timing wasn't perfect, but she steeled herself and seized the moment to change the subject.

"I made an appointment for Hunter yesterday." She set herself for the coming storm and continued. "Dr. Polisik referred me to a Dr. Keen. So, I called his office today. He can see him Friday at 2:00 p.m."

"What's wrong with him?"

Rose took a breath.

"He can't read, Pete. I told you. He can't read anything. He's in grade three already and his teacher says he's the only one who can't." Rose said it then. "Dr. Keen is a psychiatrist, the best. A child psychiatrist."

The words finally made it through to Pete. Psychiatrist?

"A shrink? You mean you made an appointment for my kid to see a shrink?" Pete's voice rose a level. "You think he's crazy? They think he's crazy? No way! Not my kid! You're not taking him to any shrink!"

Pete pushed his chair back and stood up again, looking down at his wife.

"What will the neighbors say? Jesus, Rose, think about it!" He turned his back and walked to the window, beer in his hand, but he wasn't drinking. "He's different, but he damn sure doesn't need a shrink!"

Rose stood from her chair then and walked to her husband. She wrapped her arms around him. She knew that under the rough exterior there was a damaged heart. Her husband wanted to love their son but didn't know how. She was aware of how much it hurt him to think that Hunter wasn't normal. Another failure. Another of his own father's prophecies come true. Pete saw their son as his own personal failing and pulled away from Hunter, was callous around him; his way of coping; his hard way of dealing with the truth and the pain. She knew it was made even worse for Pete knowing that others recognized that there was something wrong with their only child.

"Pete, Hunter isn't sick. He has trouble reading. That's all. And this doctor is supposed to be the best for children with learning problems. He specializes in children." Rose knew if she allowed herself to lose control, she would be crying in a heartbeat. "It will be okay. We just need to find out why he can't read. That's all."

Rose felt her husband take a deep breath and then she felt the barest of shudders.

It broke her heart to know how far Pete fell when he let go.

9

The number 4 bus picked them up not far from the school Hunter attended. Rose could see children playing in the field beside the school. Others were hunched over circles scratched in the ground, playing with marbles that she couldn't see from where she and Hunter sat on the bus seat looking out the window. Hunter was looking too, but not at the kids; he didn't seem to take any interest at all in other children. He was watching a hawk soaring high above the school, circling and then swooping down to land in a tree beside the bus.

Was it looking at them? Rose pursed her lips and shook the question out of her mind. Out of her mind was right. Maybe she was the one who should be seeing the doctor.

"Aren't you happy you don't have to go to school today?" She patted her son's smooth brown hair. She loved Hunter more than life itself and it hurt her to know she was taking him to a doctor to find out what was wrong with him. Wrong? It felt as if she was betraying his trust in her. She was his mother. She should be protecting him.

Several stops and a transfer later, Rose pulled the overhead cord, letting the bus driver know they wanted off.

"We're here!" She took Hunter's hand and helped him get down the three steps to the sidewalk. The doors hissed closed behind them and the bus pulled away, belching black exhaust.

The place wasn't institutional as she imagined it would be. Instead it was a house, old, Victorian, with cedar-shake siding and quaint gingerbread cutouts in the gables. There were beds of flowers and a nicely trimmed hedge on each side of the lawn.

Rose checked the address on the paper she pulled from her purse one more time. It was her best purse, and she was wearing her best mohair cape, like Jackie Kennedy's.

"You ready?" Rose was still holding her son's hand. Thankful that unlike the other children his age, who she often saw pulling away from any sort of handholding with their parents, Hunter didn't seem to mind; didn't seem to notice to be entirely accurate. Rose took a deep breath. The future would be what it would be and there was no way to ignore reality any longer. They would find out what was wrong, and they would deal with it as a family. She opened the low white picket fence gate.

"Here we go."

————

"We're here to see Dr. Keen. We have a two o'clock appointment. This is my son Hunter." Rose was pleasantly surprised. She'd been worried that there would be other parents in the waiting room, with their own children, parents that she'd have to make small talk with, but there were none. The office was decorated like a home. It had a warm, comforting feeling and the lady sitting behind the counter smiled nicely. Rose wasn't sure what she'd expected, but all of a sudden she didn't feel guilty; relieved would be a better way to describe it. Finally they would know. Whatever it was, they would know.

When the doctor came into the waiting room, after the nice lady at the desk had taken Hunter's information down, whatever apprehension Rose still might have harbored was dispelled. She was instantly put at ease by him. Middle-aged, he was wearing a cardigan sweater and had glasses on his nose. Round but not fat. Not short, not tall; kind of unimposing in every way, gentle and welcoming. She could not have imagined a more stereotypical-looking children's doctor.

"Hello! I'm Dr. Keen. And you must be Hunter!" He bent down to bring his face to Hunter's level and held his hand out to the young boy standing beside his mother. The boy's eyes never left the man's face. Friend or foe, the boy was making up his own mind. He didn't move.

The doctor held his hand in place. The boy continued to look in the man's eyes; unwavering.

"Hunter! Don't be rude! Dr. Keen wants to shake your hand."

For a full minute they stood.

Then the boy held out his hand too.

"I'm so sorry, Dr. Keen." Rose was used to making excuses for her son. "He's got his own mind. If I insist, it only gets worse."

The doctor didn't even seem to notice there'd been a full minute of awkwardness.

"That's okay, right, Hunter? Good to make up your own mind!" He looked up at the boy's blushing mother. "Perfectly normal for some children, don't give it a second thought."

He straightened and turned to the lady at the desk, who held out the file she'd been making notes in. Hunter's name was on the file tab. After leafing through it for a few moments, the doctor turned back to Rose.

"Probably best if I visit with Hunter alone for a bit, if that's okay. I've got some tests I'd like to give him and often having a parent in the room can make the child wary. They can pull back from freewill responses and even answer the questions incorrectly on purpose. It's a defense mechanism for some children." He looked down at Hunter, who by then wasn't paying any attention to any of the adults in the room. "It's always best if the child doesn't have any predetermined behavior patterns to fall back on, behavior they might rely on to deal with stimuli when their parents are around. What do you think, Hunter, would you like to come into my office and have a chat? Just you and me?"

He opened the door he'd originally come through, standing beside it, holding his hand in, toward the room, an offering, neutral ground.

The boy didn't answer; he was looking in the room now, through the doorway, staring at the section of the doctor's far office wall that he could just see from where he stood.

For the second time in as many minutes, Rose was embarrassed.

"He does this sometimes. We don't know what it is. He sees something and gets fixated on it, like he's gone into another world." Rose reached behind her son and gave him a gentle push forward. "Hunter, the doctor is waiting. You go ahead, I'll be right here."

The lady at the desk stopped marking dates on the pages she was sorting and was watching now, interested.

"What is it, Hunter? What do you see?" The doctor looked back into his office and then turned to the boy. "The paintings? You like art?"

Hunter nodded and the doctor smiled slightly, bemused.

"You have a good eye, young man! Want to take a closer look? Lots more than just those you can see from there. The rest are on the wall around the corner, if you want to see them."

This time Hunter didn't hesitate. He walked through the door.

"He'll be fine. We'll be about an hour, maybe a bit longer. Mrs. Truscott, please hold any calls and maybe you can see if Hunter's mom would like a coffee." He smiled and added for a second time, "Don't worry, Hunter will be fine. Right, Hunter?"

But the boy was already standing in front of the painting he'd seen from outside the office.

"You like it?" The doctor closed the door and walked to stand beside the boy, looking at the painting together. "I love art too. I bought that painting at an auction eight or nine years ago. An auction is where people bring their things from home and sell, kind of like the garage sales that I understand you and your father like."

He looked down at the boy.

"I started going to auctions when I was a little bit older than you." He chuckled to himself as he walked around his desk to sit at the chair, opening the folder he'd been carrying. He looked over his glasses at the boy, who was still standing before the wall of paintings. "I had a good untrained eye, but other than that one, I never found any paintings that were valuable. Decorative mostly; that one is the best I've ever managed to buy. It's attributed to a man called Pablo Picasso; he's starting to get popular now but wasn't that famous when I bought it. He was a Spanish artist who loved to paint in an unusual way. It's called cubism. That's why the lady looks so different."

He was looking at his pride and joy now.

"Unfortunately, Mr. Picasso forgot to sign it. If he had, you and

I would be looking at it inside a bank vault instead of here in my office." The doctor smiled to himself and added as an afterthought, more to himself than his patient, "And I'd probably be an art dealer, not a doctor."

But Hunter wasn't looking at the lady. Brown and brown.

He was looking at the small painting beside it, a poem of harmonious colors interacting with each other; it was a living entity with a three-dimensional soul; the essence of the creative process.

Triangles and circles. Watercolors and crayons. Colors. Brilliant colors.

Those triangles and circles; he couldn't tear his eyes away.

Nyala, it is me again.

Hear what I must tell you now.

Brown and brown. Brown and brown.

Then color. Triangles and circles. God so beautiful. How could anybody not feel it?

Cognitive dissonance.

The lifeblood of his art.

They say he was the best at it, but I didn't know what that meant then, I didn't know what I was looking at.

How could I know? I was eight years old.

The triangles, so cold. The circles. One inside the other. The living souls. Trapped.

Solomon and Hilla. They knew it first; saw it in Germany, at the artist's studio, before the Nazi Party assumed complete control. But he would not part with it, and they did not talk about it when they returned. They were the only ones of Our World who both felt beauty and needed to possess that beauty.

Solomon and Hilla.

They were the king and queen of the Gathering.

Secrets. So many secrets in Our World.

Solomon died in 1949, but his secret did not die with him. Entropy. Nothing stays in order. Maybe the secret escaped from his grave, the result of nature's desire for maximum randomness. Or osmosis, the unconscious assimilation of a thousand clues, a hint here and a whisper there; clues only for those who are ordained to hear the hints and whispers. It was out there to be found. Our World's leaders knew about it, had been searching for it in the decades since it was conceived. Hilla was still alive. Maybe she dreamed it and they saw it in her dreams.

Who knows how, but Our World knew.

Yet none of them saw it in the three decades since Solomon and

Hilla saw it, until that day I stood there, stood before the artist's finest work. And I wasn't one of them; not yet. Our World did not exist for me then.

A synesthete, he was a poet with a paintbrush.

When operatives gathered and we talked about the art he created, even though he was an artist and not one of us, we simply referred to him as the Poet. He did not feel beauty as I did; didn't feel its impossible colored intensity in an anodyne ocean of brown and brown mediocrity. The Poet, one of God's gifted children, heard colors. I was taught that he saw sounds. He could have been an operative, but he was not, he was an artist.

He was gone long before me, he passed in 1944, but I wish I could have met him. We had much in common, I think; so much in common that is indefinable and incomprehensible to all those who do not possess our gifts.

But that meant nothing to me then. I hadn't learned yet. I was young, naïve. I was a student without a teacher.

I did not know when I stood in that office, gazing at that painting, that I was bearing witness to a casualty of the Second World War, the war that changed everything, moved everything, lost everything. Gone. The records, the history; the "how" disappeared along with the same people who could have told the story of the "why" and of the "where." Even the "what" was long dead to all but those of Our World.

It was a continent plus thirty-long-years away from where it had been created and then, somehow, after the lost years, inexplicably it was in that place, on that wall, before me.

Farbstudie–Dreieck und konzentrische Ringe.

Triangles and circles.

Our World.

The instant I walked into his office, into that room, the instant I felt the colors, they were coming.

I liked him. He was kind. A nice man. He cared.

The colors killed him.

The triangles and circles killed him.

God forgive me, Nyala.

I killed him.

10

2020

PINEHURST, NORTH CAROLINA

God forgive me, Nyala"?

Seriously?

Who the hell was this guy and why did he drop her name like they knew each other? She was strangely intrigued about what she was reading though, and still upset as well. Who wouldn't be? It was disconcerting. This whole "*I killed him*" stuff was way crazy. The guy was basically confessing to a murder. Three so far, to be exact, if she'd read correctly; the Zhivago guy, whoever he was, the fat antique dealer, and now the kid's doctor. And if he *did* murder these people, should she report it?

Frankly, it was too bizarre to be believable or she knew she would have *already* called the police. And it wasn't like he described how he killed those people, so what would she report anyway? "Hi. I want to report three murders. No, sorry. I don't know who was murdered. Nope. Not when, either. Bodies? Nope. Motive? Nope. Suspect? Er, well, some guy I don't know called Tsau-z. Description? Er, well, he's apparently covered in sores."

She hated being confused. She liked order. She preferred to control everything in her environment. Luba called her a perfectionist. Actually everyone who knew her called her that, but she wasn't, or at least she didn't think she was. She just liked everything to have a slot, a spot on the wall, a position on a shelf, a place on the table. Nyala also hated analyzing herself, so she changed the subject.

Intrigue was a form of disorder.

Creating order from intrigue; that's what journalism was about; getting to the bottom of the story; investigation. She hadn't chosen to be a journalist, she'd often said in a half-joking manner: journalism had chosen her. You'd have to be a masochist to purposely choose journalism as a major and even more of one to choose it as a career. But that was her calling, the challenge that actually kept her brain busy. And not so coincidentally, it kept her from having to look at anything to do with herself, with who she really was; the impossible dilemma staring back at her in the mirror every day.

Her life was like a Gordian knot, only she didn't have a sword. And even if someone gave her a sword, she wasn't sure she would be strong enough to wield it, to cut the knot. Who was she? Not who she was now, not the person she'd molded herself into, but who was she really? Who had she been? Who was her mother? Who was her father? Where was she born? Who left her, literally on some cold, random police station doorstep?

Why?

A date, that's what her file said; she'd read it a hundred times. That's all there'd been. A birthdate. And a strange name. Nyala. Apparently both written on a torn piece of paper, taped to the blanket she'd been wrapped in. The file said the blanket was handwoven, heavy, coarse, made from mountain goat hair. Weird. But that was it. A nothing child from nowhere. A child who didn't fit in, didn't play, didn't have friends.

The unwanted of the world never did.

The disorder in her own life, the confusion, the lack of knowing; the mystery; she couldn't control that, but she could sure as hell bring order to the rest of the world. She could focus on her work and in so doing, avoid having to think about herself. In keeping busy, arranging the rest of the world, she could ignore the fact that there was a darkness that existed inside her, always just one self-reflective thought away. Hopelessness and despair were always there, waiting for her to give them free rein.

If she worked hard, never played, and kept to a routine, she could keep the darkness away. She could live with that, control and order, but it wasn't the blackness that really scared her.

It was the voices.

She didn't tell anyone, but there were times, quiet, alone times, when she would be overpowered by a sense that she was part of something greater than the world she could see. It didn't happen often, but when it had in the past, it was usually when she stopped for a rest on a forest trail. If she sat quietly for long enough, the natural world around her would seem to still.

The squirrels would stop chittering and the birds would light on branches around her. It was always the same, everything around her hushed, like the forest was covered in cotton. Then a gentle breeze would wash over her. One way and another, flowing around her. Almost like it was washing her, cleansing her. It would grow then, from a breeze to a wind, but the leaves on the trees above remained still.

That's when it would start.

The wind would sing to her.

Or not the wind exactly, but voices on the wind. Singing voices. Singing in a language she didn't understand, or, more accurately, couldn't speak. The light would come then with the wind. Warm. Magic light. Flaxen. Like an eternal sunset, it would beckon her to embrace it, enter it; to join and to sing with the wind.

If she did, she knew she would sing with the wind forever.

Always when it happened, she would panic. *No!* And it would all be gone in that instant of denial.

It was crazy. She was crazy. Had to be.

No other explanation. It was too real to be a dream.

Diagnosing the darkness, the feelings of hopelessness and despair, was a simple click or two away on the Mayo Clinic website . . . depression. But clicking on winds singing songs in tongues, not so much. The light scared the hell out of her. Even thinking about it made her heart speed up and palms of her hands glow.

She'd looked up those symptoms as well . . . neurosis.

And if the racing heart and sweating palms persisted for more than six months . . . psychosis.

So what was it called if you had the symptoms for as far back as you could remember?

God, what a mess she was.

The manuscript in her hands was in a strange way a welcome anomaly for her, a change from the same-old same-old tedium of the life she'd created for herself. A life she crafted to protect herself, from herself. It was a call to action. It gave her a reason to forget questioning things like why she had an intense visceral aversion to dating, to male companionship, to letting herself fall in love. The manuscript gave her a focal point, something that required more than the usual effort to organize.

She thought about it for a moment more and then set the manuscript on the desk, left her room, and walked to the kitchen, pouring herself a glass of water from the pitcher in the fridge. She leaned on the counter and sipped from the glass. Where to start?

There were two people, Solomon and Hilla, and both were part of something called Our World and the Gathering, whatever those were. Apparently they saw the same painting that the kid saw on the wall of the doctor's office, only they saw it in Germany probably in the early 1930s, before World War II for sure. That part made sense, but she'd have to do some research on the Solomon and Hilla characters. And she'd have to figure out who the artist was. He was the one who apparently created the painting the kid saw on the doctor's wall. A painting of triangles and circles.

Okay, got that part.

She took another sip of water. There was that odd name too; the guy seemed to think it was important. What was it he wrote? She put the glass in the sink and returned to the bedroom. Leaning over, she flipped back through the pages she'd read, scanning the manuscript. There it was.

"and then, somehow, after the lost years, inexplicably it was in that place, on that wall, before me. Farbstudie–Dreieck und konzentrische Ringe."

She sat at her desk again and pulled her computer closer, hit the Google icon, and typed. "Farbstudie–Dreieck und konzentrische Ringe translation."

"**Color Study Triangle and Concentric Circle.**" There it was on the screen: the English translation. Odd that a line of images, paintings, appeared only a couple of leads down the Google page; they looked a lot like a child's scratchy, nonsensical doodles. Grown-kid paintings maybe. Modern art? She didn't know anything about abstract or postmodern artistic style; squiggles and lines weren't really her thing.

Circles inside circles.

She clicked on the images. See more.

The images of the paintings were mixed up with diagrams of some obscure "**Beobachtung des unsichtba**" science formulas. Chaff. Waste. Nyala scanned the screen, looking at the paintings and ignoring the scientific graphs. She had a talent for separating the chaff from the wheat when she researched the stories she was assigned to work on. She often wondered if the ability to see what was true and what was obfuscation was somehow rooted in her nature. Definitely wasn't in her nurturing, what little of that there had been.

The paintings had to be the key. Maybe the strange kid in the story with what seemed to be a super talent for recognizing old Chinese dishes and rare watches also knew his art. The painting the boy Hunter had seen at the doctor's office was a painting with triangles and circles. And the Tsau-z guy, who seemed to be telling the story and knew her name, obviously thought it was significant.

Why?

Plus, he referred to the kid in the first person, like he actually was the kid. Disorder. Ugh.

Kandinsky. Wassily Kandinsky; it was the name that appeared under all the squiggly kid-looking paintings; she leaned forward and looked closer at the images. He was definitely the artist who painted all the abstract paintings she could see on the screen. His artwork came up when she'd typed in the German words for "study triangle and concentric circle."

"**Wassily Kandinsky.**"

She moved the cursor arrow over the name. Click.

Vasily. Not Wassily. Russian. Guggenheim Museum Collection. Interesting.

She scrolled down to Wikipedia. Thank God for Mr. Google and Mrs. Wikipedia, every investigative journalist's two best friends.

When she researched, she didn't generally read thoroughly the first time she looked through any information; instead, she let her eyes fall down the writing, expecting that some word, some phrase would trigger a response. Like opening your mind, clearing it of clutter, to *see* the trailhead, a bent blade of grass, a wilting leaf on the ground, knocked from a low branch, pointing the way. Nyala was good at finding trails, a talent she'd exploited not only on her nature hikes, but all through her school years and at her job.

"Born in Russia. Moved to Germany 1920–1933." There it was!

The date triggered whatever it was in her mind that made her good at her job. Bang! The first connection to the manuscript; a place to start making sense out of the senseless; more like a starting point in what had so far been a day of gray, unconsolidated confusion, mixed in with more than a little worry. It wasn't like she had planned to spend the day researching some obscure Russian artist. Just the opposite; she'd planned to relax, go on a hike; do some yoga. Work out. Listen to the sounds of nature.

Then she planned to return to work on Monday and on Tuesday. Repeat. Wednesday. Thursday and Friday. Repeat. Repeat. Repeat. And repeat again, week after week. Month after month. Repeat forever, avoiding the unknown, avoiding all the "what-might-happens" until she died.

The frown left her forehead for a moment and a small smile crossed her face; it was a show of begrudging respect. It was like this Tsau-z guy knew she wouldn't be able to resist the challenge.

You had me at *"they will all know me as fear."*

She started at the top and this time read instead of scanning the artist Kandinsky's bio.

"... became an insider in the cultural administration of Anatoly Lunacharsky." More blah blah. More chaff. But she read through it anyway. **"Established the Museum of the Culture of Painting."** Hmmm. Mental note. Something to check out. **"spiritual outlook ... was foreign to the argumentative materialism of Soviet society."** Interesting character trait, but probably irrelevant. **"Taught at the**

Bauhaus School of art." Bauhaus? She opened another Google page and entered "Bauhaus." Literal translation. Building house. Nope. False lead. Back to Kandinsky.

There it was again. "**. . . taught art from 1922 until the Nazis closed the studio in 1933.**" The starting point; the first bread crumb; the trailhead.

That meant Kandinsky was in Germany before World War II. That's what the Tsau-z said, something about Solomon and Hilla seeing the painting in Germany before the Nazi Party controlled the country.

She picked up the manuscript and reread that piece. "*Solomon and Hilla. They were the king and queen of the Gathering*"? Intriguing. She tried to remember her history classes. Wasn't there a King Solomon from the Hebrew Bible? Nyala thought she recalled reading somewhere about the Queen of Sheba bringing rare spices and precious gifts to the Israelite, King Solomon. Or was she mixing it up with the three kings from the Orient song? Note to self. Check on that someday.

On a whim more than intent, she typed "Solomon and Hilla" into the Google line. Not expecting much. Click.

And this time she took a deeper breath.

What the hell.

"**Hilla Rebay-Guggenheim.**" And right under that, "**Vasily Kandinsky.**" And "**Solomon R. Guggenheim.**"

The real Guggenheim? The art collector? With the museum?

Dots and lines. Connections.

She clicked on "**Hilla Rebay-Guggenheim**" and began reading, fascinated.

Hilla Rebay was a baroness. "**Died in 1967.**" Wasn't that what the guy said in the manuscript, that Hilla was still alive when the weird "*brown and brown*" kid was at the doctor's office? Nyala made a mental note. The kid was eight years old in the early 1960s when he found the Chinese plate and the Rolex watch. Okay, good. At least two dots connected. She continued reading about the Baroness Rebay.

"**Profound spirituality.**" "**Theosophy, Buddhism, Zoroastrianism,** and astrology." Not important, or maybe. Not sure. "Studied art in Germany, moved to Paris, back to Germany."

Nyala was growing to like this lady. She must have been an incredibly strong woman to stand up and be seen in those days with women barely granted the right to vote.

Ahhh. There it was. Nyala wasn't sure what it meant, but she drew another mental line between dots. Hilla Rebay moved to the United States in 1927 and painted a portrait of Solomon Guggenheim! That's how they met. What about Kandinsky?

Then she saw it.

"In 1930, Rebay traveled with Guggenheim and his wife, Irene, to Europe. Among other artists, in Europe they met Kandinsky while he was teaching at the Dessau Bauhaus, and Guggenheim purchased 'Composition 8,' painted in 1923, the first of more than 150 works by the artist that would enter the Guggenheim Museum."

Holy shit!

She sat back for a second, not wanting to continue. It was the real Guggenheim and it was in 1930, about the year Tsau-z said Hilla and Solomon saw the triangles-and-circles painting. The same painting the boy saw in the doctor's office. Isn't that what she'd read in the manuscript? For a second she considered stopping the search, stopping the hunt for whatever truth might be hidden in what was becoming an even more convoluted and confusing story. It would be so much easier to climb back out of the rabbit hole now. The way back was marked, bread crumbs maybe, but at least she could return now. If she continued, though?

She leaned forward.

For a full minute she didn't do anything, just stared at the screen. It was a photo of Solomon and Hilla. They were lovers. It was obvious. You could see it in their body language, even though it was a low-resolution snapshot in time, taken nearly a century before.

They'd been in Germany in 1930. They knew the artist Wassily Kandinsky, or Vasily, whatever his name was, the Russian.

Then she typed. "Wassily Kandinsky art."

And clicked the search button.

It only took her three seconds to see it.

"Study in Squares and Concentric Circles."

Wow! Now that was a real connection! So close, but it was *squares*, not triangles.

She scrolled down through the many Kandinsky paintings on the screen, better than grown-kid finger paintings now that she looked closely, at least to her eye. They were appealing in a funny, simple, and truthful way; New Age–looking, not her taste, but obviously painted by someone with talent. And there was the era they were painted in; that gave perspective. This guy Kandinsky was way ahead of his time. The official New Age was still eight decades away. But there was zero reference to triangles. Zippola.

So many dots connected. Verified; fact checked; but no triangles.

She clicked on **"Study, squares and concentric circles"** and waited.

"Farbstudie–Quadrate und konzentrische Ringe."

Now, that was even more interesting. It was titled by the artist in German, really close to the German words in the manuscript. No cigar though. Nyala confirmed with two clicks that **"Quadrate"** meant **"Squares."** Not triangles.

Back at the original window, she looked at the painting. She liked it, thought it would look nice in her bathroom. It was small enough to fit beside her sink according to what she was reading about the size. **"Considered to be Kandinsky's greatest work of art."** She wouldn't have guessed that.

She added the word "value" to the original search. Click. Nothing. It was in a museum in Europe somewhere; had been forever; donated by some rich guy. So she tried again; changing direction. If at first you don't succeed.

"Most expensive Wassily Kandinsky paintings." Click.

And then she drew in her breath. Wow.

Forty-one million dollars! And it wasn't even his best work! The one the art world figured was Kandinsky's greatest creation, the "Concentric Squares and Circles" painting, wasn't even listed; it hadn't sold in decades, so no way to value it; priceless probably. Crazy. Who would have thought?

She hit the back arrow and looked at the painting again. Instant respect is easy; just stick a big price on your forehead! Every outlaw from the Old West knew that.

Okay, she could see it now. When you looked at the on-screen photos of Kandinsky's most famous painting of squares and circles, the colors seemed to go together, not in a Luba matching, fashion-sense kind of way, but in more of an intimate, harmonious way, a somehow perfect way. It was growing on her. Not because of the price; expensive never did much for Nyala; waste of dollars as far as she was concerned. She would chastise Luba every time she came home with a new designer purse or pair of thousand-dollar Italian designer shoes. No, it wasn't the knowledge that the little painting was probably worth northwards of $50 million; it was because the painting was good.

She scanned down the page for another link on Kandinsky. Click. Apparently he'd written a book.

"What is odd or inconceivable yesterday, is commonplace today." Nyala sat back but continued to read. **"What is avant-garde today (and understood by only a few) is common knowledge tomorrow."**

Okay, got it. A touch laborious, but it made common sense and common sense was something Nyala had all kinds of time for. There was hardly any of it in the touchy-feely crowd she shared office space with. Scott. Ugh. Kandinsky wasn't like the guys nowadays. The painter must have faced adversity, moving from country to country like he had, from Russia to Germany, back to Russia during World War I, and then back to Germany during Hitler's early reign of terror. He'd been vilified by the Nazis and he'd defied communist doctrine. Not the smartest thing to do in Stalin's pogrom heyday, let alone exhibiting degenerative paintings with the Brownshirts Sieg Heiling around Germany at the time.

Fascinating, but it was what she read next that moved the needle on her attention level.

"A Nazi raid on the Bauhaus in the 1930s resulted in the confis-cation of Kandinsky's first three 'Compositions.' They were dis-played in the State-sponsored exhibit 'Degenerate Art,' and then destroyed."

For the second time she said it out loud. Holy shit!

"Kandinsky embarked on the first seven of his ten 'Compositions.' The first three survive only in black-and-white photographs . . ."

It wasn't just a dot. It was right there in front of her, a complete picture telling a story of ten thousand words, painted in glaringly obvious facts. The kid may have found a missing work by Kandinsky! A small painting that was lost in the reality distortion of war and then found again on the wall of a doctor's office in some small Midwest town; a painting that Mr. Guggenheim tried to purchase before the war. Could it be?

Could it be that the greatest of all Kandinsky's paintings, the "Study in Squares and Concentric Circles," was actually one of a pair? One of the pair painted with squares and one with triangles? One saved into the public domain and one lost; believed to have been destroyed by the Nazis and then found by a special needs kid in a doctor's office half a world away and more than three decades after the artist conceived the work of art?

Nyala didn't see the shadows lengthen outside. Didn't hear the wind pick up and didn't notice that her legs felt tight, cramped from so long in a sitting position. She was deep into her research.

Still there was nothing.

No reference about any Kandinsky painting with triangles and circles. Zero. Dead end. Nada. Or almost nada. She'd found only two references that she'd highlighted and saved in a file she'd labeled "Tsau-z. Man of Sores."

Probably all bullshit. The whole thing. There is no way Google and Wikipedia wouldn't know about a painting of such great value and importance. Damn.

In a way she wouldn't have been able to explain if someone had asked, Nyala was disappointed. She closed Google, moved the cursor to the "Tsau-z. Man of Sores" file icon on her screen, and clicked.

When the file opened, she read what she'd saved again.

"Kandinsky, in his book, 'Concerning the Spiritual in Art,' felt that the authentic artist creating art from 'an internal necessity' inhabits the tip of an upward-moving pyramid. This progressing pyramid is penetrating and proceeding into the future."

Not a reference to a missing triangles-and-circles painting exactly. She continued to read.

"The modern artist-prophet stands alone at the apex of the pyramid, making new discoveries and ushering in tomorrow's reality."

Nyala leaned back and rubbed her eyes; they were burning. She closed the computer.

For a moment she considered what she'd just read. A pyramid was a bit like a triangle. But it was a long, long stretch to connect that dot to the existence of a second Kandinsky painting, one with triangles and circles, not squares and circles; but possible; maybe.

For a few more moments she sat, thinking about getting up and going for a walk. Instead, she leaned forward and picked up the manuscript again.

11

1960s

UNDISCLOSED SMALL TOWN

When the door to the doctor's office opened for the second time in the three hours Rose had been waiting, she wasn't sure if she felt relief or fear.

Two long hours before, the gentle-looking doctor had come out of his office and explained to Rose that he was going to need more time with her son than he originally thought. He made a point of telling her not to worry, but then he'd spoken to his office assistant, Mrs. Truscott, instructing her to cancel the rest of the day's appointments.

Not worry? She was hoping for a simple coast-is-clear signal after waiting for that first hour. "Your son is fine" would have been nice, or "come in and we can discuss your son," but "cancel all appointments"? That couldn't be good. Rose's trepidation grew despite the doctor's reassurances and her concern would have grown to fullblown panic if she'd noticed the doctor's assistant raise her eyebrows in surprise. The look would have told Rose instantly that the request was not normal.

However, even Rose, as flustered as she was at the request for more time, noticed the doctor took care to stand in the doorway, blocking the opening, keeping Hunter out of her sight. That bothered her more than the need for more time; she wanted to be with her son, helping him, protecting him from what other people thought, protecting him from the shame of not being normal.

She felt a flush of guilt then. Hunter never felt shame or even noticed when people whispered about him. It was Rose who felt the shame.

"Everything is fine. I just need a little more time." The doctor's smile, at least, was comforting.

Then he'd turned and closed the door behind him.

That had been two hours ago. This time, when the door opened, Hunter came out first and Rose was already up and out of her chair, across the room, kneeling and reaching for him before the doctor came out behind the boy.

"I am so sorry, Mrs. Johann, I honestly didn't think it would take so long." He stood at the door watching the mother hug her son and the son not hug his mother back.

Rose pulled her face away from Hunter and looked into his eyes. Nothing there, no emotion. Her son was perfectly content to be distant.

She stood and faced the doctor, pulling Hunter close to her side, her arm around his shoulders.

"Is everything okay?" It wasn't a real question, she knew it wasn't, but she was steeling herself for the diagnosis.

"Hunter is fine." The doctor looked down and smiled at the young boy, but his brow was furrowed, as though even as he said it, he was trying to figure out if what he said was true or not. "Better than fine I would say."

Rose looked at him, trying to read the meaning of what he'd just said. The first flutter of hope crossed her face, but relieved or not, she wasn't willing to let herself fully feel thankful. Not yet. It had been years since she or her husband truly felt thankful, so it was easy to keep the feeling buried.

"Mrs. Truscott, would you see if Hunter wants something to drink? I think we have soda pop in the fridge, or orange juice." The doctor then beckoned to Rose and looked directly into her eyes as he spoke. "I'd like to talk with you for a few minutes in my office, about our young man Hunter here."

Rose hesitated for a moment, then looked down at her boy.

"Mommy will only be a minute."

Hunter didn't catch the apology. She didn't know if her son's seeming lack of awareness was that at all, or if it was more of a philosophy, a way of looking at life. Why should people notice an apologetic look? Why should anyone care?

Whatever was done was done and if everyone just did what they wanted to do or had to do, there should never be a need to apologize.

Not that Hunter understood that any more than his mother understood it.

At eight years of age, it was just who he was.

———

"First off, your son is definitely not, he's not . . ." The doctor paused as he looked for the correct word. "Not unintelligent."

Rose wasn't exactly sure what that double negative meant.

"In fact quite the opposite." The doctor paused again, searching. "Mrs. Johann, your son Hunter is certainly unusual but unusual in a good way."

Rose didn't understand the doctor's body language. He was saying the words but shaking his head. If it was good news, shouldn't he be happy? If her son was "not unintelligent," then why did the face she was intensely focused on show concern and confusion? It certainly was not the look of someone bearing glad tidings.

"Frankly, he is something I have never seen before." For the third time he paused. This time it wasn't a search for a single word, but more of a way to express a failure of sorts. "I don't think anybody has seen someone like your son before. None of my peers, at least that I know of. Nothing like it in medical school."

He waved to the wall of books beside his patient's mother.

"Nothing." The pause again, looking at the books and searching for a way to express what he wanted to say. He swiveled slightly in his chair and looked at the wall of paintings beside him and then swiveled back to look at Rose. "Once I realized that your son was, is special, I was curious to learn just how special."

He saw Rose's face change; trepidation again.

"No, no, not special like that, special as in rare, so rare, his abilities and potential are not definable. At least not by me today." The doctor smiled reassuringly at the obviously confused and bordering on distressed lady sitting in the chair in front of his desk. "Let me put it another way. What I'm saying is, Hunter is literally too fine for me to even understand."

Shafts of light cut into the office, through the mullioned window that let in the late afternoon sun rays. Dust flecks floated in the air, captured by those rays, held in suspension by the nearly still air of the room, moving only when either of the two people moved a hand, leaned in their chair, or shifted position.

Rose wasn't sure she was reassured in any way, regardless of how the doctor spun the words.

"So why can't Hunter read?" She was on the edge of tears. The fear, the emotion she'd been holding back for so long, was close to overwhelming her self-control. "Why does the teacher say he's the only one in his class who can't read?"

"Mrs. Johann. Your son *can* read." He paused for effect. "In fact he reads at a level beyond what I've been able to fully fathom. *Reads* maybe isn't even the right word. *Comprehends* is more accurate: he comprehends what he sees on the page. Here, let me show you."

He stood up and walked over to the coffee table located in front of the big diamond-tufted leather couch set off to the side of his office and reached down to pick up a book. Rose watched as he walked by the collection of framed photographs, each carefully aligned in a pleasant way behind the doctor's chair.

A lady appeared in many of the photographs. One showed the doctor and her, both dressed in shades of blue and white, clasping hands and standing in a pine grove. There was a big Happy 10th Anniversary printed on a banner across the top of the photo. Rose thought she looked nice. About her own age. Had to be his wife. No children yet apparently.

The dust swirled and curled, flitting out and then back into the divided sun rays as the doctor passed through them. As he walked back to where Rose was sitting, he noticed that she was looking at the photos.

"My better half." He stopped and as though seeing the photos for the first time he smiled. It was a look that Rose would have recognized on anyone; any woman would have. Deep respect; earned and cherished. Love. "My soul mate. Dottie. Dorothy. We married when I was still in college. I was head-over-heels in love with her then and I'm even more so now."

Rose smiled gently at the doctor. Like all women, she understood.

He looked back from the photos and handed Rose the book he'd picked up from the coffee table.

"It's *The Story of Art*. I had it in my library. I like art." He waved toward the wall of colorful paintings as he sat back down in his antique oak swivel chair. "The author, Ernst Gombrich, wrote something to the effect of 'Art seems to be as inexhaustible and unpredictable as real human beings are.'"

He leaned forward, placing his elbows and hands facing down on his desk, focused now on Rose.

"Mrs. Johann, here is the point. If you and I want to know exactly what Mr. Gombrich said, all we need to do is ask your son." The doctor looked intently at the woman sitting on the far side of his desk. He wasn't smiling; he was deadly serious. "Your son Hunter read that book, the whole thing, four hundred and sixty-two pages, including the index, while he was here. While you waited. He read it! I know that sounds absurd, but I watched him leaf through every page. I didn't believe it either, so I tested him. Your son not only can read, he reads at a speed I've only ever heard about." He was shaking his head. "Only it's not reading like you and I would read; it's like his mind copies the pages and somehow he simply understands what he's seeing."

He wasn't mocking her. Rose could see that. The doctor was sincere, but his words weren't making sense at all.

"I thought he was looking at the pictures in the book. But he was reading it." The doctor caught himself and corrected what he was saying for the third time. "No, not exactly, as I said, it was like he understood every page! Hunter is an idiot savant, but more than that, much more."

He noticed the sudden look of fear on Rose's face and his demeanour changed, tone apologetic but at the same time bemused.

"No. I'm sorry. Not idiot, like stupid person, Mrs. Johann, the

opposite. Idiot savant. Someone who generally has learning diffi-
culties, but is extremely gifted in some particular way, like your son.
His astounding ability makes him a savant. The retention . . ." He
let the thought trail off as he reflected for a moment. "But he's more
than just a savant in one area; he seems to know inherently about art,
recognizes art and understands it. I'd even say I'm jealous of him in
that regard, but unlike the classic savant case studies that I know of,
your son doesn't seem to have any learning disabilities. None at all.
Or at least none that I could find."

He picked up several loose pages from his desk and looked at them.

"I tested your son's IQ. I'm sure you've heard of that. It's a way
we try to associate a number to someone's intelligence. I gave your
son two tests for children, one the typical test that I'd normally give
to any child who comes into my office." He paused. "And once I saw
how your son performed on that one, I gave him a second test, one
that Margot, a friend of mine, came up with to test gifted children."

He paused again, looking at the pages he was holding.

"In both cases, your son scored in the top one percentile." He
looked up at Rose, his eyes betraying the incredulity, the wonder
he had been feeling for nearly the last two hours with his patient.
"Some people would call that genius. Or more appropriately in your
son's case, gifted."

He put the papers down and looked at Rose across the desk.

"Beyond gifted. He's above normal in mathematics but doesn't
seem to care much for it and he has above-normal cognitive abilities
in problem solving for his age. He's higher across the board in all the
areas we test, which is unusual in most children, but typical of gifted
children. But those children never, at least that I know of, have your
son's extra gifts."

The doctor tapped the papers into a neat stack on his quartersawn
oak desk and leaned back in his chair.

"Mrs. Johann, in a nutshell, your son simply isn't interested in
whatever his teachers are trying to get him to read, so they interpret
that to mean he can't read. And he doesn't care about his grades, or
what the other children might think of him. He doesn't care what you
and I think about him. What anyone thinks of him." He paused to let

what he'd said sink in and then as an afterthought added, "I suspect he will never care about peer pressure like the rest of us, because from what I've seen, he will have no peers."

The doctor gathered his thoughts, consolidated them.

"Did you know Hunter is fascinated with anything to do with art? Every kind of art." He wasn't asking a real question and he didn't wait for an answer. "And Mrs. Johann, I also discovered that Hunter has a highly developed disposition toward anything connected to the outdoors and nature. He's fascinated by wild animals. I believe I read in the file that you said your son likes to fish. Does your husband fish? Hunt?"

"No. No, he doesn't. And Hunter doesn't really fish. He sits in a cardboard box on our driveway and pretends to fish." She hesitated and added, "I had a great-uncle who was famous. He hunted. He collected different animals for the British Natural History Museum."

"Interesting. I would have thought Hunter received his penchant for the outdoors from his father. I certainly don't hunt or fish either." His brow furrowed in thought. "In my profession, we believe that hunting and fishing are learned avocations, passed down through generations by the teaching of mentors, but perhaps there actually is a hunting gene. I heard that Dr. Watson and Dr. Crick are up for a Nobel Prize. If anyone can find such a gene, they will, but no way to know at this point; the future maybe."

The doctor thought through what he'd observed.

"Mrs. Johann, I will say it again: Hunter is a gifted child, but he is well beyond the tests I have at my disposal to discern the level of those gifts. Really there is no test that I know of that would apply. Your son is one of a kind. One in a million, one in a billion maybe. One in possibly . . ." Again he let the thought trail off as he looked for the words. "One in all of us ever. I honestly don't know."

He looked at the lady in front of him. Compassion and concern both showed on his face now.

"I would like your permission to further explore Hunter's situation. There may be studies around the world I don't know about, probably, hopefully there are, and I'll need time to go through them all, if indeed they do exist."

He stood.

The dust shifted again. The sun rays were slowly fading as late afternoon shadows grew longer.

"No matter what you decide, Mrs. Johann, your son's gift is like a seedling, just germinated, beginning to poke up through the soil. Like that young plant, the beginning of his life is crucial. Hunter needs water and fertilizer, sun, or he will wither like that plant might do if left to the capricious whims of nature. So I strongly suggest that you or your husband immediately start taking him to the library. As often as possible. Allow him to learn. To learn his way. To learn about his art and his animals."

Rose was hearing the words, but not all of it was sinking in. She was still struggling to comprehend what the doctor was telling her.

"And frankly, don't expect great results from any school report cards. I'm afraid that regular school, for your son, will be a prison sentence.

"It's early to suggest this, but at this point, without further insight, I would even suggest that you start researching private schools for your child. Maybe not even a private school. He may need one-on-one tutoring at the highest level."

The doctor walked around the desk and held out his hand to take the art book that Rose still held in her lap. He placed the book on the desk and walked to the door, waiting for Rose to rise from her chair before speaking again.

"I'll have Mrs. Truscott set up another appointment before you go, for late next month, whatever time works best for you, if that is okay. I should have more to tell you by then.

"Mrs. Johann?" The doctor paused before he reached for the door handle. "With your permission, I would like to consult with other child psychiatrists about your son."

"Yes. Of course."

The doctor opened the door to the waiting room.

Hunter was there, sitting on a chair, glass of orange juice beside him on an end table, untouched. He wasn't looking at her, or any of the three adults in the room. He didn't even seem remotely concerned where his mother had been. Considering what she'd just heard in Dr. Keen's office, Rose had to admit, she was somehow expecting him to act differently now. Certainly she *saw* Hunter differently now.

In fact, gifted or not, he was looking out the window, watching a butterfly flit from flower to flower.

Had Rose known her butterflies, she would have known that her son was watching a butterfly called a painted lady.

Lepidoptera.

Vanessa cardui, to use the more precise scientific name.

Had Rose taken notice of the books her son found at garage sales, the ones on the shelves in his bedroom, she would have seen that two were a rare leather-bound set of first-edition books, published in the mid-1800s, written by Edward Doubleday and John Westwood and aptly titled *The Genera of Diurnal Lepidoptera: Comprising Their Generic Characters, a Notice of Their Habits and Transformations, and a Catalogue of the Species of Each Genus.*

Had Rose known as much about butterflies as these famed natural historians, she would have known that the painted lady was also known as the thistle butterfly, nearly global in distribution, and that the tiny blue dots just visible on the butterfly's black submarginal hind wing eyespots were called pupils.

Nor did Rose know that those blue dots defined it as the summer morph of the pretty cosmopolitan. Another common name.

Rose didn't know any of this.

Hunter knew all of it.

12

2020

PINEHURST, NORTH CAROLINA

HOPE HAIR WELL
CAN'T MAKE DINNER
ENJOY FRIES
DON'T BE LATE

Nyala typed and sent four separate texts. She hated long text messages and always used caps. If it was important enough, it should be shouted. If it wasn't important, then why send it at all?

She was growing to like the strange kid in the story now. Was there actually such a kid? One with superpowers? Who could read books as fast as pages could be turned? Photographic memory? With comprehension? At eight years of age? Was that even possible?

In a way, she wanted to believe it was, wanted to believe in an actual superhero, not the cartoon freak characters with superpowers that Hollywood and Marvel were spewing out by the green and red, scaled and winged, fire- and ice-breathing dozens of late, with their perfect bodies and shiny, tight-fitting suits of magic and science.

The hint of a demure smile lifted the corners of her lips as she considered the Marvel cartoon characters. In the very few moments when she was totally honest with herself, she had to admit that the actor who played Thor in those dumb movies was someone Nyala found herself quite attracted to. He was a big guy and handsome. Two important traits, for sure, but not the most important; guys like that were there for the taking if Nyala, with her exotic looks, long, straight raven-black hair, and coppery skin tone, wanted only that. They could be found by the narcissistic dozens, working out in the gyms springing up everywhere in the city.

No, it wasn't just looks, it was more about the Thor character being tragically flawed, human, naïve, and honest with an instinctive sense of justice, but super powerful.

Nyala's smile at her own childish fantasy faded. It was another one of her secrets. The secrets nobody knew. The secrets she would never tell, not even to Luba. What was she supposed to say anyway? "Yes, that's correct, I am a twentysomething orphan and I have never slept with a man"? That would go over well. Even Luba, if she knew, would think she was nuts. "Oh, and I forgot to mention that I'm saving myself for Thor to show up and sweep me off my feet. What's that? Odin? Sure! Zeus? Absolutely, bring him on! As long as the guy has the right mix of sorcerer and warrior combined with wisdom and poetry, I'll be happy!"

What was she saving herself for?

She honestly didn't know. She just knew she had no choice.

God, what an idiot she was.

The kid was kind of an antihero with superpowers. He couldn't care less about what anyone else thought. She frowned again. The Tsau-z crazy guy sounded like an antihero as well. Or at least he seemed to be searching for answers like antiheroes always did.

Nyala let her thoughts run on that trail for a bit. The guy admitted he killed somebody called Zhivago on the first page. Worse, said he "*enjoyed*" killing him. Who was Zhivago? Maybe he was a bad guy? Killing was wrong, or at least it was supposed to be wrong, but Nyala deep down felt that killing bad people was okay. She would never say that around the snowflakes in the office though; that would be social suicide! Totally taboo! The meek had definitely inherited her world, if not the real world.

Tsau-z did say he killed the doctor, or what was it he said? "*The colors killed him. The triangles and circles killed him.*" Obviously colors and shapes can't kill anyone. The painting in the doctor's office couldn't have killed anyone, but he said it did, didn't he? It had to be a metaphor.

Then there was the pudgy antique dealer; he wasn't bad. Not someone who deserved to be killed. And antiheroes or heroes didn't kill anybody except bad people who earned their death sentence. Right?

She swiped the face of her iPhone, tapped the screen, and typed in "painted lady butterfly," although she knew what the answer would be. Yep. Check. All real, all facts. No point in even checking on the purple spots. She already knew what she would find; they existed.

Formalities first. The low-hanging fruit.

She typed again, although again, she knew what she'd find.

Yep, the two butterfly authors were real. She typed in "Abe Books" and then clicked on the "Rare Books" button. She had to look back into the manuscript for the correct spellings of their names and when she found it, she typed their names in the author section, "Doubleday Westwood," and clicked.

Yikes! Twenty thousand dollars! Four months' wages to Nyala. Too bad Rose and her husband were so blind to their kid's abilities. If they had been more aware, they could have put a leash on him, like those tribal guys did with cormorants in the South Pacific. Catch the fish, but don't let the bird swallow it. They'd be rich. Hell, the kid's watch alone could have paid for their house, and more. Probably they could have bought a new truck with what the butterfly books alone were worth.

She hit the back arrow, deleting the two entomologists from the screen.

She typed "Ernst Gombrich."

Again she expected the same results. What was it they said about the definition of crazy? Doing the same thing over and over and expecting a different result?

Yep. As she had expected it to be, another checkmark; the book was real, written in 1950 just like the doctor in the story said, or at least he was close. Check. Check. Check.

Her phone vibrated and a message showed up. Luba.

WHAT??????

A one-word text appeared in caps. Nyala smiled. It was Luba's way of making fun of her texting style.

IS

Another one-word text.

YOUR

Another.

PROBLEM

Nyala was still smiling. Okay, got it; point taken. She typed her answer.

HAVE FUN

SCOTT IS YOURS IF YOU WANT HIM

THANK ME LATER

WORKING

She'd barely pushed the send button when her phone vibrated and two hearts and a thumbs-up emoji appeared on the screen, this time in one text.

Then another text displaying the boy and girl kissing emoji.

Then another with a plate of what looked like french fries and another heart.

Cute. Nyala typed now.

HAHA. GO AWAY

Send.

Now where was she? Oh right, the book; lots of copies available on Abe Books. Dead end again. The book existed. So what?

Nyala let her hand holding the phone fall to her lap, on top of the manuscript. Then she had a thought and started leafing back through the pages. What was the name the doctor mentioned? The one who designed the test for "special" children? Maggie? Margret?

She found it and typed "Margot." Enter.

Argh. Shot was too long. Waste of time. A gazillion Margot references.

"Margot . . ." She contemplated the problem for a moment and then added "IQ test."

The screen lit up with links to Margots that had absolutely zero to do with the Margot she was looking for.

Scrolling down through the list of false leads, she paused on the second page, halfway down. Hmmm, that was interesting; nothing to do with her search for Margot, but interesting because Nyala was half-curious about the organization. **"Mensa International–Wikipedia."**

Why not check it out? She needed a break from being a disciplined researcher anyway.

Click.

She'd heard about Mensa people; they were geniuses. Just a little pretentious to her way of thinking; a lot pretentious, truth be told. But pretentious or not, being a card-carrying genius did have some appeal. Rather be smart than stupid. She smiled as she remembered John Wayne's quote, "Life is hard, but it's harder if you're stupid." Ha ha. She shook her head even though nobody was around to see; imagine someone saying that around the office. Scott and the rest of them would literally go apeshit apoplectic!

Not Nyala. She liked everything John Wayne stood for, which was basically everything that was missing in the world she was forced to live in. The world she was supposed to find her Thor in. Ugh. Good luck.

Admitting to being a member of Mensa wouldn't fly in the socialist, everyone-should-pretend-to-be-equal mediocrity of her office, but she could see where a license that said you were a genius might be useful. She smiled; the image of a scarecrow clutching a diploma came to mind. Maybe the point was that a card or diploma that said you were smart wasn't really needed if you really were smart.

The kid.

Isn't that what the doctor said? The kid didn't care what anybody thought about him. Hmmm. Nyala never doubted her own intelligence, but upon occasion she did have self-doubts about other things. Maybe she could learn from Hunter. It wasn't about what people thought about you, it was about who you were. Period. If you knew yourself, you didn't need approval from anyone else; didn't need permission to be you; didn't need to apologize for being you.

But Nyala didn't know anything about who she was. How could she?

Then she saw it, down the page of information about Mensa: "Margot."

"Margot Seitelman."

Click.

Could it be? Died young. Sixty-one. Sad. Executive director of Mensa for nearly thirty years. Housewife, it said. That's cool. House-wife with superpowers. Had to be the Margot the doctor talked about. Born in Germany before the war.

Nyala got back on the track, which she had to admit was not much more than a trail of weak conjecture. The doctor could be real. No way for her to research if a specific small-town shrink from the 1960s even existed; probably a hundred Dr. Keens and ten thousand small towns that fit the description; more maybe. Mr. Google was good, but not that good; there had to be something significant about the doctor for there to be a remote chance of proving he existed.

If it was the right Margot, the Mensa Margot, then she was for sure real and since she was involved at the highest level with Mensa for so long, she probably would have had something to do with designing the tests for entry to the respected club, like the doctor referenced in the manuscript.

Nyala worked through what she knew. There was a Margot, prob-ably the one the doctor called his friend, and the butterfly books and art book existed, she'd proven that.

It was time to get serious. The formalities were out of the way.

"Idiot savant."

She paused, not quite ready to click on the Google Search button.

Was it possible that the superpowers the kid was supposed to possess were real? Didn't Tsau-z say he "*felt*" instead of saw beauty? Maybe the kid was the same. Maybe they were the same person. Her sleuthing had revealed that Kandinsky was supposed to have been able to hear colors and see sound; she had even added a note to her file on that. But the kid's abilities? Pretty hard to believe.

Idiot savant. Click.

"French. Translation 'Learned Idiot.'"

Makes sense.

"Savant syndrome is a condition in which someone with signif-icant mental disabilities demonstrates certain abilities far in excess of the average."

Okay. Knew that; got it. Like what kind of abilities?

"Skills generally related to memory. May include rapid calculation. Artistic ability or musical ability."

Wow! The kid was all of the above except maybe for the music part. Nyala continued to read. She was enthralled. Superpowers did exist, albeit in people with **"significant mental disabilities"** and **"neurodevelopmental disorders."**

Not cool. Kid was strange, but didn't the doctor say he wasn't challenged mentally?

"Condition rare. Affects one in a million people. More male than female cases. 6:1." Not too impressed with that. Probably a man figured that out. **"Estimated to be fewer than 100 savants currently living."**

Really, Mrs. Wikipedia?

Nyala did a quick mental calculation. More than 7.5 billion humans on the planet, divided by one million. That meant there had to be closer to 7,500 savants out there, not 100. Or was it 75,000? Math was never Nyala's strong suit and obviously it wasn't Mrs. Wikipedia's strong suit either.

It still didn't mean there was a savant on every corner, but there were more than a few out there.

"May not be prone to invest in socially engaging skills."

Ha ha. Nyala snickered; it was a page out of her own book. She wondered if she was a savant; had the idiot and nonsocial parts down pat.

"Enhanced perception or sensory hypersensitivity."

Not exactly a eureka moment, but the kid had the strange ability to recognize great art, like the triangles painting in the doctor's office. The one Nyala hadn't been able to track down, the one that, if it really existed, would be the second of a pair the Russian Kandinsky painted. She shook her head. Stop it. She was jumping to conclusions. It wasn't one of a pair, unless it existed, and she hadn't been able to find a word about it, so it probably didn't.

Nyala returned to scanning. **"Notable cases."**

"Tony Cicoria." Click. **"Acquired savant. Different. Wasn't born with his talent. Struck by lightning at 42, in 1994. Couldn't play a**

musical instrument, and suddenly was able to play at a performance level."

Interesting.

"Chopin's Military Polonaise, Op. 40, Chopin's Fantaisie-Impromptu, Brahms' Rhapsody, Chopin's Scherzo in B-flat Minor, Op. 31."

That was pretty superpowerish!

"Alonzo Clemons." Click. "Sculptor. Animals. See any animal and sculpt it from memory."

Holy cow! His sculptures sold for $45,000. Crazy.

"Began sculpting at school, where he would sit silently in the back of the classroom, molding bits of clay into tiny animals."

Hmmm. Nyala smiled. Sounded like her report cards from public school: sits at the back of the class; doesn't socialize. Other than the missing super talent, she was beginning to think more and more that she was one of the rare idiot savant cases. Even rarer! Six-to-one! She was a female!

"When the teachers took the clay from him, he began scraping bits of pliable tar from the pavement and working on sculptures in his room at night."

Whoa. Too close to home. Nyala spent almost her entire childhood hiding in her bedroom. Instinct? She still wasn't sure what she'd been hiding from, but knew it was better than the alternative, being alone out in the real world. It wasn't the fault of the foster parents who raised her, they did their best, but she was never able to call any of them her parents. They weren't. They were nice though, most of them; some probably loved her. No, it wasn't them, it was that she'd always felt she didn't belong to the world they lived in.

Okay, way too close to the edge. Get control, lady. She was a big girl now. Not some child with more issues than an army of orphans.

"Daniel Tammet. Author and polyglot." Nyala asked Siri for the definition of *polyglot*.

"As a noun: a person able to use and know several languages." That would be a cool superpower.

"Derek Paravicini. Blind musical prodigy. Pianist. Leslie Lemke. Musician. Matt Savage. Musician." Great name.

"Orlando Serrell. Able to do calendrical calculations."

Calendrical calculations?

Click.

"Ability to name the day of the week of a date, or vice versa, in a tenth of a second on a range of decades or even certain millennia."

Really? That was possibly the most boring superpower ever.

Nyala looked at the long list of names. "Kim Peek, Steven Wiltshire, Temple Grandin, Tom Wiggins, Tommy McHugh." Poets, architectural artists, composers. Even a professor of animal science.

She was saturated. She wasn't sure she'd found what she was looking for, but she knew it was time to change directions.

"Speed reading."

Click.

Lots about how to speed read. She noticed John F. Kennedy was a speed reader, 1,200 words per minute. Nyala thought about it. If she recalled her Creative Writing prof correctly, there were about 90,000 words in the typical novel, 250 words per typical page. So five pages a minute! Impressive! Typical postgraduates read at half that speed, it said. Mental note to self: see how fast you can read.

Jimmy Carter too; he and his wife were both speed readers.

Nyala literally sat up and took notice of what she read next.

"Howard Stephen Berg from the United States claims to be the fastest reader at 25,000 words per minute."

That's one hundred pages of a novel in one minute? Nyala frowned. Are you kidding me?

"Maria Teresa Calderon from the Philippines claims to have earned the Guinness World Record for World's Fastest Reader at 80,000 words per minute . . ." Seriously? That's nearly an entire novel in a minute! Can pages even be turned that fast? Nyala read on. ". . . and 100% comprehension."

There it was.

"and 100% comprehension."

The doctor said the kid read 450 pages while he was in the office for three hours, or at least he said "he comprehends what he sees on the page." Wasn't that what he said? She leafed through the manuscript until she found what she was looking for; 462 pages, to be more accurate. So it was possible.

Nyala deliberated with herself but decided not to spend more time chasing leads. She was deep into the rabbit hole now and it seemed like every turn had ten more tunnels to choose from.

She put her phone down and picked up the manuscript once again.

*B*efore you read more of the past, Nyala, heed these words of the present.

I have been watching you from the darkness that is my life now. I know the motion of one event is predictable; one force acts upon another, a simple calculation; a vectoring of direction. But when one event entwines with another event, and then a third and a fourth, the outcome grows more difficult to predict.

And when an infinite number of events are set in motion by an infinite number of possibilities, the result is chaos, Nyala.

And it is in chaos that they thrive. They are the masters of chaos. They control chaos.

They do not obey any law, not even those of nature. I said these words to you before, maximum randomness; the degree of disorder in a system; nothing can stay in place as much as you, as much as I need it to be. As much as WE need it to be. Our nature, yours and mine, is order.

Disorder for us is a black abyss.

That black abyss is the place they call home.

Chaos for them is comforting.

Our World.

They call it that, because this IS their world. Make no mistake; they own this world we live in.

The events I caused were colliding, wrapping around each other, spinning toward where Our World waited, bloated and twisted, like a monster, like a spider in the center of its web. Threads set in a hundred, a thousand, in an unimaginable number of directions; threads set for years, decades. Every thread connected to the center, to them.

They waited. They always waited.

The barest vibration. A hint of movement.

No matter how weak the signal, they would not miss it. They had to survive and to survive they had to eat. To eat they needed to find us. We were rare. So few of us to be found.

There was only one of her. There is only one of you.

The spider awoke that day, Nyala.

The day it learned of me.

I woke it. The events I set in motion. Colliding. Random.

Could I have changed it? Could I have saved them? Could I have saved her? And if I had, what would have happened to you? These are the questions I live with every day of my life now. These questions and one more.

Is it too late?

13

1960s

RUSSIA
UNDISCLOSED LOCATION

The single desk lamp cast light downward but did little more than show that there were two men sitting at a large wooden table, antique, age-blackened Turkish walnut; one behind, on the side with two drawers, one in front. The man behind the table was wearing glasses, reading the pages he held in front of him, his forearms on the desk, his hands holding the papers so the light would hit them.

He didn't move for a long time, except to shift one page to the back to read the next one. When he came to the last page and finished reading, he shifted that one to the back as well, so that he was looking at the first page again.

There was nothing on the table to give away any clues about the two men. There was not enough light to see what else was in the room, if it was a room at all. The light wasn't strong enough to reach the walls of whatever space held the men. It could be a cavern, the silence was so heavy.

The man with the papers wore a beard, trimmed perfectly, white, and flecked with black. He was at least sixty years of age, maybe more; maybe as much as seventy-five. It was difficult to tell. There were lines by his eyes, but they had nothing to do with smiling. The light was low and indirect, but even so, those lines looked hard, cut into a hard face by the tempered steel edge of life lived beyond the pale.

The formal-looking suit jacket he wore was of tweed, not Scottish, but the highest European quality judging by its refined roughness. There was a scarf around his neck, tucked down into his jacket. Not silk. Wool for function, not fashion. The color wasn't discernible, only that it was a darker shade, blue? There was not enough light to tell. He wore a hat and his hair was longish. Like his beard his hair was white, but with more black, especially at the back.

It was the hat that spoke the only truth about the man. It was Soviet made, of sable fur. It was called a *ushanka*, a derivative of the Russian word for "ears." The hat's "ears" were tied together on the crown of the hat. In the context of the *ushanka*, the conclusion would be that he was Russian, western Russian by the sharpness of his face, which would also imply that he was a citizen of the Union of Soviet Socialist Republics, the great red bear that was the USSR.

But to draw that conclusion would have been incorrect. The man was of Russian descent, to be sure, but he was not a citizen of the USSR. He was not a citizen of any country. He didn't have to be. He was a citizen of every country.

He was the leader of Our World.

He placed the pages on the table and looked at the man sitting across from him. On this man there was no light and therefore nothing to shed light back on; he was only a dark shape.

"Corroborated?"

"Da."

The man pondered the enormity of this for a moment.

"How?"

A one-word question, but like a gun with one bullet in the chamber, it was loaded.

"It came from a doctor; a child psychiatrist; an inquiry. We responded as per protocol."

"Our test?"

"Da."

"The data was analyzed?"

"Da. Twice. As per protocol."

The man with the beard did not say anything for several minutes. He was thinking. His position in Our World meant that he was all-knowing. He was the single point of contact. Like a spider sitting at the center of a vast web of intelligence, every bit of information found its way to him. And it was also through his hands that every treasure found by Our World's operatives passed. Decisions were his alone to make and orders were his alone to give.

He'd been in his position of power for more than three decades now and this was only the second time in his long tenure that he'd seen such a test result.

"Only Zhivago scored so high on the art indices."

It was a statement of fact. Zhivago was the best. Another fact.

"Da. Only Zhivago. And he had a second spike as well."

Again, a long pause.

"Nature."

"Da. Same. Nature."

The man in the light didn't respond to the affirmation. Instead he pondered the information once again. Even in the rarefied air the test was designed for, achieving a result so high on the primary art indices was almost incomprehensible, but the anomaly, the spike on a secondary index? The sample set wasn't large enough to know what the spike on the nature index signified. Only the operative Zhivago scored so high on the primary art indices and only Zhivago had shown a second spike, his too on the nature index.

Zhivago was not a good comparison. They'd learned soon enough what the nature index spike meant for him. Sadism. It manifested itself quickly once Our World had taken him under its possessive wing. Granted, depravity wasn't a bad thing; it had proven to be useful when properly directed. But this person wasn't Zhivago. There was no way of knowing what the second spike on the test meant in this case, a test result that intimated a deep connection with nature.

The man in the light did not like the unknown.

His body language for the first time changed. Unease? He shifted slightly in his chair, refocusing on what he *did* know, namely that there were too many fail-safes built into their test for the results to be wrong. He also knew that as with Zhivago, his decision was going to be predicated on the only important result, the child's unfathomably high score on the primary indices. Art.

"Have we started preparations?"

"Da. The instant the inquiry came in. As per protocol."

"Who?"

He knew the answer before he asked.

"Charlotte."

Protocol or not, there was nobody else to entrust with the assignment. Nobody else qualified. There can only be one who is the best, and for an assignment of this magnitude, it was Charlotte. The leader of Our World, relaxed in confidence, reflected on the absolute correctness of the decision.

She'd been tested as a child by the Soviet state for occupational aptitude, as all children behind the Iron Curtain were, and her results showed an aptitude for virtually everything. He'd directed that young girl's file be removed from state hands the day he'd been made aware of the vocational anomaly. He also arranged to have the child removed from her distraught and pleading parents' arms in Bishkek, Kyrgyzstan. She was eight years old.

She didn't cry, not a tear.

She adapted.

Unlike the other Soviet Bloc children who showed potential aptitude for a given endeavor, Charlotte was not taken to one of the Olympic training facilities to become a gymnast or track star, or to an academic institution where she might have studied to become a scientist, a biochemist, or an astrophysicist destined to work for the nascent Korabl-Sputnik aerospace program.

Nor was she taken to begin a lifetime of indentured servitude with the Bolshoi Ballet, although the leader of Our World knew she would have excelled as a ballerina, not only because her facial features were fine and of indeterminate origin, and so could easily be made up to be beautiful or bland, but also because her deceptively athletic body was made for smooth, efficient movement. No. She was not taken to learn Pyotr Tchaikovsky's *Swan Lake*.

Instead, she was taken into Our World custody, where she immediately began training in arts that existed beyond the regimented thinking of the world's most advanced military special forces units. For eight hours a day, seven days a week, month after month and year after year, Charlotte was intensively and mercilessly trained in those dark arts.

She didn't cry, not a tear.

She learned to kill.

Another eight hours of each of her days were devoted to academic study. She was taught in every subject: history, the arts, the sciences, and culture. She learned the theory behind pleasure and excelled in the practical application of that learning. Charlotte was driven, pushed relentlessly, never allowed to put her body or brain into neutral, to coast. Hers was a life of endless physical and cerebral travail.

But she didn't cry, not a tear.

She became a polymath.

For the final eight hours of each day, she was forced to lie down and sleep. But not the sleep of dreams: it was the disturbed sleep of constant stimuli, languages, spoken to her by the best linguists Our World money could buy. For hour upon hour, by her bed, they spoke to Charlotte as she balanced between the unconscious and conscious, dialects, inflections, perfect enunciation. The latest in Soviet neuroscience applied brutally and relentlessly. It would have driven most insane, but not her.

She didn't cry, not a tear. She learned to speak seventeen languages not just fluently, but perfectly, including several dialects within each language.

She became a polyglot.

Charlotte had been raised for this time, educated, groomed, cultured, trained, and finished. She became the best of the best, proving to be one in a hundred million, not one in a million as the leader of Our World originally calculated. She surpassed her own teachers and received her operative code name, a name he'd personally chosen for her.

Charlotte.

It was his right to choose. Names from history, from literature, his choice, his fancy, and his will. And it was irreversible. Who operatives had been before they came under Our World control died on the day the leader bestowed their code names. To resurrect the past, to seek who they'd been before, was a crime against his rule of order. Even to refer to themselves by their birth name was taken as rebellion, a direct threat to Our World. Punishment was swift and severe for any who dared look back.

The eight-year-old child from the Soviet hinterlands died that day and an assassin-in-waiting was born.

Charlotte.

She was ready. She'd been prepared for this moment, waiting for her chance to serve Our World.

"Send her."

He reached toward the string hanging from the table light.

The meeting was over.

"Send her now."

14

1960s

UNDISCLOSED SMALL TOWN

There was something about the late fall this year, something that made Rose happy; even happier than she had been all summer. She watched the trees pass by the bus window, red and yellow, seasons changing gear.

Hunter was reading now, nearly every day.

It had taken a lot of soul-searching, but they'd finally decided to follow Dr. Keen's advice and take Hunter out of public school. Dr. Keen helped them with the school board. He'd written a letter saying it was in his young patient's better interest to be homeschooled. Rose had never heard of such a thing, didn't even know it was legal. But one thing she knew for sure was that she wasn't qualified to teach Hunter what he would have learned in school.

Dr. Keen helped there too. He found the perfect tutor for their son, one that, most importantly, she and Pete could afford. Barely afford, but they were getting by.

Happy though she was, Rose knew the change hadn't really affected their son one way or the other. He was still the same, but both she and Pete had changed. It felt like the weight of the world had been lifted from their shoulders. Their son was still the elephant in the room, but in a good way now. He still seemed distant, contented to be in his world, but at least he wasn't fishing on the cement as much as before. Pete was happy about that.

Yes. So much had changed in their lives for the better.

Dr. Keen had been a godsend; he'd walked Rose and Pete through the process of coping with who their son really was and what his special needs were.

Rose noticed she was close and pulled the cord to ring the bell. She walked to the front and thanked the bus driver as she stepped down and off. He was a nice guy and even waited at her stop a couple of times when she was late to catch the bus. She had a job now. It didn't pay much, but it was helping to pay for Hunter's new tutor.

She stepped back into the bus stop shelter and watched the loud bus pull away, then turned to walk the two blocks to home, thinking as she walked about all that had transpired over the recent months.

"Beautiful day! Your yard looks great!" Rose liked Mrs. Hyland. She knew the elderly Mr. and Mrs. Hyland took great pride in having the neatest yard in the summer and the cleanest driveway on the block in the winter, shoveled and swept clear of every single white flake.

Mrs. Hyland looked up from where she was on her knees, pulling dead plants from a flower bed that would soon enough be frozen rock hard, and waved her off with a proud smile.

It took a few moments for her to dig the keys out of her purse. She was wearing gloves, thin cream-colored gloves that she'd found at the thrift store for a fraction of the price that a new pair would have cost. They were still an extravagance, so she didn't tell Pete that she'd spent the money. He wouldn't understand that she needed to look presentable now that she was a saleslady.

The door opened before she found the key.

"Hey, Mrs. J! I thought I heard you at the door!" Hunter's tutor stood to the side to let Rose enter; ebullient as always.

"Thank you, Wilbur." Rose smiled at the young woman holding the door open and stepped in. It still didn't sit right with Rose, calling a female "Wilbur," and at one point, when the tutor asked about Hunter's strange middle names, Powell Cotton, Rose asked the young tutor about her own strange boy's name, but let it drop when the tutor explained that it was just a nickname that she preferred to her real name.

"Did you and Hunter have a nice day?"

"For sure. All good here. He's in the living room right now, looking at a book about tribal art we picked up from the library. It's a thick one, should take him at least an hour to read it. He wanted to know more about thirteenth-century Edo bronzes from Benin. Sheesh! He's one smart cookie!"

Rose removed her gloves carefully and shrugged off the heavy coat.

"Did he eat his lunch today?"

"A small one. He definitely eats to live, but not much more." The girl called Wilbur took Rose's coat and walked it to the closet. "I wish I had the same self-discipline!"

Rose smiled as she placed the gloves in the basket on the side table by the door.

"Enjoy eating while you can. I literally look at food now and it attaches itself to my backside."

Rose bent down to unzip her boots.

"How about his math? Did you give him the math questions?" Rose wasn't much for math, and neither was Hunter, but she knew it was required as part of the homeschooling curriculum.

"Oh, yes. He doesn't like it, but he is capable. Just need to motivate him the right way. He did four extra lessons when I told him I'd take him to the Biology Department at the university next week *if* he got ahead of his math work." She shook her head and tucked back a wisp of strawberry blond hair. "He's a machine! Still shocks me how he seems to know all the work before I even show him how to do it!"

She'd laughed when she'd explained during the job interview with Rose and Pete that even though she was studying psychology, once she finished her postdoctoral studies, she wanted to go to Africa to do field studies on developmental relationships between primates and humans. She wanted to combine what she'd learned in school with paleontological discoveries about humanoid beginnings. But she'd also explained that she liked poetry and thought she might just change directions completely and become a poet. Finally, she'd admitted with a cute smile that it was all a little scattered and that she probably needed some time to sort out her future.

Rose could relate. She'd been young with dreams once too. If she hadn't thought Pete would have taken it personally, she'd have told Wilbur to live life while she could.

Rose had asked at the interview, "Why here? Why this city?" and pointed out that it wasn't exactly like where Wilbur had been having fun in the sun at the University of Southern California. Wilbur explained she'd chosen their quiet local university as far away as possible from USC because she was taking a sabbatical from the stress and distractions of big university life and mainstream academia.

Rose was the one who made the final call. She didn't know what that postdoc thing was, and she'd barely heard of the university in California, but she liked the girl, liked that she was down-to-earth and respectful, obviously the product of a good upbringing. And it was a huge plus that she had her own car.

Now here she was. The young woman with the funny name was Hunter's new teacher. And she had turned out to be even better than they'd hoped. In fact she was becoming indispensable. Rose was finally able to admit to herself that things were going to be okay. It was a relief; the last two months had been a joy.

"I can be back tomorrow morning, same time if you want. I'm planning to spend most of the weekend at the library, so I can easily swing by and pick up Hunter." She smiled and added, "I'll park him in the periodicals section tomorrow. He loves *National Geographic*. That and *Outdoor Life*. He eats up the adventure stuff! So he'll be busy and I can get some of my work done too."

"Thank you for offering, Wilbur, but garage sales aren't over yet. Pete always takes Hunter. It's probably the last weekend anyone will have a garage sale before spring. But if you aren't busy on Sunday that would be very nice. It gives Pete and me some weekend time together."

"You got it, Mrs. J!" Wilbur gave a thumbs-up and reached in to take her own coat from the closet. But then she paused and reached into her pocket. "Oh, speaking of garage sales, a guy came by today. Said he was an antique dealer. He left his card. Said he and your husband met early in the summer at a garage sale and he was wondering if he could come by and look at the old stuff in Hunter's room."

Rose took the card.

Willisford Dowan. Indefinite Art Incorporated.

"Oh yes, I remember. That's where Hunter got that watch he always wears." She was frowning, curious how the antique dealer would even know about Hunter's collection. Had to be Pete; he must have told the guy.

"Ahhh. I wondered about that watch. Hunter sure seems to like it." Wilbur shrugged her coat into place on her shoulders and pulled the scarf from where it was hanging out one sleeve, wrapping it around her neck when she did. "No way I'd let anyone take that from Hunter."

Rose smiled at the thought.

"Don't worry." Rose held the door for Wilbur. "They'd have to steal it from him when he was sleeping!"

15

'll pay one hundred dollars." The unhealthy-looking antique dealer held the beaded bag toward the couple standing in the bedroom near the door. "It's old."

Very old, actually; an octopus bag it was called. Métis, circa 1860. Over the years he'd found two of the serge cloth fire bags, but neither compared to the one he was holding now. It was in perfect condition. No beads missing. Wool tassels all there; museum quality. Even the strap was there. He had a collector of native pieces who he knew would pay $1,500 with a phone call. He'd be able to sell it for even more if he shopped it around.

If it wasn't for the two other people in the room, he'd have been showing how excited he really was. The kid's bed already had six pieces laid out and there were another dozen items that he recognized as being worth at least as much as the pieces he'd already picked out.

The wife looked at her husband, indecisive; the antique dealer could see that they obviously had zero idea as to the value of their son's collection. Frankly, it was astonishing that the kid had been able to amass such a treasure trove just from attending local garage sales.

"A hundred and twenty dollars." The counteroffer from the same clown who would have taken twenty-five dollars for the porcelain plate worth thousands; or was it twenty? No finesse. A lout; insufferable and totally predictable. But the game was the game; it had to be played.

"One hundred and ten," the antique dealer countered. "You drive a hard bargain, Mr. Johann!"

He'd only brought along $200 in cash, a lot of money for a house call; never in a million years did he think he would possibly find enough treasures in the kid's collection to spend more than that. Already he'd made deals for $450 worth of the kid's stuff, just with what was on the bed. And he was lowballing hard, devaluing the items to a tiny fraction of what they were worth.

There were more pieces on the shelves that were outside his realm of knowledge. Books. Had to be very careful with books; you needed to know your stuff for that game. Paintings. There were a couple that looked to be important, not big, but they smelled rich. It was weird, but he honestly felt that richness in an object had a quality you could smell. Maybe it was a smell that you only learned to identify if you'd been surrounded by luxury for some extended period of your life.

Back in his European days, luxury was in the very air he breathed. No doubt that was where he acquired his taste for expensive objects.

"I'll have to come back." He didn't want to leave; it was a huge gamble. They could change their minds. Or some other antique dealer could cut in and offer them more. The kid was out in the living room, looking at a picture book or something. For whatever reason, he didn't seem concerned that his parents were selling off his things, but he also didn't trust the kid; too strange. What if he threw a tantrum about his stuff getting sold? That could ruin the deal too.

It was getting late, after 10 p.m. All told, including the hour's worth of formalities, cookies, and tea, he'd been there for over three hours. The antique dealer knew he had no choice; it was last-resort time. Tell the truth and get back as soon as possible.

"To tell you the truth, Mr. and Mrs. Johann, I didn't bring enough money to pay for everything tonight, but I'll give you two hundred dollars now and take this bag. You can keep the other ninety as a deposit against the rest of these pieces on the bed."

He held out his hand to shake on the deal. The husband took it. The antique dealer could see the guy was out of his league, trying to appear as if it was no big deal, but he was obviously as shocked as his wife. It was easy to see that they didn't have much money. Should have offered them less, he thought to himself as he walked through the living room, toward the front door, past where the boy was still looking at books, flipping pages.

That's when he noticed the watch, his watch on the boy's wrist.

He would ask the parents if he could buy the watch back. He'd had second thoughts about the trade since the day he'd made it but wasn't about to risk pushing to get it back until after he made the deal with the parents for the rest of the kid's stuff.

"How about tomorrow evening. Same time good for you?"

He knew it would be. Both parents worked. That's what they said when they called him. But if he had his druthers, he'd have preferred to come back first thing in the morning, rather than wait until evening. Less risk of losing the deal.

They both nodded.

"So 7 p.m. it is!"

With that he opened the front door and exited, leaving the husband and wife holding the ten crisp twenty-dollar bills he'd just given them.

A good day.

A very good day, he was thinking to himself as he heaved into the brand-new van he'd purchased with the profits from the sale of the Yongzheng plate. Yes. Life was wonderful again. He set the beaded bag carefully on the bench seat beside him and started up the truck. It still smelled new. He loved it.

As he pulled away down the dark street, illuminated only by one large streetlight, he turned on the radio. *If I had a hammer, I'd hammer in the morning.* Good song. He turned the volume up.

I'd hammer in the evening.

All over this land.

When he turned from the crescent onto the main street, where the road was brighter, lit by streetlights on every block, he didn't notice the tow truck pull out from the dark alleyway he'd just passed. He had no reason to. Why should he be aware that the big truck followed him out onto the main east-west freeway?

I'd hammer out danger.

I'd hammer out a warning.

The four-lane, divided freeway, joining the two halves of the city, allowed the 65,000 people living on the east side of the river to cross to the west side and the 65,000 citizens living on the west side to cross the other direction easily and quickly. The obese man in the van never drove the speed limit. He liked to make up time. Especially at night, when the cops were all in the shop and traffic was light. Actually nonexistent that night.

It's a hammer of justice.

In the dark, most newcomers to the city would never have noticed that the freeway crossed the wide river, the boundary between the west side and the east. There was no real change to the roadway, no bridge superstructure over the pavement. Only low concrete barricades along both sides of the freeway marked where the road built on land stopped and where the portion of the freeway with nothing under it but a long drop to the water below began.

It's a bell of freedom.

He didn't take notice of the bridge. He'd crossed it ten thousand times. And he didn't notice the wrecker rapidly catching up to him, or he didn't until it rammed into his van's back driver-side bumper. Heavier than the van, and traveling at 90 miles per hour, the tow truck kept pushing, causing him to lurch back into his seat. Even then it took a second for his mind to register what was going on.

The tactical ramming maneuver used by the massive tow truck caused his van to careen toward the guardrail at more than 75 miles per hour. He didn't even have time to hit the brakes. In fact, when he realized there was no avoiding the collision, he panicked and instinctively jammed his throttle foot down to the floorboard, pushing himself away from the steering wheel, a futile attempt that only increased the impact speed of the now totally out-of-control van.

When his vehicle's passenger-side front quarter rammed into the guardrail, his big, soft body was thrown against the steering wheel, which in that instant was effectively converted into a blunt spear. The force of the impact drove his head forward, like a twenty-pound egg attached to the end of a sling, first onto the metal dashboard and then, already flattened on the front side, up and forward into the windshield, cracking the top as well. The new van's rear end rose at the impact, vectoring forces working together to flip it high above the roadway and over the guardrail in a wide arc.

Momentum and physics. Laws of nature. The heavy wrecker passed by the careening van as the latter obeyed those laws and pivoted over the top of the railing, falling away from the rending sound of metal against concrete and down into the blackness.

Nobody saw the van hit the guardrail. Nobody heard it hit the water. Nobody saw the splash or saw the van bob a few times and then gently sink. In fact, nobody even noticed the large white scratches on the concrete for three more days, at which time an observant city engineer thought to stop and look more closely at the marks and investigate the bits of glass and chrome lying on the pavement beside the guardrail.

Slowed now to the speed limit, the tow truck continued on its way. The driver obeyed the law now by choice, not out of necessity.

Rule of Law or Law of Nature, Charlotte was above both.

Our World laws were the only ones she obeyed.

16

He liked working after hours at the office. It wasn't his home, but it was homey. It was a quiet time for him, a time he could focus on any paperwork to do with the children under his care. Dottie didn't mind, she said she liked the quiet time for herself too, and besides, he could be home in five minutes if she needed him.

The letter in his hand had come to his office that day. It was from his friend Margot, apologizing for the tardiness in responding to his original query. For all her genius, she was hopeless when it came to details like answering correspondence in a timely manner. How she ever managed to run her Mensa organization was beyond him.

"It certainly seems as though you have found yourself a young Mensa candidate. However, my dear friend, it is my considered opinion that the child should be retested. As you know, an infinite number of monkeys will *almost surely* replicate any score possible on our test. A mathematical metaphor, dear, please forgive me. My talents lean toward every direction, excepting the literary."

He smiled when he read on.

"Have the child retake the test variant and if he does as well on that version, please offer him my job."

Better late than never, he was thinking as he refolded the letter and slid it into his sports jacket pocket to take home. He made a mental note to bring Hunter's file back to the office. It was at home, filled with two dozen similar letters, pretty much all saying the same thing, that Hunter's test results must be corrupted somehow. Something he would have probably thought too, if he hadn't seen the child with his own eyes and if he hadn't administered the tests himself and watched the boy respond.

Hunter had been a challenging patient, one that he'd found himself working long hours on. He'd pushed Dottie's tolerance to the limit by keeping Hunter's file at home so he could work late into the night on his young patient's case. There were even days when he woke up early at home to be able to make calls out east and write more letters. How many had he sent? Asking if any of his peers had heard of similar cases. Thirty? No, it was more like fifty. The larger institutions didn't even deign to respond, no doubt thinking that he was a small-town quack and that the claim was too outlandish to deserve a response.

But all that was behind him now.

The doctor poured himself a glass of "medicinal" whisky from the bottle he always kept for pensive moments. White Horse. Blended. Scotch whisky. He smiled to himself as he placed the bottle back in its spot. Prescribing hard spirits and self-medicating would probably be frowned upon by his profession and it probably wouldn't help him think clearer, but it would go well with the touch of melancholy he was feeling.

Tonight it was officially over.

He'd done all he could for Hunter and his parents. For the last six months he'd used at least part, and many days a large part, of any spare time he had available, working on the case of his wondrously special young patient. And today when he'd made his weekly call to find out how Hunter was doing with his homeschooling and his personal tutor, Rose had told him that she'd never been happier, and that Hunter was reading voraciously. It was the sixth week in a row that she'd said the same thing.

All was good!

Cheers! He lifted his glass and toasted aloud to himself. "Job well done, Dr. Keen!"

He paused, reflective for a moment, noticing the framed photos in his office. "And to you, my beautiful Dottie. No more work at home. I promise."

It was over, out of his hands now.

Funny how the first sip of whisky always tasted as good as the last.

The big break had come in the letter from the Swedish doctor who'd heard about Dr. Keen's inquiry from another doctor at a workshop they'd both attended. The Swedish doctor said the letter made him recall something he'd read in a German periodical and had included a small clipping, cut from the back of the periodical. He'd been kind enough to enclose a rough translation with his letter. It was an advertisement, a general request for child psychiatrists worldwide to contact the address in the advertisement if they had any information about case studies showing the following list of results, results that were nearly identical to what he'd found when he tested Hunter.

He must have had Mrs. Truscott check the mailbox five times a day during the days he waited for a response from the address in the periodical. He'd sent off Hunter's test results via airmail, at no small cost, and he'd included Margot's Mensa test and the standard IQ test results, as well as the description of Hunter's ability to assimilate knowledge from books at an impossible rate. He'd included a paragraph or two about his patient's incredible intuitive ability to recognize fine art.

He'd even mentioned the original Picasso in his office and how Hunter had been so enamored with it on his first and subsequent visits. As an afterthought, he'd included a photo he snapped of the painting with his Kodak Brownie Starflash. It wasn't that he needed to; it was more vanity than anything. He wanted to let the German researchers see his pride and joy.

When the response finally arrived in the mail, it wasn't just a letter; it was a big package that had to be picked up at the post office. It contained a dozen separate portfolios and at least two hundred pages of very explicit instructions on the protocol to administer the enclosed tests. Crazy complicated, but he'd studied them harder than he'd ever studied in university. When he felt ready to administer them, he brought Hunter back to the office.

He'd sent the results off as per the instructions and received a letter back a few weeks later saying they would get back to him, but it would take them several months to analyze the results. He was disappointed with the delay but couldn't say he was surprised.

He smiled to himself again, proud of his work. He'd done all he could. The German researchers would get back to him in good time.

"To Hunter! And to Hunter's future!" He downed the glass, thought for a second, and then reached for the bottle again. Why not?

How many of his peers could say they discovered a child prodigy? Not only that, but he'd made an unhappy family happy. And he'd found them the perfect personal tutor. What was her name again? It was an odd name: William, no, Wilbur. That was it. Nice girl.

It might have been a bit out of the box, but with the applications he often received from university students looking for internships, he figured he'd do a good deed and so had interviewed a few of the applicants on behalf of the Johanns. He'd even checked the young lady's curriculum vitae and phoned her references.

Pretty impressive list of references really, mostly from California. One was Robert Duncan, the author of *The Opening of the Field*, a book he'd only read himself after speaking with the author on the phone about Wilbur. Not exactly his type of book, poetry, but he did agree with one thing, that personal spiritual knowledge overruled orthodox teaching. They'd gotten into a deep discussion after the poet gave his young acolyte a ringing endorsement.

He poured himself that second drink and walked over to stand in front of his favorite painting.

There were two other candidates who had been good choices too, but both said no when he called them back for second interviews. They'd changed their minds, they said, but declined to explain why when he asked out of curiosity. Not a big deal; he'd have recommended the USC grad anyway. Given the fact that she was willing to work for little more than room and board and bearing in mind the Johanns' financial situation, she was the best choice by far.

"To us, Mr. Picasso." He lifted his glass to the odd-looking lady in the painting.

Before he could bring the glass to his mouth, the doorbell rang.

Strange for someone to come by the office so late, he thought to himself. It was 7 p.m. Probably someone looking for directions.

He was wrong.

17

knew he was full of it." Pete walked into the kitchen where Rose was working on a tray of muffins, Saskatoon berry and bran. A touch too healthy for Pete, but Hunter liked them. "Didn't even call. Guy's a jerk."

They'd waited for the antique dealer to come back the next evening, but he hadn't shown up. Rose called his store from the pay phone at work the day after that, but there was no answer.

It wasn't so much that he hadn't come back, or that he hadn't even shown them the respect to call and say he couldn't make it. They were upset about the lost revenue. It was a lot of money to them.

"But he left the deposit." Rose always looked on the bright side and she did have a point. "He'll come back. Nobody would walk away from that much money. Probably something came up."

"He probably changed his mind. He's probably going to bring that Indian thing back and will want all his money back." Pete stood up and walked to the fridge, opened the door, and took out his third bottle of beer of the evening. "No way. Not a chance."

Rose bent and put the muffin tin into the 1952 Moffat stove. It wasn't new, but it worked well enough, and Rose loved the chrome; it looked like the front end of a Cadillac; luxurious somehow.

When she was done, she untied her apron and hung it on the hook inside the skinny pantry cupboard by the kitchen nook. Pete had cooled down and was sitting again at the table by then, so she pulled a chair out and sat with her husband.

She reached for the newspaper Pete had dropped on the table and unfolded it, intending to give Pete the sports section. But something caught her eye on the front page, a small note off to the side. There was a short headline, DOCTOR DIES, and an instruction for readers to turn to page 7. Her brow was furrowed as she turned to that page.

"I think I'll go by his store this weekend. He must be open on Saturday afternoon."

Rose scanned the page in front of her.

"Oh no." Her eyes never left the page. "Oh no. Pete."

Pete stood up to look over her shoulder at the open newspaper.

They forgot about the money and the antique dealer.

It was Dr. Keen.

LOCAL DOCTOR DIES IN TRAGIC FIRE

Rose felt sick to her stomach. She'd come to know the doctor well; they'd had time after Hunter's many appointments to chat about other things besides his professional interest in their son. She'd grown fond of him, not just because he'd helped them with their son, but because she felt he was such a genuinely nice person. They'd talked about life and family. He'd even told her that he and his wife, Dottie, decided not to have children so he could devote 100 percent of his attention to the children coming to his office.

Rose never met Dr. Keen's wife and felt a wave of grief for what she must be going through.

The poor man.

His poor wife.

Pete was trying to read the article from over Rose's shoulder, but when he saw her sit back and stop reading, he reached around her and lifted the section from the table.

Rose didn't object. She was done.

"Damn. It was his office. Jesus, we were both there to meet Hunter's teacher." Pete was back in his chair now, reading. "Says the house was burned to the ground; nothing left. Firemen tried for six hours to put the blaze out. Inferno they called it."

Rose didn't want to hear it. She had already pushed herself back from the table and was up now, walking toward her son's bedroom door. She needed to hug him. She needed to hold him.

"He was working late. Alone. Lucky it was only him." She wasn't listening to her husband. "Did you know he had a wife?"

She opened the door to her son's room. He was awake, sitting in his bed, looking up at her. He had a flashlight in his hand and a paperback book on the bed in front of him. *Tarka the Otter: His Joyful Water-Life and Death in the Country of the Two Rivers.*

Rose looked at her son, so content to be who he was. He looked back at her. No guile. No guilt. No apology. No question. No worry that he was breaking a rule, that he was supposed to be sleeping. He was in his world. Wandering with Tarka on the River Taw, mourning Greymuzzle, and preparing for Deadlock. Her son was in his element. No, in a beautiful way, he *was* elemental.

She sat on the edge of the bed, leaned over to her son, and hugged him.

The tears that threatened minutes before now welled again, not only from compassion, but from a hundred different emotions overwhelming the control she'd managed to maintain for so long.

Her son didn't hug her back.

"Are you okay, Mommy?"

Rose pulled back and stared. His face showed concern. It was the first time. The first time she'd ever seen him come out of his shell, the first time he'd shown her that he cared for her, for his mommy.

The tears that she'd been holding back now spilled down her cheeks.

Her son was growing up. He was going to be fine.

Everything was going to be okay. Please. Please make everything be okay.

She hugged her son again, pulled him close to her, and cried. She cried away all the fear, all the worry, the pain, and the guilt. She cried now as much from happiness as from all the other conflicting emotions.

In the kitchen Pete was reading the sports section now. Baseball was over, hockey starting. Football would be ending soon.

He didn't notice the photo on page 3 of a van being pulled from the river. Nor did he notice the headline.

DIVERS FIND BODY INSIDE SUBMERGED VEHICLE

18

November 2020

PINEHURST, NORTH CAROLINA

Holy cow!

Nyala set the manuscript on the side table by her bed.

This was heavy stuff.

She didn't hesitate. She leaned forward and picked up her phone, hit the "Recents" button, and then hit the top number and the phone's speaker button. It barely finished ringing once.

"Nyala?"

Ugh. The voice was so hopeful. She didn't let her disdain show though; she needed him, or at least she needed his skills. The day she needed him for any other reason was the day she would kill herself with a spoon in the eye.

"Yes, it's me. Listen, remember I said earlier that I might need you to do some research for me tomorrow?" Nyala stood up from her bed. She'd moved there when her tailbone started aching from sitting most of the afternoon on the cheap office chair at her desk. She picked up the manuscript and carried it out of her room, talking as she went. "I changed my mind. I need you to do a search tonight. No. I can't tell you why."

As good as Nyala was at researching, her skill in that regard paled to Scott's, mostly because he didn't have a life. He spent his weekends playing video games with his reject basement-dwelling buddies.

Not nice. She needed him.

"No! I don't need you to come over." She set the manuscript on the kitchen table. "I want you to research a name."

She pulled out a chair and then sat at the table, pulling the manuscript closer.

"He's a doctor." She read back through the page in front of her. "Dr. Keen. No. No first name. Only know he was a child psychiatrist."

She was leafing through the pages, scanning what she'd read so far.

"No, that's part of the problem. I don't know what city he lived in. Not even the country for sure, but definitely North America. Focus on the Midwest. Include Canada. Not sure if this will help, but only look at cities where they had stubby beer bottles. What? No, I wasn't being insensitive. Okay, what's the right word? Seriously? Vertically challenged?"

Nyala shook her head and stood up from the chair, agitated. Scott was serious; his whole generation, which was technically her generation, was way over the top on the politically correct garbage that was pervading society, like a cancerous tumor metastasizing out of control. She had to bite her tongue and count to three before she spoke again; there was a more important fish to fry.

"Yeah, I'm still here. Just feeling bad that I tweaked your trauma trigger." She rolled her eyes and listened to the voice coming through her phone speaker. "Okay, got it. Microaggression bad. I'll do my best. Listen, can you go to your safe place a little later? I don't mean to change the subject, but the city has a river running through the middle of it. Yes, I know most cities have rivers and no, that's the other part of the problem. He's not alive. He practiced back in the 1950s. Early '60s. Up to about '62, I'd say. Maybe '63.

"Yes, I know what I'm asking. It's not going to be easy. That's why I'm calling you. Nobody else can do it. You're the best."

It was more of a carrot than a real compliment, but it was also true.

"The only other thing I know is he died in a house fire; it was his office. I think that's the key to finding him or finding anything about him; where he lived; what city. For sure the local newspaper carried the story."

Even as she said it, Nyala realized the futility of what she was asking. Even if Scott was able to confirm there was a real Dr. Keen and even if he discovered where he'd lived and practiced nearly sixty years before, she couldn't talk to the guy. He was dead. And if he was in his late thirties back then, he'd be close to one hundred years old by now. But at least she'd be able to confirm that someone in the manuscript actually did exist, or at least had existed back then.

There was something deep inside her that wanted the whole thing to be real, and not just because she would like to believe that people could have superpowers, but because maybe in a weird way it gave her hope that if she could prove everything was real in the story, she might be able to unravel the truth about her own life someday. Be able to research her own past, prove that she *had* a past.

Prove that she too had a story, a story with a beginning instead of just a big black void.

Nyala stopped herself. She felt a momentary hit of self-loathing. Stop that maudlin shit, girl.

"Enough. What? No, sorry. Talking to myself again."

Get back on the track.

Based on what she'd just read, there was a lot more to go on now, more than just the circumstantial stuff about paintings and Rolex watches that she'd been able to research as she read. A fire killed the doctor, not a painting, not triangles or circles. And the Chinese plate didn't kill the antique dealer, nor did the kid, despite what Tsau-z said. The antique dealer's van was pushed over the edge of a bridge.

That was another bit of confusion cleared up and another way to locate whatever city all this was supposed to have happened in. She added one more task to the one she'd just given Scott.

"If you think you found a city that fits the bill and can't find anything about the doctor, then you can also try looking for another guy. Hang on a second." Nyala leaned over and leafed through the pages again, looking for the name. "Winnisford Dowan. D-O-W-A-N. No, wait. Willisford Dowan. He owned an antique store back then. Indefinite Art Incorporated."

Nyala didn't want to overload Scott but screw it; she wanted to know the truth.

"Shouldn't be too hard; he died around the same time as the doctor. Car crash on a bridge; car was found in the water. Van, I mean, not car; a panel van I'd say." She thought for a moment, adding the west and east side numbers. "Population of the city was about 130,000 people back at that time; sorry, forgot to mention that."

She considered adding one more task but decided against it. Too much even for Scott. Every city in the Midwest would have a thousand Johanns, although locating Rose and Pete would prove that part of the manuscript was true. For sure they had a phone; she remembered reading that the doctor called Rose the day he died in the fire, so that would also help find them. They'd be in the phone book from back then. There was a library in the city, she'd read that too, so there should be a phone book archive, right? Libraries didn't shut down, did they? Nyala wasn't sure about the phone book part though; she'd never looked in one. Wasn't even sure they were still being printed.

"What? No, sorry, my bad, I was just thinking." She touched the speaker button and put the phone to her ear. "Think you can do it? Yes, I know it'll take all night. Yep, for sure, call me if you find anything. Doesn't matter what time it is."

She didn't wait for him to respond before ending the call. She walked to stand in front of the window, looking at the lake's silver surface reflecting the last light of the day. She was tapping the phone to her chin, her go-to habit when she needed to think.

If the doctor was real, Scott would find him. She was sure of that. Zero idea how. Had to be some kind of doctor list or something he could access, maybe a national registry of some sort. It wouldn't be much of a challenge to find a doctor nowadays, no matter where they practiced, but they probably weren't even entering data on computers in the 1960s. Computers? It was all slide rules, wasn't it? Not even calculators. All hard copy and paper, which she did use herself, but how did they even function without computers? It was caveman time back then.

Scott would have a tougher time locating the antique dealer; she doubted there was such a thing as a database for that type of business. Maybe there was some kind of antique-collecting association he was a member of. There had to be a record of his death though;

it wasn't like he died of old age. Both of their deaths, his and the doctor's, had to have been suspicious to the authorities.

Both deaths were apparently reported in the newspaper. Maybe the local library had digital copies, or microfiche? Wasn't that what it was called? Nyala searched through her mental hard drive, recalling her journalism history classes. Microfiche. She remembered them being mini, low-resolution photographs of the pages in local newspapers, kept in files at libraries.

If the antique dealer was really pushed over the bridge, that would mean Tsau-z was confessing to knowing about a murder. Didn't that make him an accomplice? Somebody named Charlotte did the actual killing. So *if* it was all true, Nyala would also be an accomplice if she didn't report what she knew, right? Or not? She wasn't sure what her responsibilities were in such a case. *If* it happened, it took place nearly sixty years ago. Maybe the police managed to figure out that there had been foul play involved and opened a file. Heck, maybe they had even found Charlotte and put her rear in prison. Maybe that's where she was now.

The police did pull the van from the water, according to the newspaper report Rose and Pete read, but it was conceivable the detectives didn't catch the dents and paint scrapes on the back end where the tow truck pushed the van off the bridge. Maybe they declared it an accident so there wouldn't even be a cold-case file to reopen if she did report a murder.

And what about the doctor? Did they call that an accident too? Did they think there was an electrical short? It was an old house. Or did they believe the doctor just happened to be sitting in his office and fell asleep with a cigarette in his hand? Didn't everyone smoke back then? And was there even such a thing as a fire marshal in the 1960s? Someone to investigate if a fire was possibly arson or not? Who knew how backward they were, and it wasn't like CSI was going to come to the rescue; cavalry maybe, on horses probably.

Maybe she was just being paranoid, maybe it was an accident. It didn't say in the manuscript that the doctor was actually murdered. It could have been a coincidence. Bad luck.

Nyala pondered all these things.

The 1960s were long before her time, but one thing she was sure of: she was going to keep researching. Whoever Tsau-z was, he'd taken up a whole day of her life. And she was only one-third of the way through the manuscript.

She was still pondering when the front door opened and her friend Luba swept in.

19

"Read this." Nyala didn't even let her friend take off her coat before she handed Luba the pages she'd already read.

"Uh, excuse me? *Hello?* Yes, I'm fine. Yes, I had a wonderful meal. Oh, how sweet of you for asking! Yes, I did buy the perfect blue sweater I've been trying to find for the last six months!" She took the pages Nyala was holding out to her, changing her tone from sarcasm to pained questioning. "Like now? You want me to read this now?"

Nyala had already turned and was heading toward their fridge, ignoring her friend. She was famished and wanted a drink. She'd forgotten to eat since she'd found the manuscript in her mailbox.

"How rude! Remind me again. Why I'm your only friend?" Luba didn't bother to take her jacket off; she just walked to the big, over-stuffed chair and flopped into it.

"Want something to drink?" Nyala was reaching into the fridge for the open bottle of white wine in the door. "I'm having wine, with ice and water."

"Of course. Wine. No ice. Water's poison." Luba meant it. She'd often said that even if she was dying of thirst, she would crawl ten miles across a desert filled with plain ice-cold water to be able to drink a glass of flavored sparkling water. The fact that a desert couldn't technically be covered in ice-cold water didn't in any way concern her. "'*I am the Man of Sores*'? That's gross."

"Just shut up and read." Nyala reached for the plastic container with the leftover Greek salad she'd made the day before. Then she opened the freezer door and reached into the ice tray, pulling out four cubes. She dropped the ice into a cheap wineglass.

It was dark outside now and the moon was a waxing crescent low in the sky, Nyala noted as she poured wine into each glass; it was beautiful. She liked the moon, always had, and liked walking on clear nights, under the Milky Way. She loved listening to the nightjars and the crickets and she loved the flitting little brown bats. She felt at home when she was out on nights like that, alone with the wild animals.

Funny, she'd never been afraid of being alone in the darkness of the night. It wasn't the darkness living inside her. And the wind, the singing voices didn't come to her in the night. Maybe the wind was out there somewhere, in the vast sky above, flowing around the stars.

She took a moment longer to look at the moon, before turning to her friend.

"Here's your wine."

She grabbed a fork and the container of Greek salad. Then she walked past where Luba was already scrunching her face up as she read. Nyala balanced her salad container against her chest and picked up the rest of the manuscript.

"I'll be reading in my room."

She knew that if she stayed in the living area, Luba's attention-deficit disorder would kick in and she'd want to talk instead of read.

20

1960s

RUSSIA
UNDISCLOSED LOCATION

The man with the perfectly trimmed white beard flecked with black sat back in his chair and put the palms of his hands together, then brought them to his mouth, as though praying.

But there was no higher power to pray to.

No, he was not praying, he was contemplating the painting on the table in front of him and was for all intents and purposes enjoying himself, basking in its reflected brilliance.

The legend was true; every triangle, every glorious circle; true.

When the messenger, the minion across the table, first reached down into the darkness on the side of his chair to pull the small painting from the leather case and pass it across the table, the man with the beard recognized and authenticated it immediately and only a second later had calculated its value, conservatively $150 million. Those of the Gathering would determine the pennies above or below that price, or they would to the degree he would let them decide. In the end, Our World would get exactly what it wanted from the Gathering; always had and always would. They would pay whatever he decided.

For those selected to attend the Gathering, wealthy purchasers of the world's greatest art treasures, collecting art was far more than a simple passion to obtain beautiful objects, it was a need. A need more powerful than any autonomic response, a need that usurped all human compassion. It was pathological, a sickness, but for him, for Our World, art was purely business. Prices realized in the normal world of art auctions, even at the best auction houses, were mere pittances compared to the prices being realized for the best of the best, the art treasures that never made it to the normal world channels.

He made sure of that. Our World made sure.

He scoffed inwardly at the thought of the published world-record prices for various art vernaculars; they were light-years below what the finest art was worth. If the greater unwashed only knew. But they never would.

Had anyone been able to hear his thoughts at that moment, they would have heard him giving thanks to war, the patron saint of Our World. Without it, nothing would change. Without it, there would be no chaos, no upheaval, no redistribution, and no loss; more importantly, no gain.

War.

The man at the desk knew in that single word was founded the principle upon which his profession was built, for upon the horrors of war through the ages came chaos, and with chaos came opportunity.

Whether past, present, or future, war was a necessary good.

The painting before him was on the table for one reason: war's deconstruction of morality, ethics, religion, and philosophy; the disintegration of status and quo. And to think this painting had been only a legend, a story told in the dark by the operatives of Our World.

Looking over the manicured fingertips of his clasped hands, he reflected on the origin of the legend. Solomon and Hilla had first seen it thirty years ago in Germany, but the artist Kandinsky wouldn't sell it then. They had tried to keep its existence a secret. He smiled at the futility. They may have been able to keep their find from the rest of those in the genteel American circles they spent time in, but keeping a secret from Our World? Impossible.

They were collectors, infused into the very lifeblood of the Gathering. When the pair desired an object of art, they were rich enough to bid the desire out of the other auction attendees. But the two of them were more than patrons; they also had the rarest of abilities to "feel" beauty. They were necessary, their money was necessary, but their meddling in the business affairs of Our World, their constant searching on their own, to bypass the Gathering and augment their personal collection at lower prices, had proven problematic.

As much as it hurt Our World's bottom line, he was glad that Solomon was gone. Glad that Hilla was nearly so.

He looked at the painting. It was among the pantheon of greatest works; legendary. And until that day, until it was pulled from the black leather case by the man across the Turkish walnut table and brought into the light, it was just that, a legend. It would be a highlight of the Gathering in the coming year.

The bidding would be brisk.

Zhivago would not be pleased. He'd been searching for the painting and had been getting closer. He'd requested cover for the West; nothing special: a passport, travel, and working capital. Easy. The man with the flecked beard arranged it with a two-word note to his underlings. "Do it." Zhivago was on the trail, smelling blood. He would have found the painting, with time, but he didn't. He was too late.

The man smiled slightly. That was good. Zhivago lacked humility and controlling him was a challenge. Controlling his urges even more so. Even Vlad the Impaler would shrink before Zhivago's sociopathic tendencies. So this was good. Anything that humbled the operative made the leader of Our World's job easier.

Zhivago was the best, so a final solution was not the answer.

Could it be that the child from across the water would surpass Zhivago? Time would tell.

The course was set.

He looked again at the painting, so obviously the work of Kandinsky, so obviously the lost sibling to the known work. A legend lost and now a legend found.

When the small square photograph from the doctor arrived with the child's test results, the man instantly recognized what he was looking at. It was in fact a photograph of a supposed Picasso, front and center, with Kandinsky's brilliant contrasting *Farbstudie–Dreieck und konzentrische Ringe*, his "Study in Triangles and Concentric Circles," just visible on the edge of the printed photograph.

Even in black and white, it had been obvious that the child had not been enamored with the Picasso as the doctor thought. It was the Kandinsky the child felt. It was the most magnificent piece of undiscovered artwork to find its way into the light for the last decade.

Works as important as the painting before him were the rarest of finds, even for the best operatives of Our World, even for Zhivago. It was exactly these legends of the art world that were sought out by the cloaked masters of the trade, the shadow figures, his operatives. There were certainly other legends extant, of equal import, impossibly beautiful, legends that as often as not would be proven to be just that, legends. Stories with lost origins, folk tales passed down from generation to generation, family to family, until they ultimately found their way to Our World and then to its operatives.

A legend like the "Flaming Cross" of Flavius Valerius Constantinus was merely a historic footnote to the rest of the world, deemed by academia to be a figment of ancient imagination; a fairy tale that told of the great emperor, also known as Constantine I, personally carrying the cross to North Africa and placing it in a shrine to his Christ, the Son of God, more than three hundred years after that Son died for the sins of man. It was a cross encrusted with the purest and finest gemstones, gathered through a thousand Greek and Roman conquests, over a thousand years, and said to be wrapped in the shroud of that same Christ the emperor worshipped.

It was a legend, like the Kandinsky painting on the table before him had been. A legend so many of the operatives had tried to prove true but failed. Even Zhivago was thwarted, at least so far. He'd come close. But a dead end in Ethiopia was still by every definition a dead end, a failure.

The Russian looked down at the painting. As enlightened and transformational as it was, as much as Kandinsky created the implausible, space with colors and shapes, it was not in the league of the Mongol Genghis Khan's personal standard, reputed to have been hand-painted by the most venerated Song Dynasty artists of the day, enslaved into artistic servitude by the Great Khan. Sewn and woven of the finest silk by the greatest weavers; another legend that lived on, waiting to be found.

And there was the fabled greatest single work of the Old Bering Sea Culture, carved of mammoth ivory, chopped with primitive stone hand axes from the skull of the last mammoth to walk the earth, killed by Siberian Yupik hunters on the great beast's remote Holocene bastion, the Soviet Union's Wrangel Island. Legend had it that to hold the carving was to hold all the loss and pain of the Ice Age megafauna, gone forever from the vast, cold, and wild steppes.

All these great works had been created. The legends formed around them and then all had been lost; lost and waiting in their dark recesses to be found by his operatives.

Found by Our World.

The man dismissed the thoughts of these treasures. For him, for Our World, as magnificent as legend had them all being, there was only one work of art to rule them all; one work of art that stood above them all.

The single greatest work of art created by God or by gods or by demigods.

The Soul Catcher.

Even as he thought it, he dismissed it. Our World had been looking for the Soul Catcher since the beginning, two hundred years before, when the original founder Samuel Baker formed Our World and presided over the first Gathering. That first was attended by notables such as Louis XV, who already happened to be a patron of the founder's licit enterprise, a business he would pass on to his nephew, John Sotheby.

Our World was Cain to Sotheby's Abel and it was Baker who laid down the rules of engagement that hadn't changed since day one. "Let nothing stop us. Let no force resist us. Let the wars of man be our ally. Search the world. Find the best. Vet the buyers. Make the laws. Be the law."

Now he sat in the same seat as the founder. There had been only eight over the two centuries who had. The difference between the first and the last was that the last did not require the cover of a legitimate enterprise as the first had, disseminating books to the wealthy. Our World had been making the laws as the first decreed. Our World *was* the law now.

If the Soul Catcher existed, it existed in a place that was so hidden, so deeply secure, that the best of the best, the operatives of Our World, had been unable to search it out.

No. The Soul Catcher was not real, could not be real. But what if it was? What if he could bring it to the light on his watch?

His thoughts were interrupted.

"Charlotte sent the second painting as you instructed." The man on the dark side of the table pulled a second painting from a second stiff-sided black leather satchel and laid it on the table beside the other one.

He was not happy that the mere nobody before him dared speak without being asked to do so. He would pay for that transgression. He said nothing though and instead leaned forward, looking through his glasses at the painting. From the photo, he'd been unable to confirm what he'd suspected. Seconds later he leaned back in his chair again.

"Destroy it."

His minion knew better than to ask why. His was but to do or literally die.

The Russian took his glasses off and laid them on the table, putting his hands up to his mouth again, palms flat, pressed against each other. The Picasso painting was a forgery. A good forgery, if there was such a thing. Schuffenecker's work; valueless; or valueless to the collectors of the Gathering. His order to destroy it was not literal, it was figurative. The painting would be sold into the public domain, the pathetic world of art that to him was inhabited with a million patrons of mediocrity.

The forgery would no doubt be authenticated by an academic holding a doctorate in the fine arts, a piece of worthless paper, issued by peers of equal ineptitude. What was it Sir Arthur Conan Doyle wrote? "Mediocrity knows nothing higher than itself; but talent instantly recognizes genius."

The fake Picasso would end up in a museum most likely, a private collection perhaps. It didn't matter; both were to be disdained. His world was Our World and anything less than the best of the best was not worth his attention.

To his personal regret, although he was singular in his abilities, he was not genetically endowed with the special talents of his operatives. But he was brilliantly adapted to his position at the top of the pyramid that was Our World. His knowledge of art was unparalleled, perhaps only matched by his ruthlessness.

It was he who'd recognized the Kandinsky at the edge of the photograph the child psychiatrist sent and he was proud of that fact. Charlotte was trained for her job, she was the best of Our World's enforcers, but she did not have the gift and would not have recognized the painting for what it was. It was only because he had directed her to take it, along with the potential Picasso, that both were now sitting in front of him.

He had directed one hand to take the paintings.

He had directed the other hand to slide the garrote around the doctor's neck.

And he'd ordered her to start the fire that would destroy any and all evidence that might link the doctor to the boy or to Our World.

21

2020

PINEHURST, NORTH CAROLINA

Ah-OOOOG-ah. Ah-OOOOG-ah. Ah-OOOOG-ah."

The obnoxious sound of the submarine-dive-warning Klaxon from her cell phone startled her from a deep sleep.

She jumped up and searched for her phone in the rumpled flannel bedsheets but didn't find it until it was too late. A few seconds after the offending phone went silent, still in a daze, she found it and checked the time, 6:23 a.m. She was groggy and wearing the same clothes she'd worn the day before.

The manuscript was on the floor in a messy pile, where it must have fallen from the bed during the night.

Nyala took a deep breath and shook her head, trying to clear her thoughts.

She'd been making notes about what she'd read late into the night and must have nodded off. It was all coming back to her, the strange feeling that the story was real and that somehow it was about her. One thing for sure was that real or not, what she'd been reading was getting into her head. It was like the bearded guy was in the room with her all night. Ugh.

Note to self: she needed to change the ringtone on her cell phone to something less offensive to the senses.

BAM. BAM. BAM.

The pounding on her bedroom door made her jump again. There

wasn't any reason to tell Luba the door was open. She was already walking in, shaking her pages of the manuscript at Nyala.

"This stuff is *way* weird!" She was excited. "I couldn't put it down! I love it! Been waiting for you to get up! Coffee's on!"

"Ah-OOOOG-ah. Ah-OOOOG-ah. Ah-OOOOG-ah."

Jesus! For the third time she jumped.

She waved her friend into silence and slid the answer button to accept the call, sitting on her bed as she did.

"Scott. Yes. It's me. Sorry I missed your first call. No, don't worry, not too early. Whatcha got?" Nyala didn't acknowledge Luba's questioning look, even when she plunked herself on the bed beside her. Nyala turned away, trying at the same time to rub the sleep from her eyes with her free hand. She wanted to focus on what the voice on the phone was saying.

She listened for a full minute in dead silence, not saying a word, and when she finally spoke, it was Luba's turn to jump.

"No shit! You're kidding me! If you're kidding me, I'll kill you." She was wide awake by then. "So you're saying you found the doctor? And you found the city? Saskatoon? Where the hell is that? Saskatchewan. Okay, Canada. Prairie town. Got it."

Nyala grabbed her pen and took the information down on the notepad she always kept on the night table, but motioned to her friend, pointing at the notebook lying on the floor not far from the manuscript. She mouthed "It's Scott" to Luba.

"Hang on. Give me a sec." She waved her hand at Luba, signing to hurry; the frown was all she needed to make it clear that she wasn't joking as she reached to take the notebook from her friend. "No, don't send a text with the info. I'd rather take notes. Old-school.

"I know, nobody uses pen and paper. Forests getting cut down. Yep, got it. My bad. Go ahead."

Nyala didn't say anything for another five minutes; she just listened and wrote. Slowly the page filled.

"You really are the best." It was one of the very few times she'd said something to Scott that she sincerely meant. "I'm sure it was difficult. All night. Yes, I bet. Cross-referencing data. Amazing how fast you found the information. No. Definitely do not tell me how you hacked it. Plausible deniability. No. I don't want to know how you did that either. No. It's not that I don't care. I do care. No, I don't care about you. No. I didn't mean it that way; I meant I care about your work, not about you. No. Not just about your work."

She noticed Luba making a heart sign and pursing her lips in mock kisses. Then Luba wrapped her arms around herself in pantomimed rapture; Nyala gave her the finger.

"Listen, I have to go. I'm sure I'll have more for you to research on this. And by the way, Luba is too shy to tell you how much she likes you."

Nyala mock-stuck her finger down her throat for her friend's benefit.

Luba was nodding her head and with a big genuine smile was goading with her hand for Nyala to continue.

"Not sure. Ask her tomorrow. I know she loves East Indian cuisine. Curry is her favorite."

Luba hated curry.

It was Luba's turn to give her friend the finger.

"Thanks, Scott. Really, thanks."

Nyala hit the end button and turned to her friend, her eyes wide open now.

"Holy shit." She looked at Luba, now sitting cross-legged on her bed.

She stood up and paced to the window. "It's true. The doctor is real. Scott found the newspaper reports saying he died in the fire that destroyed his office. The antique dealer is real. He died when his van flipped off a bridge back in November of 1962. Crazy. What the heck is this?"

She was looking down at the floor, where the part of the manuscript she'd been reading was lying.

"They were real. They were killed."

"Supercool! Can you imagine? You get to break the story to the world!" Luba reconsidered. "We get to break the story to the world!"

Nyala snorted.

"You're sick. Where's your heart? They were murdered. The doctor too. It wasn't an accident. Besides, what story? Back sixty years ago, two people who the authorities determined had died in accidents in some small town in Canada were actually targeted and killed? What are we going to tell the world? That they were victims of some trained assassin named Charlotte? We know they died, but we don't have proof that any of it happened the way it says in the manuscript."

She frowned, something she'd been doing a lot over the last twenty-four hours.

"And I ain't going to be the one who tries to tell people there's a superpower kid out there, or was a kid out there, that grew up and is now covered in sores. I'm *sure* we will get a Pulitzer Prize for that one."

"Okay, so probably no Pulitzers in our future, but it's still cool!" Luba said.

"There's the Kandinsky painting too; says in the manuscript that it's worth $150 million. But it doesn't exist according to what I've been able to find." Nyala considered whether to sic Scott on the question. "It's absurd to think it was worth that much half a century ago; can't be true."

Luba looked at Nyala, confused.

"What $150 million painting?"

"Oh sorry, you didn't read that far. Remember the Picasso the doctor had in his office? The one he was so proud of? It was a fake. The other painting, the one the kid was looking at, was apparently real though. I checked on that. Or I checked on any paintings with circles and triangles. Nothing came up, except a reference to a painter, Kandinsky. He painted circles and squares, not triangles." Nyala paused, reaching back in her memory to what she'd learned the day before. "Apparently Solomon Guggenheim and his mistress Hilla von Rebay bought a bunch of Kandinsky paintings back in the 1930s, in Germany. I think they tried to buy the triangle-and-circles painting as well, but it was confiscated by the Nazis."

If any of that is true, she caught herself thinking, putting the brakes on the storytelling.

She noticed the look of total confusion on her friend's face.

"Huh? What are you talking about?" Luba twirled her finger by her temple.

"Sorry, you haven't read as far into the manuscript as I have. And I forgot to tell you that I've done a little research on some of the parts of the story that you have. I've been able to at least confirm parts of it."

She looked at her friend, open and honest as she could be.

"It's totally weird, I know, but it's like this guy is reaching out to me, to tell me his story. My story."

Nyala tapped the edge of the heavy manuscript on the floor to line up the pages and then stood up.

"But I don't know why I think it could possibly have anything to do with me."

Nyala continued, weighing her words.

"There's more. Something really important. The doctor who died in the fire had a wife. Dorothy." Nyala whispered it, emotion in her voice. "She's still alive."

Luba opened her eyes wide.

"As in really? Alive? Still? Today?"

Nyala considered her response for a moment. She stood silently contemplating the correct course of action. She knew she was always too ready for the next battle, too quick to forget the last. She knew she tended to be unwilling to look back on her choices, to double-check if it was the correct decision or not.

No regrets.

"Get a bag packed. We're going on a road trip. Your car."

"Huh? Serious? Now?"

Nyala was already heading to her closet.

"Yes. Now. Right now. Bring money. I'll bring what I have."

Luba still wasn't moving.

"Where are we going? The boss is going to be pissed if we aren't back at work tomorrow morning. It's not like it's a long weekend. Tomorrow *is* Monday, in case you didn't know."

Nyala pulled a soft-shell day bag from the shelf above her hanging clothes.

"We're working on a big scoop. I need you to help me do some investigating. He'll be fine."

"Still doesn't answer the where part." Luba, normally the one given to flights of fancy, looked unsure about the idea. "Driving? My car needs gas."

"Saskatoon, Saskatchewan," Nyala added. "Canada. Yes, we're driving."

"Squasatoon? Squaskatch-wachy what?" Luba stink-eyed her friend.

Nyala didn't answer the question.

"Bring warm clothes. And bring your passport."

22

2020

YORKTON, SASKATCHEWAN

What do you mean there's no such thing as supersizing anymore?"
Luba turned to her passenger and rolled her eyes at her own
rhetorical question.

Nyala rolled her eyes right back at her friend. Tilting at windmills.
She could never understand why Luba continued with her passive-
aggressive protest against McDonald's execs because of their decision
to get rid of "supersizing." Like the message would ever get past the
tinny voice taking their order. She wasn't a fan of company CEOs
who caved like milksops to the politically correct mob mentality; let
people get fat, it was their choice. Why take away their right of self-
determination? But really, Luba? Supersizing was a hill worth dying on?

Apparently Luba thought so.

"I'm sorry, would you like me to get the manager?" The voice was
squawky through the speaker, partially from the fact that the inter-
com system hadn't been upgraded since it had been installed years
before at the McDonald's in the small Saskatchewan town of Yorkton
and partially because all sounds were squawky in the frigid fall air.

"Okay. Then just double it!" Luba ignored the "No! Not for me!"
waving-hands sign language from her friend in the passenger seat.

"So that will be two of everything?"

"Definitely!" Luba could literally eat McDonald's every day, had
eaten McDonald's every day. "And don't forget I wanted ten ketchups
and a side of McChicken sauce."

"Double that too?" The tinny voice was dutiful at least, the client was always right, but the voice on the speaker obviously wasn't getting the point of the protest.

"Absolutely! Why not!" Luba was smiling now, happy she was sticking it to the spineless McDonald's execs. Hit them where it hurts, the bottom line, the ketchup profits.

Nyala rolled her eyes again. After six days straight of eating like bushpigs on the road, Luba's two-year-old Mercedes GLE 550 looked like it needed a complete makeover, inside and out. The pearl white outside was a mud-splattered mess, compliments of a rainy-day, gunky road construction detour way back on day one, only hours north of their rented country house in North Carolina. On top of the mud was a layer of salt, compliments of the last 1,800 miles on late fall Canadian highways.

The fancy porcelain leather and the inside of the vehicle didn't need a makeover; it needed a complete overhaul, reupholstering, new carpet, the works. Nyala didn't need to be a forensics expert to piece together the crimes they'd committed on their entire debauched road trip. From where she sat, she could see their journey mapped in a mess of mayonnaise stains and ketchup blobs everywhere, the darker oxidized blobs indicating the early stops, heading north toward Ottawa, Ontario, and the brighter red ones telling the tale of their westward travels across Canada. Bits and pieces of McChicken and Filet-O-Fish sandwiches, Chicken McNuggets, Big Macs, and double orders of french fries littered the floors, center console, and even somehow the dashboard.

Nyala was filled with self-loathing for her lack of discipline and was seriously considering committing herself to a sixty-day detox program. Ugh. Filet-O-Fish sandwiches were her nemesis. Oh, and gas station Miss Vickie's potato chips—Sea Salt and Malt Vinegar flavor, kettle cooked, and approximately twenty thousand calories per bag—and Goodies, and Twizzlers and Wine Gums. Good thing she only drank diet Mountain Dew the whole way; at least that would save her a few thousand hours on the elliptical even if her insides were now lime green.

They'd laughed the whole trip and by the seventh day were tired and giddy. Now, though, with their destination two hundred miles ahead, things were about to get real, and the giddiness faded to serious contemplation.

It had been Nyala's decision to drive instead of fly. She wasn't sure why, but it seemed like the right thing to do. Like having their own vehicle would somehow give them freedom from schedules and would inoculate them from the capricious whims of airlines that were still recoiling after getting hammered by the COVID-19 scare. It seemed like a lifetime ago they'd struggled through the quarantine, Luba particularly, Nyala not so much. She liked social distancing; it made her feel like she was normal when everyone else did it too.

It had been Luba's idea to go via Ottawa, even though it was hundreds of miles out of their way, to see their old friends from college and check out their alma mater one more time. Ugh. A flashback headache made Nyala reach up and rub her forehead. Fun then, but wasn't much fun when they started on the two-thousand-mile cross-Canada drive from Canada's capital city, Ottawa, to Saskatoon. She remembered feeling hangover-ugly all the way across Ontario as they cruised north of the Great Lakes. It wasn't until they hit Lake Superior, really until the city of Thunder Bay, that she started feeling human again or at least as much as a bushpig could feel human.

"Thanks!" Luba waved to the face in the McDonald's window, already closed against the cold bite of the Saskatchewan air.

Her friend was amazing. She was as happy and excited now as she was the first day of their trip, always living in the moment, without a care in the world about what the future might bring. She was already munching on her french fries, savoring each one, like it really was the first one, not the ten millionth she'd eaten over the last week.

Nyala lived in the future. She tolerated the present and didn't have a past.

"McDonald's fries are the best!"

"I know. You told me." Nyala dug through the bag, looking for her Filet-O-Fish. "Yesterday and the day before and the day before that and the day before that."

Her plan had been to read more of the manuscript along the

route, letting Luba do most of the driving, but it hadn't exactly worked out that way. First, Luba blabbered pretty much constantly, about pretty much nothing, and second, Canada was a big place. The entire trip was 2,986.41 miles according to Google Maps and they'd driven approximately 2,700 of those miles in the six days since they'd left North Carolina. Subtracting the two-day party stop in Ottawa, they'd been driving at least twelve hours each day, which meant Nyala had to take the wheel for her fair share of the time.

Still, despite the numerous stops for gas and munchies and to load up on McDonald's, plus her own predisposition to carsickness on the winding parts of the Trans-Canada Highway, she'd managed to read another hundred-or-so-page chunk of the manuscript. Instead of answers though, she found the reading had only produced more questions.

She wasn't proud that she'd glossed over a big piece of the manuscript without concentrating. She had not been laser focused on what she was reading. Instead, she'd pretty much let her mind go with the flow of each day they'd been on the road. In a way, she'd turned her brain off, or at least turned the volume down. It was journalistic malfeasance, not her usual style. She was going to have to reread the entire section. She hated watching movies twice and hated rereading a book. It would serve her right, a slap on the wrist.

Nyala chewed on the deep-fried fish and the white bun, slathered on the inside with special sauce, and looked out the window, watching as Yorkton kaleidoscoped by, replaced by farmland, mottled with poplar bluffs and buck brush. Several deer fed in a field; one was a buck. Majestic, it stood and watched as their grotty $120,000 Mercedes swept past, eight cylinders pounding out 435 horsepower, accelerating under Luba's control to her speeding-ticket-risk-tolerance limit of 20 miles per hour over the posted speed limit.

Nyala knew she needed to get back in the figurative saddle and fire up her brain cells again. Saskatoon was only three hours away—less, at the speed Luba was going. They'd take a motel somewhere on the outskirts of the city, like they'd done every night on the road, a cheap one usually even though Luba wasn't on any kind of budget. Nyala honestly didn't think her friend's credit cards had a limit. Luba's unbreakable bank or not, they stayed in cheap places because Luba liked cheap; cheap as in $1,600 high-heel-white-go-go-boots-with-fringes cheap.

Luba fiddled with her phone, totally distracted, and then for the hundredth time played their theme song.

"There's a province up in Canada, right next door to ours. It's called Saskatchewan. And in that province there's a small town, where nothing much ever happens, called Saskatoon."

Nyala loved the songs from the greatest era of music, loved the Guess Who, loved Burton Cummings, best of all rock band lead singers, and she loved Randy Bachman. Those were the days when music was real music. She paused, midthought: she really was "Running Back to Saskatoon." Even though, technically, she'd never been there, she had the strangest feeling that she was going home; weird.

> *I been hangin' around hospitals*
> *I been learnin' 'bout dyin'.*

Learning about dyin' was right. Apparently the song was wrong. Something did happen in Saskatoon, ten years before Burton and Randy released the tune, something terrible. Two men had been murdered there, if the manuscript was based on truth.

The key that would hopefully unlock the door and reveal the truth was an eightysomething lady by the name of Dorothy, living in Saskatoon, the wife of the doctor who uncovered the boy Hunter's superpowers.

She looked out the window, but nothing had changed from the last time she looked. Farmland and poplar bluffs. It was getting darker. They'd get in too late to see Dorothy Keen tonight; it would have to be tomorrow. Nyala figured she could change into one of her less-grubby pairs of jeans when they took a room in Saskatoon.

Saskatoon. She thought about what she knew of the city. It had grown in the sixty years that had passed since the events in the manuscript had supposedly taken place, that was for sure, grown by nearly a hundred thousand citizens. There were a quarter of a million people living there now. Besides being put on the map by the Guess Who, it also happened to be the home to the world's only pierogi drive-through restaurant. She'd had to ask Mr. Google what a pierogi was and found out it was a dough-dumpling filled with savory or sweet filling, usually served with sour cream and fried onions. She'd made a point of not telling Luba about that particular takeout attraction.

It was known as the "City of Bridges" and was located on the banks of the South Saskatchewan River, undoubtedly the same river the antique dealer's van ended up in. The city received 2,381 hours of sunshine a year, although Nyala couldn't recall if that was the average or the high. One thing she was sure of: sunshine made her happier than rain and rain made her happier than snow, which meant she would never choose to live in Saskatoon. Coldest temperature recorded was minus 58 degrees Fahrenheit, even colder with windchill factored in. Yuck.

Saskatoon berries sounded interesting. And the place was supposedly inhabited for five thousand years by natives, who still made up nearly 10 percent of the population. Her own looks were decidedly native in an exotic mixed-race kind of way, and she often wondered if either of her parents was a native. That would be cool.

Ahead she could see the lights of an approaching vehicle, miles away it seemed. She was mesmerized by the approaching pinpoints of light until Luba suddenly hit the brakes hard to avoid a deer crossing the road. A whitetail buck again, like the one they'd seen earlier, not as big though; younger; dumber. The rut would be starting soon here, maybe already had started. Nyala sometimes tuned into the "Whispering Channel" on their TV, or at least that's what Luba called the Outdoor Channel, which showed hunting and fishing 24/7. She called it that because everyone seemed to be whispering as this or that animal approached.

Nyala liked the channel. That's where she learned the difference between whitetail deer and mule deer and about the "rut" and in an odd way felt comforted by the whispering hunters, as if it was a familiar sound.

In her research on her cell phone as they traveled and when they had cell service, Nyala had confirmed that Joni Mitchell had attended high school in Saskatoon, a place called Aden Bowman Collegiate Institute. Scary-sounding name, but Google confirmed it was a regular high school, grades 9–12. Nyala had been researching Joni Mitchell because as she progressed through the manuscript, essentially following Hunter's life as he grew from a young boy to a young teenager, there had been a reference to him "feeling" a report as he went through a stack of book reports that a high school literature teacher called Mr. Lowen had stored in a box at the back of the classroom.

Tsau-z said in the manuscript that the book report was written by Joni Mitchell, which Nyala immediately called bullshit on. She was wrong though; in fact the famed singer-songwriter *had* attended the school years before the teenage Hunter did.

Nyala found it fascinating as she read that Hunter's parents, or Rose actually, went against the advice of the by-then-deceased doctor and after a few years of Wilbur's private tutoring, insisted their gifted son go back to regular school, with regular children. She decided that his tutor should only be there to take care of his *special* needs. Rose had explained that she didn't want her boy to be even more socially maladjusted than he already was.

Tsau-z said in the manuscript that the tutor was so deeply involved with her gifted student's life by then that she'd put off her original plan to continue her postdoctoral studies and instead signed on long-term with the Johanns, requesting permission to write up a developmental paper on Hunter as he progressed through his adolescent years.

There were other pieces of information in the manuscript that Nyala made note of, information she intended to track down if she met with Dorothy. Nyala had made up her mind not to call the lady ahead of her visit, not to show her hand, as it were.

There was a very real possibility that even when she knocked on the door, the answer might be "No, she doesn't want to talk to some crackpot girl who is covered in ketchup and Filet-O-Fish stains and who just drove three thousand miles to interrogate a stranger. Go away."

It had been a long week.

Nyala needed a beer to calm her road-jangled nerves, a shower, and sleep, in that order.

Tomorrow, one way or the other, she would know the truth.

23

2020

SASKATOON, SASKATCHEWAN

Fifteen minutes had passed since Luba dropped her off at Dorothy's home. Nyala had explained to her friend that she wanted to do this alone, which was fine with Luba. Luba said she was headed to a car detailer she'd found online and then planned to check out the shopping opportunities in Saskatoon. Nyala hadn't moved from the sidewalk in front of the house for fifteen minutes; she just stood there, staring at the small house in front of her. She was getting cold, already shivering, the first step on the downward spiral to hypothermia. Slurred speech always came next; then clumsiness, weak pulse, lack of coordination, and memory loss; then dizziness and loss of consciousness; finally, death.

Nyala figured she was at the dizzy part and was seriously contemplating loss of consciousness and death as an acceptable alternative to walking up to the door and knocking on it.

That's when the door opened and the person standing in the doorway called out to her.

"Young lady? Can I help you?"

Even with fifteen minutes to prepare for the shock of meeting, Nyala was still taken by surprise at her reaction to seeing the old woman.

Nyala's legs wobbled and went weak and the world around her started to darken until only a tunnel with a distant spot of light at the far end remained.

Slowly though, she brought her breathing under control, her heartbeat calmed, and the tunnel widened. The darkness that was her constant life companion, always there, always lurking, retreated.

"Yes. Yes, please." Her eyes welled; emotions overwhelmed her will to resist, freed her to say the thing she fought her entire life to deny. "Yes. Yes, I need help."

———

It was warm in the house, and it smelled deliciously of coffee and flowers. Nyala closed the door and turned toward the interior, standing in the entrance, unsure what to do. She wiped her eyes dry. The wind, it was the wind that made them water.

"I saw you pull up with your friend."

The lady looked to be in her late seventies, late eighties?

"You seemed to want to come to my door." Her voice was gentle, kind, not an ounce of guile, just concern. "But my dear girl, then you just stood there and froze."

Nyala didn't answer.

Was this it? Would this be confirmation that she was on the trail that would lead her to who she was, or who she wasn't? She had dreaded this moment since Scott confirmed that the lady in front of her existed.

"Mrs. Keen? "

The elderly lady stood straight; age hadn't bowed her in any way. Although the deeper lines in her face spoke of sorrow, there were lines of joy too, a long time before maybe, but at one time it was evident that she'd been happy.

"Are you Mrs. Keen? Dorothy?"

The lady standing in the hallway that led from the entrance to the kitchen in the small house seemed to be taking stock of the unkempt young woman standing before her. Deciding how she would answer the question.

"Yes. Do I know you? I'm afraid I don't recognize you if I do. I am sorry; aging has not done my brain any favors."

She was smiling and it was evident to Nyala that the elderly lady's precise command of the English language and her self-effacing humor were not the product of a slowed brain.

"No, Mrs. Keen." Talking to the person she'd read about in a manuscript, placed in a time sixty years before, felt weird, really weird. "You don't know me."

Or did she? Nyala wasn't sure about anything now.

"I came a long way to see you. I wanted to ask you some questions."

She took a deep breath.

"Did you have a husband? Was he a doctor?"

There it was, past, present, and future colliding with two questions.

If the elderly lady was disturbed by the questions, she didn't show it. She only seemed to look more closely at the face of the young lady standing in her home. For nearly a full minute she didn't answer and when she did, it was not what Nyala expected. It was a reprieve.

"You must be cold." She turned her back and walked slowly toward the kitchen, careful with her steps. "Come in. Leave your shoes on. I'll put more coffee on."

24

1994

VICTORIA, VANCOUVER ISLAND, BRITISH COLUMBIA

Zhivago stroked the cat.

He'd picked the tabby up from the local animal shelter the week before, not normally easy to do for someone without a fixed address and on short notice, but easy for him when he explained to the lady at the animal shelter that he was closely affiliated with a big financial donor to the American version of the SPCA, the Humane Society. Based on his say-so, the middle-aged lady, who smelled faintly of wet animal hair and wood shavings, waived the requirements for reference and background checks and let him choose and take one of the dozen stray cats she and another younger hippie-looking woman were caring for that day.

It didn't hurt when he added that he was organizing an anti-hunting rally in the city the following week. In fact, he was quite sure that once they knew that, both women would have done anything he'd asked. He was their champion, and they would service his needs. He loved the blind obedience they both exhibited to the animal rights ideology that he himself had been instrumental in promulgating in the Western world for three decades. Beyond taking the cat off their hands, he had no intention of doing anything with either of the dank-smelling women. Besides, asking wasn't the way he worked; taking was much more satisfying.

He'd kept the nondescript tabby with him wherever he went for the following week and was now holding it in his arms as he looked down from the seventh-floor hotel room window at the protest in full swing on the lawn in front of the British Columbia Parliament Building, only a block away. The venerated stone Empress, an old Canadian Pacific Railway hotel, was situated perfectly for him to see his handiwork in action.

How many were there already? A thousand? More, probably. Signs and placards jabbed up and down with a rhythm that matched the violent upward fist pumps of the speaker on the makeshift stage. There was even a large contingent of First Nations members, located in their own section of the grounds, away from the thronged bobble-headed protesters.

Boom. Boom. Boom.

He could hear their drums.

"Bear killers! Bear killers! Bear killers!" The bobbleheads were working themselves into a frenzy; their chanting easy to understand from a block away, even through the closed window.

Exquisite; exactly the way he'd planned it and the reason he'd financed it. His little army of mindless orcs and trolls, doing his bidding without ever knowing the endgame. They thought they were protesting the hunting of bears in British Columbia, trying to force the weak socialist government into ignoring the science of wildlife management; to ignore the biological census studies that concluded over and over again that the province's black bear and grizzly bear population was stable and increasing.

If he played this right, the pathetic demagogic politicians would disregard the science and genuflect before his orchestrated public protest and declare bear hunting to be socially unacceptable and therefore something to be banned forthwith.

Public protest? He smiled and scoffed; it was *his* public. He owned it, he paid for it. They weren't the public and they certainly weren't representing the majority of the real public's opinion. They were there simply because he was paying many of them to protest or they were there because they were ideologues, easy to manipulate with sophistry. The truth would not have worked as well. *I have gathered all of you here today to help further my own ends and the ends of Our World.*

He was still smiling to himself. He was close now. So close. It was nearby, somewhere hidden, out of sight for a thousand years, more? Less? Nobody knew when it was made. But it was here, the Holy Grail, and he would find it. Holy Grail, no, that was to denigrate the object. It was a god of art unto itself. Legend said it was the *only* god of art.

The Soul Catcher.

The cat stopped purring and turned its head toward the door. The knocking a moment later told him it was time to go down and join the rabble, to add to the disturbance, incite, revel in the chaos he'd created. Turning, he let the cat jump to the bed.

His decades-long quest had shown him beyond any doubt that the Soul Catcher was here on this godforsaken island. The Our World money and influence served a dual purpose: to narrow the search for the art treasure, and to fuel hatred, the hatred he himself felt for those who pursued the wild animals of the world and then heartlessly, remorselessly killed them; the hunters; grinning Neanderthal egotists, posing over their bloodied trophies.

He was an avowed animal rightist.

Killing animals was an aberration, a disgusting throwback to the days when humans were nothing more than animals themselves with no higher sensibilities, abject brutes. Every chance he had to combine his worldwide search for the treasures of Our World and the Gathering with the perpetuation of his ideology and the ideologies of his philosopher animal liberation peers, he eagerly took, with a fanaticism that rivaled the greatest of the Inquisitors.

"Redoubling your effort when you have forgotten your aim." He hated Santayana's definition of fanaticism, hated his "truth" about passion. What did that charlatan and his acolytes in their academic ivory towers know about true passion for a cause? What did they know about normality? Was it normal to hunt down and kill a bear? To kill it and eat it? To make a rug out of its hide?

No. It was repellent.

The end justified the means.

It had been he who'd financed the upwelling of chaos the previous months on Vancouver Island, the ticking time bombs in the hunters' boats, the arson and mail bombs, the rat poison and razor blades sent to hunters' homes; sent to the homes of the animal murderers and their whelps. He'd tapped a friend, the heiress to an American department store fortune, to put up most of the actual funding for the movement; she was an idiot, a rich puppet who jumped on every fashionable save-the-world bandwagon, but she was *his* idiot, *his* puppet, to be used to further the cause and justifiable end.

It was that end that he sought, the end of all hunting, not just here in this backward backwater of a place, but everywhere in the world. If all went according to his plan, the left and the right would become so divided that they would turn their guns upon each other and away from the animals he loved.

He could see the end coming. Would it be twenty years? Or thirty? Either way, it was coming in his lifetime. It had taken his considerable talents and a vision only he possessed, but now the juggernaut he'd set in motion was reaching peak velocity. Antihunting and animal rights sentiment would ram through the six years that remained of the 1990s, through the 2000s, attached like a remora to the growing worldwide environmental movement.

He was the progenitor, the godfather of the hate and contempt, and yet nobody knew. He was the one who planted the seeds and fertilized the soil. He was the one who would see the harvest for what it was.

His will would be done.

The mirthless smile that came to his face then said more about the man than any other physical attribute. He was big, over 250 pounds, but not fat. He had a large frame, with the filled-in flesh of a weight lifter. The soft knock at the door came again, more insistent this time; a minion bidding his master.

"Not now." He pulled on his big leather jacket, speaking loudly. "Go to the lobby. Meet me there."

The chocolate-brown jacket was a little too warm for the late spring weather in Victoria, the grass was growing fast now, and the cherry blossoms were almost done blooming, but he liked it. It was buttery Italian lamb, and he liked the fashionable cut. He was wearing $1,200 red leather Italian shoes.

He reached down to undo the Hermès belt from where it was wrapped tightly around the neck of the young woman lying on his bed. Aerobics body, too skinny for his liking, but she'd been exactly what he needed at the time. He was smiling as he remembered picking her up the night before at a local club. He'd watched her from a dark booth at the back of the busy lounge and been attracted to her girl-next-door looks and sunny disposition. It made him happy to know she was somebody's daughter, somebody's sister, somebody's friend. She had an exquisite smile.

She seemed nice, so he'd decided to rape her.

He liked Hermès, not so much the clothing and accoutrements of the famed Paris fashion house, but for the name. He would have liked to have been named Hermes by the leader of Our World. Hermes would have been good, instead of Zhivago, although Zhivago was certainly better than his real name. Born into a poor family in postwar Europe, he had been destined for a life of repetition, like his father, like his grandfather and all his antecedents, farm laborers, generation after useless generation.

Or he was until Our World found him.

He looked back down at the naked and exposed girl on the bed. Not the Aphrodite that Hermes impregnated, but the cute student from the University of Victoria had been a passable surrogate; beauty, pleasure, passion, and procreation. Just like Aphrodite in that way. The canted H from the buckle had left a deep imprint in the girl's soft, unblemished skin, a raw brand on her neck.

As he pulled the belt through the loops on his pants, he had to admit he felt as powerful as a god. Like Hermes, he moved with ease between the mortal and divine worlds, the world of the mediocre, the greater unwashed and the sacrosanct universe of Our World, motherland to the denizens of the Gathering.

Yes, he was a god!

As he pulled the belt tight, he felt himself growing aroused at the thought of guiding the young woman all the way, instead of bringing her to the doorway of the dead and leaving her there to recover, such as her recovery would ever be after what he'd done to her.

The woman on the bed, spread-eagled and tied, shuddered then, inhaling a deep breath. The gamma-hydroxybutyric acid was wearing off. She wouldn't remember anything, and for a brief delicious moment, he entertained the idea of going back to her right then, as she awoke, to finish the job, to open the door for her and escort her through to the afterlife.

He'd been careful slipping the drug in the girl's drink, careful when he'd guided her out of the club, careful in bringing her to the room, but that is where his care ended. To do more now, as much pleasure as he would have found in the act, would be messy. Not easy to deal with. It was time for care again. None of it was Zhivago's choice, but the leader of Our World was not someone to trifle with and he'd been watching Zhivago's every move since the complications in Peru, twelve years before. The threat of incurring the wrath of Our World's all-powerful leader was the only reason he controlled his urges to the degree that he did.

He took a knife out of his pocket, touched the button, and watched the stiletto spring out, an action that always gave him a thrill. He leaned down over the girl, almost for a moment forgetting his decision to take care, and then, after the hesitation, cut the tape holding her in the position of violation. The girl was tremoring now. She would wake up soon and not recall anything about what caused the pain she would be feeling. And when she awoke, there would be nothing in the room to give her any clues as to the why and who; nothing. The room had been purged, rented in a false name, paid for in cash. Nobody would listen and she wouldn't know what to tell them anyway.

Even if she said anything, nobody would believe her. She was destined to spend the rest of her life afraid of shadows, afraid of the dark, knowing but not knowing, or at least not admitting even to herself what she knew had to have happened to her, what was stolen from her, no closure, no one to turn to, a purgatory of shame. She might even be pregnant! That brought the mirthless smile to his face again; a bastard child to add to the curse that would be her life from then on.

The blade made a snicking sound as it slid back into the slotted handle. He balled the tape he'd removed from her wrists and bedposts and gave the room one last check. No mistakes. He never made mistakes. The last thing he did was pick up the cat, pulling it to his nose, smelling it, feeling the warmth of its fur and listening to it purr.

He loved animals.

Patting the cat in his arm, Zhivago turned to the door then, the rag doll on the bed already fading from his short-term memory.

He had animals to save.

He had the Soul Catcher to find.

*T*he names will mean nothing to you, Nyala.

Moe Sihota. The Minister of the Environment. We met with him to put an end to the insanity.

Bobby Fontana. We were fighting to hold back the tide, to build a dam, to protect science and the freedom of self-determination from the mob.

John Holdstock, another warrior; a good man; they were all part of it, actors on a stage, in a play they didn't understand.

Couldn't understand.

The stage is too vast; the stage is the world, Our World. And only those of Our World sit in attendance at the theater. They are the only audience to the play.

You are on that stage, Nyala.

I too was an actor on the stage that day, in costume, long hair, a New Age thinker, above nature, a cosmic wanderer with the world revolving around my ideologies; a socialist soldier, a warrior of social justice out to right the wrongs of the right, the rich, the capitalists, the scions of the old ways, the enemy who didn't fall into line with my and my fellow protesters' think-speak.

Make no mistake, mine was an act. I was an actor in disguise on the stage that day and I walked through the disorder, searching.

Zhivago was there searching as well, we were both close; we both knew we were close.

The Soul Catcher was there, Nyala, we knew it; we could feel its beauty, but in different ways.

I didn't understand his way and he did not understand mine. His was like a predator picking up molecules from the air, the scent of prey. He was a blind horror following a smell, a creature from an unspeakable place, sniffing the air, breathing in the essence of beauty, following its perfume. If the wind was right, Zhivago fed.

Mine was to feel beauty in color.

Brown and brown.

And yet, we were the same.

We were both products of some infinite genetic recombination; adenine, cytosine, guanine, and thymine colliding in time and space to produce two identical mutant twins that were inconceivably different.

Brown and brown.

He was not my friend. I was not his. We worked for the same reasons, for Our World, for the Gathering, but we were different, so different.

For Zhivago it was about chaos, it was to take, to destroy everything, scorching the earth as he passed, to sterilize it of ideas that ran counter to his own beliefs and then to reform it in his and his kind's image, in a belief structure that did not include tolerance.

No choice.

No freedom.

No freedom unless you thought exactly like him, like them. Then freedom was your entitlement. It was a freedom born of superiority, born of a false belief that ideology alone holds the moral high ground, regardless of whether the outcome of the ideology is to irreparably damage those it professes to help.

His was the ONLY WAY; his was to state arguments in an invidious way that could not be refuted. His way was hypocrisy. His way was to stop others from having the rights he and his took for granted. Only he and his were qualified to decide what was right for you and for me, Nyala, for all of us.

Zhivago was there that day. I saw him, saw his arrogant hulking form in the background proud of his work. Proud of the destruction of a way of life, the devastation of tradition, the end of science, and the beginning of a nascent social order that would in the coming decades have his kind crowned God Emperors and their beliefs written in monumental stone that would crush any and all who dared resist political correctness.

The embers he'd nurtured for so long and fanned that day, I watched in the years that followed grow to a conflagration of intolerance.

To stand against Zhivago, his ways, his thoughts, his people, was to be vilified, publicly shamed, held in contempt, and tried in the court of the converted. Drown and you are innocent. Survive and you are guilty and burned at the stake of public opinion.

Zhivago was the leader of the coming years of Inquisition, an Inquisition that, Nyala, you know as media.

He was there that day.

He was scent trailing his prey.

He did not see me.

And that is the day, Nyala, when I truly saw for the first time. That is the day I realized how blind I had been.

Brown and brown.

A thousand strong; they thronged around the stage; a thousand weak; followers of a false prophet; freedom fighters fighting for the death of freedom.

I turned away from the mob and suddenly, color; the most brilliant color; so deep, so infinitely pure; so breathtaking, so beautiful.

I saw.

And I fell to my knees.

To behold the greatest work of art this world has ever known.

The drums. I can still hear them. Boom. Boom. Boom. Boom-boom-boom. They beat me; they beat me into something new. Boom. Boom. Boom. I was forged; shaped; I was annealed.

Nyala, I was born that day. As surely as an infant begins the journey from the womb to the world, I started on my own journey that day, a journey to me, Nyala, and a journey to you.

She was dancing. Boom. Boom. Boom. She was beckoning to me. Boom-boom-boom.

Brown and brown.

The rest of the world didn't matter. There was only her.

God, Nyala, I wish you could have seen her. She was beautiful. She was perfect.

She was the light and she was the darkness. She was all that we were, are, and all that we can be. She was dancing for all of us. She was dancing for this world.

Boom. Boom. Boom.

She was dancing for me and I saw for the first time. Saw beauty that was inconceivable, every color in the universe, every sound, every feeling in her movement.

It was Her.

The Daughter of God.

The Keeper of the Breath.

It was the Soul Catcher.

25

2020

SASKATOON, SASKATCHEWAN

Nyala dropped the manuscript on the library table and leaned back in the hard wooden chair, looking at the pages in shock.

Wow. What the hell?

She felt overwhelmed.

The Daughter of God? Keeper of the Breath? The Soul Catcher?

What did all that mean?

It was too confusing.

Tsau-z specifically wrote *"It was Her."* But the Soul Catcher was supposed to be a work of art that Our World had been trying to locate for centuries. A painting or a carving, Nyala would have thought. It didn't make sense. Was it possible that they had it all wrong? They were supposed to be all-knowing, but everyone made mistakes, right? So could it be that the Soul Catcher was a person? Some kind of living work of art? Could there be such a thing? Had there ever been?

Or was it just a typo?

Not a chance. Tsau-z wrote cryptically, but so far had never been loose with his choice of words. And he'd taken great pains to describe the scene, so that didn't compute either.

She leaned forward and picked up the last page in the manuscript.

She was dancing for me and I saw for the first time. Saw beauty that was inconceivable, every color in the universe, every sound, every feeling in her movement.

Nyala dropped the page and leaned back once more. She rubbed her eyes with the heels of her hands and then ran her hands back through her hair, tipping her head back and rolling her neck as she did.

Couldn't be.

Our World had been looking for the Soul Catcher for centuries apparently, so the "*Her*" Tsau-z was talking about would have to be an inconceivable beauty who was at least two hundred years old, maybe more, maybe a thousand years old.

Yeah, that made a lot of sense. Maybe in the twilight zone.

One thing for sure: if it was true, Luba would want in on the woman's beauty care secrets. Who was her hairdresser? Who did her nails?

Nyala smiled to herself.

Did dermatologists even exist a thousand years ago?

But Tsau-z also said "*It*" was the Soul Catcher.

More questions than answers.

And it was the first she'd read about Zhivago too, other than at the start of the manuscript where Tsau-z said he hunted him down and killed him. Was it possible that Zhivago was real? If so, the guy was a loathsome psychopathic piece of shit. Maybe it wasn't politically correct to say so, but Nyala was all for capital punishment and not just for murder in the first degree. As far as she was concerned, the guy definitely deserved to be killed if what he'd done to the young girl he'd drugged was true.

At least she was in a good place to sort out her thoughts; the Saskatoon Public Library was nice, quiet, and surprisingly large. There were only three other patrons that she could see from where she sat close to where the one librarian on duty manned the main desk.

Nyala knew she was putting off thinking about her meeting with the elderly Mrs. Keen the day before. She'd come to the library to begin the laborious task of digging into everything the elderly lady had told her.

But she hadn't done what she'd planned; instead, she'd taken the easy road and continued to read further into the manuscript, up to the early 1990s in Tsau-z's life. Wasn't that what Zhivago said when he was at the antihunting protest? That there were still six years left in the nineties? That would make Tsau-z, assuming he was the grown-up version of the superkid, somewhere in his late thirties.

She wanted to read on, to find out what happened after Tsau-z saw the Soul Catcher, just like she'd wanted to keep reading back in North Carolina, to rush to the end, but something stopped her. The manuscript wasn't simply an entertaining work of fiction that she couldn't put down; it was more important than that, something that she instinctively knew she needed to *live* through, not just read.

Instinct.

It was another of her secrets.

Instinct wasn't just a word to her, or some undefinable thing that only animals possessed. She could feel things. Strange things. Like danger. Even evil. Things that wanted to cause someone pain, not just her. It was so weird. When she was ten—or was it eleven?—she knew not to cross the street that time the garbage truck lost its brakes and careened through the intersection seconds later, wiping out three cars in the process.

It would have killed her, but she hadn't crossed the street. She stopped. She started screaming before the truck was even in sight, but the drivers in their cars never heard her. She could still feel the rush of the truck as it swept by, still remember vividly the sound of metal rending metal, and still feel the horror of lives being crushed from existence.

Instinct.

Like knowing not to cross the street, she knew reading on would have been the wrong thing to do. Even jumping ahead and reading the last two chapters was wrong; she should have properly reread the one hundred or so pages she'd skimmed over during the blurry drive to Saskatoon from Ottawa, instead of reading farther in the manuscript.

It was her bad habit again, the reason she didn't get 100 percent on every exam in school. Reading too fast, jumping ahead, wanting to fight the next battle before the last was even over. No regrets. But this wasn't a stupid exam, this was real life. Real life? If it was, it was like no real life she'd ever imagined.

Despite her misgivings, she had to admit she was starting to believe that Tsau-z *was* real. Way too obtuse in his writing style for her taste, but real.

Nyala didn't like questioning her decisions, but she should have researched and corroborated what she'd learned so far. Poor journalistic research methodology, a sure way to make mistakes. Any job worth doing is worth doing well. Most people would be able to say their father or their mother gave them that advice, but not her.

She had neither.

Wa-wa. Poor Nyala. Enough with the self-pity. The world was filled with people who would rather blame everyone else for their problems than look in the mirror. Ugh, she was starting to turn into a millennial.

Feeling sorry for herself, she knew, was just another way to avoid the task at hand, going back over everything she'd read with a fine-tooth comb to see if there was something she'd overlooked the first go-round. She picked up her pen and pulled the notepad closer, shoving the loose pages of the manuscript to the side.

Best place to start, the meeting with Mrs. Keen the day before. Think; don't skip over any points. There had to be something she'd missed, some new clue.

Mrs. Keen had insisted she be called Dottie as Nyala followed her to the kitchen, where the elderly lady had made fresh coffee, talking about the weather mostly as she busied herself putting sugar in a container and pouring cream into a small pitcher. When the coffee was ready, she set out a plate of cookies and took a chair at the table, across from where Nyala was seated, waiting for the truth that she'd driven across the continent to hear.

"Yes. My husband was a doctor."

Nyala had nearly lost control then. It was true! She remembered the hammer stroke of her heart releasing adrenaline.

"Are you okay?" The elderly lady, Dottie, was so sweet and she had looked so concerned. "You look unwell."

Unwell? Nyala hadn't been unwell; she'd been shredded by a truth that was now impossible to deny; a truth that determined her future and possibly her past.

"He was a psychiatrist; he specialized in helping children. He died in a fire a long time ago."

The doctor was real. Nyala had to fight an internal battle to control her desire to run away. She hadn't been sure she wanted to ask the next question or not; unsure if she could handle the truth.

Was there a superkid?

If it was a fact, and the boy Hunter did exist, then what?

And if it was fiction? That would be worse than fact. She wanted it to be true. By every breath she'd ever taken, by every thought and by every day she'd lived, she wanted it to be true.

No, she needed it to be true.

Yoga helped her then, square breathing; anything to get control; she took a deep breath, counting to four slowly as she did, held four seconds, and released the breath, counting four in her head, then she held for another four seconds and took a long, slow breath, calming her panic. She remembered steeling herself.

"Mrs. Keen, I am so sorry about your husband, but I have to ask you this. I know it's a long time ago, but do you remember your husband working with a patient, a young boy, a special young boy, about eight years of age?"

Dottie hadn't answered right away. In fact she didn't answer at all; she looked into Nyala's eyes for several moments and then sighed and rose from the table. She walked back down the hallway toward the front door and then turned to go into the small living room, leaving the faintest scent of warm roses and an aura of resignation in her stead.

For a moment Nyala wondered what she'd done. Was the question inappropriate? Certainly it was heartless to ask, and now, thinking back on it, she had to admit that the entire unannounced visit had been heartless. The lady's husband had been murdered and she didn't know. Or not; maybe it wasn't true. Maybe she did know. God what a mess; nothing made sense. Nyala's head had felt like it was about to spin off when Dottie returned, carrying a cardboard box full of files and yellowed newspaper clippings.

"Young lady, I don't know why you are here, and I don't know why I kept all this stuff." She set the box on the table and then sat down. "But you are here, and I did."

Nyala hadn't moved. She remembered staring at the box, paralyzed, her hands clenching at her sides.

"Yes. I remember the boy well. His name was Hunter. Hunter Johann."

———

Ah-OOOOG-ah. Ah-OOOOG-ah. Ah-OOOOG-ah.

The sound of the submarine Klaxon destroyed the library silence.

Jesus! She'd forgotten to turn her ringer off. Nyala was holding one hand up to the three other people sitting in the library and was mouthing "Sorry, sorry, sorry" as she frantically searched for the source of the noise in her purse with her other hand. It was on the third screaming "ah-OOOOG-ah" that she found it and was able to hit the decline button; she saw Luba's smiling face on the screen when she did. Next she hit the tiny switch to put the phone in silent mode.

The patrons turned back to their books, but the librarian was still scowling at Nyala, obviously not impressed. Nyala rolled her shoulders and pointed to the phone in her hand. She mouthed "Sorry" twice more before the librarian turned back to her work, making it clear with her body language that she was still not impressed.

I'M IN THE LIBRARY

Nyala typed the message in the text window.

Send.

CAN'T TALK

Send.

It took only seconds for the response.

U R FORGIVEN! THIS PLACE ROCKS!!!!!!!!! I'M MOVING HERE!!!!! GREAT SALES!!!! BOYS CUTE!!

Luba's opinion of the Saskatoon males wasn't exactly the same as a restaurant getting three Michelin stars; she also thought Scott was attractive.

Nyala sent the thumbs-up emoji, double-checked that her phone was indeed in silent mode, and then threw it back in her purse.

She looked at the pen, sitting on the notepad where she'd dropped it when the phone rang, her train of thought gone. The manuscript was sitting on the table as well, where she'd pushed it away after winning the internal battle with the discipline devil. Once again, every molecule in her body wanted to take the easy road, to read on and not to investigate what she'd just read about the psycho Zhivago guy.

Was the reference to the anti-bear-hunting protest real? Wasn't that what the bobbleheads were chanting? Stop the bear hunt? Did it happen? Was there even such a place in Victoria? What was the hotel? The Empress? Did the legislative buildings have an area in front where protests could be held? Wouldn't that be illegal?

Christ, there was so much she needed to research, but she wanted to get at it, to move forward, to the next battle, damn the torpedoes. She wanted to read on.

But she shouldn't. She knew she couldn't cross the road.

There was the obscene violation of the girl in the hotel room as well. Did it happen? Tsau-z said on the first page that he'd killed Zhivago, but she hadn't been sure then who was the bad guy and who was the good guy, Zhivago or Tsau-z. But what she'd just read answered any questions she might have had in that regard. Zhivago was the embodiment of evil. Whatever Tsau-z had done to kill the brute wasn't retribution enough. She wasn't even there, but she knew in her heart she would have enjoyed seeing the police carrying Zhivago's carcass off too, the piece of shit.

She needed to consult Google. Was there an antihunting rally back in the early 1990s in Victoria, British Columbia? Who was the minister? Moe Sihota? Who was John Holdstock? And the Soul Catcher? The beating drums. What was that about?

None of it made sense.

Nyala forced herself to start from the beginning, like a good journalist should, to ignore what she didn't know when writing a story and focus on what she did know. Again, she picked up her pen and pulled her notepad closer.

She wrote POSSIBLE FACTS at the top left of the blank page and then wrote CONFIRMED at the top right quarter of the page and UNCONFIRMED beside that word. She drew long lines down the page to make columns under the words. It was old-school and she knew it, but she hated digital spreadsheets with a passion. She needed to see and feel her work.

Then she wrote "Mrs. Keen's husband was a doctor, child psychiatrist" in the POSSIBLE FACTS column and put a checkmark in the CONFIRMED column.

Order. She needed order in her life. Without order, it was like she couldn't breathe, like she would suffocate. If it was something she could control, she did so to an obsessive degree.

She added "Dr. Keen died in a fire" to the POSSIBLE FACTS column.

CONFIRMED; another checkmark.

Dr. Keen murdered. UNCONFIRMED. She didn't have proof that he was murdered; she'd only read that in the manuscript.

"Hunter, superkid, eight years old."

CONFIRMED; checkmark.

Nyala felt like she should give her head a shake when she checked off that column. But there was no denying it, the doctor's meticulous notes given to her by Dottie were in the box on the library table in front of her, confirming everything she'd read about the boy in the manuscript. She'd scanned through the notes with the elderly lady the day before. They stated unequivocally that his young patient understood the content of certain books, the ones that were of interest to him. Art and nature; the boy was passionate about and ubertalented in both disciplines.

At one point, during the two hours she'd spent drinking coffee with Mrs. Keen, Nyala had asked Dottie if she could recall her husband having a painting with triangles and circles hanging on his office wall. The kindly lady had looked at her with a question in her eyes then, but, thankfully, hadn't asked Nyala how she could possibly know that there were paintings on her husband's office wall. But she didn't ask. Instead, after a pause, she said she couldn't recall if such a painting was there or not, only that her husband loved art and that he had an authentic Picasso in his office.

She added sadly that the Picasso had been destroyed in the fire, but it was obvious that her sadness had nothing to do with artwork. The guilt Nyala was already feeling, just for being there, questioning the nice woman, became almost unbearable at the mention of the Picasso. She knew it was a fake, knew it had found its way to Our

World, compliments of Charlotte, to the Russian and was probably a part of some institutional art collection as they spoke.

That had been the roughest part of the time she'd spent with Mrs. Keen, the saddest time. Her husband might possibly have been murdered and she didn't know. Nyala took a deep breath and tried to forget the feelings of guilt that still lingered. She leaned over the notebook and started writing again.

"Triangles and circles painting."

UNCONFIRMED; checkmark.

"Antique dealer died; van pulled from river."

CONFIRMED; checkmark. Thank Scott for that one; actually thank Scott for locating Dottie too, for locating the key to the vault that held the truth.

"Antique dealer murdered."

UNCONFIRMED; checkmark. No proof.

Nyala had tried to double-check the antique-dealer-dying point with Dottie, but her host claimed she couldn't recall anything about a car accident involving such a person. It seemed more like she didn't want to dredge up any more memories of that tragic time in her past and instead of even trying to remember, she reached in the box and pulled out an old yellow newspaper clipping.

"I kept track of Hunter for years after he was my husband's patient." She'd looked at the fragile dry clipping in her hand for a moment before continuing. "I'm not sure why exactly. Maybe it was because the boy was so important to my husband, and it gave me some comfort to see him grow up. Or maybe it was because the little boy's life was so easy to follow. I never remarried and had a lot of time on my hands, so I cut these out of the newspapers and put them in the box with the files he kept on Hunter here at home. I suppose it was my way of paying respect to my husband's memory. He was so passionate about helping children."

Nyala had been shocked at the number of newspaper clippings. The earliest one was of the kid winning gymnastics medals, while the later clippings showed that he was also a swimming star.

"He played water polo too?" It was rhetorical. Nyala already knew the answer before Dottie nodded her head and handed over several articles showing a teenage Hunter wearing nothing but a funny-looking cap with ear covers, and a tiny Speedo. One magazine photo, from when he must have been in his early twenties, even showed him aggressively checking a Russian player in an international match. The caption said it was taken in Hungary, the birthplace of the odd sport. Nyala scanned the article and saw where it said Hungary claimed more water polo world titles than any other country.

She'd looked closer at the age-yellowed press clippings, noticing with a blush that she wasn't the only one with a talent for looking good in a bathing suit. These water polo guys were hot. Regardless of the stigma associated with Speedos these days, she liked skimpy swimwear on guys, thought Speedos looked sexy on the right body.

She wrote the point on the notepad. "Accomplished swimmer H2O polo player." CONFIRMED; checkmark.

Dottie's box of newspaper clippings made the research a lot easier. Even better, without ever asking why Nyala was interested in her husband or his young patient, she'd told Nyala to take the entire box when she left. Dottie had walked back to the front door with the box and waited for Nyala to put her coat on and then handed it to her.

"You take this. My husband would have wanted you to have it, I think. I didn't tell anyone about the files being here all these years. Not even the graduate student who was working with Hunter before my husband passed away. I think she took over my husband's work with the boy after he passed."

Nyala remembered frowning.

"She asked for the files?"

"Yes, I think so, maybe, it was so long ago. I would not have told her anyway. They were my husband's. It was a few weeks after my husband passed when she came by to express her condolences. I believe my husband was the one who got her the job with the Johann family."

Dottie looked like she was trying to remember something.

"She had a funny name."

26

Maybe it was nothing. Probably it was nothing. But maybe it was something. Whatever it was, Nyala couldn't put her finger on what was bothering her about Dottie's parting comment.

"She had a funny name."

Nyala rocked back, balancing on the back legs of the library chair, a bad habit. She was careful not to lean too far back in case she went past the tipping point and crashed. The skinny sixty-something, strict-looking librarian sorting books nearby would kick her out for sure; public disturbance. She looked severe enough to kick her right out of Canada.

Nyala leaned forward carefully, making sure all four chair legs were firmly resting on the floor, and pushed whatever was bothering her out of her mind. There was nothing more to be gained by hashing over the meeting with Dottie. She'd answered the biggest questions Nyala had for her. Was the doctor real? Had he died in a fire? And was there a superkid?

Yes. Yes. And yes.

Retreating was no longer an option for Nyala. Parts of the manuscript were true, which meant her destiny wasn't behind her; it was waiting for her, tantalizingly close somewhere ahead. She just didn't know how to get where she needed to go. She took a deep breath, pondering the problems the manuscript presented, trying to recall what she'd read while driving across the country.

The pages told the story of Hunter, growing from a child to a young man, from the swimming phenomenon in his teens to a national water polo player in his later teens and early twenties. She'd even learned that his father passed away at a relatively young age, when Hunter was attending university. It was a stroke, apparently, brought on by what had become a serious drinking problem. No surprise there. There was nothing about what happened to Hunter's mother, though.

She checked the shaky notes she'd attempted to take while driving with Luba from Ottawa. There it was. "*My life was under the control of Our World from the moment they heard about me.*" The Russian had apparently been orchestrating Hunter's life, directing even the choice to switch from swimming to water polo, with the wave of a hand and two words: "Do it."

Reading between the lines on the bumpy highway between Winnipeg, Manitoba, and Yorkton, Saskatchewan, it seemed that Hunter's transition between sports wasn't as difficult as Nyala would have thought. It started when he was still in Saskatoon, when he played the game in a local league. He was tall for his age, already world-class fast in the water, and from what she'd read, he had good hands, an innate game sense, and, most importantly, a predator's instinct for scoring goals. Dorothy's newspaper clippings confirmed all that.

According to the timeline in her rough notes, while in his second year of university, Hunter quit the endless monotony of training for speed swimming and walked onto the varsity water polo team. He was physically ready, filled out to just over two hundred pounds, stood well over six feet tall, and was honed to an Olympian physical fitness level. It was then that the Russian leader of Our World arranged the swimmer's acceptance onto the Canadian National Water Polo Team with a few words in the right ears, a warning in a few more ears, and some American currency.

She checked through her notes.

Tsau-z explained in the manuscript that the leader of Our World had done it so Hunter could "*liaison with an operative closely associated with the Hungarian National Water Polo Team; an operative who was working with Our World.*"

Hmmm. Interesting, but the two chapters she'd read that morning in the library were even more so.

Nyala considered this for a moment, then picked up her pen and opened a new page in her hard copy notes and wrote SCOTT TO DO at the top. She leafed through the manuscript until she found what she was looking for and started writing.

From what she'd read that morning, the antihunting protest that Zhivago supposedly organized would have taken place sometime in 1994.

1. Who is Moe Sihota? Minister of environment?
2. Who is John Holdstock?
3. Who is Bobby Fontana?
4. Check if there was an animal rights protest in Victoria, British Columbia, in the spring or early summer of 1994.

There had to be a record somewhere if that part of the manuscript was true. If anyone could find out, Scott could. She was deep in thought, so deep it took a moment to comprehend that the librarian's scowl was meant for her. Sorry! Nyala mouthed the words. She hadn't realized she was tapping her pen on the table as she thought. Another bad habit.

She put the pen down, pulled her phone from her purse, and held it so it could recognize her face. She touched the messages icon, then went to the last text she'd sent to Scott and started typing in the message bar.

She pushed the send icon again and checked the time before she placed her phone back in her purse. Three hours already, but it was still early, she had all afternoon.

Nyala knew she had to go back and reread the pages she'd given a cursory look during the road trip. She found the marked page and read her note, "Hunter 13 years old, 1968?" and started from there.

27

1960s

UNDISCLOSED SMALL TOWN

"Check it out, Mrs. J!" The book in Wilbur's hand didn't look special. It was more of a scrapbook with a nondescript black binding, leather, worn, well used; older than newer; Rose could see that. "Hunter and I found it in a secondhand store. Well, Hunter found it."

By that point Rose was used to seeing the odds and ends that her son and Wilbur had dragged home from the city's many secondhand, antique, and thrift stores over the last five years since they'd discovered that Hunter was special. Her boy and his homeschool tutor were supposed to be going to the library, or a museum or university, not shopping, but Wilbur insisted that they always finished the lessons first and only then went treasure hunting.

Rose smiled and reached for the book. She began to flip through the pages of drawings, noticing that her son had the expectant look on his face he always did when he brought something home to show her. Was he really thirteen already? How could that be? Where had the time gone?

"Ummm. Eva Mendel Miller?" Rose feigned concentration as she read the name written on the front of the book and on many of the later drawings. She didn't have a clue what she was supposed to be seeing. "Does she have something to do with that new Mendel Art Gallery? I see thirty-two pages of very nice drawings. Is it the flower painting?"

The look on her son's face made it clear that she wasn't correct about the flowers being important. Wilbur was smiling, seemingly enjoying her employer's inability to recognize the thing that to Hunter made the sketchbook so obviously special.

"Okay, I give up. Show me." She handed the book to her son, who promptly turned to one of the middle pages and handed it back. It was a drawing of . . . she wasn't exactly sure what, other than it looked like someone had scribbled on the page for at least an hour, with no rhyme, no reason. Rose read the title, name, and date written on the page near the bottom. "Always Eva, Study The Wind. Hans Hofmann. 1939."

Her son looked happy; he seemed contented now that Rose couldn't possibly be missing what was so important about the old leather-bound notebook. But she still didn't have a clue.

"Okay. I give up again." She handed the book back to Wilbur this time because her son seemed to have already lost interest in the conversation and was rummaging through the fridge for the milk bottle.

"Mrs. J! It's Hans Hofmann!" She opened the book again and showed Rose the scribbled-up page. "It's his *Wind* painting, only not in paint, just in lines! Like a study! And Hunter says 1939 is years before the experts say he painted *The Wind*! They say he didn't paint it until 1944!"

Wilbur looked at Rose in a way that didn't need words to express her meaning: "Surely knowing all that you still can't be confused." But Rose was, not that it mattered. Her son and Wilbur were in their own world these days, discovering this or that treasure, whatever it was, learning about it and selling it. Rose was thankful that Hunter wasn't keeping everything anymore, except for his watch; otherwise his room would be packed.

Thank goodness for Wilbur and her car. She'd taken the lead over the last few years, driving Hunter around. She'd helped sell off the stuff that he had collected before she became his tutor and was also helping sell the new things the two of them brought home. She was smart and somehow figured out who in town would buy the pieces to get the best dollars.

Rose remembered Wilbur's offer. "Don't worry about it, Mrs. J, easy as pie. I'll do a little research and find where to sell to make sure you get top dollar." And she'd done exactly that and done it well. Just the pieces the antique dealer wanted to buy so long ago, but didn't return to pay for, brought the family enough money to pay the mortgage for a few months. What was his name? Willisford? Poor man; so tragic.

Rose felt bad about Pete too. He was drinking more these days; that concerned her. He was still doing his garage sailing, but mostly he was doing it alone now. He tried to make a dollar or two on his purchases, but the money that Hunter's stuff brought into the household pretty well took the pressure off the family financially. It hurt his pride, she knew that, and even though Pete was forced to accept that their son was undeniably smart, she knew he still felt that he wasn't normal.

At least not Pete-style normal. And to be fair, Pete was right, their son wasn't your average boy next door, but he was doing much, much better now that he was in school and interacting with other kids his age. Rose was thankful she'd put her foot down and insisted he go to a public school.

And he was swimming! Competitive swimming with the Saskatoon Y-Optimists Swim Club. Rose didn't know anything about competitive swimming and Pete definitely didn't. But Wilbur had suggested they might want to let Hunter try it, to work off some of his extra energy. On weekends in the winter, Pete and Rose would go and watch their son racing at local swim meets. He was good, really good, and his coach, Harry Baily, said if Hunter stuck with it, he could go to the Olympics someday.

"I'll cut this page out and donate the rest of the book back to the ladies in the thrift store tomorrow." Wilbur brought Rose out of her thoughts. "I know a guy who will go crazy for an original Hofmann! I'm betting I can get us two hundred dollars for this drawing. And we only paid two dollars for the whole notebook."

She was shaking her head as she looked at the notebook in her hands.

"Hunter is amazing; he can spot a deal from a mile away. It's crazy. He's like a bird dog." She held up the notebook for Rose to make the point. "This came from the Salvation Army! Same place he found that old crackly painted yellow document box last month, the one with the black trim; got thirty-five dollars for that one, it was Mennonite apparently, cost us a dollar fifty!"

Rose smiled. The Salvation Army was one of her son's and Wilbur's favorite haunts. Only the library and the swimming pool took more of their time. School was hit-or-miss. Once Mr. Clark, the principal at the primary school, John Lake School, realized how far beyond the other students Hunter was, he told Rose that Hunter could attend whenever it was convenient and for exams.

Rose worried about next year, when Hunter would be going to high school at Aden Bowman. She was sure the rules would be different. She wasn't looking forward to explaining to the principal there, Mr. Smythe, who she'd heard was extremely strict, that she wanted Hunter to attend school for the social part, not really for the academics.

But that was in the future.

Rose smiled again.

Right now life was good.

28

2020

SASKATOON, SASKATCHEWAN

The buzzing in Nyala's purse put an end to her reading for the moment. It was funny how in the quiet of the library, the table her purse was lying on acted like a giant eardrum, amplifying the sound of the buzzing from her phone. She leaned forward, grabbing the offending purse as she did, and rushed for a hallway off to the side of the main room, smiling sweetly at the librarian as she passed, pointing in the direction of the ladies' bathroom.

It was Scott.

"What did you find? No. Nothing's wrong. No, I don't have laryngitis, I'm in a library." Nyala rolled her eyes. "No, I don't care what he is going to think when he gets back, let him be pissed. He hasn't given me a raise in two years."

Going AWOL from work wasn't normal for Nyala, but it wasn't totally unusual either. There had been a story or two she'd tracked down in the past that kept her away from work for a week or so at a time, but having both her and Luba gone for over a week already was going to cause waves. The good news was that her boss had apparently done the same thing and had taken time off without giving anyone a heads-up. Not that it mattered what he thought anyway. He needed her a lot more than she needed the job; Luba not so much, although technically Luba didn't need the job either. Didn't want the job might be more accurate.

"Tell him when he gets back in the office that Luba says she will quit if he fires me." She snickered to herself; witty. Her boss wouldn't fire either of them even if they were gone for a month; he needed Nyala that badly. "What did you find out?"

Scott's confirmation that there had been an animal rights anti-hunting protest on the grounds of the British Columbia legislature buildings back in June 1994 didn't in the least surprise Nyala. Too many of the details in the manuscript were based on provable facts, so there was no reason to believe this one wouldn't be true too.

"Bear Watch?" Nyala frowned and repeated the question in full-sentence form for Scott. "The animal rights group that organized the protest was called 'Bear Watch'?"

Even as she listened to him, she was trying to recall anything she already knew about animal rights groups. She'd heard of ALF, the Animal Liberation Front; ELF, the Earth Liberation Front; and HSUS, the Humane Society of the United States, and she'd even heard of USFWS, the United States Fish & Wildlife Service, which, from what she understood, was part of the Department of the Interior. But nothing called "Bear Watch."

"Say again?" She was frowning. "'Really? Animal rights fanatics were classified as the number one domestic terrorists back in the nineties? Wow! Nasty people."

Scott explained about bombings and arson and the balaclava-clad "Bear Watch" protesters following legally licensed hunters and their guides and throwing paint on their guides' wives and children as they walked to school. The instigators had been charged with arson and conspiracy to commit arson, but the charges were dropped when the Sierra Club lawyer defending the animal rights members filed a petition requesting the release of the name of the FBI undercover agent who had provided the damning evidence.

The judge in the case apparently sustained the request, or whatever the legal terminology was, and the Crown prosecutor, unwilling to risk the life of the deep-cover agent, dropped all charges. Interesting, but way too much information. Nyala finally stopped Scott when he started giving her his personal opinion, saying he felt hunters deserved to be attacked and that the animal rights extremists were rad badasses.

"Bad assholes more like; what about the names I gave you?"

Again she listened, this time with even more attention.

"Moe Sihota was the minister of the environment for the province of British Columbia at that time? What about the other two?

"Yes, got it. John Holdstock. President of the British Columbia Wildlife Federation. Deceased. Bobby Fontana. President of the Guide Outfitters Association of British Columbia. Highly respected guide and outfitter. Deceased.

She shifted the phone to her other ear and turned to look into the mirror above the three sinks in bathroom.

"What? Seriously? Killed in Africa by a Cape buffalo? Jesus."

That was a fact she wasn't expecting.

She was about to ask Scott to find out whether there had been a meeting sometime around the protest with the minister and those two gentlemen.

"We met with him to put an end to the insanity."

Surely there had to be a record of all the minister's meetings, but she changed her mind. It wasn't important anyway and the manuscript said there had been a meeting, so because everything else was proving to be true, the meeting probably had taken place. Better to conserve Scott's energies for more important tasks.

The narrative was becoming clear now. The two men were obviously representatives of the pro-hunting community, no doubt meeting with the minister to try to educate him in hopes of stopping him from bowing to the animal rights demands. Tough one; she felt for the two men. It would have been an uphill battle, she imagined, especially if the government in power was weak and left-leaning with a socialist platform, as Zhivago said it was in the manuscript.

The fact that Tsau-z said *"we met with him"* told Nyala that he must have been in the meeting too, poor guy. If the politicians back then were anything like those running the planet today, the minister probably smiled a big fake smile, shook their hands, and promised them the world. The same thing he would have done with the animal rights protesters screaming for the death of all hunters.

Drown and you are innocent. Survive and you are guilty.

Burn them at the stake.

So strange; how could people want to save animals, but be willing to kill humans? What a screwed-up world. What was it the deranged sociopath, Zhivago, called the animal rights protesters? Orcs and trolls?

She dropped the phone back into her purse and took one last look at herself in the mirror before turning toward the door. Saskatoon uglies. Nice. The door to the ladies' room opened before she reached it and the librarian poked her head in, obviously checking to see what Nyala was up to.

This lady was starting to get on her nerves.

————

*"They were all part of it, actors on a stage, in a play they didn't un-*derstand.* Nyala considered the meaning of the words. *"The stage is too vast; the stage is the world, Our World."*

She was back at the table, her new home away from home, and she was tapping her pen again, but this time it was on the side of her head. Think. What did he mean by that? She read it again.

"They were all part of it, actors on a stage, in a play they didn't understand. The stage is too vast; the stage is the world, Our World."

For five minutes she worked through the possible meanings, but the only thing she could come up with was that there had to be a bigger picture that she couldn't see, some larger, unseen force directing the *"play"* that the people in the manuscript were all supposedly part of.

Instead of dwelling on it any longer, she leaned over the table and flipped back through the manuscript, looking for the pages she'd already sorted through, specifically the one with the asterisk. It was the page where Rose was looking at the notebook. Nyala knew she needed a hint, something that would guide her to a figurative vantage point.

There it was, the name that she was looking for, the name that caught her attention when she was reading the manuscript on the drive from Ottawa, the reason she'd put an asterisk on the page.

"Eva Mendel Miller," the person who apparently owned the sketchbook with the drawings inside. She typed the name into the Google bar and pressed enter.

Nyala was frowning. The artist was real, no big surprise. She was the "daughter of Frederick Mendel," who was some kind of philanthropist who apparently "endowed the Mendel Art Gallery, Saskatoon."

Rather than read further, Nyala clicked on the link to the Mendel Art Gallery.

"Major creative cultural center." "Operated from 1964 to 2015." "16th largest public art gallery in Canada." "Sixth highest overall attendance in the country."

Sounded like a cool place to visit. Too bad it was closed; it would have been nice to check it out.

Nyala went back to the original page on her laptop and started reading. That was interesting. Eva Mendel Miller passed away the previous year at the age of one hundred; wild to think of living that long, an entire century. She clicked on the *Saskatoon Star Phoenix* newspaper obituary and started reading.

"Born 1919, Germany. As Jews, fled Berlin 1933, the year Hitler came to power. Kept one step ahead of the German annexation, fleeing to Poland, then Hungary and Vienna before finally settling in Saskatoon in 1940."

Wow. Must have been a strong lady and a strong family. Nyala looked at the photo in the online obit. She looked sweet, with smiling eyes. She appeared tiny but must have had the heart of a giant. All the Mendel family must have, to leave everything they knew, to start all over again in that little place on the other side of the world where nothing much ever happens.

Not only sweet, but inspirational. Nyala read in the *Globe and Mail* online obituary that in her later years the amazing woman was quoted as saying, "Life is fantastically beautiful. I'm overly happy. It's indecent to be this happy." The article stated that the diminutive centenarian said, "I don't know if this is a dream, or if it's real, but whatever it is, it is wonderful." It went on to say that Eva was attuned to the mysterious in life, to the unspoken, to the world of the imagination.

Man, you want mysterious and imagination, have I got a manuscript for you.

Then she saw it.

"Mrs. Mendel Miller studied painting with some of the leading artists of her day, including Hans Hofmann."

Hans Hofmann was the artist who did the scribbling on the page in Eva Mendel Miller's sketchbook that Wilbur said was worth $200. He was real.

Nyala typed in the new artist's name in the Google bar, clicked search, and then clicked again on the Wikipedia hit and started reading.

Hans Hofmann was another German-born artist; lots of Germans in the art world. His paintings sold for millions, not $200. That was strange.

"Symbolism, Neo-Impressionism, Fauvism and Cubism. Concerned with pictorial structure, unity, and spatial illusionism." A whole bunch of art-speak blah blah; or it was, until she saw the next line.

"Hofmann's first solo show at Peggy Guggenheim's Art of This Century Gallery in 1944."

This Peggy had to be related to Solomon Guggenheim. There was no way that it could be a coincidence, the name was too unique, there had to be a connection. She scanned further down the Hans Hofmann Wikipedia page, looking for highlighted names, and before she finished the page she saw what she was looking for, a second name she recognized. "Kandinsky."

No coincidence; another dot connected. Did this mean this new person, Peggy Guggenheim, was part of Our World? The secret organization that Tsau-z claimed controlled the art world? The Our World that Zhivago and some psychopathic killer named Charlotte were part of?

Instead of dwelling on the questions, she typed in "Peggy Guggenheim" and hit search.

"Art collector. Daughter of Benjamin Guggenheim, who went down with the *Titanic* in 1912."

Dang, the art world was weirdly interconnected. What are the odds that a sketchbook found in Saskatoon, Saskatchewan, back in the late 1960s would have connections to a passenger who died in the *Titanic* tragedy fifty-something years before?

Scanning down she saw the name again: **"Wassily Kandinsky."** Jesus, the guy was everywhere. **"His first one-man show was in England"** in Peggy Guggenheim's gallery.

"Donated her entire collection to the Solomon R. Guggenheim Foundation in 1976." Peggy Guggenheim died three years after she donated her collection to her uncle's foundation.

Nyala picked up her pen and started tapping it against her head again. There were a few more interesting points, but probably not germane to the narrative. Peggy liked men and women apparently, slept with over one thousand of them by her own account. When a reporter asked how many husbands she'd had in her life, she asked back if the reporter meant hers or other women's.

Yikes. If it was a competition, Nyala was losing 1,000 to zero.

She went back to Eva Mendel Miller's page, looking for something she missed, clicking on each option this time, reading them all. Most were dead ends, but on the third Google results page, she saw something that piqued her interest.

"Studied under Joseph Hoffman in Vienna."

A different Hofmann? Nyala checked the name out. Not much there, but he did design some really cool furniture. The Kubus armchair he designed in 1910 looked a lot more modern than most of the crap being mass-produced and sold at the high-end designer galleries she occasionally visited with Luba. Nyala also thought his Armchair of Wood and Cane from 1903 would look good on her deck; too bad it was already in the Metropolitan Museum of Art. And even more too-bad that if the Met ever deaccessioned it, Nyala was sure it would probably cost more than she'd make in her entire lifetime.

The Wikipedia page said Hoffmann studied at the Academy of Fine Arts Vienna. Out of curiosity more than anything, Nyala clicked on the blue link and started scanning the page. Whoa! Adolf Hitler applied two years in a row to get into the art school, in 1907 and in 1908. Both times they rejected his application because of his "unfitness for painting." No shit. Unfitness for being a member of the human race, they should have added.

Hitler and his Nazi henchmen called modern art degenerative, so it was highly unlikely that he applied to the Vienna art school because of that school's progressive thinking. The Bohemian group of abstract artists like Hans Hofmann and Kandinsky wouldn't have been caught dead in a staid European institution that focused on neoclassical design and attracted narcissistic psychopaths like the future Nazi leader.

Nyala knew she had to retreat. As interesting as the internet could be, it was easy to get sidetracked. It took discipline to maintain a focus on the task at hand and not wind up watching the Kardashians giving makeup tips on YouTube. She returned to Hans Hofmann and this time read past the point she'd reached before. She stopped reading when she saw the name in the list of Hofmann's students in New York City.

"Robert De Niro Sr."

Regardless of the warning to herself only moments before, about getting sidetracked, she couldn't help but click on the name. There was no way it was the father of the real Robert De Niro, right? She would get back to her serious research as soon as she checked out the link. Literally the first line confirmed what she thought couldn't be possible.

"Robert Henry De Niro (May 3, 1922–May 3, 1993), better known as Robert De Niro Sr., was an American abstract impressionist painter and the father of actor Robert De Niro."

She whistled under her breath.

"De Niro was part of a group show at Peggy Guggenheim's Art of This Century Gallery in New York."

More connections! The same Peggy Guggenheim that Kandinsky and Hans Hofmann obviously hung out with, the niece of Solomon Guggenheim and his mistress Hilla von Rebay, from Our World and the Gathering. She read further and whistled under her breath again.

"De Niro worked for five years at Hilla Rebay's legendary Museum of Modern Art."

The famous actor's father, Robert De Niro Sr., was obviously very closely connected to Hilla Rebay. Nyala worked through the pieces of the puzzle, putting each into place, but still couldn't see the complete picture. More connections, for sure, too many to chalk up to simple coincidence and circumstance. No, there was something to it.

But could the actor's father have been involved with Our World somehow?

For a second Nyala considered closing her laptop; was she starting to lose it? She shuddered. Was this how crazy began?

But she couldn't quit, she was caught up in it now, being swept along in a current that she was powerless to paddle against.

"De Niro studied with Hans Hofmann." No surprise there; she knew that from Hofmann's Wikipedia page. **"Married Virginia Admiral in 1942 and separated in 1943 shortly after their son Robert De Niro Jr. was born and Robert De Niro came out as gay."**

Now that was fascinating. Nothing to do with what she was researching, but it would make for an interesting party conversation someday.

The next thing she read absolutely had something to do with what she was researching.

She gasped out loud.

"In 1944, De Niro entered into a relationship with the poet Robert Duncan. Author of *The Opening of the Field*."

Robert Duncan? The poet Robert Duncan?

She stood up and started to frantically push the papers around until she found the page she was looking for in the manuscript. It was the page that told of Dr. Keen, Hunter's doctor, the child psychiatrist, standing in his office, celebrating the fact that he'd done all he could for his young, gifted patient. Celebrating how he'd helped the family and how he'd been the one to check the references of the young lady with the funny name. Wilbur's references.

It was the night he was murdered.

Nyala read the page, dreading what she already knew was coming. She didn't see the librarian marching across the floor toward where she stood.

There it was.

". . . he figured he'd do a good deed and so had interviewed a few of the applicants on behalf of the Johanns. He'd even checked the young lady's curriculum vitae and phoned her references."

Nyala kept reading.

"Impressive list of references." One was "Robert Duncan, author of *The Opening of the Field*."

The library started to spin. Nyala had to reach down and put both hands on the table, so she wouldn't fall.

Robert De Niro Sr.'s lover. Robert Duncan. Robert De Niro Sr., friend of the Our World operatives Solomon and Hilla. Kandinsky. Hofmann. They were all connected.

Dr. Keen spoke on the phone with Robert Duncan about Wilbur!

Robert Duncan "gave a ringing endorsement."

"Holy shit!"

They all had to be involved; they all had to be a part of Our World!

"Young lady, I must ask you to gather your things and leave." The librarian was furious. Everybody in the library was looking over to see what was causing the disturbance.

Nyala didn't see them and didn't pay attention to the librarian.

She didn't because profound fear was the only thing she knew right then. Fear for a boy and a family that she didn't even know. Fear for what it all meant.

It was Charlotte. She was the enforcer sent by the Russian leader. She was the one who murdered the doctor and the antique dealer. The leader of Our World picked the code name from *Charlotte's Web*.

Wilbur, too. The spider's friend from the same book.

Damn. How did she miss the connection?

Charlotte was Wilbur.

Wilbur was Charlotte.

29

U h-huh." Luba nodded her head, but her eyes were looking past her friend. "Yep, got it."

"I'm telling you, all this stuff is real; every word of it." Nyala had her notebook out on the bar and was flipping through it. "Tsau-z is trying to tell me something. I know it. He wants me to understand about all this for some reason."

"I'm sure he does." But Luba still wasn't listening. She stood from the high stool and held her hand out to catch the bartender's eye, the bartender who didn't seem to know she existed. "Excuse me? Hello? Beer, please. Two. Yes, same. Thank you."

Luba sat back on her stool and rolled her eyes.

"Like really? Hellllooo!" She waved her hands up and down the brand-new yellow dress hugging her petite and available body. "Lady in the house. What's wrong with his eyes?"

The Saskatoon Inn wasn't exactly a five-star hotel, but it was certainly an upgrade from the dive they stayed in the first night in town. While Nyala was busy with Dottie, Luba had used up part of her precious shopping time to check online for a better hotel and chose the Saskatoon Inn partially because it was close to the edge of town, but mostly because she loved the downstairs lounge, which was situated in a giant atrium, complete with a fake creek flowing from a fake stone cave. The zillion trees and plants were real though, and Nyala instantly started glowing when she walked into the giant open center of the hotel. It was so humid she felt like she was walking into the middle of a jungle.

Now for the second evening at the Saskatoon Inn, they'd made their way down to the bar to grab dinner and have something to drink. Both were decked out in their best, which meant Luba was wearing the fancy designer yellow dress she found in a local fashion boutique, totally inappropriate for the cold outside temperatures, but practical in a low-cut, too-short kind of way for the heavy humidity in the jungle lounge. Nyala's best was her usual, same-old same-old best. Faded jeans and a blouse in whatever color she happened to grab that day.

She was going over what she'd discovered in the library earlier in the day, before she'd been asked to leave, forever. Swearing out loud, not once but twice, apparently wasn't acceptable library etiquette. Go figure.

"It's some kind of syndicate. They deal in art. But it's underground, totally off the grid. I think it still exists now, even today."

Just saying it out loud sounded so silly it made her feel like she was part of a conspiracy theorist's wet dream.

"Did you know that Robert De Niro's father was gay?" The question came from so far out in left field it took Luba a moment to comprehend what her friend just asked her.

"What?" She was jabbing a french fry into a bowl of ketchup when Nyala's comment sank in. "Say *what*? *No way!*"

Really, who cared; it might have been wild and crazy news back in the mid-1900s, but this was 2020. There wasn't any big deal about being gay, not at all, unless it was the father of everybody's favorite actor, Robert De Niro.

"Yep. Way. And he was a famous midcentury modern painter." Nyala reached across her notes to take a french fry. "Apparently lived with a poet lover in San Francisco. Left his wife and moved in with the guy a year after Robert was born."

A poet who gave a glowing reference for a young female grad student, who then proceeded to murder the guy who was asking for the reference. She sounded like exactly the kind of girl you'd want to hire to teach your young son. Not.

Maybe he didn't know? Maybe the reference was legit? But the coincidence was beyond the pale. No. Somehow all of them were connected to Our World, Robert Duncan, the poet, and very likely

Robert De Niro Sr., Peggy Guggenheim, Solomon too, and Hilla von Rebay. Hans Hofmann, Wassily Kandinsky, and even the sweet Eva Mendel Miller. Hell, as near as Nyala could tell, everyone was connected to Our World, though probably some of them didn't even know it.

What did Tsau-z say? They are all *"actors on a stage, in a play they didn't understand."*

She chewed on the french fry and thought about it.

"You are on that stage, Nyala."

She was part of it and didn't know it. The more she considered it, the more it made sense. They were all bit-part actors, not directly involved in the nefarious activities of Our World. They simply couldn't know what was going on unless they were actual operatives.

Easy to be oblivious back then. It was a different time, people were freer, especially artists; art was their life and life was their art. Everyone in that avant-garde era of midcentury modern art lived big Bohemian lives. They just didn't realize that the structure of their entire movement was built on a foundation that shifted at the whim of their master, Our World. They didn't even know they *had* a master.

"How'd you find out?"

"Find out what?"

"About Robert De Niro's father?"

"Oh, that. I googled it."

"Sweet!" Luba was trying to get the bartender's attention again. "Any other cool intel?"

"Peggy Guggenheim slept with over one thousand men and women."

"Whoa! My kind of girl!" Luba ordered two more beers, this time with a shot to go along.

30

Watching the news channels, even the morning shows, made Nyala want to puke. The news was fake; obviously fake. Seriously, how many times could the sky fall and the world end? Couldn't people see it? News had become a business, a big business worth billions of dollars, but for whatever reason, all her peers at work and in journalism school railed constantly about big business being the problem with the world, but then worked diligently to produce the moronic one-sided swill for their own bosses, all of them working for a big business.

She reached for the clicker.

"You hate that stuff. Why do you always watch it?" Luba never watched the news but was a big fan of any Real Housewives series and watched all the *Bachelor* episodes religiously. "I'm heading downtown, big sale today! You need anything?"

Nyala turned the television off and swung her legs off the bed. With Luba gone she could get back to her reading and research. The library was out, so it was going to have to be the hotel room. Not so bad. It had a big window looking out over the parking lot, where a few cars were running, billowing clouds of exhaust as the owners warmed them up before pulling away. Sure was drab out there. Brown and brown like Tsau-z saw the world.

"No, I'm good. Work to do."

"How about lunch today?" Luba grabbed her coat and opened the door to leave. "Sushi?"

How did she do it? How could she drink like she had the night before, and still look so up and ready-to-get-at-it the next morning? Nyala saw herself in the room's wall mirror. Ugh. The case of the Saskatoon uglies she was suffering from was getting worse.

"Really? Sushi?" Nyala rolled her eyes. "And how far did you say the nearest ocean was? A thousand miles? Two thousand?"

"Good point!" Luba giggled and waved as she closed the door to the room. "Be gone all day! Ta-ta!"

Nyala thought about fixing up but decided there was no point. She needed to keep at it. She flipped through the manuscript until she found the next page with one of her marks at the top.

She was gentle. Sweet. My first attempts at being me, at being normal, were tentative.

Brown and brown.

I was different than all of them. Different but the same. I was a boy crossing to manhood.

She understood the confusion I felt. She was different too, hurt. We needed each other. She was my first love, but not from the high school I attended. I was young, she was younger, Freshie Queen from her school. Laura. She played hockey. I took her to my graduation. We talked about getting married. We talked about love. We knew nothing of either. High school sweethearts, we were meant to be together. Fated to be together, we thought.

Ill-fated.

No way to know what would have come of her, of me, of us.

She died.

Suicide.

Laura was not part of their plan for me.

Lois too. Another Freshie Queen, a swimmer on my team. Paths crossing, joining and then dividing, going to different places and converging again. Young love is resilient. Adaptive.

Maybe it would have worked. Maybe we could have stayed together. Maybe we would have settled, had a family. Normal. Maybe. But we became too close.

Lois died.

I was too young; too naïve to understand what was happening; why it was happening.

Lois was not part of their plan for me.

It was time for me to get away from that place; find my way. Find me, I thought. But I was simply playing out my part in their plan.

There was nothing to hold me there any longer; nobody.

They, she, made sure of that.

I left then. That summer, I was seventeen.

It was what Our World wanted.

My mother cried.

There was nobody to hold me there.

I did not see my mother as a real person. Regret is deep, a cavern of emptiness. Terms are all I can come to now. I did not know. I was not me yet. Had not found me yet. She was always there, from the beginning, but I was never there for her.

She told me she could not bear to come to the bus station to see me off to university.

I did not understand the depth of her sorrow.

I never looked back as I got on the bus. Never saw my father again. He passed before I found my way.

My mother would have too, had I stayed with her. She was not part of their plan for me.

I did not see her.

And I saved her.

I did not know who I was then, did not know yet who I could be, would be.

When I learned. When I understood. When I was able to see. When I was me.

I saw her.

It is never too late for hope, Nyala.

———

Nyala whistled under her breath even though she didn't need to be quiet. It wasn't the library, but she felt whistling louder would some-how have been profane right then. She didn't have a mother, but if she did, the thought of not seeing her, not being able to show any emotion, seemed too sad to contemplate. She didn't have a child of her own, but if she did and the child didn't *see* her, didn't acknowledge her, didn't express the slightest love for her, that would be beyond sad.

Hunter was messed up, obviously struggling to fit in with other kids, trying to adapt to life in the real world, confused and going through puberty. Had to be tough to make friends when you didn't even know what a friend was. He must have been teased, maybe bullied. Kids could be brutal; Nyala knew that from firsthand experience. It wasn't his fault though, even though he probably felt it was. He was born the way he was born.

If she understood what Tsau-z was trying to say in his obscure way, Our World was manipulating every part of his life. To the point they were facilitating the deaths of anyone the young Hunter became close to, anyone who might interfere with their long-term plans for the gifted protégé.

Killing Hunter's girlfriends, though? How ruthless were these people? And did Charlotte do it? Did she somehow orchestrate the passing of these two innocent young girls at the same time she was with the family, pretending to be Wilbur? The thought was repulsive. It wasn't just beyond the forbidden; it was beyond horror.

How could someone embed themselves with a nice family, smile and call the mother Mrs. J, and be a stone-cold killer at the same time? The idea that it was even possible made her feel uneasy, like she was standing on the edge of a tall building looking down. Vertigo. She had to stop thinking about it. It was too disturbing to believe such evil could exist. She had to focus on something else. She needed to cleanse her thoughts.

She'd scattered the pages on the bed and had been sitting cross-legged, reading, but dropped the page and unfolded herself, leaving the bed to sit at the small desk where her laptop was still plugged in, charging. Go figure, but she'd forgotten to plug it in the night before, after the night of debauchery with Luba. Maybe it was time to go on the wagon for a bit.

Focus.

Nyala thought for a second and then reached for the keyboard. "Freshie Queen." Click.

Had to be what she was thinking it meant, but she also needed to know for sure, it was good research form. Fact checking was good. Control was good.

"Someone who just entered an English-speaking country."

Nope.

"Freshie was a popular Canadian drink mix that was a popular alternative to Kool-Aid for the domestic marketplace from the 1950s to the 1980s."

The timeline was right, but no way that could be it.

"A wannabe gangster/hoodlum with a bad haircut."

Nyala snickered to herself then. She doubted that was what she was looking for.

"A freshie is a first-year student at a university or a high school."

Bingo. There was no mention of a "Freshie Queen," but it could only mean one of two things: either the schools back then bestowed the title on a first-year gay student, or more likely, given the time period, it was a beauty contest, a pageant that picked one girl, put her on a pedestal, made her a target, and made all the other girls feel inadequate. Nice.

Nyala's own school years had been terrible. She was too attractive; the girls hated her for that. Lied about her, made up stories, did their best to hurt her in the meanest ways possible, with the sharpest blades of all, words and innuendo. The boys all said they slept with her, undermining her already poor self-image, her confidence, making her feel like she'd somehow violated herself, confusing her about who she was supposed to be, even though she knew she wasn't what they said. She wasn't one of them.

Never had been; never would be.

Nyala pulled the screen down and got up to open the curtains wider. It was sunny outside. Saskatoon was starting to grow on her, but she'd still never live here. She turned then and crawled back onto the bed, reaching for the page she'd been reading in the manuscript. What happened to Charlotte? Or should she just say Wilbur? If Hunter left, did she go with him? She scanned down the page and then flipped to the next one, letting her eyes fall through the text.

There it was.

———

It is easy for Our World. They live outside the cage that the rest of the world lives in. They can make a war start and they can make a war go away. Getting me into a university, Simon Fraser, on a swimming scholarship was child's play for them. No advance notice, I decided after Lois. No warning. I left for Vancouver days before the semester started; no entrance exam.

A thousand miles away from where I'd lived.

A thousand miles away from who I had been.

I was alone for the first time.

Wilbur did not come with me. She said our studies were done; she said she had nothing more to teach me. She said she would always be there when called. Always be there when needed.

I thought she meant always be there for me.

I was wrong.

———

He knew! Nyala dropped the page on the pile in front of her and leaned back against the headboard, stuffing another pillow behind her back as she did and unfolding her legs to stretch them.

He knew. She was right! Charlotte was Wilbur! At least it sounded like he knew. He had to know. Why the hell couldn't he just say it, why did he have to be so friggin' cryptic all the time? It was frustrating.

Nyala reached out and pulled her toes up, stretching. She missed doing yoga, could feel that she was starting to stiffen up from lack of physical activity, and worse, the lack of fresh air was starting to make her chest feel tight, like she was on the verge of getting sick.

Instead of doing anything about it, she crossed her legs again and shuffled through the pages, bypassing the ones she hadn't thought important when she read them the first time on the drive across Canada. When she found the next asterisk, she started reading once again.

31

1977

RUSSIA
UNDISCLOSED LOCATION

How did it happen?" The man with the white beard, barely lighted in the black, dark room, did not betray what he was thinking to the man sitting across the table from him. His face gave no hint of his feelings.

"Smuggling an icon out of Russia."

"To Hungary?"

"Da."

The discomfort evident in the messenger's body language clearly showed he was well aware of his precarious position. In Our World, "I'm just the messenger" was not a form of security.

The man with the white beard was leaning on the table, close to the light; the black room around him was a silent void. He wasn't looking at the other man; he was looking through him, considering the news he'd just been given.

It was not unheard-of for operatives of Our World to engage in private enterprise that wasn't entirely sanctioned by their leader. It happened and it was something that he tolerated within limits.

But a classic Russian icon? That was a different matter.

"Where is he?"

"Butyrka."

The answer wasn't unexpected. Smuggling icons out of the Soviet Union was among the highest of crimes. The operative code-named

Hamlet was lucky it was 1977 and not 1958. As charismatic and intelligent as he might be, as quick as his wit was, had he been caught in 1958 or the years prior, the captured operative would only have been held in the infamous Moscow prison temporarily, awaiting transfer to a gulag, from where there would not have been any hope of release; at least not release from the work camp. Release from life, yes.

Still, even now a stay in Butyrka Prison would not be a pleasurable experience for his operative. The *menti*, or warden, was well-known to all those who moved in the circles of the Russian underworld. The *menti* at Butyrka was known first and foremost for his savage treatment of the *patzani*, the prisoners incarcerated there.

"Kishka?"

"Da."

Operatives of Our World represented long-term investments, and as with any responsible chief executive officer, it was his responsibility to ensure there was a substantial and profitable return on investment. Having an operative locked up in a *kishka*, better known as the "Intestine," was not good for Our World's profit margins. The Butyrka cell called the "Intestine" was so small and vertical, it provided standing room only for the inmate. There was no way to sit or lie down, and it forced the inmate to perform all bodily functions standing up.

The valuable Our World operative incarcerated in Butyrka Prison was right then, for all intents and purposes, a piece of shit caught in the intestine that was the *kishka*.

The man did some calculations, working out the odds that his investment would be lost. Tuberculosis was a real threat, or some other equally debilitating or even more hideous disease communicated from another prisoner locked in the tremendously overcrowded prison where putting one hundred men in a normal cell, designed for ten, was the norm. The *menti* put all those suffering from tuberculosis together in one cell; all those suffering from drug addiction in another; sexual predators, mostly riddled with their own special diseases, also had the pleasure of each other's company.

As important as Hamlet had been to Our World, his judgment had not been sound; he had not lived up to his wise namesake. He'd tried to smuggle an icon out of Mother Russia without the assistance and, more importantly, without the consent of Our World. Obviously the operative had intended to transport it back to his native land and from there to the West for a private sale. The man searched for the answer to the *how* question. The *why* was obvious, for personal gain, but how the operative planned to smuggle the icon to the West was more concerning.

He'd sent out orders for Hamlet to return to Hungary, to meet and indoctrinate the new operative, the young Canadian called Hunter. The plan followed protocol. Hamlet was ordered to reveal to the future operative the truth and teach him about his place inside Our World. How the older experienced operatives did so was left up to them. They each had their own methods of teaching the lessons that would dictate the destinies of the new recruits from that point on. But it was evident now that Hamlet did not intend to follow the orders he'd received. Nor did he intend to follow Our World protocol.

Hamlet likely would have used his considerable persuasive abilities to recruit Hunter to smuggle the icon back to the West, to work together and share profits. The Canadian was grown now, and with his gift would instantly recognize the artistic value of the icon, but would have no way of knowing about Our World, about his future. He would have no way of discerning truth from Hamlet's fiction. He might have joined forces with the rogue operative and the massive investment in the greatest talent to be discovered by Our World since Zhivago would have been lost before his considerable ability could be monetized.

It would have been easy for the leader of Our World to arrange for Hamlet's safe passage with the icon from Russia to Hungary, had there been any benefit to Our World to do so. Soviet customs agents at Domodedovo Airport belonged to Our World. Hamlet would not have missed his Tupolev Tu-124 flight to Budapest and would not now be standing in the *kishka*, but it was clear Hamlet had been working toward his own ends and therefore would pay the price.

He made his decision.

"Leave him there."

"Da."

"The icon?"

"It was a Nikitin."

Hamlet had good taste. A seventeenth-century icon painted by Gury Nikitin, a piece that was fresh to the art world, unknown to the pedantic academics who felt they were somehow divinely granted executive right to all things to do with art, was truly a treasure worthy of the Gathering. It was also apparently a treasure alluring enough to make one of his best operatives go rogue.

He made a note to himself to find out how the icon came to be in Hamlet's hands in the first place. It had to have been found in Moscow, his own backyard. It was impossible that the operative unearthed it on his own, without the help of a local network of contacts; a network that would soon cease to exist, one bleeding throat at a time once he discovered who was responsible.

"Where is it?"

"With Vladimir Terebilov."

"Minister of justice?"

"Da."

He knew of the man. He was a former judge, and from what he'd gleaned over the years, reading the Our World files, a Communist Party member of the first degree, which was generally synonymous with saying "da" to every word uttered by the former leaders, Stalin and Khrushchev. The minister was cut from a different cloth, however; he had never bowed before any previous Soviet leader, in spite of being subjected to the state's number one method for changing minds, an exceedingly effective tool called coercion.

He was a rarity in the Soviet Union, a man of honor who would never bend, or at least he would not if Minister Terebilov recognized the coercion for what it was. It would take finesse, someone the minister would not suspect, someone who could find their way into his mind, into his life, into his bedroom, and finally into his vault in the building housing the Ministry of Justice of the Soviet Union.

He would need to call on his best.

The Nikitin icon, painted by the artist sometime around the middle of the 1600s, lost to the world of art for three hundred years, was already, with Our World's leader's decision, destined to disappear once again, this time from a safe in the Ministry of Justice and this time forever. It was as good as in the hands of the man with the white beard when he spoke the words, sealing the fate of the valuable icon. It was also highly probable that with his decision, the leader of the Supreme Soviet at that time, Leonid Brezhnev, would soon be looking for a new minister of justice.

"Send Charlotte."

"Da."

The messenger at the edge of the light did not move, but he tensed.

It was obvious that he was waiting to be dismissed, waiting to see if there were other instructions. It was just as obvious to the man with the white beard that his minion was thankful Charlotte was not being sent after him, to punish the messenger for bringing the bad news about the incarcerated operative.

But his fear was unwarranted, at least for that day.

With a wave of the leader's hand, the frightened man was dismissed.

The messenger rose quietly, turned, and departed silently into the blackness, like someone who wishes not to awaken a sleeping dragon.

The smell of his fear lingered.

The leader of Our World did not notice the departure; he was already contemplating the forces he'd put into play. It was convenient to have Charlotte back in Russia now, available to do his bidding after all the years she'd spent in the Canadian hinterlands with the boy. Grown now, her former ward, Hunter, was twenty-two years old, and the leader of Our World knew the Canadian was positioned exactly where he needed to be, in Hungary at that exact moment; training for his chosen sport, or so the young protégé thought. Training, yes; for his sport, no.

The leader of Our World knew the water polo tournament in Hungary was the first international trip for the future operative. He knew it because he had personally issued the order to have the athlete chosen by the coach of the Canadian national team. Certainly there had to be the talent and prerequisite skill involved, but like all coaches, judges, and referees at an international level, politics, influence, and money played the most important parts in determining who would and who would not make the traveling national teams and who would win at the competitions and who would not.

Manipulating the coach of the Canadian team had been simple. He'd defected from the Soviet Union, and it was his first year coaching; he was in over his head, barely spoke English, and had no job experience. The leader of Our World understood the young coach had been a player at the 1976 Olympics in Montreal the year before and so, based on all the factors, made the correct assumption that the coach would be far more worried about his job than he would be about who was chosen for the team.

It was time to fully indoctrinate the Canadian; time to reveal to him his future.

He'd chosen Hamlet to mentor the new operative and the reasoning had been sound. The boy was a gifted athlete, and the sport he was involved in was the perfect cover. Hamlet was Hungarian and although he was past his prime, he'd played for their national team for years. The players were gods in the Soviet Bloc countries and were highly regarded in Western Europe as well, next only in celebrity to the professional football players, soccer players to North Americans.

The aquatic national teams from the USSR traveled extensively from East to West and back again in preparation for the World Games and the Summer Olympics, doing so with near autonomy from Soviet meddling. The Iron Curtain was always open for the sports teams. Exit visas came automatically with a simple request to the authorities; travel to the West was not impeded as it was for virtually every other Soviet bloc citizen and travel into the Soviet Union was just as easy for sports teams from the West.

Hamlet should have been a good instructor, the logical choice to provide clarity for the newest and potentially greatest of all Our World operatives.

The leader's brow furrowed as he considered the young Canadian protégé.

Icarus.

The leader had chosen the operational code name Icarus for him after carefully considering the reports from the observers he'd placed to monitor the boy's development over the years since Charlotte returned from her assignment in Canada. He'd grown into a young man and although it was patently impossible for him to ever entirely fit into society, by the start of his second year in university he had seemingly come to understand that he was different and needed to at least be able to conform.

According to the reports, the young man entered the school library at the beginning of the semester and pulled *On Becoming a Person* from the bookshelf. It was written by Carl Rogers, the renowned humanistic psychologist. He finished it and returned it to its place on the shelf and then proceeded to read the works of Jung, Skinner, Piaget, and Pavlov, effectively teaching himself the social skills that were necessary to pass for normal, in Western society at least.

It took him all of one afternoon.

The reports stated that the boy walked into the library a socially dysfunctional misfit and walked out hours later as a well-adjusted university student. From that point forward, the young man excelled at the social skills required to not only fit in, but to be popular. Charisma. Humor. It was simply applied knowledge, but it made the future operative liked by all those he encountered.

The leader of Our World knew those skills were a charade, an act.

Learned behavior.

There was one character trait that was not an act, a trait that the leader took singular notice of in the reports. Confidence. Confidence that the reports said bordered on hubris. Although the young man kept it hidden from those he associated with in the classroom and on the sports team, he could not hide it from the professionals observing him. The future operative had come to understand that he'd been born with special gifts. He'd come to believe that he *was* special, capable of succeeding at anything he put his mind to, capable of succeeding at everything.

The leader knew how justifiable that belief was.

Icarus.

The chosen one who might possibly prove over time to be the best of all the operatives of Our World; the best that had ever been.

Someday the operative would try flying to the sun.

Icarus.

The future operative would never be called Hunter again.

But there was still the issue of what to do now that Hamlet was out of the picture. The man with the white beard knew now that he'd made a mistake choosing the Hungarian to bring Icarus into the fold. Good was not the same as the best. The Canadian was too valuable. As good as the operative known as Hamlet had been before his recent transgression, he was not the best. It was time to correct that miscalculation.

It was time for the protégé to meet Zhivago.

It was time for Zhivago to meet his match.

He reached and pulled the string on the small table lamp that provided the only illumination in the void, casting the space back into blackness, and then in that darkness he sat, satisfied that Our World affairs were once again in order. He relished the darkness. He liked the anonymity of the night, found enlightenment in the shadows.

Hamlet would be standing in a similar inky blackness, not knowing if he would be released from prison by the forces of Our World. The man with the white beard knew his delinquent operative would be pissing himself with the fear that would be his cell mate in the Intestine.

Punishment for smuggling a national art treasure was not what would be the cause of the operative's fear. Nor would he fear his fellow *patzani* inmates and their diseases. Hamlet was strong, an athlete, world-class, and he would certainly be able to withstand the physical tortures meted out by his new *menti* overlord. Nor would the degradation of standing in his own excrement be the cause of his fear; it would be a discomfort, a great discomfort, but discomfort in and of itself was not life threatening. He would know that, deal with it.

But he would never be able to reconcile the fear that would be his constant companion during his stay at the prison, hour after hour, day after day, week after week, month after month, year after year. It would break him; rot his mind from the deepest recesses outward. The operative, standing in his own filth, would know that his real trial would not begin until *after* he'd served his state-ordered time in the prison. He would know his real sentence would not come until he walked out of that prison a free man.

He would know that the leader of Our World would be waiting, to take him into custody, the instant he stepped from the prison.

It was a fear that was justified in every imaginable way, and it was a fear that would be realized in unimaginable ways.

The man with the white beard took great pleasure in knowing that he was the cause of it.

32

2020

SASKATOON, SASKATCHEWAN

Nyala just about jumped out of her skin when the knock on the door disrupted the upside-down world she'd been so engrossed in and, like the operative Hamlet, imprisoned in. She was aware that the longer she lived in that world, the less the chance that she would ever escape; maybe more accurately, the less the chance she would ever want to escape.

The insistent knocking saved her.

The door pushed open before Nyala could reach it.

"Honey! I'm home!" Luba loved Stephen King movies. "Jesus, did you work all day? You look like crap."

Nyala gave her friend the finger and turned to flop back on the rumpled, manuscript-covered bed.

"Love you too."

Luba was carrying a large brown paper bag under one arm and an even larger octagonal box under the other. The first she placed awkwardly on the counter near the door, across from the bathroom, and the second she dropped onto her bed as she walked into the room. "All work and no play makes Ny Ny a dull girl."

Luba didn't have any superpowers, but she definitely had a talent for making Nyala roll her eyes.

"Whatever."

"Got the coolest cowboy hat today! And by the way, Debbie Downer, I brought you a surprise!" Luba walked back to the brown paper bag and pulled a white plastic food container from inside, a container that surprisingly didn't look like it held anything deep-fried. "Ta da! Wonton soup! For me! And for you I got your favorite! Jellyfish!"

Jellyfish was not Nyala's favorite; at least she didn't think so.

"Really? Jellyfish? With venomous tentacles? Is that even a thing you can eat?" Nyala got off the bed to see what it was exactly that her friend was scooping onto the Styrofoam plate from a second plastic container. "It's not raw, is it?"

"Gross. Here." Luba handed Nyala the plate and a set of balsa wood chopsticks. "I found a place on the far side of town called Yip Hong's Dim Sum. I told them I wanted to order the weirdest thing they had on the menu for my weird friend."

Nyala laughed and used the chopsticks to pick a single strip of the jelly-textured sea creature from the plate.

"I'm not that weird."

"Yes, you are. I told them all she does is work and never plays. They agreed with me that you're weird." Luba levered a big wonton dumpling partway into her mouth, straight from the container full of soup, keeping it close to her chin so the back half of the dumpling would fall back into the soup, not on the floor. "And in case you didn't notice, you're the one eating jellyfish. That's weird. What'd you find out? How's your boyfriend with the sores all over his face?"

Nyala had to admit that the jellyfish was pretty good, with a chewy, crunchy texture, a red pepper zing, and a strong oil flavor, probably sesame. Not bad at all. Chalk one up for experimentation.

"It's a really f'd-up story. I haven't had a chance to go back through everything I read in the car though. I think I'm up to about 1977. Did you know the 1976 Olympics were held in Montreal?" Nyala talked with her mouth full, chewing slowly on the cold strands that had once been a jellyfish's mantle, or at least she thought that was the part she was eating. She wasn't up on jellyfish anatomy. She didn't wait for Luba to answer the question before she asked another. "Hey, you're Russian, ever hear of a *kishka*?"

It was Luba's turn to flip the bird to her friend.

"I'm not Russian! I'm Ukrainian!" She was trying to bite another wonton in half and speak at the same time. "But yes. *Kyshka*. Sounds the same but spelled different in Ukrainian; means gut or bowels."

"Intestine?" Nyala didn't expect an answer; it was a rhetorical question. She was asking more to get the facts straight in her head.

"Yep, can be." Luba bit a third wonton dumpling in half, letting the remainder fall into the container to join the leftover halves of the first two wontons.

Nyala didn't doubt for a second that what she'd read was true, that there was a prison cell shaped like a figurative intestine in the bowels of the Soviet prison mentioned in the manuscript. Probably every prison in Mother Russia still had cells like that. Really there wasn't much difference between Russia's present leader, Putin, and the past Soviet Union's leaders.

She set the plate of jellyfish down on the bedside table and picked her cell phone off the bed; old habits die hard. She typed in "Butyrka" and then added "prison."

Mrs. Wikipedia was on the job; a tagline instantly popped up on the top of the page, **"Tverskoy area, Moscow."**

Why had she bothered checking? She knew it was going to be a legitimate prison. And she knew there would be a warden, called a *menti*, and there would be *patzani* incarcerated there. What was the point in researching what she already knew would prove to be true?

"Want to try a wonton?" Luba fished around her plastic container, first picking a wonton she'd bitten in half, but dropping it back into the container and fishing for a second one. It was bitten in half too. "And *no*, I do not want to try your jellyfish! Disgusting!"

"Disgusting as in giving me wontons with your slobber all over them?"

"Yep! Same! You want a wonton or not?"

Nyala accepted the offering, taking it in her fingers and quickly shifting it to her mouth before it could drip, holding her cell phone out to the side in the hand that didn't have Chinese dumpling juice all over it. As she chewed, she was scanning the pages on her bed. When she saw the seventeenth-century Russian icon painter's name, she used her free thumb to type.

"Gary Nikitin." Click.

"Gary Oldman got nicotine poisoning playing Winston Churchill in the new film *Darkest Hour* . . ."

Ha ha. Wrongo, Mr. Google; the Gary she was looking for wasn't from Hollywood.

"Did you know Gary Oldman got poisoned from nicotine when he played Winston Churchill? I think the movie came out a couple years ago?"

Luba loved trivia questions, especially about movies.

"Ooh, ooh! I know! *The Dark Knight*! Great movie! Who's Winston Churchill?" She knew who Winston Churchill was, Nyala was sure of that, or she was pretty sure of that. Luba was fishing another wonton out of the container, trying not to accidentally catch a vegetable.

"*Darkest Hour*, not *Dark Knight*."

Nyala wiped her greasy hand on her jeans and sorted through the pages on the bed with her clean hand until she found what she was looking for again; Gury, not Gary; my bad. Nyala dropped the page she'd just scanned and typed the corrected spelling in the Google bar. It crossed her mind for a moment that she was getting pretty good at speed reading. If she increased her speed by a factor of 1,000 and increased the retention by a factor of 10,000, she would give the kid a run for his money!

"Gury Nikitin (1620, in Kostroma–1691, in Kostroma) was a Russian painter and icon painter."

All true. Of course it was. No surprise there.

Luba was searching for the television remote, still hanging on to her now-wontonless soup container. Nyala scanned another page and typed another word into her Google bar, fully expecting another confirmation.

"Vladimir Terebilov."

Click.

"Vladimir Ivanovich Terebilov was a Soviet judge and politician, who served as justice minister for slightly less than fourteen years."

She reached over to where the plate of unappetizing-looking but tasty Medusozoa sat on the bedside table and used the chopsticks to lever a stringy jellyfish mass into her mouth. She placed the chopsticks on the bedside table that divided her bed from Luba's and wiped the back of her hand across her lips and chin; once a bushpig, always a bushpig. Then she sorted through the pages of the manuscript, looking for the next section that she'd marked for rereading.

Luba's channel-surfing on the television didn't bother her and neither did the volume, although it was loud enough to probably get the guests in the next room upset. Only the manuscript mattered, the story and where the story was taking her.

She sat down on the floor between the two beds, leaned back on her own bed, and started reading.

33

1977

BUDAPEST, HUNGARY

It was easy; too easy. The big Cuban needed money. Cubans always needed money ever since their intrepid rebel commander Castro seized power there. And it was inexpensive, less than one hundred US dollars for the crude rearranging of a face. He was happy to let the Cuban do the brutish work. That wasn't his style anyway. His fun, the elegant final touches, would come in the local hospital. Bribing the doctors and nurses working there cost a little more but not much more. US dollars went a long way in the black market behind the Iron Curtain.

Zhivago shifted his hulking body on the hard bleacher seat, located near midpool in row 15 of the thirty tiers lining each side of the Olympic-sized Bela Komjadi Pool. It was a nice facility, new, only two years old. Being at the pool wasn't the way he would have preferred to spend the afternoon, but he did like that it was located on the Buda bank of Budapest, close to the Castle Quarter, or Varnegyed, where the Royal Palace stood.

He'd made a point of taking in the art and collections held in the palace, the national treasures of the Hungarian state, a state that was not firing on eight cylinders. It had been twenty-one years since the Soviet tanks rolled into the capital city in 1956, bringing with them the inherent disorder and instability of socialist rule. Thanks to Our World connections, Zhivago had been able to enter the palace and walk freely through the archive, a place where normally only the most trusted and highly placed Soviet officials were granted entry.

He'd enjoyed knowing that he was walking the same corridors that King Matthias Corvinus, the original Hungarian Hercules, had envisioned, if not actually constructed during the thirty-two years he ruled Hungary and Croatia; one iron fist firmly holding the reins of the Black Legion, his professional army of mercenaries, and his other fist wrapped around the throats of the countries and peoples he conquered.

The archives smelled of richness and beauty, exquisite beauty. He made mental notes on the pieces that Our World should consider requisitioning—unofficially, of course. There was plenty of time to procure the best of the pieces. The USSR wasn't going anywhere in the near future, although it was already starting to smell of decomposition. Socialist ineptitude and corruption made the job of deaccessioning nationally owned treasures easy.

The entire country was fertile hunting grounds for the operatives of Our World. It was a land filled with hidden treasures and secrets held for hundreds of years. Corvinus and his Black Legion invaded Austria in 1485, sacked Vienna, and returned to Buda with the spoils of that war and a hundred more. The Hungarians were clever people; the soldiers and officers, governmental officials, and even ambassadors did not always tell their master what they brought home with them, to be secreted away and only exhumed in a time of great need.

The crowd around Zhivago rose as one, whistling and jeering. The Yugoslavs scored against the Hungarian home team. Tamas Farago was ejected for some major penalty that only the referee had seen. The whistling did not stop for several minutes. The crowd was growing unruly. Zhivago basked in the displeasure they were feeling, surveying the five thousand or more Hungarian fans watching the match, looking for one who might catch his attention, one who might provide him with the pleasure he required to fulfill his needs.

The shrill whistling did not abate until the referee called a penalty shot against the Yugoslavian player who'd scored the goal against the hosting team. Then the crowd cheered. They did not notice that one among them was not cheering. Their goal was not his goal; he didn't care about the game; he was hunting for prey and while they'd been whistling and pumping their fists at the referees, distracted, he'd sighted his quarry. Robin's-egg-blue dress, simple, Soviet made. She was young; a sweet girl, innocent; exquisite. He could tell she was in love, puppy love with the teenage Hungarian boy beside her. That much was obvious from her shy, furtive glances at him.

He liked young love.

He really liked young love.

It did not occur to him that what he planned to do to the innocent young girl was wrong in any way. People were like rats to him, less than rats; he would not harm a rat. The mere thought of hurting an animal was reprehensible; the thought of a rat suffering in a trap, or a rat dying slowly from the effects of poisoning, filled him with an uncontrollable hatred of anyone who would kill an animal. Thinking about humans suffering in the same way, however, filled him with a deep contentment; he was as passionate about causing human suffering as he was about protecting animal rights.

The hypocrisy of his ideology, knowing that he was wearing a leather jacket and leather shoes, relished fine meals of animal flesh, and consumed the bodies of fish, did not enter his mind. The thought that perhaps he was a mutation or the idea that *he* was the sick one was inconceivable to the man in the bleachers who had already determined how he would pleasure himself that evening.

Zhivago stood from his seat then. The object of his future pleasure, the teenage Hungarian girl in the pretty blue dress, would have to wait for now. The Canadian team would be playing the Cubans next, and he wanted to be down closer to the poolside.

———

They walked like they owned the world, long bathrobes open, untied, tiny bathing suits doing little more than providing the minimum amount of modesty legally required in public. They really were gods. Zhivago considered the blond one walking by him. He was tall, but the Hungarian was taller than he was, and the athlete didn't have Zhivago's barreled-out chest and bloated paunch. Nor was the athlete hirsute like Zhivago; his skin was smooth and tanned and he was built like a gladiator.

It was the smile that told the most about the player. It had a confidence that only those who possessed everything had the right to. This was Gabor Csapo, a defender on the Hungarian team with the good looks of a Hollywood actor.

Zhivago made sure he was in place when the game ended and the two teams, the Hungarians and the Yugoslavs, left the water to walk down the pool deck, headed for their respective changing rooms. The Hungarian No. 10 walked by then, wearing the white cap he'd worn in the water, the only uniform water polo players wore. His hair was long, unusual behind the Iron Curtain, and even more surprisingly, he wore an earring in one earlobe. He was the crowd favorite, Farago.

Built like the first player who walked by, he did not have the features of anyone from Hollywood; instead the Hungarian's features were those of an Aztec. Curious morphology, Zhivago thought to himself, seven thousand miles away from any possible Aztec antecedents and two feet taller than the tallest "Indio." The next player was even more impressive, towering over the first two. Dr. Istvan Szivos, the man who played the center position on the team, was a giant, easily over seven feet tall. He'd scored two goals against the Yugoslavs.

The crowd was on its feet then, clapping for their winning team as the athletes walked in a line down the deck. The Cuban team, lined up as well, walked in the opposite direction. They were playing the Canadians next and passed by the Hungarians as close as was necessary on the narrow pool deck, but not one fraction of an inch closer. To any behavioralist watching, they were like two groups of apex predators meeting at a water hole. Both teams knew it was highly probable that they would meet in the final match.

The Cuban team ran the color gambit from Spanish olive to Nilotic black and it was that team Zhivago was far more interested in. The hulking player leading the team down the deck, toward their end of the pool, was of particular interest. Jesus Perez; sculpted body, black, and 250 pounds of rippling muscle, his six-foot, four-inch frame glistening under the hot afternoon Buda sun. It was a body honed to perfection from years of training in the pool.

It wasn't the training in the pool that interested Zhivago. It was the years Jesus trained in the boxing ring. The multitalented athlete now leading the Cuban team to their staging area on the pool deck had attended the 1968 Olympics in Mexico City, the 1972 Olympics in Munich, and the 1976 Olympics in Montreal as a water polo player, a star, but he could have represented his country as a boxer as well.

"Sorry. Excuse me?" The voice came from behind Zhivago. "Do you speak English? We're going to need to put our bags here."

The man talking to Zhivago was insignificant, red hair, red beard trimmed to expose white cheeks, nothing like the gods walking down the pool deck. His smile similarly was nothing like the smiles on the faces of the Hungarians, who were now almost to their dressing room but were still waving at the adoring fans who'd taken the day to watch the best teams from around the world compete at their national sport. The smile on the little man in front of him was self-effacing, gentle, and honest.

"Would you mind moving over there a bit so our team can get ready?" He was pointing to where he wanted the big man to go, miming the words he was saying, assuming that Zhivago, like virtually all the citizens of the satellite countries falling under the Soviet Union's sphere of influence, would not be able to speak English. The red-haired man was wearing the red and white track suit of the Canadian team, with a small blue DAVID HART stitched above the Canadian maple leaf emblem on the suit. Slightly above where his heart would be, another stitched label said MANAGER.

Zhivago instantly felt heat rise through his heavy body. He hated being told what to do. There was only one person that he obeyed and that was the leader of Our World. Normally he would have made it clear to the little manager that he was nothing but a cockroach, something to be stepped on, but instead he said nothing, just nodded and moved away, looking back over his shoulder at the approaching Canadian team. He was searching for the face he'd memorized from the photos supplied to Our World; photos of the supposed protégé.

Something made him stop and turn fully around then.

He lifted his face, sniffing.

Here? How was that possible?

What was it?

It started as the smallest of signals, a smell but not a smell as anyone else would know it. It was something else, a sense that grew and then overwhelmed him, blinded him to everything except the intensity of the message. It was a primal, primitive reaction, like a creature deep inside him that crawled toward food it sensed was close. The crowd in the stands, the noise, the referee's whistle letting the teams know they had ten minutes to warm up, the smell of chlorine, did not exist for him. Every molecule in his huge frame quivered in anticipation of a feast; there was something close by.

Something exquisite.

His was to grope blindly, to feel in the darkness, like a lurking horror from Lovecraft's beyond. Smelling for the prey he, no it, the creature he became, knew was there but could not see.

Close.

Whatever it was, it was nearby.

Something so exquisite, so perfectly crafted and formed, so brilliantly conceived, the power of the growing signal told him that whatever it was, it was the equal of anything he'd found in his years as an operative for Our World. Zhivago was not in control when the beast was in him. He was taken by surprise at the intensity of its desire. He hadn't been expecting to be on a hunt, hadn't planned for it, wasn't prepared.

It upset his finely tuned sense of self-control.

Every quivering fiber told him that whatever it was, it was near, something he had to possess, something of unimaginable beauty, something that would be his. Slowly, in the heat of the afternoon sun, in the bustle and action of that place, the primeval beast inside him began to sort out the messages, began to focus, to home in on its prey, locate where it was hiding; to expose what it was.

Revelation came to Zhivago at that moment.

It was the watch.

So exquisite. So absolutely exquisite.

It was on the wrist of the arm attached to the body that also possessed the face he'd been looking for, the face from the photos.

Tall, well over six feet, not as tall as the Hungarians who'd walked past, but built the same, muscled in a way that spoke of flexibility and endurance, endless repetition and stamina.

The face was smiling; the same entitled smile the Hungarians wore. Instantly Zhivago was filled with fury. How dare this literal nothing assume he had the right to wear his confidence so blatantly in the presence of greatness? Zhivago was not thinking of the Olympic gold medalists who'd just paraded by; he was thinking of his own greatness, his own power, a power that eclipsed the inane accomplishments of any mere athlete and with absolute certainty eclipsed achievements of the whelp wearing the watch; a watch that was concrete proof that another Our World legend was true.

Zhivago knew the legend well, all the operatives did; it was the missing Rolex Zerographe.

The kid's smile filled him with an insane jealousy then, a hatred that took an effort to control. The only thing that kept him from tearing the watch from the arrogant nobody's arm was the knowledge that the offending smile would soon be gone.

The exquisite watch the Canadian was removing from his wrist and placing in the duffel bag on the pool deck would also be gone.

As was usual when he imagined inflicting pain on a fellow human being, he felt himself growing aroused.

*B*efore you read on, let me explain, Nyala.

   All this you need to know.

What happened. Why it happened.

I did not see it coming.

How could I?

I was twenty-two years old. I was playing a game, a sport. Playing for my country.

Our World did not exist for me then.

Zhivago did not exist for me then.

We were losing to the Cuban team. I passed and crossed, expecting my teammate to pass the ball back.

I did not see the fist coming.

They pulled me from the water and took me in an ambulance to the hospital. My eyes were swollen shut; my nose was smashed, grotesque, a broken mass pushed to the side of my face. I do not remember the drive. I do not remember being prepped for an operation.

But I remember him coming into the room, Nyala. I will never forget that. I was aware by then, strapped down to the bed, my head held in a clamp. My eyelids pulled back and held open with tape. I was alone.

He had a mask on; he was dressed like a doctor. His eyes. A monster.

He leaned over me then, squeezed drops into my own burning eyes, introduced himself; his face so close to my shattered visage that I could feel the heat of his breath.

"Today you will learn some lessons. This is the first. You will know me as Zhivago. I have been chosen by Our World to teach you."

I didn't know what he was talking about. I was in pain, I was in a foreign country, I was alone, more alone than I'd ever been, and

I was held captive with a nightmare that would be mine to honor and obey, in sickness and in health, from that day forth; until death did us part.

"Second lesson. You will live by the rule of Our World."

Yes. I will.

Yes, I did, Nyala.

"Third lesson. You will never keep anything that belongs to Our World. You will go where they tell you. You will do as they say. Anything you need, they will provide. You will be contacted."

There was no bottom to the blackness in those eyes, Nyala.

"Fourth, your old life is dead. You will never return to it. Your name is Icarus. Do not seek out your past. You will never be called Hunter again."

On that day Icarus became a part of Our World, a world nobody knows, other than us and now you, Nyala. On that day an unimaginable force became the only guardian, the only guiding light to the Icarus they created after their own image. Icarus of Our World.

It made no sense to me then. How could it? Like you are no doubt struggling to understand right now, it took time for me to understand; time for me to find my own way. It will take time for you to find your way, Nyala.

I will give you that time. I do solemnly swear.

Zhivago was a good teacher.

"You will never forget what I am teaching you. It is time for your final lesson."

He was facing away from me then and when he turned back, he held two stainless steel rods, a foot long, one quarter inch thick, rounded on the ends. He held those two rods in one hand and with the other he pulled back his sleeve. Even through saline-filled eyes, I could not miss what he wanted me to see. He was wearing my watch.

He said then, "You will never mention Our World."

I have never forgotten that last lesson.

He inserted the two rods into my nostrils with surgical skill, past the deviated septum.

It was primitive. It was how they did it there, in Hungary at the time. How they levered broken nose bones back into place. Cocaine was used, inserted before, to numb the intense pain the cure caused a patient.

But there was no cocaine for me.

There was only his face. His lips were curled up, but it wasn't a smile. It was pleasure.

Deep psychotic pleasure.

"Call me Zhivago. You are nothing."

I didn't know it at that time, I only knew pain.

He was insane. And I was a threat.

Then he rammed the rods through the eggshell-thin wall of my ethmoid sinuses, grinding them around inside my nasal cavities, crushing them. The sound of the thin bones crackling inside my face was the sound of my life being forever changed. Every breath I have taken since, with effort, reminds me of Zhivago's final lesson.

I remember the blood.

I remember screaming, but nobody came.

It was wasted noise. Nobody ever comes to the rescue if Our World does not want them to. They blind and they deafen. They make dumb any and all who might stand in their way.

From that point forward, I was Icarus.

34

2020

SASKATOON, SASKATCHEWAN

Brutal." Nyala shuddered.

That wasn't a lesson. It was torture.

Could it even be possible to do that to someone without killing them?

She read the lines again, trying to recall the skulls she'd seen in her high school science lab. The sinus bones were paper-thin, she remembered, like eggshells, and they would have been easy to damage with something like a screwdriver.

The pain must have been excruciating.

Nyala shuddered again.

Zhivago was one sick human being.

She put the manuscript pages on the floor between her legs and looked over to Luba's bed to see why her friend wasn't saying anything. The television was blaring; some talk show host was asking the skinny, crackhead-looking husband of the enormous bleached-blond woman sitting next to him why he'd decided to sleep with his wife's just-as-enormous sister, who was sitting on the other side of him. Nice. Pretty evident why cable was getting its ass kicked by all the streaming video services available.

Luba was sound asleep on her bed, hand still on the television remote. So much for being able to drink like a fish and go hard the next day. Nyala had to admit it was nice to see that, in spite of all the evidence to the contrary, even Luba was mortal. Although to be fair, it was already late. Nyala reached for the Styrofoam plate.

Taking a mouthful of jellyfish while still holding the plate in one hand and her chopsticks in the other, she turned back to what she had been reading.

———

He didn't kill me. He could have.

One hard shove on the rods and they would have entered my brain.

It was simply a lesson.

Zhivago had no choice but to let me live.

Our World wanted me. Needed me.

He left me then. I passed out. Lesson taught and his point made.

He was Zhivago. I was nothing.

I don't remember the flight back to Canada. I don't remember the surgery done there to repair the damage done to the inside of my broken face, or the weeks of recovery, sedated, Valium and Demerol my only friends in convalescence.

I do remember leaving the hospital and I remember finding my bank account filled with more money than I needed. I remember being contacted by an expediter of Our World, one of the vast support team for the operatives. I have used their services constantly over the years; they are the mechanics, the ones who arrange whatever we, the operatives, need to accomplish our missions.

I didn't know better. I was young. I had no framework to base right from wrong in the real world. No empathy for the damage I was doing, no remorse, no restraint. I was freed from the fetters of conscience.

Havana, Mexico City, New York, Los Angeles, London; flights of fancy. If they wanted me to go, I went. If they wanted me to search archives and museums and arrange to put in place forgeries, replacements for the originals, I would do their bidding. Searching, always searching for the treasures that I eventually learned would make their way to the Gathering.

So many treasures.

So many stories to tell you, Nyala.

You are the only one I have to pass my life on to.

Utrecht, Netherlands, 1977, no 1978, the year after Zhivago taught me all I needed to know about Our World in that hospital room. I need to tell you about The Just Judges, *the missing Jan van Eyck predella panel from the fifteenth-century Ghent Altarpiece.*

The panel, one of the twelve that made up the original polyptych, had been stolen nearly half a century before, but had been located by an Our World operative. I was tasked with authenticating the discovery.

No doubt you will use your computer to confirm what I am telling you.

Ghent was in Belgium, 180 kilometers from where I was in Utrecht, where the team was training. Everything is close in Europe. I paid a friend on the team, Greg Drew, to steal the Dutch flag from the pole outside the training center. I was young still, audacious, and without experience in the art of subtle plans.

I know how all this sounds to you, Nyala. I know you doubt what I am telling you, but you must believe me.

Ask him. Greg will tell you if you want more proof. He may still have the Dutch flag. Or ask the American coach, Monte Nitzkowski. He was there; his whole team was there on the athletes' bus driving from the pool complex to the dormitories when the Korps Nationale Politie, the Dutch gendarmes on their motorcycles, stopped the bus.

Greg and I were on the bus with the American team, the only Canadians. I had held the bus with the American team already on board, for the time it took my teammate to get there with the flag. Someone saw him take it from the pole and called the Dutch police, but the bus departed before they arrived at the crime scene. The American coach was not happy about me holding the departure up but was even unhappier when the police caught up to us, sirens wailing.

It was an affront, the gendarmes' accusations were untrue, at least for Monte's players. He did not tell them about the two Canadian stowaways at the back of the bus. He was a good man and a great coach, who respected the laws of foreign countries, but not as much as he respected boldness and audacity. He knew we had the flag.

Nyala, if he is no longer with us, ask Jon Svendsen or Joe Vargas, players for the US team. They were both there.

The gendarmes let the bus go; they did not want to be responsible for an international incident, but our Canadian team was put on curfew, as I knew it would be. No team meetings; I was free to steal away for the night.

I was there in Ghent before midnight; only a problem reading the map going through Antwerpen kept me from being there even earlier. Maps were not on a phone at that time, Nyala. Phones were not in a car at that time either and cars were not driven by computers.

Brown and brown.

It was not the original panel, or at least it was not the complete original. There were elements. Elements I could feel in color, but not see. It was a hyper-restoration, partially authentic and partially a fake. The panel had been stolen in 1930, probably damaged a decade later, during the Second World War, maybe from water where it had been hidden in a cellar, far from the searching eyes of the Dutch authorities and then from the Nazis.

It wasn't a forgery exactly, but it was the work of a forger, Jef Van der Veken. I recognized his deft touch at once. The damaged layers had been removed and the original preparatory foundation left as the base for the restoration. It was the base that confused me. It was authentic, with hints of the original beauty, muted in nearly indiscernible colors that softened the brown and brown.

It was odd to me that the operative who found it, code name Joan of Arc, had been fooled so completely, could not feel what I did when I beheld the panel, could not see the obvious, that the muted colors were all that was left of the original work. Could not tell it was only partially authentic. It was beautiful, Van der Veken's work always is, but it was not an international art treasure.

To be fair, Goering, a Gruppenfuhrer of the Sturmabteilung, lieutenant general of Hitler's Storm Detachment, fell for the same master forger's work. He paid three hundred kilograms of gold for twenty reworked and virtually worthless masterpieces.

I wonder if that mistake crossed his mind when he closed his teeth on the potassium cyanide pill.

I called her Joan, and you will too. She didn't know any of this because she didn't grasp the contents of books, the history of art like I did; she didn't have my gifts, which by then I fully recognized and embraced but showed nobody, except other operatives.

I liked her. She was a good operative, very good, but not the best. Not Zhivago. Not me. She loved beauty, felt beauty like I did, but she told me it wasn't colors, it was a type of serenity, a peace that settled over her when she was close to a beautiful object.

The hyper-restored panel was not valueless, but it was not priceless; it was not for the Gathering. We left it in her rented flat, to be picked up by an expediter of Our World and disposed of according to the wishes of the leader. I had time before I needed to return to the team, so we drove to the St. Bavo Cathedral, where the eleven remaining original altarpiece panels are installed, off-limits for most, but with Our World influence, not us.

We entered the quiet holy place and opened the panels to reveal the eleven originals that are the artistic link between the Middle Ages and the Renaissance. Then, as the moon rose above the darkened homes of Ghent, we washed ourselves in the resplendence of the Ghent Altarpiece, her in a deep tranquil peace and me bathed in the reflected colors of ten thousand rainbows.

We became our own aureole.

———

Aureole? Nyala stopped reading and twisted around, placing the pages she was holding on the bed behind her. Then she pulled out her phone to ask Siri what an aureole was, although she had a strong suspicion that the word had something to do with sex. She was wrong. Dirty minds are us. **"A circle of light or brightness surrounding something, especially as depicted in art around the head or body of a person represented as holy."**

It had nothing to do with sex.

It had everything to do with love.

Enlightened, Nyala stood up to go to the bathroom sink to wash her hands. She hadn't been able to pick the last few pieces of jelly-fish from the Styrofoam plate using the chopsticks while she read, so she'd resorted to using her fingers, her favorite way of eating anyway. Bushpig style. As she passed by where Luba was still sleeping as soundly as a baby without a care in the world, Nyala was envious. Must be nice.

After she dried her hands and returned to the bed where the pages were scattered from one side to the other, she noticed two things: first that it was a full moon, the Child Moon, and the second that the television shows after midnight were just as bad as the ones before midnight.

She would have turned the obnoxious squawk box off, but Luba had rolled over and was now lying on top of the remote. Nyala knew that trying to move her tiny friend when she was in a deep sleep wasn't going to happen, not without a two-thousand-pound winch and a couple of horses. For some reason that defied physics, Luba turned into lead when she slept. It was simpler for Nyala to turn her own mind off than try to move Luba.

She sat on the edge of the bed and gathered up the pages she'd been reading, determined not to do any more reading or researching. She needed sleep. Nyala stared at the pages for a full minute, fighting an internal battle.

Argh.

The jellyfish she'd been eating had more backbone than she did. She'd tried to ignore what Tsau-z had said: "*No doubt you will use your computer and confirm what I am telling you.*"

As hard as she had tried not to, in the end there was no use. It wouldn't be her first all-nighter. She put the pages back on the bed, picked up her phone, and typed. "Ghent Altarpiece of The Just Judges." Click.

One thing that was really starting to irritate her about Tsau-z was how he seemed to predict her reactions and what her triggers were.

Predictable was not a compliment.

It was in the top ten of the character traits she disliked most about herself.

"*The Just Judges* or *The Righteous Judges* is the lower left panel

of the Ghent Altarpiece, painted by Jan van Eyck or his brother Hubert van Eyck between 1430 and 1432."

There it was. She'd confirmed it, just like he said she would. Great, predictable.

Nyala put her phone down and again picked up the pages she'd been reading.

*M*emories, so many returning to me now as I write to you, Nyala; they are like old friends, old friends that I want you to meet.

Bucharest, the 1981 Summer Universiade, another memory. The World Student Games. My hand was broken, something even Our World could not have foreseen happening, something even they could not fix in time, so I was unable to go. Water polo players need to use their hands and I was cut from the traveling team at the last moment.

Nicolae Ceauşescu, the president of Romania, opened the event.

We had been scheduled to meet in the village of Lăpuşna after the games. Both he and Elana desired to be invited to the Gathering and as a show of goodwill to Our World, they agreed to meet with me, to arrange for the icons covering the interior of the Mânastireâ Sfântul Nicolae to disappear. A monastery, built in 1739, with an interior that was painted by the hand of man, but composed by God. A secret kept from the world by the Transylvanian forests, it was beyond color, beyond comprehension, so deeply brilliant. The meeting never happened. It couldn't; I wasn't there in 1981. I did go there with the intention to complete that unfinished Our World business in 2009.

But I could not make myself do it, Nyala. It was my conscience. The icons were too perfect where they were. Those colors.

The monastery remains original.

Elana and Nicolae attended the Gathering the next year and many years after, until they were executed. Did you know the name Nicolae means Victory of the People? Their money has been missed by Our World.

Beyond arranging the iconography within the monastery to vanish, when the athletic competition was over I was assigned the task of locating and obtaining the legendary Doamnă Albastru, *the famed Romanian artist Ştefan Luchian's painting of Lady Sapphire. His greatest work. And believe I would have, if my hand hadn't been broken.*

If I'd gone to Bucharest in 1981.

It bothered me, Nyala. I was driven to be the best at everything. I wanted to be the best Our World operative and wanted to find that mythical work of art. It has not been found to this day, although I have searched for the last forty years. Even the Romanian Ion Țiriac could not help me locate the painting. I asked him about it in 2017. Wolfgang Porsche, the automobile manufacturer, was there with Ion. We met up outside Queenstown, New Zealand; they flew in on Ion's jet because it was bigger than Wolfgang's.

I thought there might be a chance that word of the Luchian painting would have reached Ion after all these years, but I was wrong. Ion called Nadia Comăneci during our dinner together, but she knew nothing of the painting.

My flaw, one of many: the inability to accept failure, to stop searching for the Luchian.

Until a job is done, until everything is in order, until every great work of art is in its place, I am incapable of letting go. Ever.

Ion is an interesting man but has never been invited to the Gathering. He is a hunter. Did you know that, Nyala?

I suspect not.

35

He did it again! So irritating!

"He is a hunter. Did you know that, Nyala? I suspect not."

That's rude. What the hell did he know about what she knew? Or didn't know? Zero. Nothing. Nada.

But that wasn't what was pissing her off. It was the fact that he was right again: she didn't know the guy was supposed to be a hunter. In fact, she had no idea who he was at all. She set the page down on the bed and reached for her phone. Punched in "Ion Ţiriac." Click.

"Ion Ţiriac, also known as the Braşov Bulldozer, is a Romanian businessman and former professional tennis and hockey player." She read further. **"Winner of the 1970 French Tennis Open. Played hockey in the 1964 Winter Olympics. Sports agent of tennis star Boris Becker. Born in Transylvania, nickname 'Count Dracula.' First made international sports scene as a child ping pong champion."**

Nyala frowned. Another superkid apparently, a talented athlete. Who was this guy?

"Net worth $2.2 billion."

Wow!

She thought about it for a moment. The other guy at the dinner, Wolfgang Porsche, had to be associated with Porsche cars, but there was another strange name that didn't ring a bell. Nyala skimmed over the pages until she found what she was looking for.

She typed in the name. "Nadia Comaneci." Click.

"Nadia Elena Comăneci is a Romanian retired gymnast and five-time Olympic gold medalist."

Nyala whistled under her breath. Whoever this Nadia girl was, she was the real deal.

"In 1976 at the age of 14, Comăneci was the first gymnast to be awarded a perfect score of 10.0 at the Olympic Games."

"That's cool." Nyala said it out loud this time.

"What is?" Luba rolled over and stretched, then reached under her side and pulled the television remote out from where she'd been warming it like a mother bird on a nest. She stared at it for a moment and then hit the mute button. "What's cool? What time is it? I feel like crap."

"Ever hear of Nadia Comăneci?"

"Seriously?" Luba sat up now, letting her legs hang over the edge of the bed. Her feet didn't touch the floor. She was watching the television screen, yawning. "Who hasn't heard of her? What time is it? I'm still tired."

Nyala felt a little dumb.

"Okay, Einstein, what about . . ." She searched through the pages until she found it. "Nicolae and Elena . . . Cew-u-see-cu?"

"Ceauşescu. Nic-o-li Chow-shess-ko." Luba didn't bother to turn around. "It's pronounced 'Chow' as in chow like your jellyfish and 'shess' like chess with a 'shhhh' in front of it, as in shhhhh, I'm going to watch TV, and 'ko' at the end, as in duh."

Luba was snickering at her own joke.

"Very funny. So who were they?"

Luba turned from the television and looked at her friend for the first time.

"Are you kidding me? You don't know who they are?" She tapped the back of her hand to her forehead, signing a capital *L*.

Nyala rolled her eyes.

"I'm sorry if I'm not Ukrainian royalty. Please forgive me, Princess Luba."

"Pryntsesa. It's Harna Pryntsesa Luba to you." Luba was smiling as she turned back to the TV and started channel-surfing again. The sound was still off. "Beautiful Princess Luba."

Nyala smiled. Cute.

Instead of waiting for her friend to reengage, she typed the name into her phone. "Nicolae Ceausescu." Click. She chose the Wikipedia link and quickly scanned the page.

"**Romanian. Born 26 January 1918. Died 25 December 1989.**"

Christmas Day? Who dies on Christmas Day? She jumped ahead, scrolling down to "Death," and started reading.

"**Found guilty and sentenced to death. Demanded to die together. The Ceaușescus were executed by a gathering of soldiers. The firing squad began shooting as soon as they were in position against the wall. Nicolae sang 'The Internationale.'**"

Ugh. That's violent; romantic too in a macabre way; not exactly a happy ending for two art collectors who were supposedly regulars at Our World's big Gathering shindig. It seemed that happy endings were not part of the program for Our World.

Out of curiosity, Nyala clicked on the link for "The Internationale," the song the guy had been singing when he was executed.

How much of our flesh have they consumed?
But if these ravens, these vultures
Disappear one of these days
The sun will still shine forever.

Okay, way too heavy; but pretty impressive that the guy had the strength of will to sing while he faced the firing squad.

"**General Secretary of the Communist Party from 1965–1989. Last Communist leader of Romania.**"

Enough. However important these people were in the greater scheme of things, they weren't important in her scheme of things. She exited out of the screen and turned to sort through the mess on her bed, looking for the page with the names of the Hungarian water polo players. Then she changed her mind and grabbed her laptop.

For a moment she considered asking Google if there had been an icon-smuggling Hungarian water polo player, code name Hamlet, sent to prison in Soviet times, but quickly dismissed the thought. No way. Even Scott would have trouble accessing historic records from the Cold War days. Those commie guys were way too secretive; Putin probably destroyed all the files anyway.

Instead she typed in "Hungarian water polo team history."

"Whoa!" Nyala didn't bother clicking on Mrs. Wikipedia's offering; instead she clicked on the blue **"Images for Hungarian water polo team."**

"Hey, Luba! Check it out!" She turned the laptop to the side so her friend could see it too. "Hungarian Hercules here we come!"

"What? Oh my God!" Luba twisted off her bed to get a closer look at the images and jumped onto her friend's bed, brushing manuscript pages and Nyala's notes out of the way so she could lie on her stomach. "That's what I'm talking about!"

That was what Luba was *always* talking about.

They were clicking and googling, having fun oohing and aahing at the Speedo-clad bodies on the screen, when the hotel phone on the desk rang.

They both jumped, startled, but didn't have time to get up and answer. It only rang twice and then stopped.

"Who the heck phones at this time of the night?" Nyala picked up her cell phone, shocked when she saw that she'd nearly worked the night away. "Jesus, it's already almost five."

"Probably want to make the room up because of your stupid sign," Luba huffed.

Nyala always left a Do Not Disturb sign on the door when she was in a hotel room, any hotel room, no matter how many days she was staying. Last thing she wanted was someone creeping through her private stuff.

"Way too early. Can't be the television, it's muted."

Luba wiggled up from where she'd parked herself on Nyala's bed when the phone started ringing again.

"Don't you dare look at any more pictures until I get back!" Luba lunged to get the phone before it stopped ringing the second time, stepping as quickly as she was able around her own rumpled coat lying on the carpet. "Hello."

She listened, put the phone receiver down on the hotel room desk, and returned to her spot on Nyala's bed.

"It's for you."

"Who is it?" Nyala was frowning.

"How should I know? Some guy." She pulled the laptop closer so she could see the images on the screen better. "On a scale of one to ten, every single one of these guys is hot!"

Nyala wasn't listening. She was still frowning. Who would be calling her here? Scott? What time was it there? No, he would call her mobile. Her boss? Did Scott tell him where they were? But Scott didn't know where they were.

Then who?

She picked up the receiver.

"Hello?"

Then she froze; froze in place; froze to her very core.

It was Tsau-z.

36

2020

HIGHWAY BETWEEN SASKATOON, SASKATCHEWAN, AND CALGARY, ALBERTA

Pronghorn antelope, the prairie speedsters, raced across the flat white land that seemed to end only at the farthest edge of Nyala's vision, the soft boundary where the unfathomable blue sky began and wrapped back overhead and in every direction. Occasionally the highway would dip into a ravine, a coulee, choked with wild rose and wolf willow in the low spots. In those brush-filled drainages there were mule deer and once even a coyote trotted off, looking back over its shoulder, ready to hit high gear if the vehicle slowed and a window started to roll down.

The highway from Saskatoon to Rosetown, the first seventy or so miles they'd driven through during the dawn half-light, had been aspen parkland interspersed with sandhill pastureland and arable farmland, pretty much the same type of mixed prairie topography that they'd driven through from Winnipeg to Saskatoon only a few days before.

It seemed like so long ago now; a thousand new thoughts ago, a thousand new unknowns ago.

The road ahead cut the white prairie landscape clean and so straight to the distant interface between land and sky that it appeared God himself had taken a cleaver to the Canadian plains.

Lines furrowed her brow, partially because she was leaning her head against the cold window, but mostly because she was concentrating. She hated loose ends, and right then it seemed like her life had become a frazzled ball of nothing but loose ends. Loose ends like the name Eva Mendel Miller, the artist whose scrapbook of drawings the young Hunter, Icarus, found with Charlotte. And loose ends like the Mendel Art Gallery. Nyala would have liked to check the place out while they were in Saskatoon, or at least see where the building originally stood before the gallery was shut down.

It seemed to Nyala that being physically close to where the diminutive artist had walked, lived, and breathed would somehow bring order to the chaos. Even if it was only in spirit, she wanted to be close to someone who knew Kandinsky, the Guggenheims, all of them; to stand in the same spot where someone who had been an integral part of the international art world had stood; the art world that was consuming Nyala's life, propelling it forward into the unknown.

Loose ends, too many; she hadn't had time to properly do her research. She'd wanted to locate the descendants of Eva Mendel Miller as well, wanted to speak to someone who knew her, was close to her, and for some reason she really wanted to personally see the artist's paintings. Not just see one. Nyala wanted to possess one of her paintings. Somehow the trials and tribulations of Miller's life, from her childhood in Germany, the forced exodus to avoid the coming dark age, the New York art circle sojourn, and then ultimately the move to a small city in the wilds of Canada spoke to Nyala. It was as if, by owning one of Miller's paintings, Nyala could possess a tiny part of the artist.

When she had good cell reception earlier in the drive, as they'd passed through a town called Vanscoy and without really thinking about what she was doing, or at least before she organized her thoughts properly, she'd sent a text to Scott to get him to find out if Ion Țiriac, the Romanian, the multitalented athlete and billionaire who was apparently the friend of Wolfgang Porsche and Nadia Comăneci, actually owned a private jet, a big one, and if he'd flown to Queenstown, New Zealand, back in 2017.

She looked down at her notebook, open on her lap to the POSSIBLE FACTS page, and was suddenly overcome with the depressing overwhelmingness of it all, if there was even such a word. Had to be, because that is exactly how she was feeling. The main column was filled with the shaky notes she'd been making since they departed from Saskatoon two hours before.

Bela Komjadi Pool. Unconfirmed.

Hungarians invaded Austria and took Vienna in 1485. Unconfirmed.

Hungarian king called Corvinus somehow related to Hercules. Unconfirmed.

Hercules? Might as well add the Easter bunny to the list.

Gabor Csapo. Hungarian water polo god. Unconfirmed.

Tamas Farago, Aztec water polo player on the late 1970s Hungarian team. Unconfirmed.

Dr. Istvan Szivos, seven-foot-tall monster in a Speedo. Unconfirmed.

Cuban boxer and water polo player, three-time Olympian named Jesus Perez. Unconfirmed.

International water polo tournament in Budapest 1977. Unconfirmed.

Nyala smiled when she read the next line, the only one in the POSSIBLE FACTS line that had a checkmark in the CONFIRMED column. In fact, it had four checkmarks and a heart.

Water polo players have the hottest bodies of all the male Olympian athletes. Confirmed.

Not only was it confirmed by Nyala, from personal Google creeping experience, and witnessed by Luba, but two extra clicks on the computer a few hours before had proved their opinions were in fact truth. The male nine-foot-tall headless bronze statue gracing the Olympic Gateway Arch installed in 1984 at the entrance to Los Angeles Memorial Coliseum was an anatomically correct, except for the missing-head part, figure of a superhunk water polo Olympian by the name of Terry Schroeder. He was captain of the USA Water Polo team that year and of all the water polo players in the world, already considered to possess the ultimate male physiques, his was the most ultimate.

Very anatomically correct, from what Nyala had seen with Luba when they'd expanded the photo on the screen. They'd expanded a bunch of photos on the screen, and in their female-centric opinions, any of the water polo players in their tiny tight bathing suits could have posed for the sculpture. Nyala giggled when Luba suggested that the sculptor should have made an entire team of naked water polo players for the stadium, instead of just one.

Up ahead a raven, feeding on the mangled carcass of a jackrabbit lying on the centerline of the highway, hopped up and down to gain speed for takeoff, playing chicken with the approaching Mercedes for as long as it dared. The big black bird was not transformed into an explosion of black feathers, but it was close; probably a lot closer than the raven expected. The sleek bird no doubt timed his exit based on previous experience, so it wasn't prepared for how quickly the white rocket ship closed the distance.

Nyala envied the raven, envied that its only worry was where to find food and its fun was playing dodgeball death with cars making their way across the boundless Canadian prairie. *Boundless.* She liked the word and imagined being boundless as she watched the raven flapping to gain altitude, working into the wind, already banking to return to its mechanically tenderized meal.

Nyala watched the prairie pass by. She was so tired. The poplar bluffs were behind them; the part of the Saskatchewan they were passing through was as flat and featureless as a vast white tabletop. She turned away from the window and looked down at her notes again. As tired as she was, she focused on the task at hand.

Jan van Eyck, artist of the Ghent Altarpiece, a 15th-century work of art called *The Just Judges*. Unconfirmed.

Jef Van der Veken, forger. Unconfirmed.

Goering gave 300 kilograms of gold for fake Belgian paintings. Unconfirmed.

USA water polo coach 1978, Monte Nitzkowski. Unconfirmed.

Jon Svendsen and Joe Vargas, water polo players USA 1978. Unconfirmed.

She took a deep breath and exhaled slowly. What a mess.

Stefan Luchian, Romanian artist. Unconfirmed.

She paged through her notebook, looking for any POSSIBLE FACTS that she'd missed, any notes she'd made on the drive from Ottawa to Saskatoon but hadn't added to the official list yet. She stopped when she came to the page of her own roughly written reminders.

"Check if the president of Ecuador and wife were killed in a plane crash in the early 1980s. And see if something called a Raimondi Stele is a big stone carving, old as the hills."

The president of Ecuador? Plane crash? And what the hell was a Raimondi Stele? She needed more time to research.

She added the lines to the POSSIBLE FACTS column and then paged back through the manuscript, frowning. Her notes reminded her that she'd read about Tsau-z being in Guayaquil, Ecuador, in 1982, assigned to help Zhivago.

"They were looking for a legend, the second of the most sacred Chavin Culture artifacts, the deity in apotheosis, the Staff God holding his instruments of power, the Raimondi Stele."

There it was. She'd underlined the lines in the manuscript when she read it the first time.

Apotheosis? Nyala reached for her phone. Two bars. Good enough. She typed the word in. Click. **"The elevation of someone to divine status."**

Okay. Apotheosis it is.

She frowned again. She remembered reading that something happened in 1982, in South America. Something happened to Tsau-z or Icarus to make him rethink what he was doing for Our World. She looked at the manuscript and started reading.

It was there that I first started to consider the actions of Our World.

It was there that I first questioned my own actions.

Somebody killed Roldos, the president, and his wife the year before my arrival. The Ecuadorian minister of defense died in that plane crash as well, on the border between Ecuador and Peru, throwing the country into chaos.

Our World comes alive in strife, feeds on the famine of war; breathes the smoke of a scorched earth. Chaos is their calling card. The best way to remove art from a country is when that country is at war.

Did Our World orchestrate the tragedy?

It is always Our World, Nyala.

Was it possible? Were they willing to go to that length to find and bring pieces of art to the Gathering? Would they start a war? Nyala scanned the rest of the page and then flipped to the next one, looking for something. There it was, another section she'd underlined.

When Zhivago searched, he did not just search for Our World. He searched for his own pleasure.

I saw the young boy in the village.

I saw what he did to him.

It sickened me.
For the first time I ignored his lessons.
I left.
I turned my back on that chapter of my life and started again *then, Nyala; as far away from Zhivago as I could.*

———

Nyala let the page drop back to her lap. It was too much.

Depressed, she stared down at the notebook and the pages from the manuscript lying on her lap until she started to feel carsick and then lifted her head to look out the front window. The cell tower gave her an idea. She pulled her phone out, checking for reception. Four bars.

She hit the camera icon, held the camera over the POSSIBLE FACTS page in her notebook, and snapped a photo. Within seconds she had the photo on the way to Scott.

CAN'T TALK.

NEED THESE FACT-CHECKED.

She sent the last text and immediately felt better, like a weight had been lifted from her shoulders. She didn't want to do the work as they drove; she wanted to keep rereading the pages she'd glossed over on the fuzzy road trip from Ottawa to Saskatoon.

She closed her notebook.

"Oh, so look who comes crawling back." Luba took her eyes off the road and glanced over at her friend. "Decided to join the rest of us in the fun box, have we?"

She knew Luba was being sarcastic. It couldn't have been fun for her to sit there, driving quietly while Nyala worked. It must have taken every ounce of Luba's minimum allotment of self-control not to have been blabbering the whole time Nyala was trying to focus, reading and making notes.

"You going to tell me or not?" Luba turned back to watch the road, a fundamental necessity at the speed she was traveling.

Staying on the pavement was the issue, not avoiding oncoming traffic. Nyala was pretty sure she could see the town of Beiseker, Alberta, across the prairie flatness, still at least a two-hour drive ahead of them.

"I already told you."

It was true, Nyala already had told Luba, just not everything.

"Really? You expect me to believe that's all he said? Just go to Vancouver? Don't worry, your friend Luba will drive you. Nothing more?"

She knew Luba wasn't impressed; she also knew Luba was well aware that her passenger wasn't telling the whole truth, nothing but the truth, so help her God.

Nyala was a crappy liar.

Instead of answering, she turned her head to look out the side window, trying to ignore her friend.

Even in the daylight, the white and blue world looked so empty, like she often felt. There were barbed-wire fences to keep things in and out, she supposed; and there were the gray weathered remains of old wooden snow fences, designed to block the drifts. Fields of stubble, miles and miles of it, just barely poking up through the snow, gave the white emptiness a golden sheen as the midmorning sun washed the cold land in rays that held no warmth. Another black raven speck against the distant sky was the only sign of life.

"So let me get this straight. This guy somehow figures out where you're staying, calls you up out of the blue, and doesn't say anything to you while I drool all over your computer looking at hot water polo studboy photos?" Luba wasn't about to let it go. "He takes all that time to tell you that you need to leave the hotel and drive a thousand miles farther west? Really? You suck at lying. We're officially done being friends."

Luba huffed, reached down and turned on the radio, then reached down again two minutes later and turned the volume up. She turned the volume up two more times in the next five minutes, making the motion even more exaggerated with each effort. The vehicle was vibrating with the bass hammering at full volume. Even the fancy Mercedes speakers were struggling with the wattage.

Then Luba reached and turned off the radio.

"I'm sorry. What did you say?"

"I didn't say anything."

Luba wasn't sorry, and truth be told, Nyala barely noticed the whole drama-girl routine. She'd been thinking.

Thinking of how she could tell her friend that the voice on the other end of the phone line told her that he'd been watching over her for some time. That he'd followed her and knew her routines. That he'd dropped off the manuscript at her house. That he'd anticipated her decision to go to Saskatoon. That he'd watched her go into Dottie's home and been in the library with her.

How could she not have noticed him there?

It was all too crazy-sounding.

Not that in the back of her mind she didn't have some inkling that Tsau-z had to have been crawling around her life. There were too many first-person references in the manuscript, like he was talking to her directly and knew her well. He was too familiar with her.

When she hung up, she had been in shock. She didn't want to talk about any of it and hadn't even told Luba who was on the other end of the line. Instead, she told her friend to pack up; they were leaving for Vancouver. Now. She'd gathered her few things and checked out, making notes in the lobby while she waited for Luba to gather her much larger pile of clothing together, including her new cowboy hat.

If she could have run away, in any other direction, she would have. But there was no safe direction to run other than forward. To run from the future, to go back now, would be a death sentence. Worse, it would be returning to the purgatory that had been her life. She was being followed, stalked by a guy who was admittedly a murderer and very likely an art thief and smuggler to boot. His name was Hunter. His name was Icarus and his name was Tsau-z, and doing as he said, following his instructions, was her future.

Nyala at least let Luba know before they left that it had been Tsau-z on the phone, but she knew she was going to have to say something more. Blind faith in their friendship or not, she deserved to know the last two things Tsau-z had said to her.

She looked over at her friend then.

"Luba, I'm sorry." She reached out and touched her shoulder. "He warned me. He said they were looking for me, coming for me. He said they have always been looking for me."

"Holy crap! No way? Who the hell is 'they'?" Luba checked her rearview mirror and the Mercedes increased speed ever so slightly. "Why would they, whoever they are, want to look for you?"

"I don't know. That underworld art group, I guess. He calls it 'Our World' in the manuscript."

"Why? It makes no sense; you're cute and everything, but not that cute. Maybe a long-lost aunt died and left you a fortune in art! Maybe they just want to find you to tell you you're rich!"

Nyala didn't answer and knew Luba didn't expect one. Luba was a true friend, looking out for Nyala's well-being, letting her know that they were in it together and doing what she could to make the gravity of the situation less sinister with her quirky humor. Humor in the face of adversity. The way of the warrior was not only for those going into battle; it was for anyone who was brave, anyone facing any enemy; anyone looking out for a friend.

"Why did he tell you to go to Vancouver?"

Nyala knew it was coming. Her head started to ache and she felt the familiar darkness closing in on her. The white land and bright sky dimmed and started to blacken until the only pinpoint of light was straight ahead, the highway that disappeared into the distance.

"He said I have to go there . . ." She paused, willing the tunnel to stay open. "He said I have to go there to be a witness. He said I have to bear witness at a funeral."

Tears began to flow from her eyes, blurring even the tiny pinpoint of light ahead of her, the future, the hope that at the end of the tunnel, she would find her truth.

"My grandmother; he said it was my grandmother's funeral."

37

1985

VANCOUVER, BRITISH COLUMBIA

Ron Gruber was a man who kept his word, salt of the earth, and the operative Joan of Arc knew that. He was also the one who happened to be in possession of the Our World legend, the "Ellis brants" that she'd been on the trail of for months. She'd been working the folk art circles in the east of Canada and stumbled upon her first pair of Billy Ellis carved duck decoys accidentally, a pair of pintails in a flea market she stopped at while she searched for clues to the whereabouts of the carver's legendary pair of low-head "brants." She'd fallen under the pintails' spell. They were stunningly beautiful, and she'd swooned before the colorful drake and hen's perfect simplicity.

She purchased those first two decoys and five other exceptional examples of Ellis's work since finding the first pair, none worthy of the Gathering and certainly not the famed "brants," but all were significant and important. When he was alive, Ellis produced commercial-grade carved decoys like those in her possession, to pay bills, but like all great artists who cultivated creativity, sometimes he produced work that had been germinated deep within his soul; work that was not produced simply to supply a demand.

She kept those seven Ellis decoys close to her, to keep the sense of the artist's greatness fresh, and like a hound on the trail of a rabbit, she'd been relentless in her search for his brants. It was in Ellis's hometown, Whitby, Ontario, that she'd learned of the existence of a trunk supposedly containing a "dusty old bunch of wooden decoys" according to an elderly lady who thought she recalled seeing them at a flea market. She remembered that they had been found in a shed by a member of the family from Toronto who purchased the old Ellis property years after the original family moved out.

She was incorrect about the flea market part. The trunk had actually wound up at a local community fund-raiser where another sweet local lady who'd organized the event told Joan that an immigrant man, Eugene from Ukraine, bought it. Joan found the Ukrainian, but Eugene didn't live in Whitby any longer. He didn't even live in Ontario; he'd moved to the west coast of Canada, so the operative did what she'd been trained to do: she followed the scent to the end of the trail.

The helpful Ukrainian man, not immune to the very evident attributes of the tall goddess who'd knocked on his door, didn't have a clue why she asked, but he did remember the trunk and the decoys. He said he bought the trunk at a rummage sale in Ontario for five dollars, because he needed it to pack his things in. He informed her that he'd sold all the carved wooden decoys at his own garage sale before he drove across Canada; sold them all except for two, he added. Those two were bigger, fancier than the others, "black and white," he said, "with short stubby necks," and added that he'd lugged them across Canada for some stupid reason that he couldn't explain, even to himself.

Eugene pointed back inside his home, saying this new place was smaller, had even less room than his old house in Whitby, so he'd been forced to sell off some of his excess belongings at another garage sale.

"No," he'd confirmed, he hadn't sold the two decoys at the garage sale, but there was a guy who came by early on the day of the sale and was asking about old hunting and fishing gear. So, since it was raining and wasn't busy yet, he'd taken the guy inside the house and shown him the decoys. The guy wanted them and offered him one hundred dollars for the pair. But Eugene said he didn't take the offer. The carved ducks were growing on him, even though he could have used the money.

"Do you want to come in for a coffee?"

Hopeful was the way Joan would have described the question.

"Really, I can't." She had tried to sound sincere. "I only have so much time. Did he come back?"

Eugene explained that thankfully the guy left him his phone number, so when he was let go from his construction job and things got tight just a few weeks ago, he'd called the guy, who drove out that same day and paid for the birds. Yes, he thought he still had the phone number in the notepad by his phone. Did she want to come in while he looked for it? His advance this time was verging on pathetic, but she took it as she always took the many unwanted invitations she received: with a gentle, understanding smile of appreciation, but also with an unequivocal "No, thank you."

Advances that she wanted were a different matter. She may have been protective of her mutilated body and, probably because of her experiences in South Africa as a young girl, should have abhorred the male touch, but she enjoyed using her body for pleasure upon occasion. She enjoyed changing the look on the face of whoever she'd chosen to see her naked from revulsion at first sight to pure and unadulterated ecstasy.

She felt a small pang of pity for the unwitting Ukrainian man named Eugene.

He returned from the interior of his tiny house and handed her a sheet of paper, torn from a scratch pad. There was a number and a name, Ron Gruber, written on the page in a heavy hand. There was also a second phone number, the numbers larger than the first, with Eugene written in capital letters. He informed Joan that he'd included it "just in case you change your mind."

She never would.

Rather than ruin his day, she smiled and took the proffered paper, thanking him for his help.

She didn't tell him that he'd accepted five twenty-dollar bills for a pair of decoys that would bring several million dollars at the Gathering.

———

The rest was easy. Joan followed up, found Ron Gruber, and learned that he was a decoy carver of some repute himself, as well as both a collector *of* and dealer *in* antique decoys. He wasn't exactly forthcoming when the operative knocked on his door and asked about the possibility that he might be in possession of a pair of low-head brants carved by a certain Billy Ellis, but he was an honest man, and caught with a direct question, he was incapable of telling a lie, especially to an attractive woman.

"Yes," he said after what appeared to Joan to be an internal struggle. "How did you know?"

Before she answered, he added that they were not for sale, and he hadn't shown them to anyone. Nor had he told a soul that he was in possession of the decoys.

He was a talented artist with a great natural eye and knew the pair of Billy Ellis brants were special but explained that he wasn't sure how special. She read between the lines: the decoys would be for sale; he just didn't know how much they were worth. He wasn't a rich man, he'd told Joan when she returned a second time a few days later. This time instead of making her stand in the doorway, he'd invited her into his home workshop. The decoy dealer also told the operative that his father built the house long before the upscale Spanish Banks area of Vancouver became upscale.

It wasn't until several visits later, and after she'd purchased a total of three old working decoys from the carver, that he finally relented. He told her to wait while he went into the house to get something. He returned to the workshop a few minutes later with a cardboard box that, Joan was sure from the reverent way he held it, had to contain the two "special" decoys. When he pulled back the towels covering the birds, unveiling them, she was instantly aware that she was going to have to leave.

Joan was affected in a way that she'd seldom been in all the years of searching on behalf of Our World. She was literally stunned by their perfection. It felt, as counterintuitive as it sounded, like some force slammed her body into harmonious repose. Every nerve ending quieted. The visual presence of the two decoys forced her to the serene edge that divided conscious from comatose. If she stayed, it felt like she would melt into a pool of serenity.

"Are you all right?" he asked, reaching out to take her arm, to steady her.

She'd answered when she was able to that yes, she was fine, but she was sorry she needed to leave.

"Thank you for showing them to me." Joan excused herself, telling him just before closing the outside door that she would call him the next day.

But she didn't call, at least not him. Instead she contacted her expediter, telling him to get word to Our World, to let them know that she'd located what she thought were the Ellis brants, but needed another operative to help corroborate her find. Seven years had passed since 1978, when she'd screwed up and nearly sent a forged work of art to the leader of Our World. It was a close call, the first indication that her powers to feel beauty were fading. It was Icarus who saved her from what would have been serious ramifications.

The fake predella from the Ghent Altarpiece of *The Just Judges* in Belgium turned out to be a mixed blessing; she recalled the event not so much for her narrow escape from punishment, but for the night of tranquility she'd spent with Icarus, both enraptured before the glory of the authentic Ghent Altarpiece. Many times, alone in the remote places the operatives of Our World frequented, she would recall the memory of that magical night.

Joan didn't call the carver-cum-decoy-dealer as she said she would. Instead she returned the next day unannounced and used her considerable wiles to try to convince him to give her first right of refusal on the two Billy Ellis decoys.

She didn't mention that because a certain Russian with a white beard now knew the decoys existed, any right of first refusal the carver might give would be effectively void anyway. Contracts, verbal or otherwise, meant zero to Our World. They had their own jurisprudence. But working out a mutually beneficial deal was always better than the alternatives, alternatives that often included persuasion of the Charlotte kind.

The decoy carver was a good guy, innocent and honest. Joan liked him and enjoyed their visits. But he was in way over his head and didn't know it. It wasn't his fault that he came into possession of something Our World wanted; it was just fate, his good luck and his bad. The tall operative told the carver she would pay whatever he asked.

She failed to add that her offer, on behalf of Our World, was not a take-it-or-leave-it one.

It was a take-it-or-take-it offer.

38

1985

The Ellis brants?"

"Yes."

The Russian man's white beard could have been described as severe, pointed from his chin like a conquistador's beard from days of yore. Always trimmed perfectly, it was even sharper now than it had been in the past. Just as his beard was sharper, his focus had if anything grown sharper as well, although even in the soft light cast by the single lamp on the table there were now unmistakable signs that even he, with all his power, was not going to win the fight against the ravages of time.

He held his clasped hands on the table and considered what he knew of the legendary pair of folk art carvings. The artist, Billy Ellis, was born in 1870 and died at age ninety in 1960; twenty-five years ago. His wasn't the lofty perch in the rarefied air of the European masters, those whose works of art commanded tens of millions at the Gathering. No, Ellis was a proletarian artist, a working duck decoy carver from the British colony across the Atlantic, Canada.

A simple man, maybe, and a great master not, but his carvings were already well-known to the collectors of duck and goose decoys in the outside world. The carver was to be sure a lesser light in that open marketplace, where collectors who thought they possessed sophisticated taste overlooked the far more talented Ellis works and clamored for the Warins, Lakes, and Fernlunds in Canada and the Crowells, Osgoods, and Wheelers in the United States. They were sheep moving in a herd.

Those chosen few who attended the Gathering actually did have sophisticated taste, but it wasn't their own. Like the art collectors from the outside world, they were also sheep in a herd, but it was a herd that followed a leader. He was that leader, and it was his operatives who provided the *taste* to those sheep of the Gathering, operatives like Icarus and Zhivago, possessors of that God-granted gift, the ability to recognize works of art that reached the infinitely rare state of artistic perfection.

The outside-world decoy collectors did not know about the Ellis brants. The carvings were unknown to all but those who were privy to the secrets of Our World. To the man sitting in the dim light at the table, they were another legend to track down; another fable to prove true. He knew that should the Ellis brants find their way to the commercial marketplace, it would be impossible for even those of myopic mediocrity not to recognize the artistic genius of Billy Ellis.

With that perspective, Ellis would be catapulted to the top of the pyramid of the decoy carvers by the moneyed collectors of that primitive art form. Never again would the decoy-collecting cognoscenti consider the folk artist from Whitby, Ontario, a lesser light. But thankfully, to this point, the pair of decoys had not reached the commercial marketplace and outsiders did not know about the legendary pair of tucked-head brants that Our World folklore had Ellis carving and painting secretly for part of each day, over a ten-year period during the peak of his career. It was to be his magnum opus but ended up being a secret that he took to his grave.

"Authentic?"

The man sitting across from the table, the messenger, became noticeably uncomfortable with the question, thinking how best to phrase his answer. Instead of a yes or no, he told the truth.

"Joan of Arc."

His employer did not respond, although he heard the answer to his question. Joan of Arc had been good, very good, but was losing her sensitivity to beauty. It happened; some of the special gifts the operatives were born with or had thrust upon them had a life span shorter than the body and mind that possessed the gift.

The tall operative had been fooled seven years before by the Ghent Altarpiece predella, which turned out to be a Van der Veken forgery. That had almost been a disaster. The man with the pointed white beard thought through the information, calculating the odds of both a positive outcome and a negative result. She was good, yes, but not as good as she had been.

Fakes were the bane of his existence. Since the beginning of time, humans had been copying and reproducing that which they desired to possess but could not afford to own. Originals were often lost in the storm of false prophets, all screaming for attention. Forging art was firmly entrenched as the third-highest-grossing criminal activity in the world, following only illicit drug dealing and gun running. And while Our World contributed to the chaos created by markets flooded with forgeries, they themselves had to be constantly vigilant not to become victims.

The legitimate global art market was nearing $50 billion, a number that obviously did not reflect the more than $5 billion that Our World gleaned from the Gathering each year. With a number so large, mistakes were going to happen, and it was only the special talents of his operatives that kept Our World from suffering the fate of so many museum and institutional collectors over the centuries: purchasing forgeries in good faith, only to have their mistakes embarrassingly exposed for all the world to see, sometimes decades after the original purchase.

Private collectors, the dilettantes, were even easier prey for the predators in the art world. They were amateurs who were not protected by the irrefutable Our World guarantee. But he needed Zhivago and he needed Icarus; without them, that tempered-titanium guarantee from Our World was for all intents and purposes worthless. If definitive provenance did not accompany a given objet d'art, only those two out of all his operatives could validate and authenticate artwork to a zero margin of error.

Zero margin of error. The man with the pointed white beard had the same tolerance for mistakes: zero.

246 / JIM SHOCKEY

"Where is Zhivago?"

"Honshu. Akaishi Mountains."

The messenger did not have to say that Zhivago was searching in Japan for the lost sword known as the Honjo Masamune, thought to be a myth by many scholars from the outside world.

They were wrong.

Zhivago was too far away and his search too important to call him back for the less worthy Ellis brants.

"Icarus?" He searched his memory banks. "New York?"

"Yes."

Icarus was working the jet-set circles there, crossing over, a male model blending in with the artists, actors, and musicians, moving as his operatives often did, with the left-wing liberal reformists and progressive thinkers; the vanguard that determined the tastes and values of decades still on their way to being. If there was a modern masterpiece to be found in those circles, Icarus would recognize it.

The man with the pointed white beard did not respect the far-left avant-garde—they were idiots, out of touch with economic realities—but he endured their unfocused and utopic philosophies as necessary evils. At least they were creative. For the general masses following the trends set by the socialist vanguard, he had nothing but contempt. The unwashed multitudes made the last stage of any trend the most populous, the stage that put the trends on the front pages of the newspapers and magazines and from there to the history books. They were worse than idiots.

But he didn't care about that greater unwashed. He cared at that moment only about the statistical probability that Joan of Arc's Ellis brants were real, versus knowing for sure if they were real. If he pulled Icarus out of New York and sent him back to what had become his base of operations since 1978, Vancouver, British Columbia, on the far west side of Canada, the move might cost the Gathering a work of art greater than the Ellis brants.

As rapier sharp as his mind was, there was much to consider before making a decision to remove the young operative from his present position. He wasn't on an important assignment looking for a legend, as Zhivago was, but it had still taken resources to provide

Icarus with a credible cover. Our World operatives received what they needed and wanted to effectively search for the treasures the Gathering consumed each year, and should the necessity arise for any of them to turn the heads of authority or doubters, those heads would be turned by Our World; turned so they would look the other way.

The need for years of training, making connections, and social climbing was effectively negated by Our World influence. The cattle calls for jobs, competition for spots on a team, membership in an exclusive country club, or a pass to the highest levels of society were a simple arrangement away for Our World. And if the people making the decisions refused to look the other way, those heads, with a word from on high, could be turned permanently.

As he thought through the combinations and permutations of throwing all that effort away, he looked down at his clasped hands resting on the table. There half the face of a magnificent watch showed just beyond the sleeve of his jacket. Was it eight years ago already that Zhivago brought it to him? Was it eight years already since he made the decision not to put the priceless object in the auction lineup at that year's Gathering?

He wasn't infected with the sickness that was the one commonality, the one thing shared by all the attendees of the Gathering, an addiction to collecting, to hoarding. All the art passed through his hands, but the priceless objects were commodities to him, products to be bought and sold. Rare and beautiful, granted, but still he'd never been tempted to keep anything, until Zhivago brought him the watch: the Rolex Zerographe. He had determined to keep that one single object of the thousands that passed through his hands.

Zhivago had been right to remove it from the young operative's possession. For Icarus to have kept it would have been an absolutely unacceptable violation of Our World rules. Lower quality, yes: the operatives were free to buy and sell art they found at will and for their own profit and often did, creating cover businesses. Icarus had Folkart Interiors, a storefront in Vancouver. They were often businesses that helped in their search for the one-of-a-kind treasures that belonged only to the exclusive domain of Our World.

Icarus. He reflected on the talented protégé, nearly thirty now.

The confident operative hadn't flown to the sun in the eight years since he'd been indoctrinated by Zhivago, but he'd come dangerously close to doing so. His refusal to continue to participate in the Peruvian search three years before should have resulted in severe punishment, but the man with the pointed white beard had not acted.

He'd not done so partially because it wasn't unusual for young initiates to change course in their early twenties, to balk under the spaded bit of Our World control, to buck the omnipotent authority they realized was presently and always had been controlling their lives, determining their destiny from the instant their special talents had been discovered. But that understanding of human nature was only part of the reason he hadn't made the balking operative bow before him, hadn't issued the order to Charlotte or one of the other highly trained weapons in his arsenal to bend Icarus to the will of Our World.

The other part of the reason was that he himself had balked as well, calling off the Peru operation only days after receiving word from the expediter in Peru that the young operative refused to continue searching for the Raimondi Stele. The Peruvian authorities' investigations into the results of Zhivago's personal "entertainment" rendered a continuation of the project imprudent.

The big operative's cover should have been perfect. He'd entered the country as an ordained member of the Catholic clergy from a faraway land, tasked with visiting Peru's nineteen dioceses under the welcoming approval of full communion. It was a country where 76 percent of the citizens over twelve years of age identified as followers of that faith. But the report from the expediter made it clear that it wasn't the children *over* age twelve that Zhivago took a perverted interest in: it was the altar servers, boys solemnized to act as acolytes at the age of eight. Those innocent children were the ones the robed operative set apart for his own special brand of sanctification.

But his had been a purpose that could not in any way be considered sacred.

Even with the tools of persuasion at his disposal, the man with the pointed white beard made the decision to cancel the operation instead of simply orchestrating a change of mind for the authorities.

Zhivago's deviant pleasures had been so egregious that they risked exposure for Our World, the only danger, the only threat that was cause for concern.

The leader knew Zhivago considered it to be his divine right to do as he pleased with whomever he pleased, as many times as he pleased. He didn't follow holy orders, but when the furious leader of Our World called off the expensive operation and sent *his* orders, the arrogant operative obeyed immediately, leaving a sad trail of broken children, families, and tears in his wake.

The Raimondi Stele . . . Just thinking the name sanitized the memories of Zhivago's inhuman violations and rekindled in the leader of Our World an intense desire to locate the object. Zhivago and Icarus had been close to finding it, but it was not to be, at least not then, three years ago. Times would change and Our World would ultimately have the treasure so long as the legend remained hidden from academic eyes as it had been for nearly two centuries. In the meantime, he simply considered it to be in safe storage. It would be uncovered someday, revealed to the Gathering and placed in a private collection, once again to disappear.

In Our World, time was not in short supply. For centuries it had operated without drawing attention to itself. There was never a need to hurry for Our World, but his own time as leader was drawing slowly and inexorably to an end. He wanted to complete the acquisition and placement of many objects that had so far eluded the operatives of Our World on his watch, not just the Raimondi Stele. There was Afo-A-Kom from West Africa; the Black Heart of the Dead from Mongolia, Genghis Khan's personal standard; the Flaming Cross of Emperor Constantinus; the Life Mother of the Old Bering Sea Culture; and the one that sat above them all, the Soul Catcher.

He shifted in his seat, taking the pressure off the sciatic nerve that constantly nagged at him, letting him know when he'd been sitting in one place too long. It was time to end the meeting.

He thought about it for a moment. Icarus had worked with Joan of Arc before, in 1978 in Belgium, the Ghent Altarpiece forgery. She'd found the missing piece of the polyptych, but it was the protégé who identified it as a clever forgery. There would not be an issue between them. In contrast, Zhivago and the younger Icarus were like water and fire; they did not coalesce.

"Send Icarus."

He waved his hand at the other man, dismissing him, letting him leave without further instructions. His will be done.

His minion across the small table rose and left, obsequious with every detail of his body language, but the man with the pointed white beard didn't notice his departure; he was looking at the table lamp. It was small, probably 1920s, with a low-wattage bulb and a pull string that normally he would have leaned forward and tugged, to add finality to the meeting's end; to throw the space into blackness, but he did not this time. The effort of leaning forward now took more energy than he felt. He was getting older. His joints were starting to ache and sitting for any length of time, as he had just been doing, stiffened them. It was easier just to lean back in his chair, washed in the soft low light.

He looked down, taking stock of himself, something he rarely did. He looked at the jacket he'd been wearing for years, some type of dark blue, almost black, wool felt. It was comfortable and functional, but ugly in a Soviet way. Fashion wasn't of interest to him anyway. What good was vanity to a man like him? Why was it necessary when he could have whatever he wanted, whenever he wanted it? Vanity was a waste of time for a man so powerful. Vanity was only for those who didn't already have enough power or celebrity, or respect and attention, and wanted more. The only thing he wanted more of was money.

It was to that end that he'd made the final decision to pull Icarus away from his search in New York, where he'd been consorting with the pathetic Who's Who crowd. With Reagan voted back into power by the American people the previous year, the citizens of that wealthy country, en masse, were making a hard turn to the right and his young operative had been relatively successful in finding works of art for the Gathering. They were works of art that had been freed from collections being sold due to the upheaval caused by that social movement toward conservatism.

The wealthy art collectors in America, the dilettante sheep, were food for the art-dealing predators who minded not in the least their prey's lack of good taste. As that massive nation about-faced and followed Reagan's lead, the dilettantes did their own about-face in their collecting habits, shunning the largely experimental but progressive art they had been collecting for nearly half a century. They gutted their collections, replacing their pop art pieces with classical elitist fine art, more socially apropos to the new era.

For the predators, the end of détente, Reagan's rollback, escalating arms race, and better-dead-than-red rhetoric, set the table for a feast and it was for that feast that the operatives of Our World like Icarus gathered. Chaos and change; politics and art were intertwined, interrelated; impossible to separate, like Siamese twins.

Icarus was there, picking up the pieces, recognizing with his talent what was pop garbage and what were true works of the ages, art that would survive the carnage that was all that remained of the 1950s, '60s, and '70s art scene. Andy Warhol's *Orange Solanas Gunslinger* silk screen, produced long before the famed *Orange Prince* silk screens, was unknown to the art world. It had brought a ten-times-higher price at the Gathering than any Warhol had ever commanded in the public domain.

The artist himself told Icarus, while the operative was there on a previous junket to New York, that he had been going through the Factory, cleaning the place out for the move to East Thirty-Third Street, and had come across the silk screen inspired by Valerie Solanas, the radical feminist and playwright. Warhol informed Icarus that he'd originally produced it for his eyes only just to be able to destroy it and thereby symbolically destroy the founder of the Society for Cutting Up Men for what she'd done to him.

But he said he couldn't do it. Even though the deranged creator of the misplaced play *Up Your Ass* shot him twice, directing the bullets through the artist's stomach, liver, esophagus, spleen, and both lungs, the cadaverous Warhol told Icarus that maybe the convicted psychopath was right. Maybe Solanas and the men of her *SCUM Manifesto* who were striving to eliminate themselves were simply thinking forward to the twenty-first century.

Perhaps it was moral to shoot someone and immoral to miss.

The dysfunctional artist hid his work away for fifteen years, letting nobody know about it, ashamed that he did not have the strength of conviction to be able to destroy what he felt was his finest work. In the end, Warhol loved money more than he believed in principles and he'd allowed Icarus, a relatively unknown fashion model, to take the painting in exchange for a substantial sum of Our World cash.

The man with the pointed white beard pulled his sleeve back to check the time and lingered for a moment more, savoring the knowledge that he was wearing a priceless watch.

He strained forward and finally pulled the string on the small lamp, bringing darkness to the room.

39

1985

VANCOUVER, BRITISH COLUMBIA

She walked by the Alma Street Café for the sixth time in an hour, trying not to look like she was doing exactly what she was doing, peering through the plate glass window at the six people sitting inside the trendy restaurant. The Closed sign on the door was meant for everyone else in Vancouver, including her, but evidently not for the table full of people chatting the afternoon away in the center of the restaurant. One was Loni Anderson, still on top of her game from the success of *WKRP in Cincinnati*. Another was Michele Lee, the star of the prime-time soap opera *Knots Landing*. The third was Stephanie Zimbalist, better known as Laura Holt from *Remington Steele*, one of the top-rated shows on television.

The fourth woman of the group was by far the most beautiful, even though it was the other three who were Hollywood sex symbols. She was stunning, blessed with the classic looks that separated timeless beauty from cute, attractive, striking, or the carefully orchestrated presentation of the other three. The tall woman looking in the window as she passed found that one woman of the four to be the most fascinating, although she didn't recognize her.

Of the two men at the table, the older one she knew was Laszlo George. She'd learned that from two pay phone calls to her expediter, who without doubt had made several more calls to Our World's command-and-control center. It was fair to say that the intelligence and clandestine activity capabilities of Our World rivaled those of the finest national covert agencies around the world. The Gathering was composed in part of wealthy individuals who literally ran all those nations.

Laszlo George was the cinematographer for a TV movie remake of the 1949 film *A Letter to Three Wives* that was being shot in Vancouver, the expediter explained when Joan called back, and he was apparently Hungarian, which explained part of why the sixth person sitting at the table was there. The two men were no doubt talking *vizilabda*, water polo. It was that sixth person that she desperately needed to speak to.

Envy was a foreign feeling to her, one she didn't believe she'd ever felt before, but right then she was envious. Envious that they were able to sit at the table and visit with the man she'd been in love with for seven years, since the day they met in Belgium; a man who was totally oblivious to that fact.

At six feet, taller than most men, she was attractive in a South African short-haired, androgynous Josie Borain kind of way. Knowing that, she also knew she would never have been able to be a Calvin Klein model like Josie was; she was too protective of the monster that was her body. She kept it covered, long sleeves, always pants, even when she was alone. The scars of apartheid's racial segregation were not psychological for her; they were as real as the cars passing by on the nearby Vancouver street; as real as the building beside her.

Raised in permanent red welts on her back, her legs, across her stomach and her breasts, the crisscrossed lines were a constant reminder of how deeply the apartheid blade cut. They were a reminder of the day she met a gang of teenage boys from the "Black Spot," farms owned by blacks but surrounded by white farms. It could have been worse; she could have been younger, ten or eleven instead of thirteen.

Or she could have been one of the black boys who tore the faded summer dress from her body, using their machetes to cut away the remnants that remained to cover her modesty. The black boys who tied her to the stakes they'd driven into the ground before pleasuring themselves with her helplessly exposed body. The black boys who then whipped her, using the same whip their white overlords had often used on them.

Yes, it could have been worse. She could have been one of those black boys, hunted down by the white community and fitted with car tires doused in diesel fuel. Fuel that was then ignited in retaliation and retribution for what they had done to the thirteen-year-old white Afrikaans girl who would become Our World's Joan of Arc.

The act of vengeance was never investigated by the authorities, never documented.

Apartheid. It would end someday, but what good was that for her? For the suffering she'd already endured? For the tortured black boys? It was too late. The damage had been done. The teenagers had their fun with her and left her for dead; forever soiled. But at least her scars could be hidden. She didn't die that day, but for all intents and purposes she was dead to the world of her Afrikaans family and community that she'd known.

To the well-traveled, that she was of South African descent might have been recognizable from her fine facial features, but they would not have known if they'd listened to her speak, since her accent was virtually undetectable. Too many years traveling eroded the precise South African variation of the Queen's English. She shook her head at the thought. The Queen's English? Her parents would have struck her had they heard her utter such blasphemy. They hated the queen. They hated the British.

Their rough dining table, in the home she lived in until she was thirteen, was composed of two enormous flat slabs of granite, framed by stinkwood planks. On the surface it looked like an unusual but functional design, but if one were to crawl under the table and look upward, at the underside of the two granite slabs, as she had done so many times as a youth, they would have seen the names of two British soldiers chiseled into the rock and their epitaphs.

"At the going down of the sun and in the morning we will remember him."

They'd been killed during the Boer War.

"His was honour. His was duty."

The table was made from the inverted headstones of those British soldiers, the most disrespectful gesture her parents could make to the memory of both the soldiers and the British Empire colonialists of that past day and time, the murderers from half a century before; the evil force incarnate who manned the concentration camps filled with Boer women and children; the ones who committed the atrocities. They were the evil that destroyed what was once a great country, leaving the Province of the Orange Free State a gutted reflection of its former glory.

Our World found her and saved her from that. Our World saved her from *then*.

Her gift, to fall into a deep peaceful serenity in the presence of artistic perfection, was thrust upon her over and over in the hours of terror, during the horror of being defiled. Trauma induced her gift, as surely as oxytocin induces birth; and as with a newborn, her gift continued to grow in strength, reinforced by her excommunication from family and community. To them, she was sullied, unclean.

Our World knew that some like Icarus and Zhivago were born with the gift, but that others had it forced upon them, through horrors unimaginably distressing, their minds bent but not broken. Hers was of the latter sort and was refined by Our World tutelage. She learned to associate the feeling of tranquility when in the presence of objects that should have been the creation only of God, but due to some unfathomable kind of divine inspiration, were the work of mere mortals.

A chic-looking couple left the store two doors down from where she stood. They exited a baby-blue-fronted antique store with flat snow geese silhouette cutouts attached to the square top facade, a place called Folkart Interiors, and crossed the street to another antique store dealing in English imports. The tall woman backed against the insurance agency storefront she'd been waiting in front of, making way for a group of joggers to sweat by, clad in pastel sleeveless muscle shirts and even tighter pastel shorts, each with a Sony Walkman attached to the elastic waistband.

In their wake came another person in full glow, a young woman on a ten-speed bike. She stepped off her bike close to where the much taller woman stood and walked it to the store with the snow geese attached to the front. Before entering she checked her reflection in the windowpane. She walked out again a few seconds later looking disappointed. She pulled her bike away and continued to walk it up the sidewalk. The owner, the person the bike lady was very likely looking for, wasn't in; the tall woman knew that for a fact. Only the assistant saleslady was in the antique store; the owner was around the corner having a long, long lunch.

The tall woman made a decision then, pivoted, and rounded the corner, walking in the opposite direction of her last pass by the restaurant. As she approached, the restaurant door opened, startling her. Despite the huge dark sunglasses all the exiting actresses were wearing, they were easily recognizable; Laszlo George, the cinematographer, not so much, unless you were involved with the movie industry. The striking blonde stepped out second from the last, followed by the last person in the group, the one who was the object of Joan of Arc's desire. He was fit, well over six feet tall, six feet five or six inches in his cowboy boots, late twenties to a casual observer.

The tall woman knew he was exactly twenty-nine years old, only two years younger than she was. His blue jeans were faded naturally, from wear, to a soft blue color that stonewashing tried so hard and failed to replicate; the fabric on the knees was worn to a threadbare white but not ripped. The tan cowboy boots were caiman skin; no, something more exotic. His hair was long, brown, falling wavy from under a silver-belly Stetson. He was smiling at the blond enchantress, reaching around her to hold the door for her. She thanked him.

"Gentlemen are not common in Hollywood!" The tallest of the actresses already waiting out on the sidewalk was joking, though jealousy seeped into the tone of the comment.

Eavesdropping on the group only intensified the feeling of envy the tall woman felt. She would have liked to have been the one sitting at the table and visiting with the young man. She would have liked for their relationship to be personal. But theirs was purely a business one. It was correct Our World protocol, but she wished for something much more.

She pushed the feeling of envy aside. Breaking protocol hopefully might happen organically someday, as it had in Belgium, but for now their relationship needed to be all about business, the reason she needed so urgently to speak to the young man known as Icarus. The Ellis brants were going to change hands that afternoon and Icarus needed to be there to confirm their authenticity.

"Thanks for buying lunch." The actress who played Laura Holt smiled at the young man and crinkled up her nose. Of the three famous actresses, she appeared to be the least affected by the fame, still retaining a sense of humor that was earthy and sweet.

"It was really nice to meet you." The beautiful blonde turned to the young man as the others in the group started off down the walkway, headed in the same direction as the tall woman who'd been eavesdropping on the conversations. "Maybe we'll see you at Terpsichore someday. I teach the advanced ballet jazz class."

The sultry voice was all female, and yet full of the deep assurance born of innate self-confidence, nurtured by a loving family. She reached out and shook the hand of the man wearing the cowboy hat, gracefully, her smile genuine and kind. It was pure and it was a smile that only comes to the face of someone whose soul is also pure.

She turned then and walked to catch up to the rest of the group, already moving away down the sidewalk. The young man lingered for a moment longer, watching her leave, and then he pivoted to walk in the opposite direction.

The tall woman with the face and lithe body of a supermodel stopped when she first passed the group exiting the restaurant and looked in her purse, seemingly unaware of them, but as soon as they were far enough away to not notice, she closed her purse and turned 180 degrees to follow the young man back around the same corner that she'd been standing at earlier. She caught him just as he was going into the antique store.

"Still as responsible as ever, I see." She knew he'd seen and recognized her when he left the restaurant with the actresses. "Hope New York was fun. Nice shot in *Vogue*, by the way. I kept you a copy."

Even from the one time they'd worked together, she knew Icarus would never bother looking at tear sheets from his modeling cover work like any normal human being would do. But then Icarus wasn't normal, he was the best, better than Zhivago. *He* had his adherents as well; mostly they were operatives she disliked working with. Their gifts were undeniable, their higher sensibilities honed to uber-acuteness, but that was no reason for their complete lack of compassion for their fellow human beings.

Sometimes when she reflected on her life and that of her peers, she questioned whether the gifts they all possessed came with downsides; she wondered if the gifts were subject to the checks and balances that were nature's way of giving but also taking away. Life begets death begets life begets death; nature's balance in its purest form. Perhaps her peers on Zhivago's side were no more able to repress those deviant inclinations than they were going to be able to avoid dying. Maybe their way of balancing their inhuman gift was to be inhuman themselves.

Zhivago was the worst of them all; the ugly benchmark for those operatives whose devolved actions repulsed her.

Not that she was perfect.

No, one look in the mirror after a shower was all it took to recognize her imperfections.

"Yes, I'm fine, thanks for asking. Yes, it has been a long time since we worked together." She shook her head and added, this time without the sarcasm, "We have to go now."

She turned away so he would not be able to see her face and read her thoughts. That's it? Nothing? No "thank you for caring"? No "nice to see you, Joan"? Or "I've been thinking about you, Joan"? No "thanks for keeping a copy of the *Vogue* spread"?

Icarus didn't respond to any of her unspoken questions.

She'd known he was different from the first time they met, the first time she felt the stirrings of the animal attraction that in cultured vernacular was known as love. She learned quickly that he didn't seem to need anyone but lived in his own universe, where praise and recognition had no value. Validation that was the lifeblood of most sentient beings was an irrelevant thing for him.

Contrary to what most other females would have seen as a warning sign, she found the trait intriguing. She wasn't frightened off by the fact that he seemed to have no needs and therefore didn't seem to perceive anyone else's need. From his lack of reaction to seeing her and her previous knowledge of his character, she wasn't the least surprised that the animal attraction she felt as strongly now as ever was an animal that lived on a one-way street.

Not that she expected any love; she of all people, maculate as she was, did not deserve any. He was Icarus. He was the best.

Still, unlike him, she was human in her needs; a little love would be nice.

Joan led the way back to where she'd parked her rental vehicle. She knew Icarus would follow.

*S*top here for a moment, Nyala.

Before you read on, I must tell you about the colors.

Sun-ray born prisms, rainbows against the black of a storm-blown sky. The two Ellis carvings were the essence of color.

Nyala, it is difficult to understand, I know, but I can tell you that the moment of color's creation is the product of a perfect alignment, when the artist balances opposites in magical harmony and weaves them together in a way that only the greatest of God's artists can.

It is a language only those He has chosen to bear His gift can understand. A language only those He has chosen can speak.

Artists with the gift from God recreate in that language, after His image.

It is that language I see in color.

She was beside me then, Nyala, looking at me, wondering, waiting for confirmation that the serenity flowing over her scarred body was real, wasn't false; confirmation that her gift had not failed her.

The Ellis brants were so magnificent, Nyala, and she was so pure in that instant, so vulnerable.

Joan of Arc.

Lying here all alone. A lifetime of regrets. Things I should have said when I was home.

It's too late now to right those wrongs.

I was incapable then. I still am, or I still was, until I found you.

The time I spent in Vancouver and all those other cities shaped me into something I was not, something I did not want to be. As cities will do, take and never give, it took me away from who I was. It wasn't me then. It wasn't me there.

I was not them.

I was not Elizabeth Montgomery. She was kind. Her home in

Beverly Hills so suited to her style, suited to her joie de vivre. She was taken from us too early.

I was not Goldie Hawn. She told me she was bohemian, and lived her life freely, without reservation. Nobody had a cuter smile or a happier giggle. She liked the blue Doukhobor cupboard. Kurt did not. They had two homes, in Colorado, across from each other.

Kurt Russell was a hunter. Did you know that, Nyala? We talked about pheasants. But I wasn't a hunter, not a true one. Not yet.

I was not Lisa Blount. I could not see her pain, could not feel her need. Hollywood is a vampire that will drain the very life out of its own disciples.

I was incapable of helping her then, Nyala.

I was not Joel Schumacher. He was good, smart. He laughed, said I should be a cowboy, it was his idea; the movie cameo. Cousins. He could not know that I was already working for Our World.

I was not Charles Haid. Everybody adored Renko then. We stood in front of the nightclub; Tony Geary was there with us. The bouncer wouldn't let us in; didn't recognize who they were.

Everyone else in the lineup knew who the two with me were when we walked to the front of the line. They were famous. Charles asked the bouncer, "Don't you know who this is?" and pointed to me.

He was having fun. I was having fun, but who he was pointing at was not me.

Memories now.

Nothing but memories. Memories for me only, none of them would remember. I was playing a part; they didn't know me.

I was not Gene Simmons. I liked him. We drank together. We were different but the same. Street language. He spoke it and I understood it.

I was not Tom Selleck. He could solve any crime on television, but he would not have been able to solve who I needed to be. What I needed to do. His heart was soft, like the hand that he offered me.

He didn't know that it wasn't me with him. How could he? I didn't know it wasn't me either.

I was not Michael Crichton, although of all of them in those years, he was the only one who saw who I really was. What I needed to be.

Tsau-z.

I am the Man of Sores.

Before this is done, they will all know me as fear.

He possessed the gift; he could have been one of us. I told him so. Before you, Nyala, it was for him and him only that I broke the sacred law of Our World, revelation; an offense for which the punishment is incalculable by any measure except pain. In his confidence I spoke. We had nothing in common except everything.

The unholy place that claimed so many so young seduced him.

The harm we were doing, they were doing; he saw it and he tried to tell them; tried to tell the world. Crichton said it so long ago, "Anthropogenic global climate fears, promulgated by the mainstream media, fear of crisis, fear of living instead of addressing the immoral reality of poverty, the harm." He said it and he saw it, Nyala, but like Lamia sleeping with Zeus, doomed to live in anguish, he removed his eyes to keep himself from seeing it any longer.

He blinded himself, Nyala, for money and fame, to be able to live among those who would not see the truth; his peers. They produced then and still produce what the world watches and what the world believes today.

They are liars.

He is gone now or else he would tell you all this himself. I believe we would have been closer, maybe I could have saved his sight, but time always takes what it gives. And it took him too.

I feel sadness when I think of him; sadness for me, not for him. He was a writer who lived the climax and the anticlimax, who now knows the conclusion, the ending to the narrative that is the story we are all part of. He is the lucky one.

All of them and so many more. The lost years for me, the years in that city.

I have never told her, but it was Joan of Arc who gave me direction that day, showed the way forward; the way forward to me. It was her and her discovery of the Ellis brants that directed my future.

I became a hunter that day.

When I held them, they were not art for the Gathering to me; they were manifest visions of color that told stories of wild lands, of

264 / JIM SHOCKEY

cold and fresh mornings, of flights and V-formations. And calls that pierced the chilled still air and thrilled all who heard.

They were the effort and desire of our antecedents who lived because their quarry did not. Balance. We are alive today because of them, Nyala.

They were so much more than just art, they were respect. Respect for a way of life that was as old as who you are. As old as who I am. As old as all who have ever been.

The hunters and the gatherers.

I became one that day.

I became me that day.

40

2020

HIGHWAY BETWEEN CALGARY, ALBERTA, AND VANCOUVER, BRITISH COLUMBIA

Jesus Christ, Luba!" Nyala grabbed on to the overhead handle. The semitrailer's compression-release Jake brake and air horn going off at the same instant, literally beside her head, forced Nyala from sitting quietly, reading with 100 percent focus and concentration, to hanging on for dear life. The Mercedes acted like a sound chamber and her head felt like it had been torn in two by the blast. "What are you doing!"

The green mountainside appeared out her side window, replacing the eyeball-level front tire and front driver-side quarter panel of the tractor trailer that only a moment before had been less than two feet from her face.

"Asshole!" Luba leaned over as far as the seat belt would allow and reached across her friend, giving the finger to the truck driver. Her face was nearly in Nyala's lap as she tried to get low enough to be able to look up at the giant truck's windshield, to make sure the driver caught her one-finger salute.

"Luba!" Nyala reached to grab the steering wheel, to yank it back to the right side of the road.

It wasn't necessary; Luba sat back in her seat and pulled the expensive car once again into the correct lane.

"Sorry for living. What's your problem? Safest car on the road and we have airbags all around us!" She was smiling. "Nice to have you back in the real world! Won't be long and we'll be going through Banff according to my GPS!"

"You scared the shit out of me." Nyala's heart was still hammering the inside wall of her chest.

The black spruce mountainsides on both sides of the highway ahead of them disappeared into the low pregnant clouds, hiding the scenic reason that the area had been such an important tourist destination for over one hundred years. The clouds promised to deliver the second reason the resort town of Banff was so popular: snow. It was a skier's joy; backcountry mountains and snow bowls forever into the distance on clear days, ski hills and lifts, hotels and bars. Or it would be in a couple of months when the gathering winter storms delivered enough snow to produce a good skiing base.

"What?" Luba didn't look over at her friend. "I was passing him. What's the big deal?"

Passing, yes, but with so little margin of error that even the truck driver filed a 120-decibel horn-blast protest to the fight-or-flight center of Nyala's brain.

"How about driving like a human for a bit?"

Luba ignored her. She looked happy that her friend was now tuned into her world instead of stuck nose-deep in the manuscript pages on her lap.

"So what's happening? Anything cool? Did you find out how Tsau-z knows about your grandmother?"

But Luba wasn't listening, she was peering ahead and then hit the turn signal.

"Pee-pee stop! You hungry?" She didn't let her friend answer; instead she started to slow the Mercedes to be able to take the exit without losing control. "Me too! Starving!"

The gas station was bigger than most, a truck stop, and from where Luba parked in front, the inside appeared to be full of truckers and travelers, most looking about like Nyala and Luba did: worse for wear, scruffy and red-eyed.

Nyala didn't need the stop; she wasn't the one who'd been drinking coffee since they departed Calgary two hours before, and she wasn't hungry. Both had been so sleep deprived the evening before, they'd spent the night in Calgary at a fleabag motel on the edge of the prairie town. Luba grabbed two Styrofoam cups of coffee from the lobby when they checked out, no food.

"You go; I think I'll just keep reading."

"Up to you, but don't expect me to stop in an hour so you can go to the bathroom."

Nyala knew that was a lie. Luba loved pit stops for whatever reason.

"Want me to order you something from the restaurant? French fries? Maybe they have something like a Filet-O-Fish? Miss Vickie's? Twizzlers? Oh yeah! Twizzlers coming right up!"

And with that she slammed the Mercedes door.

Nyala watched her friend until she disappeared inside the building and hit the lock button before she picked up the manuscript once again.

She leafed through it for a second and then picked up her phone and clicked to the Google search bar.

"Michael Crichton." Click.

Seemed as good a place as any to start; a place to see if Tsau-z's story could be verified. Was Michael Crichton in Vancouver sometime in the 1980s? She opened the Wikipedia page on the author.

Wow. Impressive; over two hundred million copies of his books sold, and a dozen adapted into films. She scanned down the page, recognizing most of the Hollywood movie titles, but not all the books. She wasn't sure what she was looking for exactly.

Congo? 1980. The time period was about right. She clicked on it but hit the back arrow quickly. It was only a novel. The people Tsau-z mentioned in the last part she'd been reading, before Luba tried to kill them, had a common thread, an obvious connection; even though she wasn't up on movie or television trivia, she recognized that the people he mentioned were involved with that industry. She tried *Looker*, 1981. Nothing, no lightbulb. *Sphere?* Nope. 1987 was too late. The stuff in the manuscript she'd been reading was only up to 1985 in Tsau-z's life.

Runaway? 1984. Time was right. She clicked on it.

"Science fiction action film written and directed by Michael Crichton, starring Tom Selleck, Gene Simmons, and Kirstie Alley."

There it was! The connection! She clicked on "Production." There was a quote from Michael Crichton.

"Movies are about the here and now in things you see. To me, there's no point in writing a highly cinematic book or doing a very literary movie. . . . I'm self-consciously attempting to simplify my stories. I don't want to work hard to understand it."

No shit, Sherlock. Nyala totally got it. Simplifying her own story was what she was trying to do, except that it was already simple. Simple as in there was no story.

She continued to read, drawn in by Crichton's words of wisdom.

"If we don't like atomic weapons or air pollution, we have only ourselves to blame. It's all choices, all a product of our hands and minds."

Crichton was a smart guy; common sense was something that nobody seemed to have much of these days. The more she read about him, the more she liked him and the more she saw how different he was from the Hollywood Who's Who of that time. She understood why Tsau-z related to him. Apparently the Harvard-educated author didn't buy into the blame-everyone-except-us philosophy and we-know-better-than-you position of the finger-wagging dogma dummies in Hollywood. She figured he must have ruffled a few feathers in his time.

"Filming took place in Vancouver while star Tom Selleck was on a break from *Magnum P.I.*"

Vancouver. Didn't Tsau-z write that he went there on a swimming scholarship after Wilbur said she couldn't teach him anything more? And wasn't it the white-bearded Russian who said something about Vancouver being Icarus's home base after 1978? Or was it Joan of Arc? Wasn't that where she found the carved birds?

It took her a moment to find confirmation in the manuscript.

". . . his base of operations since 1978, Vancouver, British Columbia, on the far west side of Canada."

So three of the people Tsau-z or Icarus said he "was not" were in Vancouver a few months before Joan of Arc found the multimillion-dollar decoys. It was strange that Tsau-z made a point of saying he was not like those movie people. And what the hell was a "brant," anyway? Even with all the times she'd watched the "Whispering

Channel's" hunting programs, she'd never heard anyone mention the word *brant*; turkeys, yes, and doves and ducks of all kinds, Canada geese, quail, pheasants, and sharp-tailed grouse, but never "brants."

She typed it in and clicked.

"The brant, or brent goose, is a small goose of the genus *Branta*."
The birds in the photos looked like geese to Nyala.

What next? Goldie Hawn. She typed the name into the Google search bar and then paused and added "Vancouver."

The first link was an offer to check out the old mansion that Goldie Hawn and Kurt Russell owned in the city from 2002 to 2005. Their son played hockey, so they had moved there. It was a Vancouver connection. Nyala read down through the list of movies, clicking on anything that caught her eye, but it wasn't until she clicked on the movie *Bird on a Wire* that she found what she was looking for.

It was filmed in Vancouver in the 1980s.

Nyala let her hand holding the cell phone drop to rest on the manuscript in her lap. She thought for a moment and then reached to the backseat to pull her case out. Too many unknowns again; she needed her notepad to get her thoughts organized.

A pair of youngsters, dressed for the warm weather and obviously just released from minivan prison, walked by the front of the Mercedes, pointing at a spot under the grille, no doubt trying to get their two middle-aged parents to come and look at the strange North Carolina license plate. Nyala smiled at them and waved, pulling her notebook from the briefcase only after the children looked at each other, shrugged their shoulders comically, and grinning, waved back.

She took out a pen as well and zipped the case up, returning it to the backseat. Perfect time to make notes. Luba would be at least half an hour; she was always in a rush when she was driving but never in a rush when she stopped for food. It was nearly impossible to take notes while they rocketed down the highway, so now was the chance to do some actual work.

The first flakes of snow were falling.

She opened the notepad to a new POSSIBLE FACTS page and started adding names and checkmarks, leafing back and forth through the manuscript to find the references that she wanted to check out.

"Decoy carver named Billy Ellis; carved duck decoys sell for seven figures . . . seriously?"

Nyala couldn't help but add the editorial comment. There was no way a duck decoy could be worth that much, so she crossed off seven and changed it to *six* figures.

"Duck decoy carver Ron Gruber, Vancouver mid-1980s; Warin, Lake, Fernlund, Cowell, Osgood, Wheeler decoy carvers famous; Art forgery, third largest illegal industry next to gun smuggling and drugs?"

That couldn't be right.

"Human trafficking maybe?" Nyala added the question. She didn't believe there could be that much money in forging art.

"Sword of some Honjo Masamune guy, does it exist? Afo-A-Kom, whatever it is, does that exist? Black Heart of the Dead? What is that? Flaming Cross of Constantinus; Life Mother of the Old Bering Sea Culture; Soul Catcher?"

Was it even a real thing? She chastised herself for not being smart enough to check on that right off the bat when she'd first started reading the manuscript. Jesus, girl, it should have been the number one thing she looked for. She broke her own commitment to research everything in a proper order and instead stopped writing, picked up her phone, typed the two words in, and clicked.

"A soulcatcher or soul catcher is an amulet used by the shaman of the Pacific Northwest Coast of British Columbia and Alaska."

Nyala wasn't sure how she felt about the knowledge. It was a real thing. That was good, wasn't it? Why did she not feel satisfied then?

"Keeper of the Breath."

She felt oddly disturbed by the term. What the hell did that mean? "Keeper of the Breath"? Looking at the photo on her phone, supposedly of an actual soul catcher, didn't explain her disquiet. It looked like a bone that was cut open at both ends and carved. If that was the greatest art object the world has ever seen, she was greatly underwhelmed by it.

This couldn't be the Soul Catcher the white-bearded Russian was so hot to find. And didn't Tsau-z say he saw the actual Soul Catcher? At the antihunting rally? He was some distance from the person, a woman, and wasn't she holding it? Or was it her? Nyala flipped through the pages, looking for the passage she'd read only two days before.

There it was.

———

God, Nyala, I wish you could have seen her. She was beautiful. She was perfect.

She was the light and she was the darkness. She was all that we were, are, and all that we can be. She was dancing for all of us. She was dancing for this world.

Boom. Boom. Boom.

She was dancing for me and I saw for the first time. Saw beauty that was inconceivable, every color in the universe, every sound, every feeling in her movement.

It was Her.

The Daughter of God.

The Keeper of the Breath.

It was the Soul Catcher.

———

Nyala frowned. Daughter of God? No need to look that up, no such person existed, at least not in classic Christian theology. Had to be something she was missing. Tsau-z spoke so cryptically it was hard to know if he was being literal or if he was speaking in some metaphoric tongue that nobody except an English literature professor would be able to decipher. She was sorely tempted to continue reading further into the manuscript instead of getting back to the far more tedious chore of fact checking, but she let the pages drop back to her lap again and shook her head, picking up the notepad as she did.

Keep on track.

"*Orange Salanas Gunslinger*, painting by Warhol; *A Letter to Three Wives*, movie, was it shot in Vancouver and if so, when? Laszlo George, another Hungarian, was he the cinematographer for the movie? Josie Borain, supermodel for Calvin Klein 1980s?"

Nyala thought about the tall woman code-named Joan of Arc by

Our World; what a horrible thing to happen to a thirteen-year-old girl. She shuddered at the image.

"Elizabeth Montgomery in Vancouver, 1980s? Kurt Russell, hunter? Lisa Blount, who was she? Movie? Television? And any connection to Vancouver 1980s; Charlie Haid (Renko?), who was he? Tony Geary? Who was he? Joel Schumacher, who was he and was he in Vancouver in the 1980s?"

Nyala tapped her pen on the POSSIBLE FACTS page for a few moments and then leafed through the manuscript, scanning what she'd been reading on the drive, looking for anything she'd missed. There was one more note she added just under the Joel Schumacher question. "*. . . it was his idea; the movie cameo.*" What cameo?

Then she leaned back in the chair and rubbed the back of her hand against her raw eyes.

For a moment she considered taking photos again and texting them to Scott to check out, but she changed her mind. She'd already sent Scott photos of the notepad page the afternoon before, while they'd been driving from Saskatoon to Calgary, and he still hadn't returned her text from before that, asking about whether the Romanian billionaire had a private jet and if it had ever landed in New Zealand. No use freaking him out with more work before he was done with her last batch of questions.

She picked up her phone and started the serious business of actually researching the questions she'd just written in the POSSIBLE FACTS column, typing and clicking.

There were four checkmarks in the CONFIRMED column ten minutes later. The deceased decoy carver from Ontario, Billy Ellis, did exist and did pass away in 1960 and Ron Gruber was also a real duck decoy carver from Vancouver who passed away in December 2014. The other decoy carvers: all six she looked up were real as well and she was shocked to learn that two decoys, a Crowell pintail and a Canada goose, sold for $1 million each in 2007. Wow! Who'd have thunk it? Learn something new every day. She scratched out the "sell for six figures" and changed her note back to "sell for seven figures" before she put the checkmark in the CONFIRMED column.

The only UNCONFIRMED column checkmark so far was for

the Ellis brants question. She couldn't find a single reference to the carvings and was thinking that maybe it would be a question to ask Scott when her phone's ugly "ah-OOOOG-ah" submarine dive siren went off in her hand and Scott's face appeared on her screen.

She jumped as she always did when the ringtone sounded off.

"Give me good news." She hit the speaker button and turned to the POSSIBLE FACTS pages in her notebook, the pages she'd taken photos of and texted to Scott the afternoon before.

Instead of good news, he started in on her, explaining that for any of these, except for one about the private jet, Nyala could have easily confirmed herself by taking a few minutes to google them.

"Okay, got it, Google. Thanks for that. What about the answers?"

Confirmed. Confirmed. Confirmed. Confirmed. The swimming pool in Hungary, the names of the water polo players, and yes, the Hungarian king was associated with Hercules. All confirmed. Even the Cuban player who smashed Tsau-z in the face was real. So was the airplane crash that killed the president of Ecuador and his wife. The Ghent Altarpiece was real, it existed. All confirmed.

Scott rattled off the salient points of each search and then pointed out again that there was only one question Nyala had asked him that she would not have been able to research herself, because, as he explained, she didn't have the computing power to do so.

"The Romanian with the private jet was a tough one," Scott said, but eventually he had discovered that yes indeed, the guy did have a private jet. Checking on whether it had flown into Queenstown, New Zealand, in the last few years was even more involved.

"Scott! Spare me the details! Did it or did it not land in New Zealand?"

"Yes." His voice sounded hurt. "March 2017. It landed in Queenstown."

Wow. So it was true. Crazy. But it brought up even more questions. What was Tsau-z doing in New Zealand only a few years ago and why the heck was he having dinner with an apparently uberrich Romanian and another just-as-uberrich German car manufacturer, albeit the owner of a smaller private jet? Why were they meeting?

41

Knock. Knock. Knock.

It wasn't gentle tapping on the window beside her right ear; it was more of a heavy, ham-fisted pounding.

What the heck?

Startled, Nyala jumped and at the same instant leaned as far from her side window as the Mercedes center console would allow. She hadn't seen the guy walk up and wasn't expecting the heavy, bearded face that was staring at her through the fogged glass only a few inches away.

Christ. What now?

Her door was locked; it was an old habit that she'd picked up after a friend told her some random guy jumped into the front seat of her car and tried to hijack it and kidnap her. Didn't work out quite as well as the erstwhile carjacker was hoping, since her friend happened to be holding a scalding-hot cup of Timmy Ho's finest blend, no lid, which she promptly tossed in the guy's face.

All Nyala had for a weapon was a half-empty plastic bottle containing flat Mountain Dew and a few old but dangerously hard french fries.

"What!" Nyala couldn't open the window even if she wanted to, which she didn't; Luba had the keys and so instead she pretty much yelled the word at the big face peering through the window.

He was in his forties, she guessed, maybe even thirties, and definitely low-rent. The sweat-stained MAGA-logoed flat-brim trucker hat was pulled low over his eyes. His neck and part of his florid face were covered by the collar on a dirty green camo jacket. Besides the obvious, that he resembled a hairy pig, the most noticeable thing about him was his belly; he was grossly overweight. That and his bloated cheeks told the tale of too many truck stop dinners and an aversion to exercise.

Nasty; it had to be the pissed-off truck driver Luba gave the finger to. He probably recognized the Mercedes and wanted to carry on the conversation in person.

KNOCK. KNOCK. KNOCK.

Even the guy's knuckles were hairy. He motioned for Nyala to come out of the car.

"*No!*" Her message was loud and clear. No way he couldn't have heard it, even through the closed car door.

She didn't know what to do, but getting out of the Mercedes was the last choice out of the relatively low number of options running through her mind. Wonderful, this was just what she needed. Who wouldn't want to get berated, or worse, by some random truck driver suffering from a bad case of road rage and probably indigestion?

But she was wrong; it wasn't the truck driver that Luba had nearly sideswiped.

Nyala's door lock clicked open then and a heartbeat later the driver's-side door was yanked open, letting in a blast of cold air. For the second time in as many minutes her thumping heart leapt back into action. She twisted around the other way now, to face the new threat.

It was Luba.

Nyala turned again, back to her window. It was all happening so quickly; she wasn't sure if she was thankful for the return of her friend or furious that Luba unlocked her passenger door when it should have been obvious that a huge scary chain-saw-massacre-looking guy was waiting to get at her. The face was gone, replaced with the guy's large gut, flattened against the window. He was reaching across the top of the Mercedes and was handing Luba something.

Then it was over. He turned and waddled back the way he must have come, from behind the car. Nyala leaned forward to be able to see him through the side-view mirror. He didn't look any less gross from behind than he did from the front.

"Hey, girlfriend! Miss me?" Luba threw a full plastic bag toward Nyala and then flopped into her seat, closing the door as she did. "Cold as a witch's nose out there!"

"That's it? That's all you have to say? There's some crazy lunatic staring at me through the window and all you can say is 'it's cold outside'?"

Nyala shook her head and turned away to look out the front window, incredulous.

"And it's snowing!" Luba announced. "We should have brought our skis! Oh here, that big fat guy told me to give this to you." She tossed the folded paper to Nyala and reached over her shoulder to pull the seat belt forward and click it in place.

"Really? You don't think anything strange just happened? Like some guy you don't know gives you a piece of paper at a gas station in the middle of nowhere and tells you to give it to me and nothing? No spidey senses go off?" She rolled her eyes and picked the folded piece of paper from where it had fallen onto her notebook. "How have you ever survived all these years?"

"Oh right; almost forgot. He told me some guy came up to his truck and gave him fifty dollars to hand the note to you. I know you'll be disappointed, but it's probably not the fat guy's phone number." Luba was smiling at her own joke as she hit the start button and tapped the lever upward to engage the transmission. "Got you some Miss Vickie's and Twizzlers! You strapped in? We got a license to fly!"

With that Luba backed out of the parking spot and cranked the wheel to turn the vehicle toward the highway entrance. Then she accelerated out the exit lane like she really did have a license to fly. Not enough snow had fallen to cover the road, or else the Mercedes tires would have certainly lost their grip on the cold asphalt. She was smiling and shoulder-checking for traffic as she merged at 70 miles per hour, not a care in the world. Like nothing totally weird had just taken place.

"*Luba!*" Nyala was shaking the note in her hand at her friend. "*It's not funny!* Just because you may think it's okay to talk to strangers at gas stations, not all of us want to end up dead on the side of some road in the friggin' mountains!"

"Gotcha! No more strangers!" She smiled and looked at her friend. "Unless they're cute strangers! What does it say?"

The note was folded. Nyala held it in her hands and then carefully opened it. She started reading out loud.

Nyala, I am here. I am with you.

You must trust me, do exactly as I say. They are coming.

There was more, and by the time she read the whole note out loud her heart was once again racing.

Luba said what they were both thinking.

"WTF?"

42

The snow was falling now in thick flakes that seemed to hang motionless until they were swept back over the front windshield. The road was white except for the double line of wet black vehicle tracks going forward and another set on the far side of the narrow highway, marking the way for travelers going the opposite direction.

A semitrailer tractor slammed by them, heading back in the direction they'd come from, plastering the windshield with a thick layer of slush. It was something that normally would have elicited an immediate and volatile response from her friend, but this was not the time. Instead she reached with her fingers and simply flicked the wipers to a faster speed.

Nyala knew there would be no more fact checking.

It was too late now; she was all in and she had no way of researching anything even if there was a need to. Everything in the manuscript was true. All of it, from the first word she'd read in her driveway only two weeks before, to the last word she'd read a few minutes earlier, and all the words she would read from here on. And in those truths, somewhere in those words, she would find knowledge and salvation.

"You okay, girl?" Luba reached over and held Nyala's arm, just above the wrist.

After they left the gas station near Banff and Nyala read the note out loud to her, she knew her friend Luba finally grasped the gravity of the situation. It wasn't a joke any longer, it wasn't a lark; the two friends were in uncharted territory. People had died. People had been killed. They were being stalked, followed every mile of the way by somebody called Tsau-z. He had to be close to them now. In front?

Behind them? Was he somehow above them? Tracking them and anticipating their pulling into the truck stop?

The note warned that somebody was coming for them. They'd done as it instructed and then driven in silence for a long time after that. Then Luba asked Nyala to read out loud from the manuscript and had been uncharacteristically quiet the entire time, listening.

————

She was the light and she was the darkness. She was all that we were, are, and all that we can be. She was dancing for all of us. She was dancing for this world.

Boom. Boom. Boom.

She was dancing for me and I saw for the first time. Saw beauty that was inconceivable, every color in the universe, every sound, every feeling in her movement.

It was Her.

The Daughter of God.

The Keeper of the Breath.

It was the Soul Catcher.

————

As moving as the passage was, the first tear didn't fall because of what she'd just finished reading; it fell because tears were all that she had left inside her to mark the way back to who she had been. Another tear rolled down from the corner of her eye, leaving a wet trail to the spot on her chin where the first one still hung. Joined, the two tears held on to each other for a moment, before falling away forever, blotting the open pages on her lap.

It was too much.

She felt overwhelmed.

Her tears were not tears of sorrow, or joy. They were tears of emptiness.

The life she'd known was four thousand miles behind her, a trail of wreckage away. Bits and pieces of the person she'd been ripped away, left where they fell, until she had nothing else to leave behind, nothing to mark the way back, except for the tears. They were all that was left of who she had been. But why did she need to mark the trail back, when she knew she would never return? Her future was forward now and so was her past. Going back would mean living a future of never knowing.

If anyone knew the answer to the question "What good was a future without a past?" it was Nyala. All she ever wanted from as far back as she could remember was to know who she was. The manuscript contained the answers, she was sure of that now. Tsau-z, whoever he was, was guiding her on the journey toward her own past. But the warning: it was just as real as everything she'd been able to research in the manuscript.

Was she willing to die to learn who she was? Yes. She was resigned to whatever fate awaited her and it was that inner acknowledgment, the resignation, that caused the emptiness she felt inside. She wiped another tear away.

"Ny Ny?"

"I'm good." She took a deep breath. "I'm fine."

They drove in pensive silence for a time.

A train, hanging on the stony face of the mountain across the valley, disappeared one car at a time into a tunnel, like a mile-long snake sliding into a hole. She dabbed her blurred eyes with the back of her sleeve and then watched the train over her shoulder until she couldn't see it any longer. The highway was winding now and the going slow. It was snowing and the dirty back end of a massive semitrailer several hundred yards ahead had been blocking even Luba's desire for speed for the last thirty miles. It was too dangerous to pass.

In a few more hours the two friends would be at their destination. Emptiness, resignation, and fear of the unknown were her inner companions, but Nyala knew that her friend was filled with determination to take care of her, come hell or high water.

"It'll be okay. I'm here." Luba gave her friend's arm a squeeze to reassure her. "It's what you've always wanted, right? But we can turn around, you know. Right now. Just give me the word."

No. There was no turning around. Forward was what Nyala wanted.

What she always wanted; thought she always wanted, at least. To know the truth about herself, to know the answer to the question, who she was and why she was. To make sense of what had been so senseless to her all these years, to make sense of what everyone else took for granted. Who are you? A question anyone could answer about themselves. It was a question that she had asked herself every day of her life and it was a question that she had never been able to answer.

She pulled the note from her pocket and read it again.

———

Nyala, I am here. I am with you.

You must trust me, do exactly as I say. They are coming.

Stop at the pullout twenty-seven kilometers ahead, the one just after the bighorn sheep crossing sign, and leave your mobile phone in the brush under a rock. Have your friend do the same with hers. They can track you.

Nyala, you must believe me. It is the only way. You will get a new phone when you get to Vancouver. Use only cash from here on.

Go to the Vancouver airport, check into the Fairmont hotel there. Use the valet for your car. Be sitting by the fireplace in the lounge at 5 p.m. tomorrow.

To my dying day and my last free breath,

Every heartbeat is for you.

Tsau-z.

———

She folded the note and put it back in her pocket. What did it all mean? Who was coming for her? Why? Our World? What did they care about her? Luba wasn't exactly thrilled when they pulled into the emergency parking pullout by the river. They'd looked at each other, wondering what they were doing. Luba threw her phone into the rushing waters, as far as she could, and then stomped back to the Mercedes.

It wasn't what the note said to do, but Nyala wasn't about to say anything. It was too late anyway; the phone was long gone, lost in the copper-blue glacial water. Instead, Nyala took extra care following the instructions to a fault. She searched through the undergrowth and trees to find a suitable spot and then pulled a rock over and placed her phone under it. She was mindful not to let the rock fall back hard on the phone in case it shattered the glass face.

There was a bar or two, but the battery would be dead soon. Good luck to anyone tracking the phone to its resting place under a stone by a river in the middle of the Canadian Rockies. In a strange way she felt suddenly liberated. No more obsessive-compulsive need to fact-check. How could she? The better question was, why should she? Virtually everything she'd read in the manuscript had been proven true, or if not absolutely proven true, there were too many connections for coincidence to be a reasonable conclusion.

Luba was frowning, something Nyala usually did.

"So tell me if I got this straight. This guy is the superkid and he's one of the hot guys in the Speedos. He hooked up with some tall scarred-up secret-agent chick called Joan in Belgium in 1978 and then again in Vancouver seven years later, where we're headed, back around 1985, right?" Flippant and carefree, Luba's personality presets were still evident as she sorted out what Nyala had been reading out loud to her for much of the drive through the mountains. "They both worked for some crazy Russian who was the leader of some kind of worldwide James Bond art auction place. Right?"

The windshield wipers swept back and forth, whomp, whomp, whomp, as they both thought through the timelines and names in the manuscript. Luba was the first to break the silence.

"Geez, can you go any slower, buddy?" She had both hands on the wheel and was craning her neck to see around the tractor trailer she'd closed the distance on.

Nyala looked out the streaked windshield. The wipers were going at full speed, fighting to keep the brown water kicking back from the eighteen-wheeler from totally obscuring their forward vision. The clunking of the windshield wipers, whomp, whomp, whomp, was calming, cathartic, and melancholy at the same time. Back and forth, back and forth; no real purpose other than to do their thankless job, never accomplishing anything of lasting value. Like her life had been.

It took an effort to shut the negative thought out.

"That's pretty much right. The kid's name was Hunter, but he became Icarus and then Tsau-z. And I think he lived in Vancouver starting in the mid-seventies and all through the eighties when he wasn't traveling. He went to university there and had an antique store I think and he was in New York when the other operative, Joan of Arc, found the two carved duck decoys."

"So who is that asshole Zhivago anyway? Date-raped the girl and then went to the antihunting protest with Tsau-z, right? And that last part you were reading was where Tsau-z found that Soul Catcher thing at that antihunting convention. Right?"

"Tsau-z, yes, he was at the antihunting protest in 1994. So was Zhivago, he was another operative for Our World, but I couldn't find anything about him other than what I read to you. Tsau-z wasn't the same by then though; something changed him, something about those two carved decoys he saw with Joan of Arc in 1985. Something happened."

Nyala felt herself slipping.

"He said that was when he became who he was supposed to be."

The wipers blurred, the windshield blurred, the truck ahead, the snow, all faded, and the blackness started closing in.

Something happened to him. He changed. He became who he was supposed to be.

Something happened and now she was changing too.

But changing into what? Was she changing into who *she* was supposed to be?

The blackness was about to swallow even the flashing hazard lights on the semitrailer truck ahead.

No!

Nyala willed it away; she would not open her arms and let herself fall backward into the weightless forever, the void where nothing mattered, where there was no past, no future, only existence; breathing in and out, alive but not living.

Hopelessness and despair.

Whomp. Whomp. Whomp.

It was a comforting rhythm, a gentle ally, steadfast by her side in the battle against the darkness that had been threatening to envelop her so often in the previous days.

The tight highway and Douglas fir–covered slopes were behind them now and traffic was picking up. The steep, nearly vertical mountains that had been constant for hours set the Mercedes and its two passengers free, releasing them to the wide-open pastoral expanse of the Fraser Valley. Hope was the last town, Chilliwack the next, but in a way, Nyala wished it was the other way around. She wished Hope was the future and Chilliwack was behind them.

She picked up the manuscript and began reading out loud to her friend again.

No blackness now, only the words on the pages in front of her.

Tsau-z's words.

Her future.

And her past.

*S*oon you will know, Nyala.
     Soon you will understand.
   It's in your blood.
   It's in my blood.
   It's in our blood.
   We are hunters. We feel the wild, we are the wild.
   For so long I denied it, ignored it, like we all do. I did not embrace the living thing inside me that pulled at my spirit, pulled me away from what was socially acceptable. So strange to me now, Nyala, the way we live in our cities, tens of millions, hundreds, so far from the very thing that allowed the best of our antecedents to survive and to pass their blood to the next generation and the next and the next.
   We live apart from Nature now and that is considered acceptable, but living in Nature, being part of Nature is not. Living as our ancestors did is somehow unacceptable.
   Such hypocrisy.
   Such a loss.
   We live on top of each other, content to breathe fouled air, content to eat manufactured food, content to live in the layered monoliths that with the introduction of the tiniest of pathogens become our prisons, our tombs.
   We live each day the same as the previous day; the same as the next. We rid ourselves of responsibility for our actions. Self-determination is determined by what others think. We simply redo. Redo. Redo. Redo.
   We don't know better, Nyala. How can we?
   And we follow each other around and around and around.
   We do care. Our hearts bleed for that which we know is missing

in our lives, the freedom to live in Nature, the freedom to be a living part of Nature; and a dying part.

And so we seek redemption, for a way to show penance, to sacrifice something important to us, money. The cure we prescribe to each other is to buy absolution, to tax each other; to buy carbon is more acceptable than shouldering responsibility for the monster we have created.

The monster that all of us have created.

No matter what we believe, what we eat, how or where we live or how supremely we adhere to ideologies founded on the principles of I-me-we-are-holier-than-thou, we are all responsible for this monster. Each and every one of us has contributed to the burden.

Every one of us, since the day we turned our backs on hunting and gathering.

We dirty this beautiful world and blame ourselves for it and yet it is a truth that we cannot live with. So we prostrate ourselves before the righteousness and good intentions of mass-think.

Save the world.

Civilized humanity; doctrines founded on utopia. It is a place we all want and will to be real, attainable. But unfortunately, Nyala, such a world does not exist.

So we build walls around ourselves to keep our ideas in.

And we build walls to keep new ideas out.

We follow each other around and around, living inside a circle of self-confirmation. Living with the untruths we repeat to each other over and over until those untruths become true.

In this way we justify that the damage we are doing to this world is not being done by us. How can we be responsible? We paid penance. We confessed, and by our purity of thought, have been absolved. It isn't us; it is them. It is always the others who are causing the problem.

I was one of them. I lived there. In the city. I breathed their air. I walked and talked with them and for a time I was them, but it wasn't me, Nyala.

I was caged in bars I wove around myself, like a silkworm in a cocoon of wrought iron.

I lived, unknowing, slowly transforming inside that cold cell, not realizing that there would come a day when from that larval being would emerge something so different, so much more at peace than the crude groping creature that first wrapped the melded iron around itself. Around myself.

Metamorphosis.

I entered as one thing and upon the day I beheld the Ellis brants I emerged, changed from who I was, from what my life had been, to who I am.

She saw it, she was there. She held me as I unfolded my wings and she stayed with me for those days, the weeks that followed, the months, she was there by my side. She nurtured me as one would nurture another emerging from a lifelong coma. I had to learn to live with my new nature, learn to fly. She held me in her hands and warmed me until the sun dried my unfurling wings and by the glory of immaculate transformation, changed me from what I once was to what I now am.

Nyala, I never thanked her.

She was there, through it all. Protecting me in that time when I was most vulnerable, and I gave her nothing in return.

She held me while time cured and tempered what I had become.

I was a hunter.

Tentative at first, without direction, following nothing, genuflecting to the caprices of the wind, I floated above the world that I knew before, returning to her after each flight, returning to that which I'd known. But it wasn't me.

Slowly we, the mountains, the forests, and the lakes, became one. I was theirs and they were mine. The wild lands became my home, and the wild lands came to live inside me.

She knew.

I remember her waving back at me when I left for good, when I left for my good, Nyala.

When my ship set sail for that farthest sea.

So sad.

I was not capable of returning her attentions then, Nyala. A lifetime of regrets. It's too late now to right those wrongs.

Joan of Arc.

So long since I have said that name. But in the darkness now, lying all alone, I say her name and know I did her wrong.

Joan of Arc.

I am sorry.

Nyala, for me.

Tell her I am sorry.

43

1996

RUSSIA
UNDISCLOSED LOCATION

t's a fucking fake." The Russian was furious. "Who sent it?"

"Joan of Arc."

The other man in the room, barely visible in the light's low-cast illumination, answered, but tried to make himself look even less than he was, tried to shrink further back from the vision of the old man sitting on the far side of the table.

It was a waste of time; it was impossible; the old man prided himself on being all-seeing and he'd just seen that he'd been screwed. Our World had been screwed. Someone would pay.

Unsure of how to respond without invoking additional wrath, the shrinking man said nothing. Instead, he held still and waited.

Nicolas Poussin's *The Death of the Virgin* was right in every way: the paint, the frame, the materials, even the imagery was unquestionably the greatest work of Poussin. A legend, the painting was lost to the outside world when Archbishop of Paris Jean-François de Gondi's family chapel in the cathedral of Notre-Dame de Paris was looted by French Revolutionary insurgents. That happened 150 years after it was painted by the famed master, Poussin. The masterpiece originally commissioned by de Gondi disappeared into the turmoil that was the revolution, erased from the realm of knowledge during the ensuing civil strife; erased from the knowledge of all those save for the learned and those who traveled in the most august of art circles.

Lost to the world of art is how it remained, for nearly two hundred years, until the moment it was presented to the leader of Our World by the shrinking man.

The problem was, the real *Death of the Virgin* by Poussin had been discovered exactly thirty-two years before Joan of Arc's discovery of the painting lying on the table. The only people who would or could know that fact were those selected few who attended the Gathering three decades ago, most of whom were now long gone from this earth. The old man, the leader of Our World, was sitting in the very seat he sat in now when the original *Death of the Virgin* was shown to him for the first time all those years before.

The leader of Our World showed no emotion now, because he wasn't feeling any. His fury was replaced with cold-blooded professionalism. There were business decisions to be made. Joan of Arc's gift had been failing incrementally for the last decade. In spite of the early promise and some early successes, she'd come up with nothing of note for the Gathering since the Ellis brants back in 1985, and even then he'd been forced to pull Icarus off his work in New York to confirm they were real.

It was time for the operative he'd code-named Joan of Arc to be decommissioned.

The years had caught up to the leader; his sunken, rheumy eyes and the lines on the sides of those eyes betrayed the decades he had been sitting alone in absolute power. The lines were deeper than ever now and spoke of abominations and atrocities he had sanctioned during his tenure on top of the Our World pyramid. The lines had nothing to do with laughter or joy.

His time would come. That fact entered his mind now, even as he came to the conclusion that Joan of Arc's time had come. He wondered, even as he made the decision to decommission the faltering operative, how his own "decommissioning" would happen. His would be a different ending than hers and he didn't like it. As with the animal kingdom, where the father sires offspring who grow strong and eventually best him in a battle for dominance, so too had it always been for Our World leaders.

As his predecessor had chosen him, he had chosen his own successor, a successor who was through the training period now, waiting for the moment of his graduation. Although it would not be an official act, graduation would come, and it would come sooner rather than later. For the second time in as many minutes he let his professionalism slip, for the thought of his unseating angered him. Decades of being in absolute power, as power was wont to, had corrupted him and made him only want to possess it longer.

Like all the operatives of Our World, who were chosen for their gifts, so too were the leaders of Our World chosen for the singularly rare qualities that he himself possessed. The Our World web that cloaked the globe in unseen silky fibers would vibrate when the one special human being out of billions touched one of the threads. And that child, the future leader of Our World, would be brought into the fold.

His own successor had been found, guided, and indoctrinated thirty years before, near the beginning of his tenure. Time did not stop for the powerful any more than it stopped for the most insignificant living thing. His time was almost up, but until that moment, he was still all-powerful.

The smell of fear was strong in the darkened room. The man sitting before him was afraid for his life, as he should be.

The leader of Our World stared at the offensive mutation lying on the tabletop. It was good, really good. Only Zhivago or Icarus would have been able to tell it was a forgery without the prior knowledge that the authentic *Death of the Virgin* had already been discovered and sold at the Gathering decades before.

There was only one forger capable of being the father of such a creation. Hebborn. Eric Hebborn.

The leader of Our World leaned back in his chair far enough out of the light cast by the small lamp so that his pale eyes were shadowed. His features were softened, but the lessened light did nothing to soften his heart. It had been his predecessor's decision, decades before, not to recruit the young and extremely talented artist to work with Our World. The decision was not made without foreknowledge of the potential downside if the young artist lived up to his test results.

The leader at the time had been informed that there had been a vibration in the Our World web; a young artist with the "gift" had been discovered in London. It was during World War II and the then leader considered bringing the eight-year-old future forger into the fold, but there were disturbing warning signs in the test results that confirmed, even at his early age, that the artist was resistant to authority. So the connection was cut and instead the youth was placed under a loose surveillance, a watchful arm's-length attention that would last his entire lifetime.

Hebborn's artistic talents were comparable to the greatest of masters but destined from a young age to be squandered in protest over perceived slights leveled at him by the venal curators and art historians vested with the power to choose who would be a contemporary artist of repute and who would not.

In their unjustifiable arrogance, they inadvertently inspired the young artist to commit his life to forgery. They disdained his work and so he forged and fed them the forgeries.

He was an asset to Our World, not as the operative he might have been, but an asset nonetheless. Hebborn created chaos in the outside world of art and that was something Our World not only understood but nurtured. What was it? Three? Or was it four separate times the forger should have been arrested, charged, convicted, and neutralized, banished from the art world, but every time, the leader of Our World stepped in, saving the unwitting and proud Eric Hebborn the ignominy of certain incarceration.

Years later, when the forger announced to the world that the works in so many galleries and museums were his forgeries, he was not charged with a crime, or even investigated by any authority. Scotland Yard turned the other way. The FBI turned the other way. After 1991, even TRACFIN, or Intelligence Processing and Action Against Clandestine Financial Circuits, the newly formed French agency based on rigid adherence to the tenets of law and order, looked the other way.

They turned their heads thanks to Our World intervention.

It was all good for the leader. Turmoil in the outside world of art was a ringing endorsement for the secret attendees of the Gathering, where forgeries were deemed to be an impossible happening. Disruption and chaos created opportunity that the leader of Our World took full advantage of, slipping forgeries into the mainstream, forgeries that his operatives discovered or that other operatives produced for Our World. Forgeries had always been used by Our World to instill distrust in the real-world customers for fine art. Although he was never fully indoctrinated as an operative, Hebborn was to a degree brought into the confidence of Our World, to avoid the chance of one of his works finding its way to the Gathering.

But now, by virtue of the fake painting on the table, purposely passed to an Our World operative, it was apparent that the forger wasn't content with the turmoil he created in the international art markets, wasn't satisfied that his forgeries had fooled the authenticators from such erudite institutions as the British Museum, the National Gallery of Art in Washington, DC, even the Met in New York. It wasn't enough for him that the forgeries created by his hand had been purchased for display in venerated institutions and private collections—he wanted more.

Vainglorious, he wanted recognition. Wanted everyone to know that he was as good as the masters of old and better than the modern-day experts who had judged his own original work to be inferior. To this end, he had taken on the experts at Our World.

The leader tolerated Hebborn but had also sent clear warnings to the forger to never try to pass off one of his works to the operatives seeking artistic treasures for the Gathering. As honor exists among thieves, so did honor exist for the leader of Our World. But when that trust was breached, honor for him meant something very different. For him honor was the antithesis of Newton's law stating that an action always had an equal and opposite reaction. The forger's action would result in a reaction that would not be equal and opposite; it would be very unequal.

The forger, in his vanity, was not satisfied with fooling those of limited ability; he had now chosen to test his mettle against Our World, to denigrate the very thing that had allowed him to continue his war on the art establishment. He had placed a fake into the hands of Joan of Arc. She didn't feel it. She was worthless to Our World now and protocol would be followed for her decommissioning. If she was deemed to be duplicitous, somehow working with the forger to pass on the fake to Our World, protocol would involve decommissioning of a different sort.

The forger's fate was sealed when the next words came from the leader's mouth.

"Charlotte. Where is she?"

The messenger, who had been balancing on that sharp blade that often separates life from death, felt the blade shift, almost causing him to lose that balance.

To lie was to die.

"Here."

The old man frowned into the soft light cast by the table lamp, illuminating him, but barely so; it did not illuminate the space behind where he sat, leaving that space as black as the emptiness on the far side of the moon. Used to making decisions quickly, without a second thought, he hesitated. All-seeing meant also possessing intuition and there was something in the answer that alerted him to that which he could not see with his eyes and could not hear with his ears but knew was there.

Something, what was it?

Maybe it was before or maybe it was after, but either way, whenever comprehension came to him, it came too late. His minion's answer "here" was not meant in a general sense of "here" as in somewhere in the city or country, but instead was meant in the very literal sense, as in "here," right here, right now.

The thin high-tensile wire fit around his neck nicely, sliding with a whisper over his head, and then it settled above his larynx, but under the angle of his mandible, between the jaw body and the ramus. The pressure, only four pounds per square inch, didn't increase until the wire was in perfect position a tenth of a second later; about as long as it took understanding to flood into the brain of the about-to-be-former leader of Our World.

The transition of power from the past leader to his successor took the exact same amount of time for the compression of the carotid arteries to cause irreversible global cerebral ischemia. In those ten long seconds, the old man with the pointed white beard, his head tipped back, looked upward into the eyes of that very same instrument of death that so many times before he had, without remorse, ordered to do his bidding. She was still the best, a point that under normal circumstances would have filled him with pride.

All that he had been, all that he had accomplished, all that he thought, all that he desired was erased in the ten seconds it took him to lose consciousness. There wasn't time to struggle and even if his brain had been able to function, there wasn't any point. His term as leader of Our World was over. It had ended as it should, as he had known it had to, the same as his own tenure began, with finality, with surety. Power of the powerful was never relinquished; it could only be taken.

If the smell of fear in the room, emanating from the messenger who had not moved a fraction of an inch while the events before him unfolded, had been hinted at before, it was now a stench.

Five minutes later, the body, soiled and adding its own odor to the smell of fear in the room, ceased twitching. The body was still on the chair when the wire was carefully removed with some difficulty because it had cut so deeply into the skin. From the darkness behind the body, the assassin, dressed in black and holding the garrote, moved to the side of the chair and lifted the lifeless left arm.

The hands that undid the clasp holding the large watch on the former leader's wrist did not appear to belong to someone capable of what those hands had just accomplished. They were gentle, deft. One of the hands placed the watch on the table to the side of the gold-framed painting and then both hands pushed the body off the chair. It fell to the floor, where the head, without functioning neck muscles to hold it from hitting, bounced hard, like a heavy wooden ball.

The hands then reached down and with a strength that seemed to defy physics took hold of the former leader's jacket collar and dragged him away from the table where he'd held court for so many decades. A few moments later, the dragging sound stopped, and a door closed in the blackness. Another few moments later, another door clicked open somewhere far in the distance and footsteps told of someone approaching the light.

A youngish-looking man appeared out of the blackness and stood by the vacant seat. His slim body was covered in an expensive suit. Dark blue, the fine woolen weave soaked the light in and blended into the darkness behind. His skin was perfect, his ascot perfect. Everything about him was perfect and in place. His glasses, with thick white plastic rims, were perched high on his sharp nose and his face was clean-shaven. His hair was evenly cut, straight and black. That he was descended from Guangdong peasantry, working ant laborers in southern China for the previous three thousand years, would have been impossible to tell from looking at him. He was about to turn forty and he had been groomed for this position since he was taken from his parents at ten years of age.

It was his time.

The messenger, traumatized by the event he'd just witnessed, still had enough awareness for his survival instincts to kick in. He jumped from his chair, took hold of it, and brought it to the other side of the table, switching it for the chair with the unclean seat. That chair he took back to where his chair had been and then sat down again.

The new leader sat then on the clean chair and reached for the watch. His slender manicured fingers easily and quickly slid it on his thin wrist and connected the clasp.

He admired the watch for a moment and then returned his attention to the forgery on the table. If his predecessor was ruthless in directing the affairs of Our World, the new leader knew his rule would make the former leader's time in office be remembered as a gentle rain, a soft warm summer drizzle. The young man of peasant ancestry would bring the fury of a thousand-year storm to the office he now held. The precision of his features belied a thinly veiled arrogance. Under his leadership, he planned to build an empire. Our World would rise ever higher, and his name would bring dread to any who would stand in the way of his ambition.

The transition was complete. As had the previous leader and the leader before that and the leader before that, he'd done exactly as they had done and exactly as the new King of Beasts does to his own father: he kills him. Unlike the new leader of the lion pride, the man with the white glasses and precise features didn't have to do his own wet work. He had Charlotte to do that. In fact, he had a hundred of Charlotte's kind at his command.

There was unfinished business to attend to.

"Where is Hebborn?"

It was easy to see in the low light cast from the lamp on the table that the messenger's eyes were open wide. The lamp had not been dislodged, even when the legs of the former leader stiffened to rigidity in the throes of his death.

"Rome."

"Send Charlotte. She is done here." He paused, savoring the delicious image that came to his mind. "Instruct her that there will be no garrote. Tell her that it is now reserved, as it was always intended, for nobility. Tell her to use . . ."

He paused for a moment.

"Yes. Tell her to use a hammer. Make it messy." He smiled at the image.

The operative Joan of Arc was another matter. The new leader did not have a working relationship with her and so held nothing for or against her. She was simply used-up inventory, excess baggage now, and he was unwilling to spend a moment more than necessary thinking about her. The operative was now a liability to his upwardly mobile plan for Our World. If she was no longer endowed with the gifts that made her a valuable operative, she was nothing to him.

"Was she involved?" The new leader, should he be seen in the streets of Shanghai, could have passed for someone who had just returned from the Far Eastern version of a *GQ* magazine photo shoot; the "Who's Hot" in Macau or Hong Kong. He knew it and embraced his own vanity.

"Nyet."

"Decommission her."

"Da."

An operative losing their "gift" was something that happened with surprising frequency, especially if the original gift came to the operative under duress as opposed to the operative being born with the gift. Such operatives, bereft of their gift, were kept in reserve, allowed to choose a place of residence, provided it was a major urban center. They were given cover stories, permanently embedded in their community of choice, and used as expediters when and if the need arose for a functioning operative to work in that area. It was protocol.

Knowledgeable in the ways of Our World, operatives represented a substantial investment. To simply eliminate them made little financial sense. With a trained eye for art, they still had value. Demotion, in the vernacular of Our World, meant indentured servitude.

If Joan of Arc refused, if she balked, if she tried to run, if she did not comply, if she questioned, she would not be decommissioned, she would be terminated according to protocol. If she dared speak about Our World secrets to anyone, the protocol for such a transgression was also termination, but a much, much more distressing, slower, and torturous one. It was intended to make a point to all other operatives. Talking about Our World, outside Our World circles, was unacceptable.

The new leader sat straight up in his chair. Unlike the former leader, he did not lean back. He looked down at the forgery on the table. Charlotte would soon be on her way to Rome to take care of Hebborn and send a loud and clear message to the operatives and all associated underlings of Our World. A new leader was in power. The thought made him happy. In a way, he hoped there would be another who might cross the line so that he could turn that person into a message as well.

He dismissed the thought and raised his eyes to stare at the wretched creature before him. Like a cat focused on its prey, he considered the pleasure he would get from playing with the messenger, but then freed his prey with a wave of his hand.

"Go."

When the frightened minion rose and reached to take the forged painting away, the man wearing the white-rimmed glasses held up his hand, stopping the action.

"Leave it."

The minion did as he was told, turned, and left, quietly disappearing into the blackness.

The new leader of Our World wanted to savor the memory of his rise to absolute power. He did not see the forgery as an aberration to be destroyed, as the previous leader did, or sold back into the unknowing public world of art. No. He saw it as a trophy to remind him of the day he so easily took the life and the position of the old man with the pointed white beard.

It would stand as testament to this moment, his moment. It would become the symbol that represented the death of what Our World had been for over two hundred years and the birth of what Our World would become under his stewardship, an empire that would last two thousand years.

An empire risen on this day.

Woe to those who would stand in his path.

44

2020

VANCOUVER, BRITISH COLUMBIA

Nyala's heart did a flip when she saw him. Tsau-z?
Maybe.

The man entering the Fairmont Vancouver Airport hotel lounge moved with a purpose, passing the bar where several patrons interested in watching sports on television sat on stools, nursing their drinks, separated by the new socially acceptable distancing rules. It was 5 p.m. and he was about the right age, sixtyish, tall, carrying himself like a former athlete. Plus he'd definitely noticed the two of them sitting by the fireplace. Fair enough. They were both dressed in the only clean jeans they owned, the only clean tops they owned as well, and Luba, cute as ever, was wearing a cowboy hat. All the men in the room noticed them, all the women as well.

"It's him," Luba hissed.

She'd already announced the arrival of three previous Tsau-zs, all three of whom Nyala was sure her friend purposely chose because they couldn't possibly be the man they were waiting for, the operative known as Icarus. The first Tsau-z had to be ninety years old and was using a walker when he trudged into the lounge with his equally aged wife holding on to his arm, another couldn't have been out of university yet, and the third of Luba's Tsau-zs was an enormous fellow who obviously hadn't seen the inside of a gym for the forty years he'd probably lived on planet Earth. Somehow Nyala didn't believe the actual Tsau-z would look like that, no offense intended.

Nyala knew Luba was just being Luba; flippant, incapable of being serious for long, no matter how dire the straits. As Luba had done for all the previous non–Tsau-zs, she went into full pantomiming pretend-spy mode, leaning forward dramatically to reach for her beer glass, making it clear to Nyala and to anyone who was paying attention that she was really only trying to get close enough to be able to hiss her loud "It's him" to her friend. She couldn't have been more obvious, confirming what Nyala already knew about her friend, that besides her attention-deficit disorder she would make the world's crappiest spy.

But the fourth Tsau-z wasn't him either. The new visitor to the lounge continued past the low table where the two young women had stationed themselves on two of the four overstuffed chairs nearly an hour before. The big stone fireplace beside them was gas, so it didn't throw off much heat, but it did add a pleasant ambience.

Not bad for an airport hotel lounge, but Luba had bitched a blue streak about the price of a glass of draft beer when they first sat down to order. Nyala knew the usual cash supply Luba always carried with her had to be running low, especially since she'd filled the Mercedes with gas in Kamloops and she'd also paid more than $300 in cash for the Fairmont hotel room. French fries weren't on the menu either, which only added to her displeasure, but fortunately deep-fried calamari was, which made Luba happy and stopped her price-of-beer tirade. Between stuffing the crunchy rings into her mouth, she redirected her negative energies toward the fact that she was unable to use her credit cards and that throwing away her cell phone was plain old dumb. She wasn't about to let either issue go.

"It's not him." Luba pointed out the obvious and turned to try to catch the attention of the lady who was serving them.

Luba was disappointed, but Nyala was relieved. She wanted to meet Tsau-z but wasn't sure she was ready for what she hoped he would be able to tell her. And if she was honest with herself, she was starting to grow angry at the whole absurd situation, especially sitting in a normal place, surrounded by normal people who didn't have to worry about kids with superpowers and secret agents. The more she thought about it, the more her anger grew. Really? Assassins?

And intrigue? It was all so far-fetched, it should have been laughable, but here she was, like a gullible idiot.

She wished she had never opened her mailbox that day.

There was a young lady setting up what looked to be a vintage Gibson amplifier not far away. The evening's live entertainment had arrived. The girl looked to be in her late twenties, the same age as Nyala, and she had an acoustic guitar with her. After the musician reached behind the amp to make sure it was plugged in, she went about organizing her stool and microphones.

Nyala was thankful the musician was there setting up. It offered her a few moments' respite from the stress of not knowing what might happen next and why. The note from Tsau-z hadn't been cryptic, as most of his writing had been. It was evident he'd been following them from the day they left North Carolina. Nyala didn't like the feeling of being stalked. The note contained a clear warning. They needed to be careful, but she didn't have a bloody clue what they were supposed to be careful of and she was pissed-off about that as well.

The anger she was feeling wasn't so much about not knowing what she should be watching out for; it was more that Tsau-z's uninvited entry into her life had caused her to lose control of that life, at least the day-to-day part that she was used to keeping under such tight wraps. That and the fact that she was angry with herself, angry that she was frightened, filled with doubt and trepidation about meeting the man who she now believed held the answers to the questions she'd asked for so many years. Who was she?

There were so many other questions she had to ask him, all that he would hopefully be able to answer. Who was her grandmother? What was her name? How did he know she was her grandmother? How old was she when she died? Why didn't her grandmother reach out to her when she was alive? Whose mother had she been? Her own mother's mother? Why didn't her mother reach out to her? Would she be at the funeral? What about her father? Was he alive? Were they alive? Where did they live? Why did they give her up?

God knew she'd tried to answer all those questions herself. Over the years she'd searched findmypast.com and adopted.org. She'd done it all, birth, adoption, and orphanage records. She'd tried everything to find out who she was. She'd even sicced Scott on the project, but then put a halt to his efforts when he hit a dead end and started asking even more personal questions to help him in the search, questions she had not been prepared to answer; some that even she didn't want to look in the mirror and ask *herself.*

As pathetic as her life may have been before Tsau-z entered stage right unannounced, it was hers to live as she saw fit, but now even that was being taken away from her. She was starting to feel swept along by forces she couldn't understand. The whole cloak-and-dagger routine was growing old. If this Tsau-z guy was going to turn the world that she knew upside down, he'd better show up and he'd better be able to answer her questions.

"Excuse me?"

Nyala looked up and Luba glanced over at the tall woman as well but turned away when the waitress showed up holding a tray with two more glasses of beer and the glass of grapefruit juice Luba ordered. It was her new thing, mixing the grapefruit juice in the beer, something she'd learned from the cowboy named Jay in Saskatoon. It had to be a hazy IPA beer though, she'd explained to Nyala earlier in the evening.

The woman who'd walked over to them was the woman who'd been sitting at a table against the windows by herself the entire time they'd been in the lounge. Nyala noticed her when they first arrived but hadn't really paid any attention to her since she was just another traveler, spending the night at the airport hotel, enjoying a drink by herself. But now that the woman, who appeared to be in her fifties, was standing beside their table, looking down at her, Nyala couldn't help but notice how striking she was.

How tall and striking she was in an androgynous Josie Borain kind of way.

Nyala felt the rush start at her feet and hammer through her body. A jolt of electricity that was as old as mankind: fight or flight.

Joan of Arc!

———

"No, it's true. He used to take truckloads of his ethnocentric folk art furniture down to Hollywood. Primitive painted pine mostly."

The woman reached down and pulled a manila envelope from the vintage bag she'd placed by her seat. It was more of a shoulder bag than a briefcase; beautifully cut and made from what looked to be shark skin, maybe eel, it had to be a designer product from the 1920s. Somehow Nyala doubted the woman sitting beside her would settle for a modern reproduction. "He'd set the furniture up in the home of one of his movie star clients who would host furniture parties, valet parking, open bar, catered affairs. They'd all come."

"I love your bag." Luba was like a crow, dropping the conversation for a brighter, more interesting bauble. "I like your shoes too."

The tall woman smiled at Luba.

"Thank you. And that is quite a hat you're wearing. Very nice."

"So the stuff about being with those movie people was true? All of it?" Nyala also appreciated the tasteful accoutrements, but right then an atomic bomb going off in the room would not have distracted her from the conversation. Vaporized her maybe, but not distracted her. Once the initial shock wore off, that it wasn't Tsau-z they were to meet, but instead it was Joan of Arc, Nyala had all but turned the meeting into a rapid-fire question period.

"I'm not sure what you know." The tall lady spoke gracefully, and her voice was strong but not harsh. She was sure of herself. A gentle, confident sureness that told of a life lived at the outer edges of imagination.

"I know about the *Bewitched* lady. And Goldie Hawn. And a few more movie people, I think. I didn't get a chance to research all of them. Michael Crichton was one. I looked him up."

"Oh God, child, there were more than a few, so many more; they'd all come to the parties in Hollywood, or to his store on Tenth Avenue here in Vancouver. Do you know he furnished James Taylor's home? Kathryn Walker chose the pieces. He traveled in those circles, always on the search for art. He was so different, and I think that was probably what fascinated those people." She stopped and seemed to think about what she was about to say. "He wasn't the kind of person they would bump into every day. He didn't play by their rules, didn't care if he fit in. He was independent and he was also kind of mysterious. Dark."

"What was Goldie Hawn like?" Nyala knew Luba couldn't help herself.

The older woman had taken the chair next to Nyala and now that she was closer, it was apparent to Nyala that she was probably in her late sixties, maybe even early seventies, not in her fifties like she looked. It wasn't her appearance that gave away her age; it was the nuances in her voice. Besides telling of a life lived beyond most people's imagination, it was a voice that exuded wisdom, of an understanding that could have only come from living longer than fifty years on this earth.

"I never met her, dear. But Icarus told me she was sweet." The tall woman smiled at Luba. "She was a good customer of his, came to his shop all the time when she was in Vancouver. He mentioned that Kurt came as well and their son. Mel Gibson even picked up one of his folk art pieces, a carved fish by Philip Melvin, if memory serves. I was with Icarus for a time in 1985, helping him. As I said, they all came in to see him. Vancouver was called Hollywood North in those days."

She reached into the envelope and pulled the page out, handing it to Nyala.

"You asked if he was a model. Here, September 1984. *Vogue* magazine." She was smiling, remembering. "I told him I had it, but he never cared about things like that. I kept the magazine for a few years, but eventually just tore his page out."

"Wow! I really like the jacket! Is that real sheepskin? Did they do faux leather way back then?" Luba stood up from her chair to look over Nyala's shoulder. "Who's that with him?"

The older woman leaned over to see the page as well.

"It's been so long since I looked at any of this." She reached over to turn the page slightly, to get rid of the reflection off the paper. "She would be a model, a real one. He was working as a model to gain access to the right people in New York, people who might have great art pieces."

Nyala looked at the tear sheet. Tsau-z was a good-looking guy, no question about that.

"So cool! Who else?" Luba sat back in her chair and picked up her glass, taking a sip of the citrus-infused beer. "Who's the most famous person he hung out with?"

"Hard to say. Ralph Lauren furnished all his Country Stores with primitive furniture that Icarus picked for him." She looked at Luba with a kind smile. "You seem like you are a girl who would appreciate that."

"That's crazy!" Luba set her beer down and leaned in closer. "More! Don't stop!"

"Well, let's see, I can tell you that the editor of *Country Living* magazine, I think it was Rachel Newman at that time, published several articles about him over the years. She wrote that he had the finest collection of *country* folk furniture she'd ever seen. But she didn't know what Icarus was *truly* capable of when it came to folk art, or any art for that matter. He was the best." She paused and thought about it for a moment, before continuing, smiling. "Even when I wasn't working with him, I'd see articles about him in magazines. He was in *W*, he and Diego Maradona, they were 'What's Hot' around the world. As an operative, with Our World behind him, he had the ability to make anything happen; anything that would further the primary objective, to find masterpieces. He was even in *Sports Illustrated* when he was swimming."

Nyala set the tear sheet down on the table.

"Why does he call himself Tsau-z?"

"I'm sorry, honey, who?"

"Tsau-z." Nyala frowned, not quite understanding. "Tsau-z. Icarus. Hunter."

"Icarus, I know." The tall woman reached out and touched Nyala's leg. "But I don't know him by the name you mentioned. Or by Hunter. I'm sure you have many things you want to ask me and things you can tell me about. Perhaps it might be helpful if we start from the beginning."

"Wait. Before you start, do you like calamari?" Luba was looking at her hopefully. "I'll order more if you do."

Luba didn't wait for an answer to the question, just waved for the waitress and pointed down at the empty plate in front of her and then held up two fingers. Then she pointed at her empty beer glass and held up three fingers. While she had the server's attention she reached down and picked up the empty grapefruit juice glass and held up three fingers again.

"Wait! Don't start yet. I've got to go to the bathroom." She stood up and started to leave but turned back to where Nyala and the tall woman were seated. "Don't say a word until I get back!"

Nyala smiled. Not a chance.

They watched Luba leave, wending her way between the tables; all the seats around those tables were now filled with travelers stuck on overnight layovers.

It had been instantly gratifying to shoot from the hip instead of starting at the beginning, asking the woman fifty disjointed questions instead of being methodical; she was the first actual live connection to Tsau-z, the first connection to the entire bizarre Our World side of the narrative. Nyala had wanted to get as much information as she could before the woman suddenly shapeshifted and disappeared. But now that it was apparent that the former operative wasn't going to vanish in a puff of smoke, it was time for Nyala to fall back on her journalistic training. She hadn't asked to be part of this insane narrative, but since she *was* involved, she was going to find out what was going on.

"Okay; the beginning." Nyala looked at her own notepad, open on the table, searching until she found the right page. "When did you meet Icarus? Was it in Belgium? That Ghent Altarpiece?"

They both waited for the waitress to change the empty pretzel bowl, compliments of Luba, with a full one. When the lady left to look after other customers, Joan of Arc answered the question.

"Yes. It was Belgium. That was the first time we worked together." She looked at Nyala with a quizzical expression. "You should know, I haven't heard from Icarus since 1985. It's been thirty-five years. I received a note, like you did. It was on my kitchen table. He said to meet you here. He asked me to help you. I'm surprised he told you about the Ghent Altarpiece. I'm surprised he told you any of this, especially about Our World."

"Why?" It wasn't a question Nyala planned to ask; it was more of a reaction to what she'd just heard.

"Because they won't tolerate it; he broke the rules telling you anything." The tall woman paused for a second, as if she was trying to decide what she would and would not say. In the end, she seemed to resign herself to accepting that no matter what she said, it was already too late. "They will terminate him. They'll do the same to me, to you, and to your friend, if they find out we spoke."

"Who will? Who's they?" Nyala stared straight into Joan's eyes to see if it was hyperbole or if it was the truth. "Our World?"

Joan raised an eyebrow and appraised the young woman she'd been asked by Icarus to help. If it had been anyone else who asked, anyone else in the world, she would have fled; left everything she'd created for herself in the city that she'd called home since she'd been decommissioned in 1996. Such a request from Icarus meant life as she'd known it was about to come to an end.

"What do you know about Our World?" She looked back into the eyes of the young lady beside her, unblinking.

"I know it's an organization that searches the world for idiot savants who have some kind of gift to recognize great art and then uses those people as operatives to find art treasures that they bring together and sell at something called the Gathering. I know they murder people to get what they want. They have some crazy psychopath called Charlotte, maybe more, probably more, at least a hundred more, I think. People trained to be teachers and who do the killing. I know there was or probably still is a deranged Chinese megalomaniac in charge of the whole thing and that he killed the previous leader, a Russian with a white pointed beard. And I know there was a depraved lunatic Zhivago who used to be the worst of the bunch."

Joan stopped her.

"Was?" She was frowning.

"Yes, was. Used to be. Apparently Icarus killed him. It's how he started the manuscript; he said he killed Zhivago. I think it had to be recently. Here, read for yourself."

Nyala turned the manuscript to be able to show the tall woman the first page. They both read it.

———

Zhivago is dead.

I hunted him down and I killed him.

The police are gone and the street is dark now. Quiet. I stood right here and watched them carry him away. No. Watched isn't the right word; I enjoyed them carrying him away. He will never say "exquisite" again. He will never hurt you.

Zhivago is only the first. Before this is done, they will all know me as fear.

You knew me a long time ago by another name. Know me now as Tsau-z.

I am the Man of Sores.

All this you need to know.

Soul Catcher.

This is all you need to know.

When she was done reading, Joan shifted in her chair to face Nyala and considered her words.

"I didn't know about Zhivago. And I don't know why Icarus calls himself Tsau-z or why he says he is the Man of Sores. I don't know why he thinks it's so important that you need to know any of this." She reached out and took both Nyala's hands in hers. "But I do know that whatever he's done, he's done for a reason. If he killed Zhivago, something dreadful had to have happened. Honestly, I can't believe it took that long for someone to do it."

She shook her head and held Nyala's hands.

"I don't know why you are involved. But that's why he warned you, that's why he told you to be careful." She paused and then let go of Nyala's hands, turning in her seat to reach down into her shoulder bag. "That's why he wanted you to have this phone and the money."

The taller lady handed Nyala two envelopes of the same size. One obviously contained a cell phone and from the size and weight, the other had to contain cash, a lot of cash.

"In his note to me, he said to tell you not to use the phone unless it's an emergency. He'll contact you if he needs to."

"I have more questions. Please don't go." It seemed Joan was preparing to leave, as though the information about Zhivago's death had brought an end to the conversation. "Tell me about the Ellis brants. You found them, right? What happened when Tsau-z saw them? What happened after?"

The tall woman settled back in the chair slightly, as though she realized that her body language was sending a message she didn't want to be read.

"I'm sorry, don't worry, child, I'll stay until I've answered all your questions, but then I'll have to go, and you and your friend will have to go too; early tomorrow. It isn't going to be safe here for either of us now, not for long." She leaned forward and took Nyala's hands in hers once again. "Yes, I found the Ellis brants. I remember how proud I was of myself. I still had the ability to feel the serenity then, when I was in the presence of great art, but really my gift was already beginning to fade."

The waitress brought them the drinks Luba ordered, breaking the conversation unintentionally. Once she was gone, the tall woman continued.

"It's a long story. Are you sure you want to hear it?" She looked intently into Nyala's eyes.

"Yes. Please. Yes. I want to know everything."

The female musician walked by them then, smiling as she made her way to the stool and her 1953 Gibson SJ, Southern Jumbo, acoustic guitar that was standing vertically, held in place by a metal stand. The low-profile vintage Gibson amp clicked loudly and buzzed for a second when she plugged in the cord that powered the guitar mic. She fiddled with the knobs on the amp and then took a few cursory strums, an A-minor chord, C, and then an F, before twisting two of the tuning keys on the guitar.

Once she was settled on her stool, she introduced herself to a room that for the most part wasn't listening and then turned purposely to where Nyala and Joan were sitting. "I hope you like this song. It's called 'The Greenest Grass of All.' "

The tall woman stiffened when she heard the title of the song, shifting her eyes away from Nyala to look at the singer, who smiled back at her, nodded, and then turned to the room and began working through a relatively long and complicated instrumental legato phrase in A-minor, hammering on and pulling off the notes.

"Well, that's something I didn't expect." She turned back to Nyala, smiling at the younger woman and shaking her head. "Nice touch, my Icarus; very nice touch."

She raised her beer glass then and toasted in several directions around the room, to nobody.

"He's here, dear. It's his way of telling us he's watching over us." She put the glass back down on the low table without taking a sip. "Did you know it was Pete Seeger who invented hammering on? She's hammering her fingertips on and off the fretboard to make the notes."

"Wait. No, sorry, I didn't know that. You mean he's here now? In this room?" Nyala felt her heart rate rise as she looked around the room, searching for a face that she might catch looking their way. "Where is he?"

She felt the gentle squeeze on her arm again.

"You won't see him, sweetheart. He's not sitting here in the room, but he is watching us. Neither of us will ever see him unless he wants us to." She made sure Nyala was looking in her eyes. "I haven't seen Icarus in all these years, haven't heard from him since 1985 until I found his note on my table yesterday. When I was with him for those few months after we picked up the Ellis brants, he used to sing that song, 'The Greenest Grass of All.' I'd hear him play it on the balcony.

"I think he wrote it about the woman I saw him with in the restaurant the day we bought the Ellis brants. She was a stunning blonde. The most beautiful woman I have honestly ever seen. There was something about her that was special, something pure. I think he loved her, as much as he was capable of loving anyone."

Nyala stopped looking around the room.

"I read about that. You mean the restaurant he was in when you waited for him? Right? When he was with that *WKRP in Cincinnati* star and those other two actresses?"

"Yes." Joan didn't say anything for a moment and when she did speak again, there was the slightest hint of sadness in her voice. "I heard later that he married her. They had children, at least two from what I'd heard. But something happened. I don't know what. Something bad, I think."

"He was married? With children? Is that even allowed? And you're telling me he wrote music? And that he had her play his song?"

Nyala was trying to organize her thoughts, but they were tumbling around in disarray.

The tall woman smiled and reached to take her beer, declining to add grapefruit juice. When she spoke, the tone of sadness in her voice was gone.

"Yes. It was allowed when Icarus married her, but that all changed a few years later, before the new leader took control. And yes. He could play guitar and sing; his songs were lyrical more than instrumental, haunting sometimes. Listen." She took a sip and put the glass down, motioning for Nyala to turn toward the female musician. That same moment, the artist looked directly to Nyala and leaned toward the mic.

> I met an angel in a park one day,
> I was kind of in a bad way,
> She told me it was time for me to go away,
> And she said she could send me there.
> I asked her what she meant by there,
> And she told me that I shouldn't care,
> That it would be somewhere,
> Where the grass was always greener.
> She handed me some tiny pills,
> From someone else's doctor's bill,
> And I swallowed them against my will,
> And oh boy.
> It wasn't long,
> Before my mind,
> Left my body and soul behind,
> I guess it has to be, if you're to find,
> A place that isn't so bad.
> A place where things are fair and just,

Where Janis sings for all of us,
And Jimi still plays guitar,
Like a man possessed,
And God damn, I think I found the way.
And God damn,
I died that day.

"Hey! What's goin' on? Did I miss anything?" Luba's return was as disruptive as her departure. "Sorry I took so long. I was talking to a guy from the Yukon! Said there's moose and grizzly bears there! And he's single! Great, the beer's here! You can start now. Za lyubov! To the Yukon!"

She took the hint when neither of her tablemates lifted their glasses, but instead remained focused on the girl playing guitar.

And now I'm in heaven,
Hangin' with old St. Pete,
Janis is here and she's driving
A brand-new Mercedes.
And there goes John Lennon,
Teaching Mozart to play "Hey Jude."
But I'm all alone and I can't get back to you.
Ey yi yi yi, I was such a fool,
Because the greenest grass of all,
Grows next to you.

"Fine. I'll just drink by myself. Not like I don't appreciate my own company." She lifted her beer. "Don't worry about me. All good here. Yessiree, Luba is having fun. Hope everyone else is too."

Nyala and the tall woman looked at each other smiling. Nyala shrugged. The song was over; Nyala hadn't been able to hear the last verse over her friend's blabbering. It was just Luba being Luba. A smattering of applause came from various spots around the lounge.

"Please go on, tell me more. I apologize for my friend." Nyala rolled her eyes in Luba's direction.

"What did I do?" Luba took a sip of her beer and tipped her hat up higher on her forehead, watching the musician already playing the next song on her playlist. Nyala could see that her friend had already forgotten her grand entrance, and her attention, such as it was, was focused on a new shiny bauble.

"They put me out to pasture in 1996, forced retirement. Our World calls it being 'decommissioned.'" She reached down and lifted her beer, waving off Luba's attempt to pour grapefruit juice into it. "That was twenty-four years ago. They didn't keep me informed about what was going on with Our World, but I did follow Icarus's career as much as I could. My last news of him was only a few years ago. He was looking for Robert Johnson's guitar, the famous blues musician from the 1930s. It was the guitar he was supposed to have played when he wrote 'Cross Road Blues.' He sold his soul to the devil in exchange for his musical ability."

She took a sip of her beer and placed the glass back on the table.

"Icarus needed credibility in blues music circles to get to the guitar. So he wrote a song and had Our World influence promote it; they pushed it alright, pushed it to the top of the iTunes Blues charts. I think he did eventually find the guitar, but I'm not sure. As I said, they didn't exactly keep me in the loop on Our World affairs or the Gathering."

Luba wasn't listening; she was clapping to show her appreciation for the musician's last song.

"Really? They can do that? A number one hit song?"

"Of course. They can do anything they want. Make anything happen." She thought for a moment. "I believe he called it 'Howl With Me.'"

"What else can you tell me about him?" Nyala purposely didn't go back to the Ellis brants, instead succumbing to the desire for instant gratification once again, asking questions without order. "What happened to his mother, Rose? I know his father died of alcoholism."

Joan didn't say anything. The ex-operative looked thoughtful, but then sighed and answered.

"He looked after his mother. I know he mailed her money, but I don't know if he ever went to see her. He wasn't capable of giving or loving in a normal sense, but he genuinely cared about her. I don't know what happened after we parted company. I imagine she is gone by now."

Nyala listened to the words, feeling a pang of sadness for the selfless lady who seemed to have been resigned to accepting her lot in life.

"What else? I'm sorry. I need to know."

"Well, let's see. Did he write in the manuscript that he was in the Canadian Armed Forces? He held the rank of honorary lieutenant colonel. That wasn't that long ago either. Our World arranged it, probably had to go all the way up to the Canadian minister of defense to make that happen. Maybe they did it from the queen down." The tall woman paused. "I think he was probably searching for something called the Hoard of Bactrian Gold, twenty thousand ancient objects, molded from gold. Knowing Icarus, he likely figured out that it had been smuggled out of Afghanistan by some high-ranking Canadian officer who served in the theater of operations there after 2001.

"The Hoard was reputed to have been looted by the mujahideen after they overran Kabul when the Russians left." The tall woman paused and thought about it for a moment. "I was there in 1978, after Belgium, at the Tillya Tepe site in Afghanistan, trying to locate the Hoard. I don't know if Icarus found any trace in Canada, but from what I heard, he served for six years in the Canadian Armed Forces, using those connections, trying to follow the trail and locate the Canadian who smuggled the Hoard out of Afghanistan."

She looked at Nyala and shook her head.

"They announced President Hamid Karzai found it in the palace in 2003, locked away in a vault, but it wasn't Alexander the Great's Hoard from 327 BC. I know. I put it there. The pieces were real, but not from that period. It cost Our World a fortune. I was supposed to switch the real Hoard of Bactrian Gold with the gold hoard I brought with me." She paused and thought for a moment. "I personally think the Russians have it, already had it when I got there."

"Fucking Russians. It's always the Russians." Luba was barely listening to the conversation at all; it was long past her attention span. Instead, she was listening to the lounge singer, tapping her leg to the beat, but her hearing got substantially better when the talk turned to disparaging the Russians in any way. "Pardon my French."

316 / JIM SHOCKEY

Nyala's head was spinning, so much new information. She really needed to get back to the beginning, back to the things she knew about.

"The two decoys, the brants. What happened?"

"Do you mean how I found them? Or how Icarus and I managed to get them the day we both went to see them? Or after? What happened to Icarus?" The tall lady looked at Nyala, waiting for an answer.

"I think I know how you found them, some Ukrainian guy in Ontario that you followed out here. But I don't know what happened when you met up with Tsau-z." She shook her head. "Icarus, I mean. Something happened, or he said it did. He saw something in the decoys, something that changed him."

"It's a long story."

That was all Luba needed to hear.

"If you don't mind, I'll be excusing myself, had *so* much fun driving yesterday. I'm tired." She smiled and was about to hold out her hand, but remembered the rules of engagement for meetings, greetings, and goodbyes had changed in the post–COVID-19 era. "Nice meeting you. No, don't stand. I feel short enough already hanging with Nyala, let alone standing beside you."

Nyala and the tall woman watched Luba walk away. She didn't pay the bill.

"Guess I'll be using some of this cash." Nyala pointed to the envelope.

"That's what it's for. Nice friend. She's devoted to you."

"Among other things." Nyala smiled. "Like every guy who catches her eye."

Clapping came from various tables around the room as the artist with the guitar excused herself, saying she was going to take a break for a few minutes. She set the vintage guitar back in its stand and stood up from her stool. She glanced at the two women, who both nodded to her, and then she walked around the far side of the fireplace.

"He would have had someone give her the music to his song, so she could learn it. He probably paid her to play it. Smart." She turned back to look at Nyala. "Icarus was different. He was unable to show anyone he cared. It wasn't that he was heartless; it was like he didn't know how to show affection. Nowadays he'd probably fit somewhere on the autistic spectrum. Not sure. I remember not being happy with him the day we were supposed to get the Ellis brants."

"The day he made you wait while he was having lunch with those actresses, at the Alma Street Café, right? His antiques store was right around the corner, correct?"

"Yes, that day. But he wasn't at lunch to be with the actresses, I know that. He was there to meet Laszlo George, the Hungarian cinematographer working on the movie they were in town for. I'm sure Icarus wanted to talk water polo with him." She stopped and added, "I didn't recognize the blond woman, but I think she must have had a part in the movie. I think it was the first time Icarus met her. Are you sure you want to hear all this?"

"Definitely. Please don't stop." Nyala had a pen in her hand and was prepared to take notes if need be.

"The fellow who had the Ellis brants was an honest guy and he didn't want to sell them to me without first being sure his two best clients, who had the money for the decoys, wouldn't be upset that he sold them to me. One was a guy named Randy Reifel and the other guy was known as the Vancouver penny stock king back then, a guy by the name of Peter Brown." She stopped for a moment to make sure she was remembering correctly. "I had six or seven other Ellis decoys, I believe."

"Seven." Nyala interrupted. "You had seven other Ellis decoys and three more antique decoys you bought from the carver guy. Sorry, I'm a stickler for details. I made a note when I read it."

"Seven then. Thank you." She smiled at Nyala, who smiled back. "I told the fellow, Ron Gruber I think his name was, that if he didn't tell anybody about the two decoys I wanted, I'd make sure his client Randy Reifel would get the seven Ellis decoys I had. And that I would make sure the penny stock guy's latest junk stock would go through the roof. I didn't tell him about Our World's ability to make that happen and he didn't ask. He agreed with me that Mr. Brown probably wasn't collecting for the love of decoys and would more than likely donate his collection for a tax write-off someday. It was an easy prediction to make; the guy was a stock promoter. It's always about the money for guys like him. I paid $20,000 for the two decoys. Not much more to it than that, although it's funny, sometimes I wonder if Mr. Reifel still has the seven Billy Ellis decoys."

"Just curious, but what would have happened if the decoys had ended up with that Peter Brown?"

"I've never spoken to anyone about Our World. It's something they make sure every operative understands is a capital offense. It's hard for me to tell you these things." She gathered herself and continued. "Our World works around the edges of public awareness, an amorphous entity that flows in and out of situations, never leaving a telltale trace of their trespassing. No trace, except that when Our World does trespass, another art treasure disappears forever. If Peter Brown somehow beat me out of the brants, they would not have been his for long, at least not the real ones."

"I read that. That your offer to the decoy dealer wasn't a take-it-or-leave-it offer, it was a take-it-or-take-it offer."

"Yes. In a perfect world, I would get the decoys and no one from the outside world, except the dealer, Ron, would be aware they'd even surfaced." She reached down and picked up her beer, taking a sip before continuing. "If Ron had not sold them to me, or if the wealthy collector managed to buy the decoys out from under me, Our World would have taken steps to replace the originals with forgeries. Or they would have simply stolen them. That is Our World's last resort, but it's a pathway they are not afraid to go down if it comes to that."

The singer returned and readied her equipment for the second set of the night. The room was already thinning out; people were heading to their rooms as Luba had already done.

"I needed Icarus there, to tell if the decoys were one hundred percent real. It wasn't the money that worried me; it was the chance that they were fakes. I knew I was losing my gift and ever since I'd made a mistake on the missing corner piece from the Ghent masterpiece, I was on notice. Unlike Icarus and Zhivago, I was not invaluable or indispensable to Our World." She looked off, remembering, before returning her gaze to Nyala. "But they were real. Icarus knew that instantly."

"What happened?"

"It was strange. It was like he was there but wasn't even there. Really I can't tell you what happened. Something did though." She was frowning. "What did he write about it?"

Nyala looked through the manuscript until she came to the page she was searching for and turned it to the tall woman so she could read it.

_____

I have never told her, but it was Joan of Arc who showed the way forward to me that day. It was her and her discovery of the "Ellis brants" that directed my future.

I became a hunter that day.

_____

Nyala let Joan read the passage and then turned the manuscript so she could search again.

"He wrote this too, '*the serenity flowing over her hurt body was real, wasn't false.*'" She looked at Joan of Arc. "The hurt; I know what happened to you, when you were thirteen. I am sorry."

Joan of Arc looked away. Even though more than fifty years had passed, the horror of that day so long ago was always one glance in the mirror away, one thought, one passage of her hand across her welted arms or legs. The raised scars were there and always would be. It was a secret she kept hidden away, covered, a secret she'd shared with Icarus only once, that night before the Ghent Altarpiece.

Nyala held the manuscript out for her to read.

"I think he really regretted not being able to show you how he felt about you. I think he would want you to read this."

_____

The Ellis brants were so magnificent, Nyala, and she was so pure in that instant, so vulnerable.

Joan of Arc.

Lying here all alone. A lifetime of regrets. Things I should have said when I was home.

It's too late now to right those wrongs.

I was incapable then.

———

"There's more." Nyala leafed through the pages and again, when she found the passage she was looking for, she handed the manuscript to the tall woman, who was quiet now. Sad maybe? Drained of emotion? Nyala knew the feeling, the deep lethargy, the hopelessness and despair that came with the blackness.

———

She saw it, she was there. She held me as I unfolded my wings and she stayed with me for those days, the weeks that followed, the months, she was there by my side. She nurtured me as a newborn, because that is exactly what I was, a newborn learning to breathe, learning to fly. She held me in her hands and warmed me until the sun dried my unfurling wings in that glory of rebirth, another immaculate transformation from what once was, to what now is.

Nyala, I never thanked her then.

She was there, through it all. Protecting me in that time when I was most vulnerable, and I gave her nothing in return.

———

Nyala looked at the woman beside her. It wasn't possible to know how she was feeling, but compassion was something Nyala understood. Her heart went out to the woman whose body was covered in scars that had never healed. She knew that the love unrequited, held in hope of validation by Joan of Arc for so many years, was in the words she was reading, a love finally and fully acknowledged.

———

Slowly we, the mountains, the forests, and the lakes, became one. I was theirs and they were mine. The wild lands became my home, and the wild lands came to live inside me.

She knew.

I remember her waving back at me when I left for good, when I left for my good, Nyala.

When my ship set sail for that farthest sea.

So sad.

I was not capable of returning her attentions then, Nyala. A lifetime of regrets. It's too late now to right those wrongs.

Joan of Arc.

So long since I have said that name. But in the darkness now, lying all alone, I say her name and know I did her wrong.

Joan of Arc.

I am sorry.

Nyala, for me.

Tell her I am sorry.

45

2020

FERRY BETWEEN VANCOUVER
AND VICTORIA, BRITISH COLUMBIA

J36, also known as Alki, received a disrupted echolocation signal, confusing her and causing her to miss her intended target, a five-pound quillback rockfish. She wasn't desperate yet, but like the other twenty-two members of J Pod and in fact all the members that made up the total of the greater J Clan, the eighteen members of K Pod and thirty-five members of L Pod, she was distressed. It wasn't about polychlorinated biphenyls, although that did mean her body would have to be disposed of in a hazardous-waste site if it washed up on a beach somewhere along Vancouver Island's rugged coastline. And it wasn't about oil spills; she could simply swim away from that.

It wasn't about the sonar from the submarines and ships she passed daily, sonar that caused her sleek black head to hammer and then hemorrhage if she didn't vacate the area immediately. It wasn't about the powerful churning thump, thump, thump coming from the two massive 15,000-horsepower, controllable-pitch propellers driving the largest double-ended ferry in the world, the Super-C Class ferry called the *Coastal Inspiration*, through Active Pass. It made little difference to J36 that it was the ferry's second passage of the day between Tsawwassen on the mainland of British Columbia and Swartz Bay on the southern end of Vancouver Island.

No, J36 was distressed because she was hungry; they were all hungry.

Hers was instinctive, not schooled and trained in thought, like the humans who followed J Pod day after day, whale-watching from the safety of their powerful and fast eco-tour boats. She didn't know about science or what scientists postulated, but her instinct told her the herring were not coming again that year and if the herring didn't come, the Chinook salmon that made up 78 percent of her diet wouldn't come either. Instinct dictated her behavior; she would not procreate.

In fact, she hadn't done so since J52, her son Sonic, had been born five years before. It seemed right, it seemed okay, there was food, but it turned out so horribly wrong. Her child died by her side not far from Desolation Sound. The Salish Sea, which had for so long sustained J Clan, was dying; it was starving as her own son had starved.

Commercial Chinook salmon trollers catching salmon to supply the growing demand in the large urban centers of North America had been fishing the herring since the 1980s, as did the ground fishing trawlers, both in effect creating noncatch mortality that decimated the herring populations the Chinook relied upon to fatten themselves for their once-a-lifetime journey to rebirth and demise. Life begets death begets life begets death. The Salish Sea was in balance until urbanization multiplied the pressure on salmon and ground fish and incidentally on the herring, by factors of 100 times and then 1,000 times and eventually 10,000 times.

J36, Alki, knew nothing of this. She didn't know about the billion dollars spent by concerned humans to restore salmon spawning watersheds, while zero dollars were being spent for herring conservation, for spawning nets and panels. She only knew instinctively that without herring, the salmon she relied on would never return and she would die like her son J52, Sonic.

Thud. Thud. Thud.

Hers was to be instinctive. She sounded then, with the rest of J Pod, to get away from the pounding that carried through the water like a shock wave, assaulting their echolocation senses. She didn't know about the humans lined up on the *Coastal Inspiration*'s portside fifth and sixth decks, trying to catch a glimpse of the orcas, the killer whales.

"They're starving." Nyala was frowning. She didn't know how she knew; she just knew to her very core that it was true.

She was, like most of the other 1,200 passengers on board the monster ferry, watching the killer whales. Hers was a prime spot; she could look out the window where they had taken positions on the bench seats after climbing several flights of stairs from the lower deck where they'd left Luba's Mercedes.

"I'd be starving too, if all I had to eat was raw seals. Ugh." Luba had flopped down on her seat again. The spectacle was over. "I can't believe you got me up so early. Nobody should get up before the sun does."

Nyala picked up the manuscript she'd intended to read on the ferry ride to Vancouver Island but hadn't gotten to yet. There was so much to think about, so much she'd learned from Joan of Arc, not the least of which was the very clear message from Tsau-z, passed on by the ex-operative; instructions telling Nyala to catch the 9 a.m. Tsawwassen ferry to Swartz Bay on Vancouver Island. Whatever awaited her at the destination was a mystery, nothing but an X on the rough map she'd drawn in her notebook, based on the directions from the tall woman who had helped fill in so many blanks the night before.

"Have you ever heard of James Patterson?" Nyala wasn't really asking Luba the question and she wasn't asking herself either. She knew who he was, and that Alex Cross was one of his main characters, but only because she'd connected to the hotel wireless late the night before after Joan of Arc departed with a final caution to be careful. Nyala checked out the author because the tall ex-operative of Our World told her that Patterson had sold over 250 million books.

"Nope." Luba wasn't a morning person and morning for her meant all the hours before noon. "Don't care."

The huge ferry was listing noticeably as the captain of the ship turned the helm, making the adjustments necessary to direct his 525-foot ward safely through the narrow passages between the Gulf Islands that separated the British Columbia mainland from their destination on the southern tip of Vancouver Island.

"Apparently James Patterson wrote Tsau-z into one of his Alex

Cross novels. *Cross Justice.*" Nyala didn't think Luba would care and she was right.

"I don't care." Luba was watching the surprisingly nearby Douglas fir–clad islands slide by the window.

"She said Tsau-z needed it to gain access to the collection of some huge Patterson fan." She shook her head. "Crazy that Our World has so much influence."

"Crazy? As in crazy like throwing your cell phone into a river? Crazy like driving across an entire country, meeting ten-foot-tall Amazon secret agents, and getting up at six in the morning?" She pushed herself up from her seat. "You want a coffee? Never mind, I do."

Nyala didn't answer and didn't watch her friend leave. She was already leafing through the manuscript to the place where she'd left off when they'd arrived in Vancouver.

She checked her notes before she started reading; the whole story was getting hard to keep straight. The last she read, the old man with the pointed beard had been killed and the new leader was younger, from the Far East. Nyala paused for a moment; it was so weird. She'd read about a murder, like it was some fictional happening, a passage in a novel, a scene from a movie, but it wasn't. It was real. Joan of Arc was real. She had confirmed everything.

The notepad was starting to look like her brain felt, lines and scribbles, a mess.

As much as she wanted to read on, she had to get the dates right.

Okay. Tsau-z was born sometime in the mid-1950s. She opened a new page and wrote it down. His name was Hunter Johann. She added the word *autistic* and a question mark.

Sometime in 1963, he was discovered by Dr. Keen, who notified Our World inadvertently. The doctor also inadvertently helped the Johann family hire Wilbur, who was actually Charlotte, a maniacal killer who murdered the doctor and an antique dealer who happened to be in the wrong place at the wrong time. She added a note, "What's with the watch? Why does Tsau-z keep referring to it in his manuscript?"

Flipping back through her notes, she looked for the dates. In the early 1970s he was a swimmer, a good one. Then Hunter, as he was still known, switched to the sport of water polo sometime after he left Saskatoon to go to university. By then Charlotte was out of Hunter's life and Our World had taken over orchestrating the future operative's destiny.

In 1978, an operative code-named Hamlet, somehow associated with Hungary's national water polo team, was thrown in a Russian prison for smuggling an icon. Because of that, a psychopathic operative Zhivago was fingered to indoctrinate the young Hunter, who would have been around twenty-three years old at the time. Zhivago then hired a Cuban player to smash in Hunter's nose. Zhivago then took Hunter's watch and finished the work the Cuban started. He also told Hunter of his Our World name, Icarus.

Nyala added a note: "Tsau-z killed Zhivago recently and changed his name from Icarus to Tsau-z for some reason. Why?"

She thought about it for a moment and then added, "Killing Zhivago and reason for giving me manuscript related? Must be connected." She underlined the last words.

Okay, 1978. That's when Icarus met Joan of Arc; they worked together in Belgium. After that, nothing much went on until 1982, when Icarus refused to work with Zhivago in Peru. And then Icarus left his Our World water polo cover and went back to Vancouver, where he'd gone to university, to start up a new cover, as an antique dealer with a store in a trendy part of town. He was hanging with movie stars and moonlighting as a model at that time, trying to locate artwork in New York. Not a bad gig if you can get it.

Simple so far; she tapped her pen against her lip, looking out the window but not noticing the seagulls wheeling in the wind, twenty yards from where she sat. She was thinking.

In 1985, Joan of Arc found the Ellis brants and the leader of Our World sent Icarus to confirm they were authentic. He did so and somehow the carvings acted as the catalyst, causing Icarus to take a 90-degree career turn. He became a hunter.

That was the point where the story got complicated.

There wasn't much in the manuscript about the years after 1985, at least not until nine years later, in 1994. That's when the shit started hitting the fan, not that Tsau-z's back trail wasn't already littered with piles of it. Several dead bodies clearly qualified as shit piles in your life as far as Nyala was concerned.

In 1994, Zhivago and Icarus were on Vancouver Island, attending an animal rights protest. Icarus was a hunter by then, an advocate, while Zhivago was the opposite, an antihunter, bent on fanning public opinion against the practice. Icarus saw the Soul Catcher there.

That much was clear.

Nyala stopped writing in her notepad. Then what? There hadn't been anything in the manuscript about what happened right after that; nothing. Why? She looked down and leafed through the pages. It jumped from 1994 to 1996. That's when the old Russian was killed by Charlotte and the new leader took over. Joan of Arc told her that the new leader made the old leader look like Mother Teresa.

There was no answer to the question, "What happened when Tsau-z saw the Soul Catcher at the protest on Vancouver Island?"

Did he get his hands on it? And if he did, why hadn't he said anything about turning it in to Our World? Two years had passed from when he saw the Soul Catcher. Why was he silent for two years? What was he doing?

Then there was the forger, what was his name? Hebborn? He was sure as hell going to die; the new leader ordered Charlotte to take care of him. "Use a hammer." Jesus, who were these people?

That was all in 1996. And Joan told her that was also the year Icarus or Tsau-z resurfaced. "I read about him in the *Wall Street Journal*," she'd explained. "A big article about Icarus's bear-hunting operation on Vancouver Island." The article was probably done, she said, to help Icarus gain access to wealthy international clients who might possess objets d'art.

It was another thing that Nyala would have normally called bullshit on, but coming from Joan, she had to take it for what it was, gospel. Still, the *Wall Street Journal*? And on top of that, an article about bear hunting? Nyala shook her head, imagining the look on the editor's face when some Our World expediter, tasked with making it happen, explained to the editor of that respected news source what the coming weekend *Wall Street Journal* feature was going to be all about.

She couldn't help but wonder what would happen nowadays if an editor of a major newspaper or news network was forced by Our World to look the other way, while a pro-hunting article was published or aired. Turning their collective mainstream media heads away from whatever the left side of the body politic was doing was de rigueur, but turning away from what the right side was doing, especially hunting, would probably make their communal bobbleheads explode.

Nyala closed the notebook and put her pen back in her computer case. She picked up the manuscript and turned to the last page she'd been reading. The new leader, the Chinese guy, was still on the page in front of her. It was 1996 and he'd just sent Charlotte to kill the forger. The only way Nyala would find the answer to what happened with Tsau-z and the Soul Catcher was to read on.

Within seconds, it was all gone for her; the people around her, the *Coastal Inspiration*, and the spectacular British Columbian Gulf Islands sliding by on either side of the ferry.

Like Alki, she sounded.

Only Nyala didn't slide down into the still depths of the starving Salish Sea.

She slipped back into the story that would tell her who she had been and who she was.

Who she would be.

46

1996

RUSSIA
UNDISCLOSED LOCATION

The Chinese leader of Our World had only been in his new position for three days, but like his deceased predecessor, he was all-seeing and all-knowing. He'd been chosen because his brain was uniquely qualified to assimilate information from a thousand sources and compute probabilities and, more importantly, possibilities. It was his gift, nearly identical to the previous leader in that regard. But he was different than the previous leader in three ways: he was far more ruthless, he was young, and he was alive.

Even with more than one hundred operatives scattered around the world and one hundred times that number of expediters, plus several dozen enforcers and an uncountable number of influencers in high places to keep track of, he knew that Zhivago was 420 kilometers east of Yaoundé, Cameroon, at that moment. He knew the big operative, already his favorite, was in a small village on the shores of the Boumba River and had been in-country for months already, arranging for the second disappearance of the famed Afo-A-Kom from under the nose of the *foyn*, or king, Jinabo II.

Carved from the iron-hard wood of a four-hundred-year-old iroko tree, the full-size statue of a standing man was not *art* to the Kom people, it was a deity that held both power and promise for those who worshipped at its feet. Face sheathed in hammered copper and a body sealed within a cloak of a hundred thousand crimson and seafoam-blue beads, the divinity was not carved by a *foyn* of the Kom people in the early twentieth century, as the cognoscenti of the art world believed. Our World knew it was created by Abazu Massimba, an unknown but inspired village artist of the day.

It took years of his life to complete the masterpiece, but slowly, one primitive adze chip at a time, the deity trapped inside the heavy iroko blank was released. Massimba personally placed each seed bead with a hand and eyes that could only have been guided by a power greater than himself. With his final touches, the artist added the animistic powers of three carved forest buffalo to the base of the statue, there to keep the material universe in order.

He named his life work then.

Afo-A-Kom.

The Kom thing.

And he died.

The leader of Our World knew all this, but he had already moved on, thinking of Zhivago's situation. The operative was not in West Africa arranging for the famed statue to disappear as it had the first time in the 1960s, only to reappear in a New York tribal art gallery. No, the amateurs of the outside art world botched their one attempt to emancipate the monumental work of art. Now it was Our World's turn.

The carving had been escorted back to the royal palace at Laikom from the American gallery by Warren Robbins, the director of Washington's Museum of African Art, in 1974, effectively ensuring by his good deed that the work of art would find its way to the Gathering at some future date. Altruism and good intentions fed Our World's needs like blood flowing from a victim's exposed neck into the vampire's sucking maw.

Zhivago was at that moment arranging not only for the repatriated Afo-A-Kom to take a second transatlantic journey, but also for the central figure's two attendant female monuments, carved later by lesser lights than Massimba, to disappear as well; the three that made up the sacred ancestral grouping would all disappear, only this time it would be at the hands of an Our World operative and go from there to the Gathering, where they would vanish forever.

CALL ME HUNTER / 331

"Tell Zhivago to leave Cameroon now." His command was to the dimly lit man sitting on the chair across the table from him.

"Da."

He could see the man across from him wanted to add to his obedient one-word answer and he was aware of the reason why. The minion wanted to warn the leader that if he reassigned Zhivago, the opportunity might never arise again for the operative to complete his present assignment, to procure the Afo-A-Kom trio.

The effort had been prodigious to that point, even by Our World standards; replacements were there in Africa, perfect forgeries to supplant the originals. They'd been artfully crafted by the best of Our World's stable of genius forgers, each one selected as the operatives were, for their gifts. Even with the time he had put into the project already, Zhivago needed still more to replace the originals with the fakes and then would require several more months to arrange safe passage out of West Africa for the authentic works of art.

The colossal costs associated with the logistics to that point in the Afo-A-Kom operation, an operation begun by the former leader years before, and the extreme cost to extract Zhivago on short notice from the middle of nowhere in darkest West Africa didn't enter into the new leader's calculations. The cost, compared to Our World revenues, was dust; less than dust, it was nothing. But losing the opportunity to acquire the trio of Kom carvings, that was another matter, a serious consideration; they would have been the centerpiece of the coming Gathering.

He had given the matter the full attention it required, but for all intents and purposes, he'd known from the start of his thought process that his answer was preordained; the Soul Catcher always took precedence.

From the beginning, when Samuel Baker invited Louis XV to the first Gathering, that one legendary work of art, the Soul Catcher, stood above all others in the pantheon of Our World desires. Unlike Massimba's carvings, there were no photos, no etchings, no biblical descriptions. There was nothing but the knowledge that this greatest artistic endeavor of mankind absolutely did exist.

It was real.

But it was also an absolute truth that without a reference, only those possessing the God-given gifts of an Our World operative would be able to recognize the masterpiece in situ.

Its size, its shape, and its color were mysteries.

How many times during his own training had he seen his predecessor send operatives on the scent of that single most important work of art known to Our World? Any clue was worth the effort and every step that brought the Soul Catcher closer to the Gathering was worth whatever burden Our World would incur, financial or otherwise.

The most recent information on the Soul Catcher had come only two years previously, in the spring of 1994, when he'd still been a leader in waiting. The former leader had sent both Zhivago and Icarus, Our World's top two operatives, to the far west of Canada, based on the tiniest tremor in the web. The barest hint, a word whispered from one ear to the next until it reached Our World. The Soul Catcher was going to surface.

The amorphous whisper had been wrong.

Zhivago failed to find the Soul Catcher on that operation on Vancouver Island, at a place called Victoria, and strangely, Icarus had disappeared off the Our World radar at that same time. The operative had been AWOL for the two years since then.

Strangely was not a word the new leader of Our World tolerated. In fact, *tolerate* was another word he did not tolerate. Unlike the old Russian, who had put up with Icarus's two-year truancy, the new leader was already, in the first few days of his tenure, making plans to rectify what he considered to be a personal slap in the deceased leader's face and in his own face. It was disrespectful, and as such, could only be taken one way, personally. The new leader was not about to let an operative, no matter how talented, dictate the rules of employment.

Icarus.

If the new leader of Our World recalled correctly, something he was incapable of recalling any other way, for the last two years the operative, the protégé, had failed to report in, failed to send anything to the Gathering. Icarus's assigned expediters knew nothing of his whereabouts, nor was the about-to-be-decommissioned operative Joan of Arc any help when she received a formal Our World summons and questioning. Stationed though she was in the part of the world Icarus had last reported from, she had been unable to shed any light on the wayward operative's present location. He had simply vanished.

The Chinese leader of Our World was sitting stock still, back straight, and had anyone been able to see him, other than the man across the table, they would have wondered at his stillness. He was rigid in the low light cast by the single lamp. But his mind was active, calculating the probabilities to nearly an infinite degree, the combinations and permutations all taken into account.

The previous leader had let it happen, let Icarus have his head, instead of forcing the truculent operative back into the circles where the Gathering's insatiable appetite for artistic discoveries could be sated; and where, just as importantly, the operatives could easily be tracked. The new leader had no choice but to witness and accept the old man's decision; he'd still been a leader in waiting for his day then and as such, was powerless to correct what he considered to be a mistake. He watched, but he also knew that when the time arrived for him to sit in the position of absolute power over Our World, he would change the policy with regard to the long-lost operative.

Icarus, as good as he was, needed to be halter broken.

"Tell Zhivago that I want him to find Icarus. Tell him I want Icarus corrected. Tell him to make sure Icarus understands that he serves Our World and no other."

He reached up and touched the side of his glasses then, adjusting them ever so slightly.

"Tell him I have word that the Soul Catcher is going to come to the surface again. Tell him to find it."

"Da."

With a wave of his hand, he dismissed the man sitting in the chair across from him.

47

1996

UNDISCLOSED VILLAGE ON THE SHORES OF THE BOUMBA RIVER, CAMEROON

Africa was not to his liking; too crude; too rough. The smells were not polite, and he did not like sweating, something the 100 percent humidity and oppressive fetid jungle heat of West Africa made impossible to avoid. His collared poly-fiber long-sleeve shirt, while expensive, wasn't designed to breathe and so adhered to his hirsute body like a second skin. The heavy black hairs that grew from him like a thick living carpet, without space to breathe between his natural skin and the petroleum-based material of his shirt, opened their homes to the myriad local bacteria strains, allowing unhindered entrance for the legion to feed on the rotting follicle roots. The by-product of the bacteria multiplying and dying not only resulted in body odor, a foul stink, but also created suppurating raw boils that the man could not help but scratch until they bled.

The baby red-tailed monkey sitting on the only bed in the room, a bed canopied by a diaphanous mosquito net tied at the top for the day, scratched itself too, but because of fleas, not boils. The man with the thick chest and heavy paunch smiled sweetly and reached for the little primate, gently holding it in one of his heavy arms while he scratched a scab on his own large belly with the other. He was waiting for his afternoon pleasure to be delivered.

Unlike what the nongovernmental organizations might want the world to think about their peace initiatives in West Africa, intertribal relations were still strained, as they had been since the beginning of humankind. All of which the sweating man couldn't have cared less about. What he did care about was that the social unrest resulted in an endless supply of exquisite young flesh from all over the western part of Africa.

Africa wasn't to his liking, but the dark pleasures of the continent were.

The monkey jumped from the operative's arm to his shoulder and proceeded to pick through his master's thick black hair, looking for the vermin that were guaranteed to be living there. Zhivago walked to the small bedside table, the only piece of furniture in the thatched-roof hut, other than the sweat-stained single bed where he'd enjoyed so many pleasurable afternoons of late. He picked up the dossier lying there and started to leaf through it.

The previous months, working Our World connections between Douala and the Republic of Cameroon's capital city, Yaoundé, although tiring, had been productive. The Cameroon Airlines flights were easy to arrange; the airline was 96 percent owned by the government, so Paul Biya, the highest paid of all the African presidents, could with a simple decree avail himself of the public airline's only remaining Boeing 737 for his personal use. Our World connections meant that the president's "personal" use wasn't always in the strictest sense personal use for the Cameroonian leader.

Zhivago didn't care in the least about the inconvenienced passengers whose flights were canceled because he needed the airliner to take him to Garoua in the north of Cameroon, or Bangui in the Central African Republic to the east, or Accra in Ghana along the coast. And like most experienced world travelers, he didn't dwell on the fact that spending any amount of time in the air, on airplanes belonging to West African countries, especially Cameroon, wasn't safe.

In fact, the sister airliner to the one he had been so often flying on crashed the year before, in December 1995, while on a go-round after a second aborted landing attempt at Douala International Airport. Thankfully the forged Afo-A-Kom trio, crated and waiting to be imported as air freight from Cotonou, Benin, to Cameroon, were not on Flight 3701 that fateful night.

The big operative slapped at a mosquito, missing it.

He hated them. Besides carrying malaria parasites, they were vectors for a dozen other diseases. He'd already self-diagnosed and treated himself twice for subcutaneous filariasis, after feeling the loa loa worms crawling under the skin of his forehead.

Fortunately, he hadn't contracted any of the more debilitating sicknesses during his time in Africa, nothing that kept him from organizing the complicated switch, replacing the originals with the forged Afo-A-Kom trio on behalf of Our World. Nor had any illness kept him from using his time and a small fortune in misappropriated Our World dollars to sour the milk for the hunting safari operators working in the jungles and in the northern savanna regions of Cameroon and other nearby countries. It was that work that he was checking in the dossier he'd retrieved from the bedside table.

Many nations in that impoverished part of the world, without realistic options, tried to help boost the remote villagers out of poverty by creating viable hunting industries. The idea that international hunters could be used as a solution to solve the many social and economic problems facing the villagers, by infusing foreign funds into places that would never have a hope of seeing a single photo-tourism dollar, was reprehensible to Zhivago. To think that hunter dollars should be used to provide hospitals, schools, and clean water to the stricken villagers was, frankly, abhorrent to him, and totally irrelevant.

An animal being killed by a trophy hunter was wrong. It was depraved and indefensible.

Destroying the safari-outfitting industries in Cameroon and surrounds had been like picking low-hanging fruit for one so passionately against hunting as Zhivago, especially with his Our World connections and money. A few thousand dollars into the right greedy bureaucratic hands ensured that legally operating safari outfitters never received the permits they required to operate in their hunting concessions.

Zhivago congratulated himself.

He knew full well that the consequence of his successful battle to abolish international sport hunting, as counterintuitive as it was to the well-meaning animal lovers who donated money for his cause, was the wholesale slaughter of those same big game species they thought they were saving. Zhivago knew that because of his efforts, the destitute villagers, deprived of the revenues they counted on from international hunters, had no choice but to turn to poaching to survive.

He considered it to be collateral damage.

He knew the wire snares set by the villagers did not discriminate. All the animals, young and old, female and male, died. He knew that to kill the larger species, the local villagers started making their own firearms, fabricating the gun barrels from the steering rods of the ubiquitous Toyota Land Cruisers. They concocted gunpowder from saltpeter, sulfur, and charcoal and loaded their homemade firearms with one-ounce chunks of rebar.

But none of that mattered.

The trophy hunters were gone.

Honest scientists, those who did not rely on the grant funding that most often Zhivago indirectly provided, pled with the outside world to take notice. The butchery was unsustainable, and extinction of the very species that had been protected from international hunting was imminent.

Zhivago knew all this and kept meticulous notes on the scientists who needed to be dissuaded from speaking out.

He knew about the rose-colored ivory of the pygmy forest elephants, the diminutive jungle-dwelling cousins to the behemoth savanna elephants, and how that ivory brought a premium in Asia. He also knew that it had only been a matter of months after he'd put a stop to international trophy hunting, effectively defunding the safari operator's anti-poaching patrols, that Russian-made Avtomat Kalashnikova 7.62x39mm assault rifles, in the hands of Sudanese rebels working for organized poaching syndicates, started making their appearance. What elephants the local villagers were unable to kill by poisoning waterholes, the professionals killed with their AK-47s.

But none of that mattered to him. What mattered was how many trophy-hunting operations he'd destroyed. He paged through the dossier, making a mental note of his successes; by his estimation, he'd put fifty-five safari outfitters catering to the international trophy-hunting community out of business; not a bad day's work considering it wasn't his primary focus while he'd been in-country.

Zhivago scratched at his bulging side and when he felt the scab pull off, he looked to see if the blood had stained his pale salmon colored shirt. It had. He scratched another lump above the first, awkwardly trying to get his hand twisted around to reach the spot.

Trophy hunters were evil, a throwback to a time that had long passed. They practiced their depravity on animals that had no way to fight back. High-power rifles releasing thousands of foot-pounds of energy into the bodies of helpless animals enraged him. Even as he scratched, he could feel his ire begin to rise. They needed to be eliminated from the earth and the best way to get rid of predators was to get rid of their food source.

That's why he accepted the poaching as a necessary evil. It was the new civilized age, the age of reason, not instinct. There was no need for hunters in the world any longer and so it stood to reason that without animals to hunt, there would be no hunters. It was simple common sense to Zhivago, and it was a constant source of irritation to him that the moderates of the antihunting movement perceived his to be perverted logic. They were his people, but they were idiots who were hurting the antihunting and animal rights cause, in effect condoning animal cruelty.

Even so, the momentum of his worldwide movement was growing one country at a time, one donation from one well-intentioned animal lover at a time, one payoff at a time; the movement that he was such an integral part of starting and maintaining was effectively dismantling the worldwide hunting industry he so detested, brick by brick.

His tactics had been effective.

Fight them on the front lines, protest them in the field; fight them in the courts, drag them through one frivolous lawsuit after another until they bled like the poor animals they hunted. Defeat them at the polls, shame them publicly, drown them in rules and regulations; attack their laughable belief that they had a right both to bear arms and to self-determination.

Trophy hunting or hunting for sport, for entertainment, had to be stopped, no matter what the cost to the wildlife populations of the world. Better dead than a head on a wall. Hunters would never recover from the death blow he had been financing, that he had empowered, and that he intended to someday personally deliver.

Zhivago was working himself into a deep anger, an anger that could only be calmed by consuming a different type of flesh. He was itching with both hands now, the dossier thrown on the bed and the red-tailed monkey forgotten. Where was the girl? What was taking so long for her to be delivered?

He heard the thumping before the Bakundu orphan girl arrived. The pretty young child, caught in the reality of West Africa, was a form of currency, traded from village chieftain to village chieftain. Her name was Fidele. Her parents gave her up to their own village chief when she turned six, to work as a slave until she turned ten, old enough to perform the duties expected of any nubile cast into service by her own fate and bad luck. Zhivago had been looking forward to her arrival for some time, but his attention was redirected when he heard the thumping.

Helicopter?

In a place that was never assailed by the sound of a jet passing high overhead, let alone the sound of a helicopter, the approaching chopper could only mean one of two things. Either a foreign mercenary force was entering Cameroon from one of the many unstable bordering countries, Chad, the Central African Republic, or Nigeria, maybe even Congo-Brazzaville, or he was about to receive a summons.

Regardless, it was time to go.

The heavily armed warrior who appeared at the hut door didn't make small talk while Zhivago finished packing, something he'd started to do only seconds after he heard the helicopter's blades chopping through the dense jungle air.

"Where to?" Zhivago wasn't concerned about his safety. He was untouchable, protected by Our World. Once the soldier informed him that he had orders to take Zhivago to Douala, there wasn't really much need to talk to the hulking barbarian. What would have been the point; his monkey was likely more informed than the brute at his door and certainly was more civilized. He was being summoned by Our World and that meant his work in the jungle was over, which also meant that there was something out there more important than the Afo-A-Kom.

The Soul Catcher?

What else could it be?

Nothing else.

In a way he felt offended, even though he was escaping the fecund stickiness and stink of the jungle. It meant the end to his fun; *kukfini* was over. He reached down and gave the monkey one last pat on the head and then turned to follow the soldier down the trail to where the helicopter pilot and three more warriors stood at the ready.

Kukfini; to make someone suffer; he felt himself growing aroused. It was early in the morning and the Air France flight to Paris didn't depart until midnight, so there would be time in Douala at the Ibis Hotel to arrange for a full afternoon of *kukfini*.

Maybe a young boy.

Yes.

One more exquisite afternoon and then he would leave this horrid, backward place and return to the culture and civilization of his own kind.

*T*ake a moment, Nyala, to let the revulsion subside.

I am sorry you had to read about Zhivago's depravity.

But all this you need to know.

There is so much more I need to tell you.

Most I will tell you another time, Nyala; if there is another time.

So many stories. So many secrets to tell.

For now you need to know that I hunted them all, the Flaming Cross of Emperor Constantinus. It was in Ethiopia, on the smuggling lines between Somalia and Sudan. The Mursi people; Sumu their sky god protected it for nearly 1,600 years. They did not want me there. It took time to gain their respect; they are warriors. Life has little value there, beyond whatever is an immediate want.

When we met the first time, their leader pulled the sunglasses from my face and put them on his, waiting for my response. His was a primordial act, effective; two new species meeting, two new species determining who would be the predator and who would be the prey. I reached out and snapped the cord holding the gris-gris amulet around his neck. It was a trade, Nyala, a simple one-for-one trade, a tit for a tat. If he did not like the terms, the next trade would have been for his life.

Or mine.

Jason Roussos didn't know what I was looking for; he thought I was there for the Nile buffalo and the Chandler's Mountain reedbuck.

I wasn't.

Nassos laughed at me in Addis Ababa. Junk, he called it.

Brown and brown. He was right. Most of it was.

But he didn't see the color of the Flaming Cross in the crates I packed for shipping, didn't feel the weight of its ancient beauty.

There has been nothing like the great emperor's cross and never will be again.

Cloaked in the mantle of God's Son.

So many years I searched, so many years I traveled. The second Raimondi Stele, I found it. But I did not remove it. I was there many times, in Peru, since 1982, when I had to steal across the border from Ecuador. Perhaps someday I will go back. The antiquities there are breathtaking.

There was the Afo-A-Kom in Cameroon. Our World sent me back a decade after they pulled Zhivago from the project. I was there many times, and I could have brought the magnificent carvings out myself, but I did not do so. It wasn't because the deities were too closely guarded; my friend there, Prince Mbouombouo Mamadou, could have taken care of that. Not that I would have asked him to help and possibly cause him to be punished with anlu. *The wrath of Cameroonian women is not something to take lightly. No, Nyala, I left the Afo-A-Kom, because when I saw it, I was overwhelmed by the colors and the mystery, ancient and so vivid.*

I left them. I lied. They thought I failed; thought there was an immovable obstacle. There was not. There was only my sense of respect for the Kom people and their beliefs. But Our World will try again unless I stop them, unless we stop them.

I sought out the Black Heart of the Dead in Mongolia, the Great Khan's standard. To Our World it was another failure, but to me it was anything but.

I followed Genghis Khan's tracks from the Gobi Desert to the Altay Mountains; to Duwant in Bayan-Olgii and back across the Mongolian steppes with my friend Tugso Maugmarsuren, to Bayan-Unjul in Tuv, the Hangay Mountains.

Nyala, I was there, the sacred spring of Zorgol; one thousand sky-blue ribbons fluttering in the heated breath of the Mongol desert wind. I could see them, Nyala. Color. So blue, so endless, like the skies of Mongolia. The rest of the world brown and brown, the Black Heart of the Dead was close, but the Great Khan hid it well. Or did he hide it at all? Was the tapestry of that nomadic land his standard?

With the ring finger of my left hand, I flicked spirits to the Sky, and to Mother Earth and to the sides for Nature. I was a hunter by then, Nyala, I understood the shaman. I embraced animism. And I poured vodka on the rocks by the sacred spring of Zorgol.

Out of respect, I bowed.

In those years, Nyala, I was a peregrinator. I never stood still; I traveled to the remotest corners of this earth.

I listened and I learned.

I learned what it truly means to be a hunter.

Maybe the sacred spring was the Black Heart of the Dead.

I learned in the lost mountain reaches of this earth and in the hanging valleys, on the wildest seas and in the forbidden forests. I learned, no, I was taught, as we all can be if we choose the life of a hunter; taught that the most wondrous art ever created is not always a thing, an object. Sometimes it is animate, alive; sometimes the finest work of art is a place.

The Life Mother of the Old Bering Sea. I found it too, Nyala; so spiritual, so beyond anything I beheld before. Tikigaq, Point Hope to us, with the whalers of the Iñupiaq, together we paddled into the past, ten thousand years into the past, to pay respect, to live and breathe our respect. There we joined the whales in a dance that is as old as life. We rejoiced at the Celebration. They are my friends now, Popsy and Eva Kinneeveauk. All of them are my friends, and we share the past and the future. We share the forever that is the balance of Nature. Life will always beget death and death will always beget life.

The whales we hunted were the bond that keeps the future connected to the past and the past in sight of the present. Without that bond, without seeing the past, we are doomed. Ours would be an aimless future of living, but without a life.

Sadly, I believe half of us, more perhaps, have already lost sight of the past, Nyala.

The Life Mother of the Old Bering Sea. I will tell you the story someday but not now. I will tell you about Chad, the warriors painted on the rocks. David Coulson was there, documenting and saving; I saw him. He didn't see me. So many memories; the wed-

ding; to honor them, I brought the body of a gazelle to the feast and was honored in return.

Pakistan too. With the Kakara people, the Jogezai tribe, on the border with Afghanistan. Nawab Taimoor Shah Jogezai was a great man, a visionary. Amir Khusor follows in his footsteps. Khaushali, Ubaidullah, Abdus Rehman, Sattar, Jabar, Gull, Wahib, Bari Dad, Noor Khan, and his brother Ejaz Ali Khan, and I have never forgotten Farhad Magpoon.

They were looking for Sulieman markhor, but I was looking for the divine inspiration of Sadequain's calligraphy. As he had done, I thirsted for the limit of potential.

But all those are stories for another time; Somalia too, and Iran. China, Russia, Azerbaijan, Kyrgyzstan, and Kazakhstan. In Afghanistan, the queen's palace, I flew with the Black Hawks in the air over Kabul.

I did not find a kindred spirit in Tajikistan. Heed my words, Nyala, do not expect to find truth along the Wakhan Corridor. You will find only lies.

I will tell you about their lies someday, Nyala, but I will never tell you my lies.

I promise, to you I will always give the truth.

Liberia and the Congo. I would have liked to know him, the explorer Pierre Savorgnan de Brazza. We would have been friends. Zambia, Uganda, Mozambique. Brown and brown. I sought the colors of the world, the pieces of art, the singular objects created by the hand of man, but inspired by God.

Do you know that once I became a hunter, once I understood and embraced Nature and in so doing was embraced back, animals stood out in color, so vivid, so incredibly perfect? Who knows, maybe someday you can learn to feel their beauty as I do. I have hope of that.

Nyala.

Do you know what is considered to be the most beautiful of all the antelope in Africa? They are there, in Mozambique. Marromeu in the province of Sofala. That is where you will find them.

Nyala. Yes, Nyala. Nyala.

Papua New Guinea with the Baining people, searching for the carved stone divinity that was the god of their volcano. I found it. It was small. I held their god in one hand. In a primitive dugout, with a crocodile-carved prow, I paddled the Sepik and the Fly Rivers, so untouched and wild. I was always on the hunt, always looking for the treasures that would come to me in color, brilliant hues of red and blue, green and ochre. Did you know the average human eye can see seven million colors? Multiply that by a thousand thousand and you will understand beauty as I do.

Nepal, New Caledonia, Paraguay, and Argentina. Tasmania and the Chatham Islands and Zanzibar; too many places; too many treasures to tell you about now.

All this you need to know. But now is not the time to share those memories.

No.

It is time for you to learn the truth, the truth I have been trying to protect you from. A truth I did not know myself until recently.

For over two decades, I did not know why she left. Did not know what happened to her so long ago. Did not know of her sacrifice.

It's too late now to right those wrongs.

I am so very, very sorry.

To my dying day and my last free breath.

Every heartbeat is for you.

I cry for you.

I cry for her.

God help us.

I didn't know.

I swear to you.

I didn't know.

48

1996

UNDISCLOSED LOCATION, VANCOUVER ISLAND, BRITISH COLUMBIA

The cat, a calico female, purred and rubbed against the woman's bare leg; then it turned and rubbed against the leg again. When there was no response, the cat arched its back and rubbed against the woman's other leg. It was also bare and like the first leg the calico cat rubbed against, it was attached to the leg of the chair by a thin black synthetic thermoplastic polymer strap, better known as a zip tie. The cat grew tired of receiving no response and jumped onto the woman's lap, where it paused and looked up into the woman's open eyes.

They were glazing over.

The cat's tail twitched for a moment as it sorted out the messages it was receiving and then it jumped to the ground and ran into the darkness.

Blood that had for a moment been held back by the smashed ends of the small arteries and veins began to pour out the gaping wound in the back of the woman's head, forced through the traumatized vessel endings by the pressure created from the woman's still-beating heart. It ran down through her long black hair, saturating it in thick red. It ran in rivulets down her bare shoulders and down her bare arms, across another nylon zip tie that held the woman's wrists together behind the chair back, and finally down through her fingers, still clasped together as though in prayer.

The blood dripped first and then began to pour in streams to the cement floor. It pooled there, spattering the surrounding cement, but quickly grew to encompass the droplets. The pool grew to take in the chair legs and continued to grow until the woman's two bare feet were standing in a sea of red. The pool did not stop growing until the woman's heart, deprived of oxygen, finally slowed and with one final weak flutter, stopped beating.

In that moment her soul returned to the village of her ancestors.

Zhivago watched, marveling at how it looked like someone dumped a five-gallon pail of red paint on the floor. When the edges of the pool stopped creeping outward and started to coagulate and darken, he turned and put the hammer back on the hanger that was marked with the outline of the tool. There were other tools hanging from hooks and holders on the dusty cobwebbed plywood wall: saws, pliers, wood files, tin snips, and several different screwdrivers. All were designed for the construction of a building, or if need be, the deconstruction of a human's will to resist.

Zhivago had been pleasantly surprised. He would not have believed he would someday meet a human capable of withstanding his considerable abilities to persuade, at least not until he encountered the naked woman tied to the chair. To be fair, she hadn't been naked when he brought her to the garage located on the rural property that his expediter rented for him while he searched for both Icarus and the Soul Catcher. And obviously she hadn't zip-tied herself to the chair either; he'd done that too. In fact, he'd done everything to her, everything he could think of, and still she refused to tell him what he needed to know.

She'd been drugged and was comatose, so it was no easy matter carrying her to the garage situated at the back of the heavily treed Vancouver Island property. Zhivago wished he'd picked up more drugs from Henri Laborit before he died the year before.

He looked over at the result of his handiwork again; so exquisite, so perfectly exquisite.

He was proud of his skill, but somehow, mixed in with pride was a niggling sense of unease. The nakedness was intended to remove her dignity, but it hadn't. There were no windows in the garage, and he'd left her alone in the cold blackness, tied to the chair for several days before he started to work on her, a process meant to soften her desire to keep any secrets. But it hadn't worked. The foodless days and frightening unknowns were meant to break her spirit, like the hammer he'd finally used to break her skull, but the woman died defiant to the end. He'd never seen anything like it.

The calico cat returned from the darkness to the working, shop side of the garage, the side lit by the single bright bulb hanging down from the exposed roof rafters. The cat looked sideways, giving the pool of blood and cooling body a wide berth, arching its back and holding its tail straight and high as it rubbed against the thick calf of the man who was now sitting in a chair looking at the body tied to the only other chair in the lighted area.

He reached down and picked the cat up, setting it on his ample lap, where it did two circles and then flopped down, licking its paw and purring. Like the cat, Zhivago felt nothing for the woman whose life he'd just ended. She was a means to an end, or she was supposed to be a means to an end. The Soul Catcher. The trail was dead. He wasn't any closer now to the Soul Catcher than he had been when he'd been extracted from Cameroon.

He patted the cat as he reconsidered his last thought. Well, technically he was closer, physically closer. The Soul Catcher wasn't in West Africa. The leader had been right to pull him from that wretched continent; the whispered hint that had reached Our World was accurate. It was here, nearby on Vancouver Island. Or at least it had been.

He liked that the cat was purring; it comforted him. Animals were so pure, so innocent, not like the cancerous tumor on the earth that humans had become. If he had his way, they would all be treated as he treated the woman, with extreme prejudice.

The new leader of Our World would not be impressed. Zhivago knew he'd failed at both of his assigned tasks, to find Icarus and to find the Soul Catcher. Not finding Icarus wasn't really a failure. There simply hadn't been any *reason* to find him. He'd crawled out from whatever rock he'd been hiding under for two years and contacted Our World of his own volition. Like nothing had happened, like he hadn't been off the grid for two full years, business as usual. From what Zhivago had been told, Icarus had requested Our World support to help and validate his cover: hunting and killing animals.

Hatred and disgust roiled and mixed, causing the operative sitting in the chair to clench his fists involuntarily, startling the cat, causing it to twist upright reflexively, tail twitching, agitated.

"It's okay, love. Shhhh." He patted the cat's back gently, surprisingly so, considering the size of his heavy bloodstained hands. "Daddy will protect you."

If he had his way, Icarus would die, operative for Our World or not. He should die like the wild animals he hunted, like the wild animals he killed and cut up, like the wild animals he consumed. Zhivago clenched his teeth and felt his hands tightening into fists again. Living a field-to-table lifestyle, Icarus called it, as though that somehow justified murdering wild animals.

He was a mutation, a disgusting throwback, vile. The world needed to be cleansed of hunters and their spawn, wiped free of the animal killers, the pestilence.

The purring in his lap served as a form of tranquilizer to the angered operative, calming him.

"That's okay, my love." He pulled the cat up to his chest and looked at the woman who so recently had been alive. He felt better; pleasure slowly replaced the hate. Looking at the woman brought back the memory of her smell; not smell as in perfume, it wasn't olfactory, it was the *feeling* of smell.

He'd sensed it on her.

The essence of the Soul Catcher.

She had to know of it, she had to have held it recently for the scent to linger on her, however so faintly.

He'd been closer to finding it two years previously. The scent was stronger that time, much stronger, overpowering. Two years before at the antihunting rally he'd sponsored and organized in Victoria, the same scent had roused the primitive response that was his gift just as it had when the woman tied to the chair literally walked by him on the forest trail the week before.

It had been overwhelming two years before, there among the throngs at the rally all chanting, "*Kill* the hunters, *not* the bears." "Kill the murderers. Murder the killers."

Someone attending the protest had to have brought the Soul

Catcher with them and the blind creature inside him, as it always was when awakened, had been hungry. When it happened, he was powerless to control the force that took command of his body. A stupid person, smelling the air, sniffing and blind, crawling through the crowd; like a massive maggot in search of the rotting stench of putrefaction, he made his bloated way toward the scent.

The Soul Catcher had been at the rally and then suddenly the scent vanished.

The trail went dead.

He could still *feel* the smell of it on her now, indistinctly. It was strange, almost as though the woman, even in death, had some vestigial connection to that single greatest work of art created by mankind. The scent wasn't strong enough to awaken the beast inside him, but it was strong enough to make it stir. He hadn't experienced that before; it was almost like, in her having held the Soul Catcher recently, molecules of it slewed off and, like the spray of a perfume, coated the woman in the hint of its exquisite fragrance.

She'd known where the Soul Catcher was, of that he was certain; she could have led him to it, but she didn't. Not for the days he'd done his best to persuade her. She died when it was apparent that she would never tell him anything, despite the operative's best efforts.

The cat turned its head quickly, ears perked, and then jumped to the ground; a mouse, maybe a rat drawn to the smell of blood? His work here was done. The expediter would clean up the mess, make the body disappear; probably pieces of it, small pieces, would feed the crabs and bottom dwellers in the nearby ocean bay, but whatever happened to it, Zhivago didn't care.

The Soul Catcher was hidden from the world once again.

Before killing her, he'd left her tied to the chair and returned to the trail where he'd originally found her, or more correctly, where she'd found him. The scent in the rainforest that confirmed the Soul Catcher was close and caused the creature inside to stir had vanished. It was as though a wind had come up during the days he'd been with the woman and cleansed the forest, purified it.

There was no smell, no *feeling* of the Soul Catcher ever having been there.

The beast inside him remained still.

He'd have to report to the new leader that the Soul Catcher had once again gone dark to Our World.

He rose then and walked to stand under the bright lightbulb, considering the woman. It was curious, how she almost seemed to seek him out, how she seemed to have made sure he would find her and follow her.

He'd been close. Very close.

He'd narrowed the search down to a specific area on the east side of the four-hundred-mile-long island and had been haunting the remote wilderness trails he found there. He wasn't at home in the dripping temperate rainforest, but it was where the search led him. The Soul Catcher was nearby. The smell of it, diffuse as it was, permeated the dank, clammy air.

Then suddenly it grew stronger, unmistakable, when he encountered her on a secret, deeply canopied forest pathway. She made eye contact and nodded at him as she passed by.

Strange.

He'd continued, but stopped farther along the trail, beside a weathered and moss-covered figure, a carved totem with hands outstretched toward him. He had waited there, a predator biding its time, before turning and following the smell of her back down the pathway, the scent of the Soul Catcher. She hadn't put up much resistance when he caught her, making the abduction easy.

It puzzled him. It wasn't normal behavior.

He saw no fear in her eyes.

He saw only peace.

No, not peace. Something else. Transfiguration?

In spite of his distaste for the human race in general, he knew the most basic human instincts were to survive and to procreate. Yet this woman defied those instincts, seemingly giving herself up to him. It was as though she offered herself to crucifixion by his hand.

He reached up to pull the string that would throw the room into blackness.

As physically attractive and alluring as the woman had been when she was alive, somehow in death she exuded tranquility, as if the abrasions, the punctures and cuts, the burns did not exist. Her long raven hair, now matted and gobbed with coagulated blood, still spoke loudly of her native heritage. Her high, fine cheekbones and lithe body too told the tale of someone who lived an active life, far from the comforts of any city. Her hands were callused; she used them.

With a gentle pull, he darkened the room, turning at the same time to carefully make his way to the door he knew was three steps away.

The new leader was a man he liked. His instructions were clear. Do whatever it takes, use whatever means. Satisfy yourself that all the alternatives have been explored. Zhivago took the instruction to "satisfy yourself" literally and he had, in front of the tied woman several times, before he raised the hammer high above her head.

*I*t is too sad, Nyala, to think back, to remember all this again.

I know it hurts you to read this.

It hurts me to know I was not there for her.

She felt the evil coming. She sensed it. Prescience. One of her gifts. She left me; she sacrificed herself to protect us. For the last twenty-four years I didn't know. When she left me, she told me to never speak of us, never come back; never try to contact her; to never look for you, forget that you existed. Like a killdeer, feigning injury, she drew the evil to her, away from what she loved.

She sacrificed herself.

I never saw her again.

She distracted the beast for days and she died.

I swear, Nyala, I didn't know what she was doing. I didn't know what happened to her.

It was not until recently that I received word from Our World that there was a vibration in the web, the Soul Catcher was going to surface again. They didn't know when. They only knew something was going to happen and they were sending their best two operatives to find it. Me, Nyala. And Zhivago. They wanted both of us on the quest.

In preparation, as they always did, they briefed me. Everything they knew. And it was then that I learned what he'd done to her.

The tears have not stopped since.

Nyala.

I hunted him down and I killed him.

I told you; I stood in the darkness and watched them carry him away. I told you watched isn't the right word. I enjoyed them carrying him away.

Now you understand.

Nyala, he will never say "exquisite" again. He will never hurt you. Zhivago is only the first.

More will come.

Before this is done, they will all know me as fear.

You know that.

But you do not know what happened that day on the grass, with the drums; the day I first saw her dancing, at the back, behind all the people at that antihunting rally, the day I saw the colors of fantasy, of impossibility. The colors of dreams and other worlds. The colors of everything, distilled to the essence of who we are, what we are. Every question answered. The colors of God.

That was the day I saw how blind I had been.

Brown and brown. Brown and brown.

When I turned away from the mob, I saw color; the most brilliant color; so deep, so infinitely pure; so breathtaking. God, so beautiful.

I fell to my knees when I saw, Nyala, when I beheld the greatest work of art this world has ever known.

The drums. I can still hear them. Boom. Boom. Boom. Boom-boom-boom. They beat me; they beat me into something new. Boom. Boom. Boom. I was forged; shaped; I was annealed.

I told you already, Nyala, that it was my birth. I started on a journey that day, a journey to you.

She was dancing. Boom. Boom. Boom. The rest of the world didn't matter. There was only her.

God.

Nyala, I told you I wished that you could have seen her and now I wish it again; wish she could be here to teach you.

I think of her now and wish for so much more.

I wish she told me why.

Why had she chosen to sacrifice herself?

I had no way of knowing. She bore no cross for me to see. There was no desperation in her eyes when she told me I must go. No. There was only faith and absolute conviction.

In the face of such conviction, mine was not to question.

So I did as she bid.

It saddens me beyond sorrow's deepest depths, to know she

walked alone, down a Via Dolorosa and to a Calvary that only she knew of.

She would have told me not to weep for her.

I did not see fear. Why should I? She felt none. She wasn't like the rest of us, who live dreading death. For her, leaving a physical body was simply part of the journey we all must take to be with our ancestors.

I cry now, knowing nobody was there to offer a sponge to kill the pain.

I cry knowing the pain it caused you, Nyala.

Someday I will join her in Paradise, but for now the only solace I have is knowing that she believed it was the only way. Knowing she believed giving up her mortal life was worth the price of protecting the Soul Catcher from the grasp of Our World.

Too sad to remember, to think of what might have been.

Too sad to remember her as she was.

How can I describe her to you, Nyala? When I saw her for the first time that day so long ago, she was all things spiritual; she was the embodiment of all those who have gone before and all those who will come after.

It was Her.

She was the Keeper of the Breath.

She was the light and she was the darkness. She was all that we are. She was dancing for all of us. She was dancing for this world.

Boom. Boom. Boom.

Every color in the universe, every sound, every scent, every feeling in her movement.

The Daughter of God.

It was Her.

She was the Soul Catcher.

49

2020

VANCOUVER ISLAND, BRITISH COLUMBIA

Damn, girl! Hello? Earth to Ny Ny!" Luba hit her friend on the arm to break the spell Nyala was under. "Come on! Time to close up shop, we're here!"

Nyala looked up, confused. She was so engrossed with what she was reading, she hadn't been aware that the massive *Coastal Inspiration* was slowing down, preparing to dock. She had no way of knowing that most of the passengers were already down in their vehicles or waiting by the passenger walkway to get off the boat.

"Didn't you hear the announcement?" Luba turned and started toward the exit door that led to the bowels of the ship where the Mercedes was parked. "Got you a coffee to go!"

It took a moment for reality to register, but once it did, Nyala gathered the pages together and followed her friend, through the door and down the stairwell to the door marked DECK 3.

"Ny Ny, just asking, but what deck are we on?"

Nyala was in a daze, on autopilot. The words she'd been reading confused her. What was Tsau-z saying? What did he mean? Why "us"? Who was the Soul Catcher? How was it connected to her? The answer was there, but she couldn't see it, or was it that she didn't want to see it?

"Deck?" She answered but was too preoccupied with the questions she was asking herself to be engaged in what was going on around her.

It took Luba several stressful minutes to locate their white Mercedes. Nyala knew her friend would have found it sooner if she'd been any help at all, but she wasn't.

Nyala had just pulled her passenger door closed when the vehicle in front of theirs started pulling away, following the vehicle in front of it. Slowly, like the mother of a thousand babies, disgorging her children one at a time from her bowels, the ferry released her wards back to the land.

"Wow! Pretty place!" Luba wasn't paying attention to the car in front of them or the car to the side, or any of the cars and trucks all jockeying for position as they headed south toward Victoria, away from the Swartz Bay ferry terminal. Instead, she was gawking at the emerald and verdant green on each side of the highway. "I could live here!"

Nyala wasn't listening to her friend, and she wasn't watching the cars, trucks, or the fields and forests they were driving by. She was pulling the manuscript out again. They had directions from Joan, directions that the ex-operative of Our World had passed on to Nyala, from Tsau-z's note. "Go to the Quq'tsun Hwulmuhw. They will prepare you for your grandmother's funeral." It was the usual cryptic Tsau-z style; the words were there, but it took an effort to understand them.

She'd asked Joan what it meant, but the tall woman wasn't much help. "Be careful. Remember to do exactly as he says and . . ." She'd paused and then reached out her hand. "Thank you. Thank you for everything."

Nyala asked as she was walking away if they would see her again and the tall woman had turned then, thought for a moment, and answered, "Maybe. Depends." Then she'd lingered, looking into Nyala's eyes. "I hope so."

With that they had parted. Exhausted, Nyala had left the lounge and returned to the room, already occupied by a soundly sleeping Luba. Overtired from their own drive and too emotionally spent from the meeting with Joan to do any more research that night, Nyala tried to sleep until she finally gave up, fired up her computer, and logged onto the hotel wireless.

By the time her phone alarm went off, she'd discovered what a Quq'tsun Hwulmuhw was. Surprisingly, it turned out to be both a place and a people. The English bastardized version of the un-pronounceable indigenous name was "Cowichan," as in Cowichan Valley. Once Nyala googled the valley, she learned that Quq'tsun Hwulmuhw also meant "People of the Land Warmed by the Sun."

Luba laughed when Nyala told her the meaning of those words early that morning, when they'd checked out of the Fairmont hotel at Vancouver International Airport.

"Sun as in Hawaii sun? Or Canada sun? Big diff!" Luba had never been to Hawaii, but Nyala caught her gist. "A little warmth would be appreciated; it's been frigging cold the whole way. FYI, if I had my *phone*, I could tell you for sure that it is eighty-two degrees back at home in North Carolina today. But since I'm a total idiot, who throws their *phone* in a river, because her idiot friend told her to, I don't have my *phone* anymore. So you'll just have to believe me."

Luba plugged the destination into the Mercedes GPS when they left the hotel, so at least they knew approximately where they were headed. It was more than a little disconcerting to know that Tsau-z had most likely been on the ferry with them, watching them. In a way though, it was also comforting, especially considering what she'd just read about Zhivago and what he'd done to the poor woman tied to the chair.

Nyala had a sudden urge to keep driving. She wondered, if they did, if they simply kept going, right through the Cowichan Valley and beyond, would Tsau-z catch up to them and flag them down, redirecting them back to the funeral? Or would they be able to go on, to leave the future behind them?

No, not likely.

Nyala shuddered involuntarily. It wasn't from the cold. It wasn't a joke anymore; it was all kinds of scary. It was real, all of it. Joan of Arc, Our World, Zhivago; no, he was dead, Tsau-z killed him. And there was the woman Zhivago tortured. Who was she? Why did Tsau-z say they were coming? Was he out there somewhere, watching them because of that? And what the heck was he going to do about it? She felt herself losing focus for a second. Canada's gun laws were crazy strict. It wasn't like he could just go pick up an Uzi or assault weapon at the corner store.

The absurdity of even thinking someone needed to buy a weapon to protect her from something or someone brought a wave of anxiety to Nyala. She felt herself sliding into the dark side of herself. *Anhedonia* was the big word for it. She'd never talked to a doctor about her feelings of hopelessness and despair, but she'd looked it up. The inability to feel joy. The root cause of clinical depression.

It took all her self-control to banish the line of thought from her mind, too many questions. She didn't need questions; she needed to focus on what she knew.

It had only taken her a few more minutes of researching that morning to learn that the Cowichan people were a part of the Salish tribe, an ethnically and linguistically related group of approximately fifty-five thousand Pacific Northwest Coast natives. She learned their traditional lands stretched down into Washington State and even extended eastward as far as the interior of British Columbia.

Nyala was shocked to learn that after the first European contact, after Captain Cook and later Captain Vancouver and a dozen other intrepid explorers landed on Vancouver Island in the late 1700s and early 1800s, the estimated population of the Salish people dropped to fewer than two thousand remaining tribal members. There had been over 90 percent mortality from diseases introduced by the explorers: smallpox, measles, and influenza.

When she read that, an intense and inexplicable feeling of loss clouded her senses; the sadness she felt was so real, her eyes welled with tears. It had to have been horrendous for the native people who suffered from those introduced epidemics two hundred years before, but she felt a much deeper sense of hurt than she would have thought. Why? It didn't make sense that her response to the knowledge, as horrifying as it was, should have been so visceral, so personal.

Every day as a journalist she was subjected to news about disasters, people dying and tragedy on a mass scale, but it was just that, news, and news was something that happened to other people in faraway places. She justified the lack of compassion she felt in the past by telling herself she was simply being objective and professional.

Besides, the world wasn't fair. Bad shit happened and it happened all the time; somehow, though, this was different.

When she read the words **"dreadful skin disease"** and **"loathsome to look upon"** and **"men, women, and children sickened and died in agony by the hundreds"** she felt like she'd been punched in the gut. It hit her in a personal way that shocked her. The feeling was so intense that she was thrown off balance. It was like her own family died, or at least what she imagined it would be like if she had a family and they were suffering.

It was really strange, and in that quiet time, before she'd awakened Luba to depart for the ferry, she'd thought about it, imagining what it would be like to lose nine out of ten of your friends, your family members, and everyone living in your community. She didn't personally know anyone who died from COVID-19 but did know of a friend of a friend who almost did. Apparently it was a terrible experience, five weeks near death. But the person survived. Survived or not, just the thought of catching something that could possibly kill you, as remote as the chances were, scared Nyala just as the pandemic had terrified 7.5 billion other people in the world.

How would she react if she'd been in the shoes, or cedar bark sandals, probably, of the Quq'tsun Hwulmuhw people in those days? How did they cope? They couldn't close their borders to the invading sailing ships that infected their people. How did they not lose their minds from fear? Did they pray? Certainly they were not Christians back then, although the missionaries would have followed closely on the heels of the explorers, bringing with them salvation, the word of God, and more disease. Did they have a god they worshipped? Did they have a place their souls went to? Was there some kind of great thunderbird that swept down and carried the spirits of the dead to the infinite sky, to native heaven?

Was the Keeper of the Breath literally that for them, the Soul Catcher? Was the Soul Catcher their heaven?

Keeper of the Breath; she frowned and shivered. What did it mean?

"It's okay, don't worry, I got this." Luba wasn't used to being ignored. "No, it's my pleasure to be your driver bitch. I'm fine. I'll just find a new friend when you sell me."

Nyala knew her friend was being as patient as she was capable of but wasn't thrilled that Nyala wasn't interested in small talk and probably would not be for the entire drive down the Saanich Peninsula and back up north, at least sixty miles through the temperate rainforest of Vancouver Island. No, small talk wasn't going to happen.

"Sorry, Luba." She reached over and touched her best friend's arm. "Really."

A raven black pickup with SHELBY on the front quarter panel and passenger door caused Nyala's insides to vibrate as it accelerated past on the driver's side of the Mercedes.

"Holy cow! How cool is that!" Luba ignored her friend's apology. "I didn't know Shelby made trucks! I want one!"

Nyala knew that *want* and *get* were the same word for her friend. She also knew the Mercedes's days were now numbered.

"Luba." Nyala was still touching her friend's arm.

"Yeah. I know. You're sorry. I got it. Read your stupid book. I know you have to." She kept her hands on the steering wheel. "Let me know how it ends."

How it ends?

Or how it begins?

Nyala let go of her friend's arm and picked up the manuscript.

*S*he was the light and she was the darkness. She was all that we are. She was dancing for all of us. She was dancing for this world.

Boom. Boom. Boom.

Every color in the universe, every sound, every scent, every feeling in her movement.

The Daughter of God.

The Keeper of the Breath.

She was the Soul Catcher.

She chose me, Nyala. She came to me.

I struggle now, thinking about it. What right did I have to be with her? Who was I? I was nothing in comparison to her. I was unworthy.

She was the Soul Catcher, Nyala. The Soul Catcher wasn't a thing; it was a living, breathing human. It was her.

She was the Keeper of the Breath.

She was their high priestess, the heir of her own mother's birth-right and her mother's before that and hers before that, for five thou-sand years, longer probably, passed from mother to daughter, mother to daughter, mother to daughter since that time beyond time.

I should have known; it should have been so obvious; the great-est work of art produced by us, of course, had to be one of us. And it was her. But I didn't understand until she was there, dancing, radiating colors, shimmering; playing with the sun's rays, bending, colliding, and fusing them into new colors that I never knew existed.

I was an outsider. She chose me.

Like you, I didn't understand.

Zhivago was there, a heaving creature from another dimension, lurching through the portal. A Lovecraftian horror creeping from the unknown, the darkness, smelling the air for the perfection it knew was there, close by. He was groping for her, for the Soul

Catcher, sniffing at her, closing in on his prey. I saw him. He didn't see me. He knew the Soul Catcher was there, but he couldn't see it, couldn't see her. He was blinded by the beast that had been awakened inside him. The beast whose appetite would only be sated by the possession of the object that brought that lurching evil forth from the inferno.

Nyala, she knew. She knew Zhivago was coming for her, knew he was there; knew he was hunting her. She had so many gifts, one was that. Prescience. The ability to sense the presence of evil. She knew the evil that was coming for her, for her people. I suspect she knew before she left her home in the forests and wild lands to be there that day on those lawns, dancing with her people. I didn't know it at the time, but she was searching for me, just as I was searching for the Soul Catcher, for her.

We left then. All of us, her people. They and she had come to fulfill a destiny, not for the protest. The drums stopped and I followed her. I was a hunter, so it was easy. There was nothing I missed of what I left behind, what had been my life in the city.

Living off the land, hunting and gathering with her people; we lived as they have always lived, the way we should all live. I was with them, learning, at home in the fog-shrouded forests of the West Coast, under the towering old-growth canopy. The red and yellow cedars and Douglas fir, the white spruce, we lived in harmony. Ferns and salal, elk and bear, we hunted and ate what we killed. We fished the streams that her antecedents fished for a thousand years. In the night we danced to the beat of the drums that were the heartbeat of her people and their land.

I know she would want me to tell you about her people, about your people. She would want you to know the legend.

Be patient. Understanding will come.

I can tell you, but they will prepare you.

Your people will help you understand.

For now, I can tell you that your story starts in the first village, before the time we know, not far from your destiny, Nyala. It is gone now, wiped out in the years of horror, the pestilence, the foreigners from across the ocean; grown in and grown over, the village will *never rise again in our lifetimes, maybe not in a hundred lifetimes, but the legend of that place lives on in the oral tradition of your people, Nyala; the Quq'tsun Hwulmuhw.*

She told me the story of her beginning. The story of me. The story of you.

Legend has it that there was an odd child, a boy. The parents of the child asked Owl to take the boy but regretted their choice. They stole him back from Owl, but when they passed the hut of Tsau-z, crippled and covered in sores, the boy was drawn to help the distressed man. He entered the house and never left. Soon the villagers forgot him. When Tsau-z passed, the boy climbed into the frightful skin the damaged man left behind and the odd boy became the new Tsau-z, Man of Sores.

At that time, in the beginning, there was a beautiful girl in the village; all the boys wanted to marry her, to possess her, but she knew in her heart that none were worthy. She was the Keeper of the Breath, the Soul Catcher, the first, and she was saving herself for only one; one who would be worthy; a warrior and a sorcerer, one of wisdom and poetry. One who would be naïve, just, and powerful.

But the villagers grew angry with her.

She told them she would marry the Man of Sores because he was better than any of the men who wanted to possess her.

She went then to Tsau-z, Man of Sores, and he told her to go away, that he was hideous and that she should choose another, but she would not. She chose him not for what he looked like, but for who he was. He was overwhelmed and to show his appreciation, every night he would remove the skin of sores and dive deep into the ocean, bringing dentalium shells to the surface. He would leave them at the home of the fair maiden's parents, until they became rich from trading the valuable seashells. Before she would awaken, he would don his skin of sores once more.

During the day, the villagers teased the ugly youth and made him hunt deer with them. They carried him on their backs, laughing at him. The first night when they slept, he took off the skin of sores and killed four deer. In the morning when everyone in camp awakened, he was back in his skin of sores and the deer were hanging from the meatpole. With no one to question them, the other men told the rest of the villagers that they killed the deer.

The next day they carried Tsau-z again into the forest to the hunting camp, but that night they did not sleep, they waited quietly in the shadows, and when Tsau-z rose and removed his skin of sores to hunt, they stole the skin and threw it in the fire, which created a fog that blanketed the land.

She told me, Nyala, that is the reason fog to this day smells of burning skin.

When he returned and found his skin of sores gone, the young man had no choice but to appear before the beautiful maiden who'd chosen him, the Keeper of the Breath, the Soul Catcher, as he was; purified, unclean no longer.

She brought the stone carving to him then, more ancient than the people, made in the time before time, when Ravin was the shaman and Dzoo-Noo-Qua the giantess roamed the forests, stealing children.

It was sacred.

It was the Secwepemc; the Soul Catcher's fertility.

And that day they had a child, a girl. The powers flowed to the girl child from the mother upon the child's birth. The mother in that instant was no longer the Keeper of the Breath. The infant in that moment of birth became the Soul Catcher and the mother became like everyone else, save for the power to sense evil.

The mother became the protector of the Soul Catcher then.

The people lived in the forests like that, the Soul Catcher of each generation, choosing her Man of Sores, and passing on the powers that had been theirs. Each girl child became the new Keeper of the Breath, the Soul Catcher.

And so it has been ever since the beginning.

Nyala, I know you are confused. You will understand. Be patient.

I did not understand either when she told me the legend, but she brought the stone bowl to me that night, the Secwepemc. It was her offering to me.

She offered me her fertility.

I was her Man of Sores.

I am the Man of Sores.

Nyala, that night a girl child was conceived.

The child was born at full term by the warmth of the fire and under the flickering light of the stars. The ocean waves grew silent when she breathed her first breath. The creatures in the forest stilled, listening to the mother whispering to the firstborn in her arms. The new Soul Catcher was born that day; the new Keeper of the Breath.

I was there. I saw with my own eyes the sky brighten to daylight in the night.

I saw the colors fade from one and grow in another.

I saw the colors fade from your mother to you.

Nyala.

I asked if you knew the most beautiful antelope in Africa; do you remember?

It was me.

I was the one who chose your name that day.

Nyala.

I am your father.

50

Nyala let them do it. She had no power to resist, no will to question. She saw them bring two stone bowls, one filled with a thick red paste and the other black. Four wizened women, Elders.

It was their way.

She felt it being applied. One side red, the bird kingdom, and the other side black, the animal spirit world.

You are both.

You are everything.

They crowned her in a hat of long hair and grass, animal and plant, hair tied at the top, pointed upward and grass tied at the front. Then they shrouded her in a cloak of woven cedar bark, her regalia.

Her will to wonder did not exist.

The sound beat through the walls of the room. The pounding beat told of another coming, told of the return. Then a hush. Silence. The Keeper of the Breath was here. They led her then, the four Elders, through the door past the silent breathing, past the massed Quq'tsun Hwulmuhw seated in tiers. They led her to the center of the longhouse.

She felt the heat of the first fire as she passed, following the four women, each with their own faces painted in black or red. They stood her between the two roaring balefires that provided the only light in the windowless, massive, and rough-hewn longhouse, the place where the People of the Land Warmed by the Sun had assembled since the start of time. There was no center pole, she was it, and the Elders left her there disoriented and alone. The rattling started then, the dried hooves of a thousand deer, slowly at first, filling the blackness, joining the crackling and popping from the sparking logs.

Chang. Chang. Chang. Chang. Chang.

Then the drums.

Boom. Boom. Boom. Boom. Boom.

She stood alone in the center, the floor of dirt that the Quq'tsun Hwulmuhw had danced upon throughout their history. Five hundred strong around her, they pounded the ground with the carved polychrome dance sticks. It was a primal ritual, the paying of respect, the integration of knowing animals and being known by the animals, the hunter and the hunted, the balance that is the flavor of life.

Nyala felt the pounding beat penetrate her body, the strength in their belief becoming a part of her. She tried to fight it off but failed. Standing there alone, with her people around her, hundreds strong, she knew it was *her* belief, and always had been.

You are a witness to your grandmother's passing, they told her. Three years before, the venerated woman had died, releasing her spirit to return to the village where it all began, to the ancient place where Nyala's mother's spirit had gone so long before, and where Nyala's spirit would one day go. They said Nyala had been summoned to bear witness, called from beyond, from the past and from the future. It was time for her to return to her people.

They started to file down the steps then, entering the light of the balefires, one at a time at first, and then in groups; they stood at the edge of the light and told stories of the wild animals and their bodies that fed the people. They danced and they moved away, miming animals, crouching, hopping, some of the time weaving side to side, arms outstretched.

The voices. She'd heard them before.

Her secret.

The sense that had always frightened her, the sense that she was part of something greater than the world she could see.

A gentle breeze washed over her then. Flowed around her. Almost like it was washing her, cleansing her. It grew then, from a breeze to a warm wind.

And with the wind came voices.

Singing in a language she didn't know, couldn't speak but understood. In a tongue she knew by heart. The light came then with the wind. Magic light. Flaxen. Now she saw, it was the firelight. Like an eternal sunset, it beckoned her to embrace it, enter it; to join her people and to sing with them on the wind.

If she did, she knew she would sing with the wind forever.

They came to the edge of the firelight, sang their ancient songs passed down through matrilineal lines, and then as quickly left, back beyond the light of the fires, to the darkness and their seats. Slowly the hooves quieted and when the last of them left the light, the wind died, and she was alone again in the center of the floor.

Only the firelight remained.

The shaman came from the darkness then, wearing a headdress of curled eagle feathers split down the spine; he was covered in a cedar blanket as she was, but his dripped ropes of wound mountain goat hair. He touched her, held her right arm outward, her palm to the blackness above; both of his hands were tight around her wrist and forearm. He spoke, and although she did not know the words, she knew the meaning of every single intonation, every sound.

Then he left too and the vast open room, smelling of the smoke from the fire, grew silent, silent as a tomb, no voice, no whisper, no cough, and no movement from the five hundred seated in tiers, her people.

She was numb by then, numb to the blackness, the unknown. Numb to all thought, she shrank into herself. What was happening? The blackness, impossible, grew even blacker at the edges of the baleful firelight and then began to seep into who she had been, began to overpower her. The constant companions, hopelessness and despair, always waiting, always there, crept toward the center of herself where she was hiding. When it touched her, she recoiled.

No! She screamed then. Over and over and over she screamed from the deepest part of her soul. Screamed into the silence as the hundreds who were her people bore witness to the struggle.

The wolves started then. In the darkness. A single growl. Then a second and a third. More. Uncountable. It grew and built. Louder and louder, until it was a crescendo of animal roars, filling the longhouse, drowning Nyala's screams with a power greater than the world she could see. Tearing her from that world.

They appeared at the edge of the firelight then, the Nuu-chah-nulth from the western shores of the island, each led by a shaman. Each tied to a rope of cedar, joined to her grandmother by family, a secret society, masked, primordial, painted creatures from the beginning, they crawled on hands and knees across the floor toward where she screamed and screamed.

The wolf dance had begun.

The Soul Catcher was with them.

The Keeper of the Breath was back with her people.

And she screamed.

51

2020

PINEHURST, NORTH CAROLINA

His last thought was not of his mind leaving his body and soul behind. There was no soft guiding light at the end of a tunnel, no wrought-iron gates in the clouds, and no Saint Peter welcoming him. His life did not pass before his eyes in that last moment. Nor did he ask the question, why me? At least not in that moment. It was a question he'd already spent two agony-filled days pondering.

It had been a normal day. He'd kissed his wife goodbye, tousled his youngest son's hair, hugged his oldest daughter, told the middle twins to stop fighting, and walked out to his Lexus GX 460. He'd driven his pride and joy along the usual route, stopped for a Starbucks latte, parked in his usual spot marked with his name, and walked up the wide stairs fronting the building where he worked. Everything routine. Everything normal.

Even the day at work was the same as the workday before and the workday before that. Normal. Or almost normal. His best investigative journalist hadn't shown up for work, not that it hadn't happened before, but this time she'd apparently taken his worst investigative journalist with her. No word, no email, nothing, just the two of them gone and not one person on the entire staff at the newspaper had any idea where they'd gone or why. He'd been pissed. He hated dealing with personnel issues. It was the worst part of being the editor.

The first indication that it wasn't going to be a normal day after all was the cold touch of the gun barrel on the side of his neck.

"Drive."

Nothing else, just "drive."

He'd been preoccupied and wasn't paying attention when he got into his Lexus to head home after the workday was done. He hadn't noticed the passenger who'd been waiting, crouched down in the backseat. Not that it would have been easy to see the stowaway even if he had been more aware. Shortly after he purchased the vehicle, he'd paid to have the windows tinted to protect the inside of the car from the blistering North Carolina summer sun. Everyone did it even though it wasn't technically legal by the motor vehicle laws in the state.

"Turn right."

After the initial shock wore off, his first thought was that he was experiencing a carjacking, something that wasn't common in Raleigh, but wasn't unheard-of either. He'd regained at least a portion of his wits by then. Just do what the carjacker wants. Wasn't that the advice the police gave? Drive. Turn right. Turn left. He just wants the car, wallet too, his cell phone and probably his watch. Then the intruder would dump him off on some street corner and he'd have to try to flag down a passerby to give him a lift to the nearest police station. Just don't do anything stupid. Don't do anything that might give the carjacker a reason to turn violent.

"Turn in here. Stop."

It wasn't a street corner. It was a parking lot in a part of the city he normally tried to avoid.

"Turn the engine off."

The second he put the big vehicle in park, another person stepped up to his window. Another gun pointed at him.

"Get out."

They didn't want the car, or his wallet or his watch. They did take his cell phone, but only to check his contacts list after they held the phone in front of his face to gain access. Then they'd thrown it back onto the seat of his Lexus. That was when it occurred to him that if they didn't want any of those things, the only thing they could want . . . was him.

"Get in."

He noticed that the SUV had the same aftermarket tinted windows his Lexus had, even darker than his, nearly black. His two abductors made him stay down on the backseat, one holding a gun to the side of his head the entire time, the other driving.

It even occurred to him during the drive that maybe they'd made a mistake. He didn't have money. He'd worked his way up through the ranks to his position at the newspaper, and even though he had yea-and-nay power over stories and headlines, he certainly wasn't getting paid enough to afford much more than a middle-class-comfortable life for his family. He kept the thought to himself though and they certainly did the same. They didn't say a word for the entire thirty-minute drive, until they arrived at their destination.

"Get out."

They didn't manhandle him when they walked him from the vehicle to the side door of the nondescript house located at the end of a grown-over cul-de-sac.

That gave him hope.

But it was short-lived.

There was a third man waiting inside.

He had a hammer in his hand.

That was two days ago. He'd told them everything he knew about her. He'd told them where she lived and with whom. He'd told them that she was a highly skilled journalist and that she didn't socialize with anyone else in the office. He told them that she hadn't shown up for work that day and he even told them that he had a crush on her. Every guy in the office did, not just the straight guys either.

She was mysterious and alluring. He told them it wasn't appropriate, but he did pull her human resources file, not creeping her, but more to get a better sense of who was working for him. At least that's what he told himself. He found out where she lived, that she loved animals, and even what gym and yoga classes she attended. He'd told them about her short friend and that he didn't have a crush on her, but he did occasionally fantasize about her.

They'd gagged him and driven him to the place in Pinehurst where he told them she was presently living, leaving him to watch as they ransacked every inch of the place, obviously looking for the thing they constantly asked him about. Something they called a Soul Catcher, whatever that was. They didn't pay attention to him, he wasn't going to run away, he couldn't run away, his feet were the first thing they'd smashed two days before.

Now, after so long under the care of the three men, he'd learned a hard but valuable lesson: how to disassociate from his physical being. The incomprehensible pain was no longer his problem, it was his broken body's problem. They hadn't even asked him any questions until after he'd regained consciousness that first day. He'd passed out almost immediately from the initial impossible hurt, the first blow from the hammer that crushed twelve of the twenty-six bones in his right foot.

When he came to, he'd answered all their questions truthfully and fearfully, including telling them that he had absolutely no idea what a Soul Catcher was.

That's when they started on his ankles.

No, they were not worried that he would run away.

And no, there was no soft guiding light, no end of a tunnel, no wrought-iron gates in the clouds, and no welcoming Saint Peter. His life did not pass before his eyes in that last moment. Nor did he ask the question, why me?

His last thought was of the young woman called Nyala. He was thinking to himself that the little house she'd rented was quite pleasant, calming. The lake and the ducks, the trees and the dappled sunlight, the squirrels chirring and the peacefulness of the place. He could see why she'd chosen to live there.

He didn't notice one of the men pick up the hammer once again.

Designed to drive three-and-a-quarter-inch spikes into hemlock and fir two-by-fours, the framing hammer had a longer shaft than the everyday handyman's hammer and the claw end wasn't as curved. But more important for stick-frame construction workers who used such a tool was the fact that framing hammers weigh thirty-two ounces, nearly double what a regular hammer weighs, which meant, in terms of physics, that Newton's second law of motion applied.

As the longer-handled and heavier hammer accelerated through its wide arc, the hammerhead hit its intended target at nearly twice the speed that a regular hammerhead would have been traveling, resulting in a force of impact that was four times greater than it would have been had it been of a normal weight and length. Perhaps more telling was the effortlessness of the swing. It was the practiced swing of a pro.

Slow is smooth and smooth is fast.

The second and third and in fact all the many swings that followed the first were equally as efficient, but he didn't notice.

The erstwhile carjackers had what they were looking for, names, descriptions, credit card receipts, a starting point, a direction, and a destination written on a scrap of notepad paper. Canada.

The three men didn't make any attempt to clean up the mess they left behind.

52

2020

VANCOUVER ISLAND, BRITISH COLUMBIA

For more than one thousand years the red cedar grew, towering and massive. Its roots reached a dozen yards in every direction. It was already ancient, almost 750 years old when the Spaniard, Captain Juan Perez, at the helm of his frigate the *Santiago*, anchored nearby and traded beads for sea otter pelts with the cedar-bark-clad inhabitants he found living there.

The majestic tree had been standing deep in the temperate rainforest of the fog-shrouded island when famed explorer Captain James Cook made the first European landfall, claiming the four-hundred-mile-long island for Britain; the island stood guard over the coastline of what would become known as British Columbia. The 150-foot-tall tree stood through the following centuries of great sorrow, witness to the sad disease-ridden aftermath of European expansion into the area.

It still stood, but this time over a small cedar bark hut, barely tall enough for a human to sit cross-legged without their head hitting the rough rounded ceiling and barely wide enough for a human to lie straight on the floor within, which was covered with woven cedar mats. Unlike the lone inhabitant of that primitive hut, the great tree was not aware of its surroundings. It didn't feel, didn't worry, wasn't cold, wasn't damp, wasn't confused, and wasn't lost. It was home.

So too was the hyperaware woman in the hut. She just didn't want to admit it to herself yet.

It had rained most of the morning and now was midday from

what she could tell by the gray light showing on each side of the hanging woven cedar bark mat that blocked the low entrance to the hut, light that had filtered down through the forest canopy. Surprisingly, inside the dark hut the young woman was damp and cold, but not soaking wet like everything else on the dripping moss, salal, and fern-covered forest floor.

"Pssst?"

Nyala didn't move. She listened. Had the four female Elders returned? The Elders who had taken her by the hand and led her through the forest to the hut in the dark of the night? Taken her in shock, after the longhouse, the fires, and the ceremony? Taken her after the changing, after the Soul Catcher returned to her people? It was too surreal to contemplate. The Soul Catcher? She was the Keeper of the Breath?

Nothing made sense.

With warmed cloths from woven baskets, they'd gently wiped the colored paste from her body and placed a heavy blanket of handwoven mountain goat wool over her shoulders. Then they'd stayed with her in the hut all night, until the forest began to lighten. They'd rocked and chanted in low tones, singing the songs of their ancestors. Occasionally they would stop and tell her a story of her grandmother, of her mother and her grandmother and theirs before, the Soul Catchers, the Keepers of the Breath. Ancient stories, the oral history of their people.

They told her of how her mother handed the swaddled baby to them with directions to take her infant child to a faraway city, to a police station. Leave it there at the door with no trace, nothing that would lead the baby back to the people.

Just a name, Nyala, and a birth date.

During the night, in hushed voices they told of how with her gift, her mother knew doing so was the only way to keep her daughter safe. And how she told them Nyala would grow from an infant to a child and then to a woman, suffering in darkness and confusion, never knowing her birthright. Safe, but without the teaching of her people to guide her and without the knowledge that she would someday be called upon to return.

And of how at the last, she touched Nyala's forehead and told them that when that day came, her daughter would call upon the courage that was hers by lineage, by inheritance, and would assume her role as the Soul Catcher, the Keeper of the Breath.

They told her they did as her mother instructed and of how her mother left the people then, alone, to face the evil that had entered the Land Warmed by the Sun.

They said Nyala's mother never returned.

Too numbed from the overwhelmingness of it all, Nyala gave in. She didn't question, didn't doubt. She was too far removed from the real world that had been hers before, too far removed from her own will to resist or to protest.

They'd left a small flashlight switched on and pointed upward during the night, lighting their faces with an eerie, incongruous glow that was at once primal and modern, adding to her already deep state of unbridgeable disparity. Upon occasion during the night, the four Elders would go silent in unison and sit stock still for several minutes, as if in a trance. Then together they would hold the backs of their hands up to her and speak.

"Hych'ka Siem."

It was both a welcome and a thank-you. Somehow Nyala knew the words, knew the meaning as though she'd heard them before. In fact, she understood all the words, knew the songs, and could have joined the women in their chanting, which only added to her confusion. The world she had known only days before was gone, replaced with a world that should not be, could not be, but was. Only, unlike the world she had known, this was a world she could not run away from.

They left her after first light, only to return midmorning to drop off a bear-grass handwoven basket filled with dried salmon. They left the offering at the entrance to the hut before slipping silently away once more.

"Pssst?"

Still she remained quiet, trembling when the image of the frightening shaman from the ceremony the evening before slipped through the retaining wall she'd built around her imagination.

Could it be him?

The thought frightened her, not because she feared him physically, but because she feared the power he possessed, the power to reveal to her the *why* and the *who* she was.

"Nyala?" The voice was close now, just outside the low entrance. "Girlfriend? You in there?"

It was at that moment that the smell of french fries penetrated the flimsy barrier that separated her two worlds, the present world from the world of her past, the new bewildering world from the real world she had known. The woven cedar bark barrier that kept the two friends from seeing each other.

"Luba?" Nyala twisted to her knees and reached out to sweep back the woven mat hanging down to cover the low doorway. "Luba!"

The face that greeted her was smiling.

"Whoa there, cowboy!" Luba, on her knees, twisted her full hands away from her friend, who had crawled out and on her own knees was now reaching to pull her friend closer. "Careful! I've got hot coffee!"

———

"I followed them to you this morning! Those same four old ladies who took you away yesterday when we first got to that big barn place!" Luba was pulling food from the bags marked with the big golden arches, setting the items on the mat floor. "I followed them back out of the forest too and got takeout to bring you! This place sucks! I got soaked! Totally ruined my boots! I saw a slug that had to be a foot long! Disgusting! Think there's any bears around here?"

Nyala didn't care about the muddy cowboy boots on her friend's feet. All she cared about was having her close by. She was content to quietly swirl the wooden stir stick in the paper cup filled with lukewarm, creamy coffee.

"What the hell was that all about anyhow? I saw the whole thing! I was there, in the audience! Crazy! Like way crazy! Soooo cool!" Luba's eyes were open as wide as they were capable of opening. "That whole chanting and wolf mask thing was wild! Jesus, girl! You never told me you were some kind of queen or whatever!"

She dipped a french fry into the small white paper container filled with ketchup.

"Why are you in this hovel anyway? Ugh. By the way, you smell like smoke."

Nyala smiled then. It was true. She did smell like smoke. And dirt. And Spanish moss, wet red cedar, and dank forest.

"They told me that I am the Keeper of the Breath. They say that I am the Soul Catcher of their people." They both sat quietly then. "Just like Tsau-z wrote in the manuscript."

Nyala held her coffee with both hands, close enough to her face to feel its waning warmth.

"My mother was apparently one too. And her mother all the way back in time. Tsau-z or Icarus, Hunter is my father." She looked across at her friend, dim in the half-light of the hut, lit only by the daylight coming through the now-clear doorway. They'd left the woven mat folded back on the domed roof to let as much light as possible into the hut. "They told me that I need to stay here for a month. Cleansing, they said."

Nyala gently shook her head and looked down at the coffee cup in her hands.

"A month! Geez, girl, we are so going to get fired!" Luba dipped another french fry in the ketchup. "Not that I care. I only took the stupid job because you wanted to work there."

Nyala didn't respond. Her friend was telling the unfiltered truth as she always did.

"So you have some kind of superpower?" Luba was chewing her fry. "Like you can see through people's clothes or something? What color is my underwear?"

Nyala smiled again.

"Pink."

"Damn, girl! That's amazing!"

Of course, Luba always wore pink underwear.

"Oh yeah! I almost forgot!" Luba leaned to the side to be able to reach into her back pocket and remove an envelope. She sat back up and held it out to Nyala. "Got another note from your pops! Last night, after all that crazy dancing and singing stuff, when they took you away, I went back outside of that big barn to see if I could follow you, but my car was gone! And guess what?!"

Nyala frowned and reached for the envelope.

"Look!" Luba contorted again to be able to pull something from her tight front jeans pocket. "Ta-da! Look what we got! A new truck!"

Nyala frowned, looking at the key fob, confused.

"Keys? New truck?"

"Keys? New truck? Are you kidding me? These aren't just normal keys; these are keys to a supercharged 750-horsepower Ford Shelby F-150!" Luba dangled the fob in front of her friend. "It was him! Your pops! In that black Shelby truck we saw on the highway after we got off the ferry! Remember? He took my Mercedes and gave us his Shelby! Too bad it's black though. I wanted a white one."

"You saw him? Did you talk to him? What did he say?"

"No, I didn't exactly see him. When I saw my car was missing, I checked my pocket to see if maybe I left the keys in the console and these keys were in my pocket instead of the Mercedes keys! That's when I looked around and saw the Shelby truck sitting there! It was weird! I clicked the door button and it unlocked! The envelope with your name was on the front seat!" She held her hands out, palms up, and opened her eyes wide, shaking her head at the same time. "It's nuts! He must have pickpocketed me while you were down there playing with that witch doctor guy! Your old man is a freak! He's a ghost!"

Nyala wasn't listening any longer. She stopped hearing what her friend said after she heard the "no" answer to her question.

She was looking at the envelope in her hand.

The envelope with her name on it.

Another page in the manuscript?

Why wouldn't he meet her in person?

He wasn't a ghost.

She hesitated, thinking about it.

Was he?

53

2020

HIGHWAY BETWEEN CALGARY, ALBERTA,
AND VANCOUVER, BRITISH COLUMBIA

For three days he'd been waiting on the cutbank that rose sharply from the river's outside curving bend. He hadn't moved in those three days, other than to perform bodily functions, and even then he'd simply rolled to the side. For the same three days he'd been waiting, he knew that she'd been waiting as well, at a quiet Vrbo ski chalet back down the road a few kilometers toward Calgary, waiting on a text from his Garmin inReach satellite communicator.

They had met up in the mountains, he in the Mercedes and she in a nondescript rental car. She'd done exactly as he'd instructed, something he never doubted. He had her follow him in her car, up the remote logging road to the landing where he told her to wait until he returned. He'd then continued to drive to the point where the logging road was cut precariously into the side of a deep brush-choked ravine. It was the spot he'd chosen for the Mercedes to spend eternity.

He methodically destroyed the vehicle's communication systems, ensuring the car would not be telling tales of its whereabouts, no matter how many satellites tried to talk to it. When he was done, he'd sent it over the edge of the logging road and watched it tumble down the ravine for hundreds of yards before it finally disappeared from his sight. For all intents and purposes, in that moment, the expensive car ceased to exist, untraceable and unfindable.

Cold as he was, his focus hadn't wavered for a single moment during the three days since she'd dropped him off along the highway, close to where he now waited. Even when he dozed intermittently through the long, frigid nights, it wasn't the deep sleep of dreams; it was more of a profound meditation where he was conscious, but able to lower his corporeal body on a thread, into sleep, a thread that he could cut at the barest hint of stimuli or ripple in awareness. He was able to let sleep fall away from his body then, instantly bringing him back to full physical control and focus.

The degree of difficulty wasn't great, a challenge, yes, but nothing he hadn't done before. He was a hunter. He'd waited for twenty-three days straight in the steaming jungles of Congo-Brazzaville, waited for the most elusive of the forest spiral-horned antelope, the bongo. He'd spent two weeks in a treetop machan in Siberia, in the Mezhdurechensky Urban Okrug, on the banks of the Reka Usa, the River Usa, waiting that time for a Siberian brown bear that had been terrorizing a local mining camp.

As with the bongo and the brown bear, he knew his prey would come this time too. Maybe not today and maybe not tomorrow, but his quarry would eventually make its way to where he waited, silently, patiently, letting time do the work of bringing those he was hunting to within striking distance.

Yes, the ones he waited for would come and when they did, he would spring his trap.

There could be no mistakes. He knew that. Those who followed the trail were trained professionals, they were the best, so he had to do it right, the trail had to end here. These were his same thoughts later during that day when an SUV with heavily tinted windows approached the pullout, slowed, and turned in. When it sat for a full ten minutes, engine running, he suspected it was time to prepare the text. When the engine shut off and two capable-looking men stepped from the vehicle, carefully checking in all directions, he pushed the send button.

Take position. One kilometer. Wait for my next text.

When the two men seemed satisfied, they nodded to each other and both reached back into the car, pulling out Saab Bofors Dynamics CBJ-MS 9mm machine pistols with what looked to be hundred-round magazines, but the distance was too great to be sure. Not that it mattered. Events were in motion. They'd taken the bait; it was time to move.

———

"Found it." The man leaned down into the thick brush alongside the river and lifted the object they'd been seeking. An object that had taken the latest in detection technology to track to the turnout on the remote section of the Trans-Canada Highway and two hours of actual searching in the forest to locate.

It was a cell phone, hidden under a rock. The bait Nyala had so carefully and unknowingly placed.

The second man, fifty yards away, ceased his search and made his way over to get another set of eyes on the phone and confirm that it was indeed the item they sought.

Situational awareness was their stock in trade, so regardless of their immediate intent to identify the cell phone, when they heard a vehicle slowing, to make the right-hand turn from the highway into the pullout, the two of them with a simple hand signal spread apart. They lost sight of each other within seconds. The band of forest they'd been searching, bordered on one side by the highway and on the other by the river, was choked with underbrush.

Not that it would have been an unexpected occurrence for a car or truck to turn off the roadway into the pullout; the small rest stops were common along most Canadian highways and were designed for easy access and egress, places for tired drivers to stop and take a nap or change a tire. No, it wasn't unexpected, but highly trained as they were, taught to assume every change of circumstance was a potential threat, the two men acted in unison.

They hadn't voiced their intentions, but each of them knew exactly what to do. They slipped back through the thick brush to the edge of the turnout, hunkering down in positions that kept them hidden but gave them each a visual on the nondescript four-door sedan that had by then pulled in and stopped a few yards behind where the third member of their group sat in their SUV. Once they were in place, out of sight of each other, but with clear shooting lanes, they waited. Their partner, the driver and the third in the group, also waited, remaining in the driver's seat, eyes focused on his driver's-side rearview mirror, watching the newly arrived vehicle.

None of the three relaxed their vigilance for the entire time they watched and if anything they became even more focused when, five minutes later, the driver of the vehicle finally opened the door, stepped out, and stretched. It was a woman, older, tall, and attractive in a South African short-haired androgynous Josie Borain kind of way. All three classified her as a nonthreat, at least by appearance, but still, they didn't drop their guard. From the years they'd spent training under the tutelage of Our World's legendary enforcer, a woman about the same age as the one in front of them, they knew that appearances could deceive.

To be deceived by Charlotte was to die.

The female driver of the new vehicle turned to look back down the highway then, watching an approaching semitrailer truck. It was relatively quiet at first, but the sound grew in intensity as it approached, the frequency of the sound waves compressed by the Doppler shift. It was nearly deafening when it roared by a few yards away at 100 kilometers per hour, but once it passed the sound receded quickly.

Still they watched, like predators, evaluating an unknown prey species.

Or at least two of them did.

The other was dead.

The tall woman walked to the front driver's-side fender of her vehicle and, smiling, waved at the driver whose face she noticed looking back at her in his side rearview mirror.

The smile was disarming, but it didn't disarm the driver of the SUV. He was holding his fully automatic Diablo MK-107, with its 7¾-inch barrel, close to his chest, aimed at the window. He, like all criminals who intended to use a firearm in the commission of a crime, hadn't acquired it through legal channels. His was provided through illegal channels built and kept flowing with Our World influence. The difference between the Our World international cross-border conduit of illegal firearms and the normal everyday criminal supply lines for prohibited arms was that the Our World channels were created and maintained for the exclusive use of the organization's worldwide network of enforcers.

The next semitrailer that blasted by shook the heavy SUV, slamming it with a shock wave caused by the flat front end of the reefer passing through the dense and cold mountain air. The driver in the SUV wasn't jumpy, but he'd flinched when the truck went by. There was something about the woman still standing at the front corner of her vehicle, smiling at him, that was disconcerting. Maybe, if he wasn't so sure that he had two compatriots watching from the darkened forest, covering his flank, ready to deal death and destruction at the merest hint of trouble, he might not have made this last mistake.

He believed his back was covered.

It was not.

The second of the two men he was counting on, highly trained as an Our World enforcer or not, was at that moment lying on the ground where he'd fallen. Like his former partner, he too fell without ever knowing what hit him.

The driver, the only one of the three still breathing, had made his first mistake when he'd opened both his and the passenger-side window two inches just before he'd turned the engine off, his second mistake. He'd opened the windows to allow fresh air to flow through the vehicle and in so doing keep his breath from fogging and eventually frosting the windows of the SUV. He had turned the vehicle off so his partners would have their sense of hearing working at full capacity. Both decisions were based on sound reasoning and training, but the reasoning part was about to be proven deeply flawed.

Those were not his biggest mistakes though. His biggest mistake had to do with tunnel vision, the human tendency to focus exclusively on a single objective to the exclusion of all other possibilities.

The thick carbon-fiber barrel on the Christensen Arms Traverse hunting rifle, topped with a Leupold VX-6HD scope and chambered in the new state-of-the-art 300 PRC caliber, slid easily and quietly through the two-inch passenger-side window opening. To see this happening, all the unsuspecting driver had to do was turn his head away from the mirror and the tall woman, but he was too deep into the tunnel of his visual choosing to do so.

Had he looked to his right, once he got over the shock of what he was looking at, he would have instantly realized why he would never be a legend like his instructor. He simply wasn't as good.

Charlotte would not have made four errors in judgment.

Not that it would have mattered.

Even though he was still breathing, he was a dead man by then anyway.

If he had turned, long before he could have reacted, the 212-grain Hornady bullet, designed for military sniper use at ranges of two miles, would have impacted his body from point blank range, with approximately four thousand foot-pounds of energy. Enough to stop a charging thousand-pound grizzly in its tracks.

He was a dead man then and he was a dead man five seconds later when the man holding the rifle touched the trigger, sending the big expanding bullet through the driver's near-side shoulder and from there through the driver's backbone, destroying any and all bone, muscle, and lung tissue it encountered along the way. A nanosecond after it started its journey, it exited the far shoulder bone to lodge in the driver's-side door panel, its momentum finally spent.

———

As the three professional executioners had acted with unvoiced efficiency, so too did the man who'd waited for three days on the cutbank and the tall woman who'd arrived only minutes before act wordlessly. Their actions were not efficient from training, however; theirs were efficient from decades of experience. They'd both been schooled to a higher and more varied degree than the dead men that they dragged to the back of the SUV. With an ease that belied their ages, they lifted the bloodied corpses into the cargo space of the vehicle.

Before they parted, the man took a few minutes to search through the duffel bags that contained the effects of the three deceased Our World assassins, searching for the one thing he knew would be there.

When they parted company, there were no tears, just a simple nod to each other. The mutual respect would have been obvious had anyone been there to see. But there was something else in the eyes of the man and the woman. Resignation? Understanding? Empathy?

Love? The two knew well what they'd started, knew the storm would come. It didn't take any special clairvoyant abilities on either of their parts to see what the future would bring, but for now they both knew that by their efforts the trail had gone cold.

The one thing an observer would not have seen was any indication of fear.

They would have time to prepare.

Before she turned back to her vehicle, the man handed her the object he'd found in the duffel bags, the object he knew would be there.

She had his instructions; she knew what to do with it.

54

2020

Unlike the previous leader of Our World, the Russian he'd replaced twenty-four years before, the present leader of Our World was entirely capable of feeling at least one emotion besides pride.

It was hate.

Deep, oceanic hate.

His hands were clenched in fists of rage.

First Zhivago.

Dead.

And now this.

He stared at the object on the table.

It was only through the force of his formidable will that he kept himself from lashing out at the messenger sitting in front of him, the one who had placed the object on the table. Seething and barely under control, he focused on sorting out the disconcerting events of the previous weeks, putting them in order, searching for answers.

It started when word of the Soul Catcher filtered down through his vast information network. For only the second time since he'd assumed his rightful position at the top of Our World, he'd received information confirming that the greatest work of art known to mankind was about to be brought forth from where it had been hidden. It hadn't been an obscure hint or whisper and neither was it a rumor.

The sources were solid, and even more importantly, the word had come through several different channels at the same time.

It was going to happen.

And it was going to happen soon.

He didn't consider *how* the information found its way into the Our World web, nor did he care *why* the work of art he coveted more than any other was going to come to light after nearly a quarter of a century in darkness. Those were irrelevant details, unworthy of his attention, but he did take notice when he was informed of *where* it was going to happen: Raleigh, North Carolina. When he'd first received the information, he recalled thinking it was a strange location, thousands of miles from where Zhivago had been so close to finding it on Vancouver Island, first in 1994 and then again in 1996.

But that incongruity only gave him pause for the briefest of moments before he made his decision.

He gave orders for two Gulfstream 650ERs to be dispatched to pluck Zhivago and Icarus from the opposite sides of the world, where they'd been working, and to have them flown to the East Coast of the United States. He'd given instructions to have Icarus briefed in the air on the details of Zhivago's failure to extract information from the woman he'd interrogated more than two decades before, on the remote Canadian island.

The Chinese leader of Our World felt it was important for Icarus to know how fanatical the people in possession of the Soul Catcher were. He wanted the operative to clearly understand that despite Zhivago's considerable talents in the arts of persuasion, the woman defied his best attempts to make her talk. It was also necessary for Icarus to understand that Zhivago had reported that he'd sensed the presence of the Soul Catcher on the woman and that he believed she'd handled it not long before he began the long but ultimately unsuccessful process of breaking her will.

"Find the Soul Catcher."

The orders he wanted passed on to his two most experienced operatives, the best that had ever been, were clear.

"No limitations. Do whatever it takes."

Zhivago died one week after he ordered the two of them into action.

He'd been furious when he'd received the bad news and became apoplectic when he read the reports outlining the cause of death. The official North Carolina pathologist's report, converted to layman's terms, stated that some type of weapon with a two-and-a-quarter-inch cutting blade had entered the unidentified victim's left side, just below the rib cage, cut the lower edge of diaphragm, sliced through the middle of the spleen, and opened a wound channel that sheared the stomach wall and split the liver before exiting the victim's right side. Whatever the murder weapon was, it had been razor sharp and never touched bone.

That was the official autopsy report.

His own forensic pathologists added that it appeared the slicing wound could only have been caused by an arrow tipped with an expandable, surgically sharp broadhead, likely of the type used in North America by deer hunters. They added that the only commercially available broadhead capable of creating such a massive wound was something called a Rage. But it wasn't that knowledge that initiated the course of action chosen by the Chinese leader of Our World; it was the final summation of his own people.

They were of the opinion that the arrow had been purposely targeted so that it would miss bone and would completely pass through the body of the heavy operative, likely to allow the arrow to be easily recovered before the local police showed up. They stated that as massive as the wound channel through his body was, the operative would have lived for several minutes, completely aware, albeit physically incapacitated and bleeding out. It was their opinion that Zhivago would have been in a great deal of pain.

"Unimaginable" was the word they used to describe the level of pain.

They concluded that whoever released the arrow was, first, an expert archer, and second, wanted the stricken operative to be fully conscious and feeling excruciating pain in the last few minutes of his life.

Icarus.

It had to be him.

Deducing who was responsible for Zhivago's death and the motive for the killing was simple. Icarus. He must have found the Soul Catcher. It was logical. He had to be keeping it for his own personal gain.

The leader's assumption was based on his knowledge of human nature. Humans were greedy. He deduced that Icarus must be in possession of the Soul Catcher and had killed Zhivago to eliminate the only other operative capable of recognizing the priceless work of art. The previous leader, the Russian, had been prescient when he'd chosen the name Icarus and predicted that someday the operative would try to fly to the sun.

Our World's leader hadn't taken his eyes off the object on the table the entire time he worked through the events that led to Zhivago's death. He'd been furious when the messenger brought the news but remained ice cold and in control, calculating.

He remembered asking how many enforcers they had in the area.

"Three."

"Send them." His decision to send whatever Our World professionals were working within quick response distance of Raleigh, North Carolina, was one he'd made in the hatred of the moment, but even as he thought back through that decision now, he knew it had been the right one. "Send them. Tell them to bring the Soul Catcher to me. Bring Icarus to me."

He'd never second-guessed himself in the near quarter of a century that he'd been leader of Our World and wasn't about to question whether he should have waited until more enforcers could make their way to the location. There had not been a doubt in his mind that three would be enough to do the job tasked to them. In fact, that should have been overkill.

And now this.

He glared at the offending object.

His fists were still clenched, his teeth too. His jaw muscles were ropes under the skin of his smooth cheeks.

When he'd received the news of what happened to Zhivago and

after he'd ordered the minion to send the three trained enforcers after Icarus, his hatred necessitated that he issue another order once that messenger left the room. It was an order he gave directly to the person who now sat in front of him, on the other side of the dimly lit table.

"Get rid of him."

No harbinger of bad news had immunity in Our World, or at least none did except the messenger sitting in front of him at that moment. The only one who would dare to place the object on the table before the leader of Our World, the only one who would survive the message that had audaciously been sent through a regular commercial courier service.

Charlotte.

Her days as a field enforcer had ceased when the leader of Our World determined that she would be a better teacher to the army of professional assassins he'd set his sights on raising, an army that he intended to use to further his limitless ambition to manipulate, to own, and to control. Already, since he'd taken over the leadership of the organization, his will had come to dictate the decisions of half the world's Third World governments and a quarter of the arrogant remainder.

"How many will you take?"

He didn't need to tell her that he was only talking about the best of the best. Those she would handpick, those who would accompany her to do what the first three had failed to do. Those who would be tasked with picking up the trail, a trail that had somehow gone inconceivably cold.

"Nine."

"Go."

She rose.

"Take it."

His hatred was so intense, he didn't trust himself to touch the object.

He didn't trust that he could control himself from exploding, swinging the object at the messenger and in so doing ensuring that he would die long before it struck the woman in front of him.

No. It was hers to wield.

"Use it."

With those last two words, the woman reached down and picked up the object.

Designed to drive three-and-a-quarter-inch spikes into hemlock and fir two-by-fours, the framing hammer had a longer shaft than the everyday handyman's hammer and the claw end wasn't as curved. But more important for stick-frame construction workers who used such a tool was the fact that framing hammers weigh thirty-two ounces, nearly double what a regular hammer weighs, which meant, in terms of physics, that Newton's second law of motion applied.

Charlotte knew all of this.

There was dried blood on the hammerhead.

There was a lot of dried blood on the hammerhead.

Now you know, Nyala.
     All this you need to know.
  The story of you.
  I saw you by the balefires last night. I saw you fighting for your
life, fighting against yourself, fighting to keep who you were. Let it in,
Nyala. It is who you are now. I saw you in the throes of transforma-
tion and I know you are hurt. I want to help you, but who you are is
a battle that you and you alone will have to fight.
  There is pain in birth.
  Every color that has ever existed and every color that has never
existed; it is how I see you, Nyala. It is how I found you. Once I
learned what Zhivago did to your mother so long ago, I sought out
every source, worked through every clue; every hint of your passing
through the life you lived.
  Brown and brown.
  I found you.
  In that city. Brown and brown. I saw all of them, the people who
worked with you. I saw your friend. I watched. You did not see me;
they did not see me. I am the hunter.
  In the darkness now, all alone. A lifetime of regrets. It is too late
now to right those wrongs, Nyala. But know that I am here for you.
  I discovered where they left you on the steps of the police station
when your mother went to face Zhivago, the evil she knew was
searching for you.
  The evil that was searching for the Soul Catcher.
  Our daughter.
  When she went to die for you.
  I didn't know.
  The tears have not stopped.

I felt your beauty. I found you. Leaving your workplace, walking down the steps in front of that building in the city; all of them, brown and brown, and then suddenly, there you were. Alone in the middle of the crowd. Vivid, impossible, indescribable color.

You are color. You are your mother.

Nyala, you are the Soul Catcher now.

And they are coming for you, Nyala.

Before this is done, they will all know me as fear.

Do not call me Icarus. He is dead. To them. To me.

Do not call me Tsau-z. He died with your mother.

You must find your own Man of Sores now.

I am your father.

I will protect you.

Call me Hunter.

ACKNOWLEDGMENTS

I started my first novel at the age of ten.

I'd write secretively and hide the *manuscript* pages behind a loose brick in the wall of our home.

It wasn't a big space. It didn't need to be.

Within a few pages, I realized I hadn't lived *life* yet and so, desirous or not, I didn't have a story to tell.

I needed to *live* my life first and write later.

Thirty years later, at the age of forty, I penned the first lines of the novel that would become CALL ME HUNTER.

"Zhivago is dead.

I hunted him down and I killed him."

But once again, I realized that I still hadn't lived *enough* life to have a story to tell. There were still too many treasures to be found and experiences to experience.

So, I peregrinated for another twenty years, living a life that would add 125,000 words to the initial lines.

Sitting on an escarpment, gazing out at the distant fog-shrouded bamboo rainforests of Ethiopia, trapped in cold canvas wall-tents in Arctic blizzards with my Inuit friends, sweating in the fetid jungles of West Africa, or climbing in the Himalayas and even when I was hanging out for endless hours in Customs offices around the world, waiting for export permits to be approved . . . I would be writing CALL ME HUNTER in my mind.

Finally, when I was ready, just before COVID-19, I sat down and started writing the novel you have in your hands, or that you listened to.

And when I was done, the truth of being a novelist hit me like the Bura winds of Croatia.

I needed help. I needed a lot of help!

It is time to thank all those who helped get the story into your hands.

To Jack Carr, author of so many bestselling novels and someone I call a friend (even if technically I haven't earned that right quite yet). Thank you for reading my manuscript and thank you for passing it on to Emily Bestler, along with your ringing endorsement. It gives me hope for the future to know good people like you, who make an effort to help others, are out there in the world.

And lest I forget, thank you to Jon Dubin for introducing me to Jack Carr.

Emily Bestler. What can I say? How about WOW! Wow to your talents. Wow to how you can take a chunk of rough granite and recognize that if enough of the rough is chipped away, CALL ME HUNTER will be left. Truly I am in awe of your editing abilities.

Libby McGuire. Thank you for believing in and publishing this novel. I promise to do my best to make the second one even better.

Dana Trocker. Thank you too, for all you have done as associate publisher to make this book a reality.

David Brown. I've never had a publicist before, but I'll be over-the-moon thrilled if you stay on as my publicist forever.

Dayna Johnson. Having you as the marketer of my novel has made me lazy. You are too good at what you do!

Karlyn Hixon. That all marketing directors be as good at what they do as you. Thank you.

James Iacobelli. Art director for CALL ME HUNTER. In the beginning, I honestly thought I was as good at directing art as you! Ha! I stand corrected . . . and humbled by your artistic talent!

Paige Lytle. Thank you for being my managing editor. This amazing crew is even stronger for your participation.

Shelby Pumphrey. Managing editorial assistant means doing all the work that I had zero idea how to do. Thank you.

Tom Pitoniak. Your skills have shown me that I need to go back to school . . . and listen this time!

Nicole Bond. Without you watching my back, as rights director, I'm not sure I'd have been able to accomplish more than to twirl in circles, going nowhere.

Hydia Scott-Riley. Great associates are not easy to find. But I found one in you! Thank you for all you've done to make CALL ME HUNTER a success.

Lara Jones. Thank you for your patience when I asked the hundredth dumb question in a row and thank you for teaching me how to work my computer. Jobs is jealous.

And to everyone else on the Simon & Schuster team, a giant, heartfelt thanks! If I wasn't already well over my allotment of words for the acknowledgments, I would mention every single one of you.

Esther Fedorkevich. My unbelievable agent! I've met some inspiring human beings in my life, but I've never met anyone as positively ebullient as you! You *believed* in CALL ME HUNTER from the beginning and for that I will be eternally grateful.

Brittney Bossow. I'm sure Esther and I added to your workload with this project and I know this is too little in return, but thank you.

To everyone else on the Fedd Agency team, with special thanks to those of you who first read my manuscript and liked it enough to hand it on to Esther, thank you.

Mark Sullivan. I remember the day, standing with you at SHOT in 1996, talking about your first novel, PURIFICATION CEREMONY. I was in awe that you were going to be a published author. And I'm still in awe of your string of bestsellers since. Thank you for your advice on my first.

James Patterson. You don't know me and you don't know Icarus, Tsau-z, or Hunter, but we thank you for the super cool shout-outs in CROSS JUSTICE.

Ken Bailey. Your sage *writing* counsel over the years has meant more to me than you could ever know. Respect and thanks.

Gregg Gutschow. Thank you for being there all those years, editing my *raw* work for the periodicals. CALL ME HUNTER was better from the beginning, because of your teachings.

Davy Lawless. Your words of encouragement, reading the chapters as I wrote them, helped me leap the hurdles of time and effort. Thank you also for being my golf sensei . . . which is the same as being my sanity sensei during the writing process.

Aaltje Ottens. Our dear Aaltje. You were *all-in* on CALL ME HUNTER from the beginning. Thank you for the decades of friendship. I'm sure Clarke would have loved it too.

Alain Smith. Thank you for paving the way. Seeing you publish novels made me understand that anybody can do it! LOL. Sorry, couldn't help myself, my friend!

Pete and Rose Mandziuk. Thank you for teaching me the art of picking. I know you are both attending farm sales in heaven.

John McGowan. The treasure king of the Indefinite Article. Someday in the not-too-distant future, we will meet again.

Barbara Goldeen and John Selmer. Love your book! Nobody has a better *eye* for great art than the two of you. Thank you for reading my manuscript and for the editing suggestions.

Billy Dunbar. You were always there with a *Billyism* when I needed one, and thank you for Point Hope.

Blaine Calkins. Hold my spot in the House of Commons. As you can see, this is what I needed to do before I follow in your footsteps.

Cam Hanes. You inspire all of us to *keep* hammering, to be better . . . but it's not going to be easy to do better than you when it comes to discipline and bestselling books.

Joe Rogan. Seeing your success and how you have embraced the *field to table* lifestyle makes me proud to know you. And thanks for having me on your podcast.

Corey Knowlton. Thank you for listening to me blabber the entire CALL ME HUNTER storyline before it was written. You are a good friend to me and to our family. We need to get back to Katmandu . . . and Papua New Guinea . . . etc.

Steve Kobrine. Thank you for opening doors to the parts of the world nobody has been to. We need to get back to Somaliland . . . or maybe Liberia!

Bob Kern. Nobody does it better than you. Tajikistan? Iran? No problem.

Kathi Klimes. Yep. That's correct. I need to get to the middle of nowhere, then to the other side of nowhere, and from there I'd like to head to the far side of nowhere . . . can you please arrange it? And you did.

Pieter Baljet. Thank you for reading my rough manuscript . . . the version without an ending. And thank you for the camaraderie on our Mi-8 helicopter expedition up the Kamchatka Peninsula and back down the coast of the Okhotsk Sea. Dawn's and your friendship are deeply valued.

Don Ellis. The real deal when it comes to the world of art.

Gary MacDonald. Hey Mac! Really appreciate that you read my manuscript in the earliest stages of development.

Greg Drew. It was time to confess and tell the rest of the story.

Guy Shockey. My cuz. There is nobody's opinion that I value more than yours. And nobody that I know who has read more books . . . except maybe my sister Geraldine. Thank you for taking the time to read my manuscript.

Jay Shockey. I don't think I have met anyone who reads slower than you. What chapter are you on now? What do you think of my novel so far? 😊

Jason Roussos. Yep. Now you know what I was up to. Please thank your father, Nassos, for letting me borrow his truck and driver in Addis Ababa.

Jason Anucinski. Thanks for the use of the black Shelby pickup. Still waiting for my white one to be delivered.

Jeff Bradley and everyone at Christensen Arms. Thank you. And Hunter wanted me to let you know that he will be heavily relying on you in the future.

Bruce Pettet and everyone at Leupold Optics. Thank you. It's been forty years that you've believed in me and forty years that I've trusted my life to your optics.

Steve and Jason Hornady. You two are the best! Hunter and I thank you for your support.

Jeff Goodenow. Your knowledge of artifacts and support has been greatly appreciated.

Jim Zumbo. A gentleman and a great author. You always were and always will be my hero.

Jimmy Johns. Thank you for your support on this journey that was CALL ME HUNTER.

Johnny and John Paul Morris. You set an example for all of us who love the outdoors and believe in conservation. Your actions inspired me to greater endeavors.

John Stockdale. Your love of books and wisdom have been an inspiration for the last fifty years.

Judy Hill. Your knowledge of Northwest Coast First Nations customs and art is unparalleled. Thank you for sharing.

Tom Stark. Kindred spirits in the collecting world are hard to come by. Thank you for being a part of my learning curve in the arts.

Kevin Keen. Thanks, Doc! For letting me borrow the use of your name! And thank you for all you've done to help make this journey even more beautiful for Louise and me.

Lucas Fairchild. I really appreciate that you read my manuscript, and thank you for the positive reinforcement and advice.

Matt Ziniel. You walked the walk with me for all those years. Respect.

Oleg Stupar. I'm not a feral philosopher quite yet, but with your help in the choice of books to read, I'm hopefully getting there!

Popsy and Eva and all my friends up at Point Hope. Thank you for showing me how to get in touch with my *ancestral soul*.

Deep respect to my Quq'tsun Hwulmuhw friends, the People of the Land Warmed by the Sun. For me, there has been no greater honor than to be chosen to bear witness.

To my own team, all of whom have had their workloads increased because I was too busy writing to pull my own weight. Wojo. Ryan. Todd. Gerry. Kristian. Taylar. Corinne. Amanda.

And thank you to everyone who has helped me on this journey over the last forty years. Too many of you to mention here.

Finally, I would like to thank my family.

Barbara. My little sister. Thank you for reading my manuscript and thank you for comparing it to I AM PILGRIM. High praise.

Geraldine. My middle sister. You have been the greatest support through the entire writing process. Your knowledge of contemporary authors is frankly astounding. You always did read more than me . . .

with greater retention. Just so the world knows, my sister Geraldine is the best writer in our family, *if* she ever decided to sit down and write.

Eva. Tim. Leni Bow and Boone. You have all filled my heart with joy and pride. The focus it takes to write has meant that I don't always have the bandwidth to tell those closest to me how much I care about them. Know that I do. And Eva, also know that I will be doing my best to outsell your book, TAKING AIM! Although, yes, I will always have to admit that you were first and it was you who enabled me to meet Esther, *our* literary agent.

Branlin. Ashley. Flynn and Wilder. To see how close you are and how well you are doing makes my heart whole. And Branlin, thank you for reading your father's manuscript at the earliest stage in its development. You were right. It was too long, and it needed an actual ending. As always, you *see* what your father often cannot. I can't wait until your novel, DWELLERS, is published! It truly is a wonderful read.

Last and by far the most important. My soulmate Louise. For the last forty years we have lived a fairy tale. You are there, in my novel. The most beautiful woman I have ever seen. Elegance and grace and strength that I could only hope to aspire to. Without you, there would have been no point in writing this novel. Without you, I could never have *lived* this one life we are all granted.

Without you . . . no.

There is no *without* you.

We still have eternity to look forward to . . .